The
HALF-LIFE
of RUBY
FIELDING

ALSO BY LYDIA KANG

FICTION

Opium and Absinthe
The Impossible Girl
A Beautiful Poison

The November Girl
Toxic
Catalyst
Control

NON-FICTION

Quackery: A Brief History of the Worst Ways to Cure Everything
Patient Zero: A Curious History of the World's Worst Diseases

The HALF-LIFE of RUBY FIELDING

A NOVEL

LYDIA KANG

LAKE UNION
PUBLISHING

Published by Lake Union Publishing, Seattle

www.apub.com

Amazon, the Amazon logo, and Lake Union Publishing are trademarks of Amazon.com, Inc., or its affiliates.

ISBN-13: 9781542020084
ISBN-10: 1542020085

Cover design by Kimberly Glyder

Printed in the United States of America

There are no secrets about the world of nature.
There are secrets about the thoughts and intentions
of men.
—J. Robert Oppenheimer

PROLOGUE

"Ruby!" Felix screamed.

It wasn't the scream of a man whose heart had been shattered by a lover. It was the exclamation of a spoiled child who, for once, had not gotten his way. I galloped to the curb and flagged down one of the checkered cabs that had become plentiful now that gas rationing had made private cars scarce. It took several fumbling tries to open the door before I threw myself inside.

"Where to, lady?" the cabbie asked.

I swung the door shut. Through the window, I saw Felix running out of the grand front doors to stop me. His face twisted with livid fury.

I pounded the back of the cabbie's seat and yelled, "Gravesend. Brooklyn. Two hundred fifteen West Sixth Street. Go, go, go!"

"Okay, lady! Stop hitting my car!"

He stepped on the gas pedal, and I fell backward with a thump just as Felix reached the curb, his hand nearly touching the door. His car and driver were not out front; all the servants had been told to leave so that no one could witness what he'd done. I turned in my seat and watched as he grew smaller and smaller in my field of vision.

Everything felt terrible. I could barely keep my eyes open, and when I did, the city flew by me in ghastly twists and turns. I would have vomited but for the fact that there wasn't much in my stomach after days of no food *and hardly enough to drink. I pulled on my coat, buttoning it up but still shivering.*

Deep in the pockets, I could feel the bottle of zinc chloride. Such a simple compound—a fluffy white crystalline substance composed of one zinc atom bound to two chlorine atoms. A tiny little gift that could tip the balance between having a warm, beating heart and being cemetery fodder. That is, if I could use it properly. If I could survive this nightmare.

I had been so focused on the beauty and violence of the chemicals and plants around me that I'd forgotten there was a larger game to be played. Half the world would win, and half would lose in this second world war. A bullet could kill or save a life; chemicals could do the same in the right or wrong hands, and my hand was being forced. I would have to step into the light, instead of letting the war swirl around me as if it were a play on stage and I were merely a spectator. This was my time to do something. It would take every skill I had to survive and come out on the winning side.

I must have lost consciousness, because I remember waking up.

"We're here, lady."

I tried to open the door, but I could barely find the handle. The cabbie got out and opened it.

"That'll be three dollars twenty cents."

I had no money. I remember him screaming at me, something about useless, drunk broads, and then I was tripping forward, onward and onward until I was stumbling behind a section of small houses, some attached in a row. An old woman in her backyard raking leaves looked at me aghast. I didn't know who I was. I didn't know where I was or what I was doing. But when she saw me, I spewed out the only lucid piece of information in my addled brain.

"Two hundred fifteen West Sixth Street?"

She pointed to a detached house a few doors down, and I followed the direction, weaving drunkenly around nonexistent obstacles. My legs grew so weak and wobbly that I fell to my knees at the back of the house, which looked terribly old and sad, with brown shutters and stairs splintering from overuse and too many New York winters.

I couldn't take another step. My body was exhausted, wrung out, and scrambled from whatever had been laced in my tea and in the absinthe.

I'll just rest, I thought. Just for a bit. I'll save the world after I get a little breather. No one will find me here. Felix won't find me here.

I'll be safe. For now.

And under the steps I crawled.

CHAPTER 1

They say that a nuclear chain reaction begins with one simple event—the absorption of an extra nuclear particle—before calamity inevitably destroys everything it touches.

For William Scripps, the chain reaction started on a fall day when he arrived home from work, the day his world changed irrevocably. Later, he would say inevitably.

It was October 20, 1942. It had been a blisteringly long day of work, hauling two thousand barrels of uranium onto a barge in the shadow of the Bayonne Bridge. After the Staten Island ferry and the Brooklyn trolley ride, Will was finally nearly home. It had been backbreaking work, and he felt twice as old as his mere twenty-five years. He wanted beef, and beer, and a book. He would likely only get one. Beef was scarce, expensive, and would be rationed soon. Some meatleggers would sell more than they should, but Will's sister would never submit to doing something so horribly unpatriotic as buying from them. Beer was pricey. Whiskey too. A third of the beer being brewed in the country was saved for servicemen, and as of January, whiskey distilleries were producing alcohol for industrial torpedo fuel.

Will snorted. Nazis. Ruining his dinner and his drink, every damn night.

Maggie would be finishing up cooking whatever was cheapest from the grocer, along with a precious dessert, thanks to their sugar ration stamps. She would nervously ask about his day, wince when he asked if she'd found a job yet. Later, after his classes at Brooklyn College, he'd fall asleep on the sofa with a book on thermodynamics split open on his chest. Maggie would switch off the lights in their small house in Gravesend, and all would be quiet. For a while.

Gravesend. What a name for a place to live, in such a time. The name had an old Dutch origin, something to do with the one and only female founding colonist. Less macabre than it seemed, but to Will, it felt like a dead end. While American boys fought on ships and land, he stayed in America, toiling away, getting nowhere, the name of his hometown reminding him that he would likely die here. Most certainly in a forgettable, irrelevant way. He'd rather have been overseas, but his one deaf ear prevented him from heading to the front lines, a casualty of an accident when he was fifteen.

Even as a kid, he'd thought physical altercations were inelegant and brutish, but he was picked on because he didn't fight back. Still, Will had his limits. After an older boy smashed a Coca-Cola bottle against his head, he'd punched the offending bully into the dust and stomped on his thigh. The crack of his snapping femur was a shocking sound. Worse, the ease with which he broke the bone was terrifying. Once in a while, he would see that kid, now a father and a shoe salesman, limping down the street. Regret would etch the edges of his conscience. Will had not left that quarrel unscathed. His ear had become infected, those inner bones—hammer, anvil, stapes—all swollen to hell and disintegrated into a nonworking chunk of scar tissue. Now his work as civilian personnel was as close as he could get to doing something useful.

A block or so from home, Will's stomach growled in anticipation of dinner. He passed piles of scrap metal—car parts and ornaments, dishpans, balls of foil chewing gum wrappers—destined to be melted down into sheet metal and ammunition. In the dim light of dusk, kids hooted as they added to the pile and metal clinked against metal. Must have been another scrap drive that day.

The war did funny things to people. It made them live harder, and fiercer. It made them so eager to prove their patriotism that they, like Maggie, volunteered for every cause under the sun. Maggie, who was so quiet that she barely squeaked when Will said his good mornings to her, had finally found her voice. She'd walk up and down West Seventh Street, yelling at people to turn down their lights at night for dimouts. She always apologized as she yelled.

"Pardon me! Mrs. Browning! Turn your lights off! Please?"

"Oh, dear, I am so sorry to bother but you really should paint your windows with blackout paint, Mr. McClure! Or black kraft paper? So sorry! So sorry!"

Pure Maggie.

Only ten months had passed since Pearl Harbor was bombed, though sometimes it felt like yesterday. Other days it seemed like a decade. The uncommon, a year ago, was all so common now. There were the surprise sirens that went off in July to announce a blackout. Before that, simulation bombing drills in all five boroughs, complete with magnesium flares and sulfur pots. When the SS *Normandie* became engulfed in flames on Pier 88 while it was being transformed into a troopship, Will had casually noted the smoke in the sky, shrugged, and kept working.

It was a funny thing: when every day was extraordinary, it was the ordinary that became ever so odd.

His first thought when he saw the shapely pair of legs poking out from beneath the back stairs of his house was that they were ordinary too. Soldiers on leave often canoodled with V-girls and cuddle bunnies, weaving drunkenly together on street corners. He'd seen people passed out on sidewalks, sleeping against doorframes of houses they didn't belong to, and girls too sauced to stumble home without a body to lean on.

They were nice legs, though, so at least there was that. As he approached, he could see they were clad in real silk stockings, not the fakery of eyebrow pencil drawn onto calves, bisecting the flesh and pointing upward like brown line markings on a highway.

Real silk stockings. Nice shoes too. The heels were hardly worn down. She'd probably wake up soon, find her friends, go home with smudged makeup, and do it again tomorrow night.

Will climbed the steps, boards creaking beneath his two-hundred-plus pounds of muscle. Faintly, he thought he heard the woman moan.

Good. She wasn't dead.

A dead body by his house was a bad thing. His entire job depended on him living his life discreetly, and he didn't need police and gawkers swarming his home. However, a drunk and unconscious person? Not his problem.

He unlocked the door and headed to the washroom to rinse off all the uranium ore dust. Maggie wasn't home yet. Though she wasn't employed, she filled her days as a volunteer spotter on the roof looking for German planes and reporting to the local offices that nothing was amiss. She'd later do her neighborhood rounds to gently nag the residents to dim their lights. It had taken several American sailors' bodies washing up on the Jersey shore bathed in fuel oil before the East Coast had woken up to reality: their dazzling city lights cast patrolling American ships in silhouette and practically invited the German U-boats to sink them.

Will scrubbed his hands and nails thoroughly of the dark dust from today's work. The barrels he'd hauled from the warehouse were well contained, but one of the tops had buckled in the process. The longshoremen working alongside him had balked at the spill. They hauled, and they transported, but they did not like to clean up messes, especially when the messes were so secret that they weren't allowed to inquire why the barrels were unusually heavy. Will had recognized the dark ore as pitchblende. Rich in uranium. One of the heaviest metals.

He'd shoveled the precious pitchblende back into the barrel, hammered the top back on, and used pliers to bend the seams back into place. Only a brief radiation exposure, and likely not harmful. While the other workers grumbled about when they would get paid, Will had thoughtfully considered why two thousand tons of pitchblende were being sent up river from the Dean Mill Plant on Staten Island, then onto a train to Port Hope in Canada.

What was in Port Hope?

This was the question he was left with when he boarded the ferry at the end of his shift. He thought of how radium was extracted from pitchblende to use in some hospitals for cancer treatments. When he'd gotten off the ferry at Sunset Park, Will had made a few calls, first to a Brooklyn hospital pharmacist, then to a radium bead supplier. He'd scribbled the list of companies they'd named on a scrap of newspaper, but he had his answer. Port Hope housed a Canadian uranium ore refinery. There were others in upstate New York as well. The info would come in handy.

He'd had dirtier work before. Shoveling coal. Laying asphalt. Painting ships. That had stopped for two years while he was a student at Columbia, but even then, he'd been covered in sooty dust. At the behest of Professor Fermi, Will and the rest of the football team had been asked to haul some thirty tons of slick graphite blocks into one of the research buildings. There, he'd helped pack eight tons of uranium oxide powder into square iron cans and then carry them to a basement lab as well. It was easy, thoughtless work, and Fermi expected the football team to disappear as quickly as they'd been summoned. But he was surprised when Will had stayed behind to query him on the quality of the graphite for a reactor pile. Will was soon tasked to help Fermi's team whenever he wasn't in class or football practice, but it wasn't for long.

It had been a little over a year now since he'd quit Columbia to keep a closer eye on Maggie. He'd even started college late, at age twenty-two, to be around more, but here he was, back at home. Luckily Brooklyn

College was free and had some evening classes. It would still take years to complete his degree. But if Maggie needed him for longer, then it would have to wait again. Possibly forever.

He only wished they didn't have to live in Gravesend. Or any place that reminded them of so much disappointment.

Freshly bathed, Will ambled into the empty kitchen to start dinner. There was a sliver of slightly dried ham in the icebox. Milk, not yet soured. Flour in the countertop crock. Maggie had forgotten to put away the bread this morning, and now it was hard as a rock.

He began crumbling the stale loaf into a pan, poured in the milk, sprinkled salt and pepper, and let it simmer on the stove. The ham would be cubed and added, and the resultant mushy panada would feed the two of them. It was baby food for adults, but he and Maggie had made do by themselves for ten years now, since he was fifteen and Maggie twelve. Survival was more important than flavor.

Will was scraping the nauseating mess into two bowls when a grunt and cry came from the kitchen door. He shut the burner off, set down the bowls, and opened the door. The temperature had dropped precipitously, and the icy October air slapped his face, but he didn't flinch. It took a lot to make him react with true surprise.

Down the seven steps to the dim back alley, Maggie was tugging hard at something. Even in the darkness, he could see her face was animated, eyes wide and perspiration on her brow and upper lip.

"Will! Help me! There's a woman here . . ."

"I know. She was here when I came home."

"Well—" She tugged what he could now see was an ankle and then grunted with another tug. Was she trying to steal the woman's shoe? "Well, help me! She's sick or something!"

"Mags. Leave her be. She's probably drunk. The cold'll sober her up, and she'll go home."

"She'll freeze first! Anyway, she's not like those V-girls. I've never seen her around here before. Look at her clothes, Will. Look at her face."

The one thing he had decidedly chosen not to look at when he came home. Faces made everything personal. He didn't have time to care. Maggie, work, and school took up all the space in his mind. Damn. He probably should have called the police and had her removed before Maggie had come home. He could have avoided this.

"Will!" Maggie's voice became higher, shriller with every tug of that slender ankle.

"Good God, Mags. You can't pull a body like that."

He sighed, and descended the stairs. Now the unconscious lady was flat on her back, one arm trapped beneath the stairs, the other making a deep gash in the moist soil beneath the landing. She had glossy hair that looked chestnut brown in the gloom, and her pink lips were open as if surprised by her predicament. Maggie gave one last artless tug of the stockinged ankle, then dropped it gently to the ground.

Will bent over and crammed his bulk beneath the stairs, wood scraping against the fabric of his shirt. With some difficulty, he pulled her body out. Her skirt—embroidered with pink roses—caught on the gravel and began to peel upward like the skin of a banana being removed. The tops of her stockings hugged her thighs.

"Will!" Maggie whispered hoarsely. She darted forward to pull the woman's skirt chastely down.

Will ignored her, intent on getting this lady off their property. Once he'd freed her from beneath the stairs, he could see her better, even in the rapidly fading light. Maggie, in her drab gray sweater and brown plaid skirt, seemed like a dirty smudge next to the elegantly dressed woman, who was an agate cameo come to life. Inwardly, he didn't consider thinking of his sister this way as an insult. He was terrifically proud that Maggie wasn't some addled bobby-soxer. She didn't elicit stares, whoops, and hollers from the seamen on leave. Having a stunning sister would have only added to his woes.

For a moment, he and Maggie simply stared at the body lying before them.

"Is she . . . dead?" It was just like Maggie to verbalize what Will was thinking. In the cold, her breath puffed out in weak clouds. It made him realize that the woman's chest wasn't rising and falling as it had before. He couldn't see any vapor coming from her. Maggie's hand went gently to the woman's wrist. "She's got a pulse. And yes, she's breathing. But barely." Maggie looked up pleadingly. "She's ice cold. We should bring her inside."

"God, no, Mags! I have to go to work early tomorrow. You have to look for a job."

"I have a job."

"You do?" Will blurted. He didn't mean to sound so aghast, but Maggie had proven all but unemployable. Sometimes it was crippling nervousness, sometimes outright ineptitude, but it was always costing her a job, like when she dropped too many dishes at the Automat. After the day when Maggie'd had her terrible accident, Will had quit Columbia, packed up his dormitory room possessions, and moved back in with his sister. It was that, or lose her. And lose the house. The house he hated. Two months after he came home, Japan attacked.

"I'll tell you about it later," she said impatiently. "Let's get her inside."

"Mags, no. We're too busy. Busier now that you have a job, I guess. I'll call the police to pick her up."

"She'll freeze before then!" Maggie cradled the woman's bare hand in hers. "She's already half-dead!"

Will sighed, the plumes of his breath only accentuating her point. Maggie might not be good at helping herself, but her heart certainly bled for everything else. At least once a week, Will came home to find her making a shoebox nest for some helpless creature. Last week, it was a half-frozen pigeon she'd found in the front yard. The week before, it was a butterfly pupa she was afraid would freeze. It was now living in an old pickling jar on her dresser.

"Fine. Until the police come."

"Well, but—"

"Maggie!" Will raised his voice.

"Very well, then! Pick her up gently!"

Will leaned over, then scooped the woman up beneath her shoulders and knees. Her head sagged back listlessly, exposing a creamy white neck, an invitation of sorts. Inviting . . . what? He shook his head and looked away, willing his body from continuing in that direction. Maggie ran to prop open the kitchen door. As he carried the woman carefully up the stairs, he stole a quick glance down at her unconscious face—a mere flick of his eyes down and up—as if anything longer would risk him becoming more than passively involved.

Her hair was carefully waved. She was pale, and a sickly sweet scent wove through her perfume. Spirits. Drunk, as he'd thought. Was she beautiful? Yes. No. Something in between. Despite his efforts, Will had a vague inclination to kiss her, and he immediately reeled back that ridiculous thought.

Get rid of her, was his second thought. She could ruin everything. There was a reason Will had no friends, and no guests were ever invited over to dinner. Casual conversation meant asking about work and discussing the war. Giving away answers of any kind—be they subtle truths or outright lies—might ruin everything he'd been planning for months.

"In here. Bring her in my bedroom." But Will had already started lowering her to the kitchen floor. "Oh, Will!" Maggie moaned. "Not the floor! She isn't a dog!"

"Fine. If she vomits, I don't want to hear a complaint about the mess. And I'm not cleaning it up." He straightened, then carried the woman through the narrow hallway, with its peeling wallpaper and absence of photographs. There were only two bedrooms in the small house. One was uninhabitable, crammed with pieces of broken furniture yet to be fixed and relics belonging to their childhood that Maggie refused to discard. The other bedroom was hers. Will slept on the sofa.

Maggie's bedroom reminded Will of their mother, which was why he never went in if he didn't have to. Fix a splintered floorboard, oil the creaking door. Otherwise, he pretended the room wasn't even part of the apartment. It smelled of cloves, Mother's favorite spice, and trinkets of her existence haunted the corners. A stained doily here, beneath two new books recently purchased with precious spare dollars: *How to Dress in Wartime* and *Army Guide for Women*. A scarf hanging over the lampshade. A striped blanket at the foot of the bed. Usually a glass jar or box with some ailing animal Maggie was nursing. An image flashed in his mind, of flesh that looked like sodden gray clay. Brackish water in an open mouth that would never speak again. Will had had to identify his mother at the morgue, and the images were permanent acid burns in his memory. He felt queasy, and forced the images away.

"On my bed. Careful!" Maggie pulled the coverlet down and clasped her hands together as Will laid the woman down. His sister smoothed the woman's skirt down to her calves and pulled her shoes off. "Oh! Such pretty shoes," she murmured, setting them on the floor as gingerly as if they were fine crystal. They moved to the doorway.

Will could still smell the woman's lavender fragrance on himself. He waved his hand and brushed off his biceps, but the scent remained irritatingly intact. Maggie looked expectantly up at her brother. He knew exactly what she wanted. She wanted to keep the woman, like a trinket. Like a kitten.

Little Mags. So sweet. But her naivete would only get her in trouble. It was good he was back.

"Maggie. Call the police. It's time."

"But Will, she's so cold! Maybe we could just watch her—"

"Maggie."

"I could make a little tea, and perhaps in the morning she could tell us what happened."

"Mags!"

Maggie went silent. He rarely raised his voice at her, and guilt immediately flooded him. She tugged at a braid that was pinned to the back of her head, freed the rope of hair, and began chewing on the end instead. Sometimes it seemed she was still twelve. That was the age she'd been when their mother had killed herself at Brighton Beach. And a year ago, Maggie had nearly followed.

He sighed. He was a generous brother, but there were limits. In a firm but gentle voice, he said, "Mags. It's time to call the police."

Her eyes went glassy, the way they did whenever he asked her to do something she disliked but knew was inevitable. She sighed.

As they turned away from the bedroom, a tiny voice issued from beyond the closing door. Tinier, even, than Maggie's.

The woman's voice.

"Please. I beg you. Don't call the police."

CHAPTER 2

It was a startling sound, her voice.

Maggie was used to only ever hearing Will speak within their small apartment. Even then, there had been scant words between them, and not an iota of discord. Without a syllable uttered, Maggie knew when Will wanted another cup of coffee, or an extra serving at dinner. When she was more tired than usual, Will would soundlessly rise from the kitchen table, touch her shoulder to gently pry her away from the sink, and wipe the dishes himself.

The only other feminine voice that had ever existed within these walls was their mother's ambivalent one. She had always sounded like she was asking a question, even when making a statement. *Dinner's ready? I think I have a cold? I'm not sad?*

This woman's voice was so very different.

For one, it was deeper than Maggie's girlish voice, and her mother's hesitant one. Husky, almost, as if cigarette smoke had entangled the woman's vocal cords and lured them to a permanently deep register.

"Please," the woman rasped again, just as Will pushed the bedroom door back open. Maggie was filled with a thousand questions. Who was this stranger? Why had she been unconscious? Where did she come from?

But as Maggie started to ask, the woman's eyes fluttered. She pushed herself off the pillow in an attempt to sit up, but the muscles of her forearms spasmed, and she sank back onto the bed. Her eyelids flickered closed as unconsciousness took her again.

Will turned toward the kitchen, but Maggie tugged his sleeve. "Will. No. She asked us not to call the police."

"She could be trying to rob us, Mags. She could be a s—" He stopped before saying *spy*. Everyone in the country was paranoid about spies. It was only a few months ago that German spies had been dropped off by U-boat on the beaches of Amagansett, a hundred miles east of New York City. And six days before Pearl Harbor, thirty-three men in a Nazi spy ring had been rounded up.

Saboteurs and spies were not fiction. Will was always suspicious, more than an ordinary citizen. He didn't want Maggie to know much about his work, but he'd let it slip once—just once—that General Groves was the boss of his boss. Rumor had it that Groves's work, and hence Will's, could end the war.

"Look at her," Maggie whispered, leaning toward Will's good right ear, as she did whenever she needed to speak softly. "What could she steal? Her clothes alone are worth more than our rent."

Will hesitated. She knew what he was thinking. There was no telephone nearby. Mrs. Jardin in the house next door had been wanting to buy one, but installations were on hold due to the war—so he'd have to ask someone else. Their neighbors would surely want to know the who-what-where-why-and-hows of the phone call. Even if they didn't ask, the entire party line would be listening. Maggie's brother was mortally allergic to gossip, and not only because of the secrecy of his work.

Maggie, though—she had a weakness for gossip. She lingered at doorways to hear snippets of conversations when she made her dimout rounds, and leaned closer to the neighbors waiting in the long lines at the grocery. Everyone else's lives seemed vastly more interesting than hers. And now, Maggie was on the verge of owning her very own kernel of gossip.

"Please, Will. We ought to help our fellow human beings, don't you think? She's probably running away from a beau who's been cruel to her. Or had a fight with her parents. Leave her be, just one night! I'll nurse her better, and she'll be on her way."

"You'd open up an infirmary if I didn't protest," Will growled. But Maggie felt elated. The joke meant he was near to giving in. It was time for him to leave anyway. His classes started soon, and the trolley trip to Brooklyn College took nearly forty minutes.

She gave him one last puppylike eyebrow raise.

Will sighed. "All right. One night."

She clasped her hands together like a child who'd just been given a new Raggedy Ann doll and followed him to the kitchen. Will gathered his shoulder bag with his schoolbooks, scooped the congealed supper of panada into his mouth. His portion was gone in three swallows. He tore off a hunk of stale crust from the bread box and left.

Maggie watched out the window of their tiny parlor as he lumbered down the street and disappeared around the corner. He wouldn't be home until ten o'clock or so, later if he stopped by a bar. She hurriedly ate her portion of dinner, saving a bit in case their guest woke up hungry, then tiptoed into the bedroom. She stopped first by the dresser and peered into the glass jar at its temporary tenant—the dark-brown pupa the size of a pinky finger, attached to a thick twig. She tapped lightly on the glass with her fingernail. Whatever it was, it was still safe and sound. Then she looked at her patient.

Oh, the woman was beautiful all right. Not beautiful like Veronica Lake or Hedy Lamarr. Those faces on the screen were inhuman. Perfect. This woman had an all-too-real beauty that Maggie didn't. She drew closer, just to get a better look.

The woman's lipstick matched the vivid red of her nails—Victory Red. Maggie had to stop herself from reaching out to touch her stockings. Real silk! It said something that she hadn't donated them to the war effort. Or if she had bought them recently, they would have been an exorbitant price.

She should undress the woman and put her in more appropriate clothes. Maggie hesitated. Her only experience with the care of human beings was being taken care of herself: Mama unbuttoning her dress, filling the washtub with a mix of cold tap water and boiling water from the kettle. A sprinkling of soap flakes. The smell of her mother's hair— the rose oil she always dressed herself with.

Maggie shook her head, the memory threatening to shut her eyes, clench her teeth, bite her tongue. She forced her eyes open and remembered. This person needed her help. It was such an astonishing sensation, the idea that someone else needed her—and not the reverse.

"It's the right thing to do," Maggie said again, to no one, as she knelt by the bed. She began gently pulling the coat off the woman's arms but realized she'd have to roll her over to get her fully undressed. She didn't want to wake her. She wasn't ready for that yet.

In the end, she managed to get one arm of the coat off, the woman's shoes, and her stockings. Maggie carefully wriggled out each pin in the woman's hair and placed them in a painted clamshell ashtray next to the bed. Maggie never smoked—cigarettes made her feel like she was disintegrating from the inside out, choking her in the process. The ashtray was there because she *planned* to be one of those ladies who smoked, who looked glamorous encased in a plume of gray.

And yet . . . Maggie plucked a chair from the corner of the room and set it by the bed. She watched the cadence of the woman's breath as her chest rose and descended. On the woman's left pointer finger was a thin gold ring set with an emerald-cut stone the color of blood. A ruby. It shone in the dim light, like a lone pomegranate seed. Maggie stared at it, wondering who she was and why she'd been under their stairs.

It was only when she awoke with a start, chest thumping with an unexpected, agonizing fear that the woman had left without a word, without an explanation, that she realized she'd dozed off. It was nearly midnight. She hoped Will wasn't home yet.

Normally she found Will's company comforting, but for some reason, she'd rather be left alone with her new companion. The house was quiet, and it felt as if the world outside had dissolved away. Maggie smiled, looking over at her mysterious guest, who slept soundly. It wasn't long before Maggie dozed off again.

She woke to the light of dawn and the sound of dishes clicking in the kitchen.

Quietly, so as not to wake the woman sleeping in her bed, she massaged her neck, bobbing her head this way and that. Her eyelids felt swollen and baggy. As a child, she could sleep curled up in a box—because it was fun, and because it somewhat shielded her from the noise of her parents endlessly shouting at each other. Now, her body betrayed her by showing how easily its comfort was thwarted. Even in her mere twenties, aging was not enjoyable.

When she walked into the kitchen, Will was wiping soapy water off his hands with a dishcloth. "It's time to call the police," he said, barely glancing at her. "I have to go to work soon. And you have to . . ." He turned to face her. "Didn't you say you got a job?"

Maggie sighed miserably. Yesterday, she'd been briefly incandescent about the news. Now, a job was the last thing she wanted. "I did. At the Navy Yard. I start today, actually."

"The Navy Yard?" The incredulity in Will's voice was both embarrassing and delightful.

"Yes. I passed the civil service exam. I got my acceptance letter yesterday. I'm going to be a welder."

Even for Will, the silence stretched on too long. She rushed to fill it. "Well, they said they needed help in the sewing loft, but I'm not that good at sewing. I can't drive, so I couldn't be a chauffeurette. And they just filled positions for ship riggers and toolroom attendants." She puffed out her chest. "Apparently welders make the most money. And they'll pay me while I'm training too."

"I see." It was Will's turn to sigh. It was obvious he didn't think she'd be able to keep this job either. "I'll call the police. You'd better wake her up."

Maggie nodded, resigned, and returned to the bedroom. The woman was still sound asleep. She hated to wake her, and yet, a part of her was excited. She'd finally get some answers.

She patted the woman's shoulder. "Miss," she whispered. "Wake up, miss."

When the woman didn't stir, Maggie tried her hand. It was warm, and so soft. It reminded her of her mother's hands after she'd slathered them with Pond's Cold Cream. Reflexively, Maggie slipped her hand into the woman's, palm to palm. She allowed her fingers to close around the woman's hand and waited.

The woman squeezed back.

Maggie's breath caught.

She'd never really held anyone's hand before, aside from her mother's. Her brother shied away from physical contact, and she'd had no beau to speak of. Even when she was a child, her teachers always seemed to guide her using a single hand pressed like an iron paddle between her shoulders. Maggie watched the woman's eyes open slowly and a pink color begin to suffuse her cheeks.

"No," she moaned.

The hand squeezed Maggie's harder. It tightened from soft, tentative pressure to a relentless grasp. The woman's body spasmed, and she cried out like a stricken dog. "No. God, *no!*"

She clawed Maggie's skin with the nails of her other hand—so hard Maggie yelped with pain. "Will!" she screamed.

Will was in the room in less than a second. He always came so swiftly, as if he'd run, and yet his movements were so controlled and slow that it defied explanation. He assessed the situation in a blink.

His large hands grasped the woman's wrist and pried her fingers off Maggie's, now scored red where the fingernails had gouged her. He grabbed the woman's shoulders and shook her, hard.

If a person could roar quietly, Will did. "Wake. Up." The walls nearly shook from his command.

The woman's eyes seemed to gain focus. She looked wildly at the ceiling, at Will, at the bed.

"Oh God," she gasped, shaking her head violently. "Don't hurt me. Please don't hurt me."

Will immediately released her shoulders, and she scuttled back against the headboard, eyes still wild.

"No one's going to hurt you here," Will said gruffly.

"Oh no! Not at all," Maggie said, moving closer to the bed. "You were unconscious outside. You were going to freeze to death, so we brought you here. Into our home." Reluctantly, she added, "We're about to call the police."

"No. No police," the woman said immediately.

"But—" Maggie began, and the woman clasped her hands together. "Please. He'll know I'm here. He'll hurt me. I can't go back."

Maggie and Will looked at each other. He gave her a look that said, *Don't you dare ask. Don't get involved.* But she couldn't help herself.

"Who?" Maggie said.

The woman was still shaking her head and had gathered her knees to her chest. In the light of morning, Maggie saw what had been unnoticeable last night. Faint purple marks on her leg, near her calf. How had Maggie missed them when she'd taken off her stockings? And where the collar of her half-removed coat had come away from her neck, there were more bruises.

Will had seen them too. He hesitated, but shook his head. "I'm sorry, but that's not our concern. You can't stay here. Why don't you get your things and go home now?"

"I don't have a home," she said in that same low voice, so penetrating and direct.

"Of course you do. You've had some disagreement with your friends or your family," Will said in his let's-be-reasonable voice. Which was, to be honest, his all-the-time voice.

"I'll pay you . . . for the room. For your trouble. I just need some time. Please." She looked down at herself, then wrested the ruby ring off her hand and held it out as an offering. "Take this. It's worth a lot. It's all I have. Just a few days. I promise I won't be any trouble."

Maggie looked at Will, afraid. He'd become so hardened over these last years. He'd taken care of her and, yes, was even tender on occasion, but . . . good God, she prayed, there must still be a heart in there somewhere. If he was unable to help even a woman in distress, Maggie would know somehow that it was all her fault. Perhaps she had wrung dry all he had to give.

The woman seemed to sense the battle going on behind Will's still, amber eyes. Moisture gathered on her lower lashes, and her eyebrows knit together. "If you turn me away, I might as well be dead." She still held out the ring, but now her fingers trembled. When Will still didn't move, she put the ring on the night table next to her. "Keep it. As a thank-you for taking me in last night." She blotted her face with the back of her hand. "Give me a minute, and I'll get out of your way. I'm . . . I'm so sorry."

Maggie, anxious to avoid being witness to the embarrassment of the woman putting herself together, began to back out the door. But Will continued to stand there. There was a hollow look in his eye, as if he recognized something in this woman that he loathed to see. Something he'd seen in Maggie.

Maggie knew what it felt like when death was a better option than living. Even though they'd shared their meals together this past year, listening in silence to Mayor La Guardia on the radio every Sunday afternoon, there was always something else, something enormous, taking up space in their home. That bleak desolation that belonged to Maggie and their mother and that they never discussed.

Will was still staring at the woman, who was wiping her face again and trying to put on the other half of her coat. But her hands were shaking, and her face had the pasty pale complexion of someone about to pass out. Her forehead was speckled with perspiration. After struggling with her coat, she began to cry. Like a child.

"Will." Maggie spoke his name less as the segue to a question and more as a statement, the way a person might say, "It's cold out" or "The sun is golden." She had come to her decision. She was no longer asking.

He turned to her and sighed in resignation. Then he looked away and headed for the door.

"I'm going to work. There had better not be anything stolen when I come back."

"There's nothing to steal," Maggie reminded him, following him out of the bedroom. "Nothing of worth, at least."

He clamped his hat on his head and grabbed his coat. Before he shut the back door behind him, he said gently, "There's always something worth stealing, Mags."

She knew he wasn't talking about the teakettle or the worn sheets. Maggie put her hand on her chest, took a deep breath, and returned to the bedroom, where the woman was still quietly sobbing.

"It's okay," Maggie said. "You don't have to leave. Everything is going to be all right." Maggie wasn't sure if she was speaking about herself, or the war, or the mysterious predicament that had landed this woman in Maggie's bedroom, but she felt more optimism than she had in a year. The certainty that things were about to change for the better.

It was a lie she embraced, no matter how often she told it to herself.

CHAPTER 3

Will was astonished at how he had let Maggie convince him to allow a complete stranger into their home. They knew nothing about her but what they could judge by her looks. And looks lied. They lied all the time.

Will was a perfect example of that. His tangled hair, broad shoulders, and sheer poundage of muscle made people think three things when he walked down the street:

Dumb as a rock.

Violent.

A danger to women.

He was used to people eyeing him with fear. It made his life easier in many ways. Sidewalks became less crowded; people rarely challenged him. But lately, with the war, the looks were more of confusion and slight disgust. He knew what they thought—his muscle ought to be doing something worthwhile in France. Instead, the words spoken by his mother to his fifteen-year-old self stayed with him every day, every hour.

Help Maggie, she'd said. *It's your duty now. I can't anymore.*

I just can't.

She had spoken these words a week before she killed herself. And a decade later, Maggie attempted to walk into the same icy waters of

Lower New York Bay with the goal of never returning to land alive. Will's guilt was an incessant burden, heavy as a leaden cloak. He should have been more careful. More caring. He should have seen the signs, but he was too consumed with college and all the subatomic work with Fermi and what it could mean for the world. Luckily, Maggie had been found half-alive washed up on Brighton Beach, because she hadn't had the foresight to weigh herself down before she'd tried to drown herself. All that, because she had been fired from a sewing job.

His mother. Maggie. The failures were watermarks upon his conscience that would never rub out. Coming home had been the only answer.

Will got off the trolley in Sunset Park and boarded the ferry to Staten Island. His work at the Dean Mill Plant would only take another day. Though they'd loaded 114 drums onto flat-bottomed barges yesterday, there was more ore to be shipped. The barges would float to the Lehigh Valley Railroad Company pier and be loaded into railcars there. He didn't know if today's shipment was destined for Port Hope again, or a refinery in upstate New York.

The ferry was not terribly crowded. Most people were commuting into Manhattan and Brooklyn from Staten Island, not the other way around. Many would go to the shipyards. Which reminded Will— Maggie was starting work today. He wondered if she'd last more than a few hours.

While the ferry traversed the Narrows, he realized that he was being watched. Or at least, he thought so. He'd been grooming his ability to sense when eyes were on him. Will looked up from his physics book as the ferry approached the dock, motors rumbling louder as it positioned itself and slowed. There had been a man in the corner of the benches where he sat with a few other people, but when he looked up, the man had turned away. All Will could appreciate was his size. Six feet. Sloping shoulders. Clothes of an everyday working man, but hair that was salt and pepper, like someone a generation or two older. Will looked away, hoping the man would turn around again so he could catch a face. But when he looked up again, the man had left.

The book disappeared into Will's canvas shoulder bag, and he took the railway to the Tower Hill stop. The Dean Mill Plant was a short walk from there. Beneath the Bayonne Bridge, there was always a pall of gloom. The few boats sliced silently through the water between Staten Island and Constable Hook, as if being graded for good behavior. The dirt underfoot was crumbled pavement, stone, dying weeds, and grass.

Today, the longshoremen were absent. Instead, one of General Groves's men waited for him—an active duty army man but clad in civilian clothing, so as not to bring attention to himself. He stood as stiff as a board. You couldn't have squeezed the army out of him if you tried.

"William," he said, exhaling on a cigarette. "You're late."

Will paused. It was that woman's fault he was late. *See,* he would tell Maggie. *She's already messing up our lives.* In his mind's eye, he saw the pulse beneath the smooth skin of her neck, her steady breathing as she lay unconscious on Maggie's bed. His heart snapped an extra beat, and he coughed. "Won't happen again. So. Not shipping today?"

"No. Here are your orders." He handed Will an envelope and gently kicked a box at his feet. "You'll need this too." Will didn't open the envelope; he simply stared for a long minute. If there was one thing that made humans uncomfortable, it was silence. They didn't know what to do with it, except to fill it with words that gave away their inner thoughts—an arsenal of useful information.

The man stayed unhelpfully silent, turned on his heel, and was gone.

Will lit a cigarette, then opened the envelope. The note was simple. Perform inventory on the remaining barrels. Make sure they were full and gather samples for purity testing. His bosses needed to know that everything African Metals sent was as expected, and not a thousand tons of dog shit. The next line gave him pause.

Mrs. Rivers will be by at 15:00 to speak to you.

"Mrs. Rivers?" Will said aloud to nobody. Mrs. Rivers was the secretary for her husband, Archibald Rivers, who worked directly under General Groves. The secret murmurings were that Groves was working on a project at the Manhattan Engineer District that would end the war. Possibly a weapon. But what Will mostly heard about were the tasks meted out by Mrs. Rivers. He reported only to her, and his entire world revolved elliptically around when he would next see her to report on a job completed or to receive a new task. Otherwise, Will spoke to no one at the MED. He wasn't army personnel or a scientist, like many involved at the level of Rivers and Groves, but his was the work that made the entire project possible. Finding places and items, moving precious metals, occasionally bending rules, all without bringing undue attention to the project. The army couldn't work in the shadows. Will could.

He'd only ever met Mrs. Rivers's husband once. As for General Groves . . . well. That would never happen. People like Will didn't speak to such men.

Mrs. Rivers. Coming here. The hackles on his neck rose. Usually, he met her at the towering building on Chambers and Broadway where the MED headquarters lived.

Will took in a deep breath that smelled of New York bay water, and tossed his spent cigarette into the cloudy water of Kill Van Kull. When he was a child, he used to think the smell was like sewage mixed with rotted algae, but now he recognized the scent for what it was. The peculiar tidal mix of salt and fresh water, of wooden piers and docks succumbing to the moisture, of a port alive and thriving. Possibly hiding U-boats.

Will was alone to do this work. He was never sure if he was being watched or not, so he simply assumed he was, most likely by the MED to be sure he wasn't selling secrets. He stared up at the vast three-story warehouse that normally stored vegetable oil. Several large steel tanks stood next to it, along with a seed elevator that went unused for the moment. The factory building was shut with double padlocks since the MED was now using the rest of the facility for the war effort. He picked up the unmarked box and walked around to a smaller storage building.

Inside, the remaining barrels took up most of the space. Will opened the box to find sampling jars, gloves, and scoops. He started on the third floor, prying off the tops of several random drums, scooping the dark, dusty, crumbly black uranium ore into glass vials and labeling them. By the time he finished, there were thirty vials, and the samples showed (at least to Will's eye) that the barrels contained what they should—pitchblende.

No one had ever told him what greater project he was working on. He'd heard the hushed title "Manhattan Project" mentioned on the eighteenth floor of the MED, though never to his face. But what Mrs. Rivers asked him to do fit in with what he surmised about it. H. G. Wells had written fiction about an atomic bomb. And in 1932, James Chadwick had discovered the neutron—another particle in the atomic nucleus. It was a Hungarian, Leó Szilárd, who'd postulated that a nuclear chain reaction could occur with these particles. A chain reaction that could unleash untold amounts of energy. Enough to destroy towns. Perhaps even entire cities. A single weapon to bring the world to its knees.

It was no wonder that the eighteenth floor of the MED practically reeked with anxious desperation.

Somehow, working on this theoretical weapon felt mostly like a game. Will couldn't actually fathom that it would be used. One test would be all it took to force the other side to negotiate an end to the conflict. But if Will played the game correctly, he'd find himself in a prime position after the war. Right now, he was one of many trying to help move mountains. One day, he wanted to be the person ordering the mountain to be moved.

The rest of the work didn't take but a few hours, counting barrels and hand weighing several at the station on the ground floor. By early afternoon, he was done.

Now, he waited. For two hours, he smoked and sat on the pier by the locked doors of the warehouse, box of samples at his side. Presumably Mrs. Rivers was coming to collect the samples, but he had a feeling she wanted to talk about more than just that. Will was oddly wound up and tense, despite the quiet of the unmanned warehouse.

He couldn't stop thinking about that mysterious woman in the bedroom of his house.

It would be simple enough to find out who she was. If the police didn't know something about a missing woman, then the papers might mention it. But what if they didn't? What would he and Maggie do? What if they got in trouble somehow . . . with her family?

Damn. See, that was what Will was always trying to avoid. He had to be clean as a bar of soap or his job with the MED might be in danger.

A woman's voice punctuated the relative quiet. "Did you spend our bond money staring at New Jersey all day?"

Will turned abruptly. Usually women's heels made more noise, but she had walked up behind him and he hadn't even noticed.

"Mrs. Rivers." He stood and flicked his cigarette into the water, then wiped his hands on his trousers. Not that she'd shake his hand. She usually kept a distance, which he preferred anyway.

She smiled. She was of medium height, had brown hair and brown eyes, and wore one of those newfangled dresses that tied around her tiny waist. He remembered Maggie saying something about how zippers and buttons wasted materials that could go to the war effort. The fabrics were mostly drab browns and grays, but the one part of her person that stood out was the violent shade of velvety red lipstick. When she delivered an order from her husband, the words were always like a razor blade. However, coming from those particular scarlet lips, the message felt more like a rusted blade meant to give you a terminal case of teta-nus. Even her smiles felt unsafe.

"Go ahead," she said. "Tell me what you were thinking, all these hours."

About that woman? God, no. "I was thinking you should have shipped the rest of these barrels today," he said. "And tested them earlier when you had the chance."

"They haven't decided where to put them. They might need them here, in Manhattan."

"No, they won't." Will took out his cigarettes and offered one to her. She took it between tapered fingers with nails painted an identical shade as her lips. Her hand gently leaned on his as he held the lit match.

"And why won't they need them here?" she asked at the end of an exhale.

"It's unrefined."

She nodded. It was a test, to see if he really knew what he was talking about.

"But when it returns from wherever they've sent it, it's going to have to go somewhere."

Her face was hidden in smoke. "Go on."

"Somewhere nearby. Columbia is going to do the testing on the refined pitchblende, aren't they?"

Mrs. Rivers said nothing. That was as good as a yes.

"And somewhere in all that refined pitchblende is a tiny amount of the right kind of uranium you need to start a chain reaction. But you need more. You need to enrich a large amount of the right kind, the right isotope."

This time, Mrs. Rivers froze, the cigarette an inch away from her lips.

Ah. It was an educated guess, but it must be correct. Somewhere in this pile of unrefined uranium was the isotope of uranium that would be the one—the atom that could start the chain reaction, but only if they had enough to keep it going. But it would be incredibly difficult to separate that isotope out, scarce as it was. How to get enough of it?

He'd heard a location slip out of Mrs. Rivers's mouth once when she was exiting her husband's office: Tennessee. Something was being built there, something enormous. No doubt other countries were racing toward the same goal. If he could help the Allies win, Will's life would change in a way that would make up for all the disappointments up until now.

He was getting ahead of himself. If he didn't keep his eyes in front of him instead of on the sky, he'd fall on his face.

She spoke so softly it sounded like a flutter of a bird's wings. "Be quiet."

"There's no one listening."

"There's always someone listening, Will." She relaxed her shoulders. "So. Who told you?"

"You just did," he said.

She smiled a tiny bit. "There are days when I can't figure out if you're a liability or an asset, William Scripps."

"Don't worry. I'm the latter."

"Good. But I won't stop worrying," she said. "So about the warehouses."

"Yes. There are several nearby that would suffice. But not this one," said Will.

"Obviously." She inhaled deeply, and let the smoke curl out of her lips. "Mr. Rivers has a list already, but he needs someone to scout them out."

"When?"

"By end of next week," she said. "But I'd appreciate a report in ten days, if you can manage that."

"That I can. And when we find these warehouses, you'll have to gather more guards. That soldier who delivered your message this morning is the only one watching over this place." He cocked his head toward the bridge. "Isn't he?"

She smiled again. "Is your sister as clever as you, Mr. Scripps?"

Will shrugged. He didn't like to talk about his personal life at work, though he had been as open as possible about his life when he was first hired. One shy sister, no friends, and two dead parents with no relatives? He was perfect. He knew Mrs. Rivers knew plenty about Maggie already. The question was whether he'd answer her.

"I suppose one of you takes after your mother, and one after your father," she continued.

"We don't have the same father," Will said, and immediately regretted speaking. It was instinct, when people asked why he and Maggie were so very different. Not just in looks, but nature. One was quiet from shyness, the other because he wielded silence almost as a weapon. They seemed as well related sometimes as a tortoise and a grizzly bear. After Will's father had died in the Great War, his mother had been despondent and nearly desperate to remarry. And she did, the first man who'd have her. She was pregnant with Maggie even before they got married. Her body, soul, and pocketbook were dependent upon a person who seemed to loathe the responsibility. And then he'd died, too, from an unglamorous work accident. Not from serving his country.

Will realized he'd stiffened and clenched his jaw. Mrs. Rivers never asked anything about his personal life. The shift in their conversation made him wary. Was she wanting a more personal relationship with Will, or was she, God forbid, flirting? Will had no interest in being doll-dizzy, chasing skirts. Two lightning-bolt events had happened yesterday—Maggie finding a job and the appearance of the mystery woman. Was Mrs. Rivers trying to get him to admit something? Her eyebrow lifted ever so slightly.

"Also, I have the samples that you requested," he said, forcing himself to relax before she asked any more questions.

"I'll take them."

"You'll dirty your dress." He lifted the box, which was smudged with dirt.

"I'm not afraid of dirt, Mr. Scripps." The box was heavy, nearly thirty pounds, but she tucked it against her hip as one might a toddler. He noticed she had a gold pin on her dress, embellished with scrolled *H* and *R* initials. What was her first name? Harriet? Henrietta? He had an urge to ask, but she began to walk back to an idling car he hadn't noticed before, off to the side of the building. They'd been watched the whole time. Mr. Rivers himself might be in there.

"What are you afraid of?" he asked quietly, half expecting her to not hear him. She was ten feet away now. She stopped and pivoted, but didn't face him.

"It doesn't really matter, does it? We all have our own nightmares, custom made. For me, and for you." She turned her head just enough to make eye contact. Will wondered exactly how much of his file Mr. Rivers had let her see. He knew somehow that even without a glance inside it, Mrs. Rivers could probably bring Will to his knees if given the opportunity.

Good God, Will, he thought as the car drove away. The women in my life are going to be the death of me.

CHAPTER 4

October 21, 1942

Dear Mama,
Something interesting happened. But first there is other news!
Today I begin work at the Navy Yard. I passed the civil ser-
vice exam, and before spring, I'll be welding on battleships
instead of just for practice. I'll know them inside and out,
can you believe it? I know what you're thinking. A little girl
like me can't do a man's work. But I can try. Don't give up
on me yet! I can be stronger than anyone believes me to be.

It's so cold today. No snow yet, though. Small mercies!
Meatless Tuesdays are apparently going very well in the
city, though I do not think William likes to go without
meat on any day. Apparently our good country and the
Britons have sunk five hundred and thirty U-Boats. And
yet, the war does not seem to be progressing in any good
way. How long will it last? I wish I knew.

I am still making my rounds helping with the
dimouts every night on our street. Mr. Potts, four houses
down—do you remember him?—is very ornery about
the whole thing. He likes to read at night and dislikes it

when I ask him to turn the lights out. He has also resisted buying blackout curtains, or trying the black paint or window paper. He is incorrigible.

Next week, I am hoping to double my time airplane spotting. They always need more spotters. They prefer to have the women stay in the offices to collect the information, instead of actually standing guard on the roofs to spot planes, but I'd rather be outside. Abercrombie and Fitch is selling steamship chairs, rugs, and foot warmers for spotters. What an extravagance I don't need!

The bomb shelter I've been working on in my spare time is going very well. In our basement, I have gathered some dry food that should not spoil for a long while, plus water, a small supply of bandages, and blankets. It is not enough. I never feel safe. I think I should start sleeping there instead of my own bed.

Speaking of which, I did not sleep in my bed last night. This is the interesting thing that happened! We have a new guest, and her history is a complete mystery. Please don't be angry with me. I know you always say to be wary of strangers, but if I needed help, I would be a stranger to someone else, and oughtn't they to help me too?

Please, don't be angry.

I shall tell you more soon. William is livid about it, though of course he doesn't say so.

I am writing this letter on the trolley, heading to the Navy Yard, so excuse my terrible penmanship. I am very nervous. I am afraid I shall ruin everything. Wish me the strength to stay there, so that I may do my duty as best as I can.

Much love,
Maggie

———✦———

Maggie folded the letter into an envelope and put it in her pocket. Writing the letter on the trolley had soothed her nervousness. She wasn't even sure what to wear, so she had pulled on a pair of pants, her second-best shoes, and a warm coat over her cardigan. She knew the letter, addressed to her deceased mother, had no true destiny ending up in those hands. God knows, she'd never tell Will she had such a habit. But describing her daily doings helped her live with more intention, and so it had become a ritual. Some days, she unburdened her heart further and would write, "I miss you" or "I loathe speaking to new people" on a slip of paper. Those ended up scrapped in the trash can. Even she couldn't go so far as to declare her softheartedness to the universe. During wartime especially, there was only duty. No room for wasted sentiment. Still, if not for the almost daily exercise of putting pen to paper, she might not have the courage to go to the shipyards today.

Before she had left home, Maggie had ducked into the washroom and opened the tiny medicine cabinet. There was a small bottle of Luminal that was a few years old. The doctor had prescribed it for her when she'd begun having nervous attacks, and it always settled her into a complacent stupor with a brutal efficiency. She doled out one tablet and curled her fingers around it, then filled a glass with water.

The stranger still lay in her bedroom, curled up on her side. Maggie could tell from the rise and fall of her back that she wasn't sleeping. Too quick, and too shallow. Maggie walked around to the other side of the bed. Streaks of moisture drew a path from the edges of the woman's eyes down to the pillow, where they darkened the cotton coverlet.

"I . . . I brought you something. To make you feel better." Maggie dropped to her knees and held out the pill. "I have to go to work, see, and I'd like to take care of you, but I can't. Will would be so disappointed if I don't actually go to work, and we need the money . . ."

The woman opened her eyes, blinking rapidly. She pushed herself to a sitting position and blotted her wet face with the backs of her wrists. Even this movement was painfully elegant compared to Maggie's general bumbling. Maggie was the kid with snot running in torrents from her nose during a cry, mopping her face with her sleeve, dragging mucous trails and ropy muck all over her face and hair.

"I'm so sorry. Of course you have to work," the woman said, again in that entrancing, husky voice. "I won't be much trouble to you or your husband. I promise."

"Oh." Maggie blushed. "Will isn't my husband! He's my brother. Our parents died a while back, and . . . it's cheaper to share a place. Everyone is packed together these days. Here. Take this." Maggie pressed the chalky pill into her hand.

"What is it?"

"For your nerves. It'll do you good."

"What is it?" she repeated. "An opiate? Barbiturate? Chloral hydrate?" The quickness with which she rattled off medications alarmed Maggie. Why did she know them so easily? There was a wary look on her face. Maggie's heart began to beat fast. She didn't want to be mistrusted. But she didn't want the woman to leave either. At least not until tonight, when she could learn more about her. This stranger was the most interesting thing that had happened lately.

"I . . . I'm not really sure," Maggie stammered. "They gave it to me when I was having a . . . crisis. During the years after my mother died. It calmed me down."

The woman studied the pill, then looked at Maggie. Her eyes had stopped tearing, and she tilted her head ever so slightly.

"I trust you."

Maggie's heart wanted to blurt out, *You do? Wonderful!*

The woman went on. "I think you're trying to help."

"What else would I do?" Maggie said artlessly, before realizing what she was saying. Oh. Someone had been hurting her, like she had said before. "I wouldn't hurt you," Maggie added.

"No. No, I don't think you would." The woman smiled, as if coming to the resolution right then and there. She took the pill from Maggie's hand and drank it down with the glass of water.

"There now. Go back to sleep. The washroom is down the hall. We'll lock the doors so you're safe. When I get home, we'll get a bath running, and have a nice dinner, and . . ."

And she didn't really know what next. But she could hardly wait for it. Tentatively, Maggie reached her hand toward the woman, who stiffened at her approach. Maggie tugged out one hairpin that she must have missed the day before. The last of the woman's curls tumbled to her shoulders.

"There. Now you can sleep without this dreadful thing poking your head."

The woman smiled. She leaned forward, and this time it was Maggie's turn to stiffen at the closeness. Gently, she kissed Maggie's cheek.

"You're an angel," she said, sighing, as she lay back onto the pillow. Maggie pulled a blanket over her, and the woman closed her eyes. As Maggie went to shut the door, the woman spoke again, her voice muffled against the pillow.

"Pardon?" Maggie turned back.

"I said, my name is Laurel."

Maggie had tried not to grin like a child who'd just been given a bag of candy. "I'm Maggie Scripps."

"It's nice to meet you, Maggie. Finally," Laurel had said before yawning.

This morning's events already seemed too long ago. When Maggie looked up at the morning rush crowd filling the trolley, it occurred to her that perhaps none of this—the woman's arrival just as she was about to start her new job at the Navy Yard—was a coincidence.

But Maggie brushed the feeling off.

She wished she didn't have to work, that she could just go home and watch Laurel sleep. Laurel! What a gorgeous name! Like trees, and green leaves, and perfumed, fragrant things. Not like Maggie, which sounded like *baggy*, or *saggy*. It was anything but beautiful.

Saggy. Sad Maggie, who could barely survive on her own. Who preferred to follow in her mother's footsteps to the depths of the Lower Bay rather than face another failure. Despite her pounding heart reminding her of all those past truths, she straightened her back and decided that today would change her life in another way. Will hadn't believed her capable of holding down a job, let alone even qualifying for a Navy Yard position. To be honest, Maggie herself hadn't believed it. But this time, with this job, things would be different.

She would be different.

The trolley rang and jolted to a stop, emptying its belly full of workers. Some looked as nervous as she, the women clutching their purses as they cautiously lined up at the Sands Street Gates a few blocks away. If the gates were meant to elicit awe and patriotic pride, they did. The gates were flanked by what seemed like two squat castles, the gatehouses, complete with battlement-topped towers, as if awaiting siege from bowmen below. Large stone eagles perched atop the columns on either side, wings spread. Maggie saw a post office letter box, dropped her letter in, and stood in line like the other workers. When it was her turn to enter, a guard checked her ID and looked in her purse.

"No booze?" he asked.

"No."

"No newspapers?"

"Uh, no." What was wrong with newspapers?

The guard noticed her quizzical expression. "They're bad for morale," he said.

"Oh."

He kept looking. What else was there to search for? She didn't carry lipstick. Just a handkerchief, peppermints, aspirin, money, and sometimes a Kotex. A single scribbled note about where to arrive, and when. She would be late if this took any longer.

"You're new," the guard said gruffly.

"Yes."

"Punch in over there. You have papers in your purse. Don't do that again. You could be a spy smuggling notes for all we know."

"Oh. All right." Maggie blushed. She wouldn't make the same mistake. She was glad she'd already mailed her letter.

"You know what's good for morale?" The side of his mouth stitched up into a lopsided grin as he handed back her purse. "Lipstick. I like the red kind."

Her blushing went from 99 degrees Fahrenheit to 212 in half a second, but before she could say anything—or even decide if there was anything to say—the guard was searching the woman in line behind her.

She punched in, put the new ID they'd given her yesterday in her purse, and made her way to Building 4. Here, she would learn how the sinews of a ship were put together, how to keep them strong, how riveting something correctly or incorrectly could mean a win or failure in a crucial battle. She wanted to show everyone that she was capable of something that would truly affect this damned war. Make it end for good.

There were a dozen other girls walking with her toward Building 4. She couldn't see any of the dry docks from here, just brick and metal buildings. Barracks. A pipe and copper shop. The smithery. Across Wallabout Bay, a watery indentation of Brooklyn, she could see the lower east side of Manhattan. To her left, the top of a huge hammerhead crane turned and loaded a gun cannon onto an unseen ship. There was nothing but noise surrounding her—the chatter of workers, the insistent whirr of riveters, screams of metal being cut, the hiss of steam. Eyes wide, Maggie tried to pair sounds with actions or tools or people, but there was simply too much going on.

A group of workmen carrying cables over their shoulders walked by.

"Go iron something," one of them hollered at the women.

"Look at those arms! Won't be able to lift more than a hanky!"

"You can put that red pucker right here." That one pointed to his bristly cheek.

A few of the men stopped and tipped their caps. Maggie blushed, and then blushed more furiously as the hollering got louder. Walking faster, she stumbled from a divot on the pavement. The men whooped louder.

"Can't even walk, how can she weld?"

Maggie was one more catcall away from turning on her heel and running home to watch Laurel sleep all day. That would be infinitely better than this.

"Never mind them," a woman behind her said. She hooked Maggie's arm before she could protest, and practically dragged her forward. "Bunch of silly mutts. Those dolts forget we're all on the same team."

"Thank you," Maggie said breathlessly.

"It's nothing." The woman clutched her arm harder. "I'm Holly. And I'm scared as heck to be here."

Maggie glanced at her, finally having enough courage not to just stare at her shoestrings. The woman was her height, but appeared strong—wide shoulders, ample bosom and hips. Her eyes were large and clear brown, nose like the edge of an envelope, and thin lips covered in red lipstick.

"You're scared?" Maggie asked. "I thought it was just me."

"Mmm." Holly shook her head. "I've never had a hard day of work in my life, but I got to start somehow, and there are bills to pay."

"And it's our patriotic duty," Maggie added.

"Oh. Of course!" Holly said, lips curving into a friendly grin. "That too."

Building 4 was large, an awning protruding from the side painted with white letters: SHIPFITTER SHOP—TRAINING PROGRAM B—ANNEX—WELDING SCHOOL. The women punched their cards, and one by one passed inside the building. Their supervisor was waiting for them—an imposing woman with serious, crinkled eyes who launched into roll call. Maggie was agog but tried to pay attention. The twelve other girls here were from all backgrounds—every shade of skin and texture of hair. They were shown to an area where they stashed their purses and confronted orderly piles of protective welding gear.

The supervisor started the training immediately. "You'll have dungarees to wear over your clothes or a welding apron, plus a cape." She held up a funny-looking shirt that seemed like it only had sleeves connected at the top—nothing to cover the torso. It was made of thick material, like layered canvas or leather. "We'll also provide welding gloves, and goggles or a helmet. Everyone will be fitted today, and you're to keep your things here, in your labeled cubbies. We recommend you wear practical clothing to work. Please purchase your own steel-toed boots. You'll be lifting and moving heavy sheets of metal, and you will get your toes chopped off like carrots if you are not careful. And it's easier and faster to get ready if you wear trousers. Many of you will be working out of doors, so wear flannels beneath your clothes. No heels whatsoever!"

Maggie was proud that she was already dressed sensibly. She was used to wearing Will's hand-me-downs, large and ill fitting. Many of the girls had worn skirts and heels and were blushing about being dressed so inappropriately. The supervisor glanced at Maggie and nodded approvingly, as if to say, *Thank goodness you have a smart head on your shoulders.*

Pride. What an odd new feeling. It fit Maggie strangely. But she liked it.

"We recommend you cut your hair short, and keep your bangs out of your eyes. No hang-down hairdos. Pin your hair up in victory rolls like Veronica Lake does, and always wear a kerchief or safety cap. Hair is extremely flammable, so if you don't want a burnt scalp and singed hair, you'll be on your guard."

"Veronica Lake," Holly whispered. "Even she couldn't look glamorous in those welding aprons."

Maggie glanced around at the other women surreptitiously touching their hair. This time, when the supervisor nodded at Maggie's kerchief, the other girls noticed the approval.

"Pay attention!"

The other girls' heads snapped up.

"Now, just because your clothes are practical, doesn't mean you ought to stop being beautiful." She looked pointedly away from Maggie this time. "Lipstick and powder are acceptable, so long as your primping does not take away time from work."

Holly smacked her lips together, and the women laughed.

Perhaps she should wear lipstick more often. Maybe that guard was right. But at the thought, her mind went to Laurel's beautiful lips, and how she was sleeping in Maggie's bed right now.

The rest of the morning was a blur of new experiences. The welding cape was smothering and quite heavy. It felt hilarious and unfinished, covering her arms, shoulders, and upper chest only. She was told how to lift the helmet up or down, when to use goggles. The women wiggled their fingers within the thick gloves, testing how they felt. Everything smelled burnt. And yet, the gear didn't bother her at all. She felt all the more powerful wearing it, and couldn't care less if it made her unfeminine. It was such a wonderful feeling, not being the weakest link in the chain.

There was a long lecture on the science and techniques behind stick welding, and Maggie learned all sorts of new words, like *flux* and *arc* and *electrode*. She was nervous each time the instructor called on her, but she found she could answer the questions. Holly winked at her every time she got the answer right.

At eleven thirty, the lunch whistle blew. Maggie was exhausted, and only half a day had gone by. She was rubbing her tired eyes when Holly nudged her as they left the building.

"Come on. You'll be fine. Let's get some grub."

Crews were leaving the shipways in search of food. Some exited the Sands Street Gates to eat outside, but many headed to the canteens and purchased brown boxed lunches for forty cents. Maggie bought a cheese sandwich, but she wouldn't do this again. She ought to save money. Because of the stranger in their home, she hadn't even thought about making time to shop or preparing a lunch today. She wondered if Laurel was still sleeping. What Laurel usually ate for lunch. What those elegant fingers would look like holding a cheese sandwich.

She and Holly wandered over to an area by Dry Dock 1, the smallest one. They peeled the wax paper off their sandwiches and bit deeply into them. All around Wallabout Bay, workers were scurrying over ships of various sizes, under repair or being built. A destroyer was being repaired in Dry Dock 4. Maggie gaped at the size and at the enormity of the tens of thousands of workers around them, seen and unseen. She had read in the paper about how the dry docks were filled with water so boats could be floated in, then the water drained for the repair process. The huge battleships were constructed in the slipways, or "ways," that would eventually launch them into the bay.

"I heard the USS *Missouri* is in one of the ways. Wish I could see it," Holly said.

"We probably will be welding on it, eventually." Just saying the words made her proud.

Holly shook her head. "I didn't think it would be like this."

"It's dirtier," Maggie said, chewing mechanically. The sandwich could have been cheese; it could have been clay. She hardly noticed. Her mind was tired yet buzzing. What a day so far.

Holly took an enormous bite. Her lipstick left crescent stains on the white bread. "This wasn't my first choice for a job," she admitted, brushing crumbs from her lips. "I didn't want to work here."

Maggie considered that. "I thought that women aren't meant to do this kind of work. But I'm glad I'm here."

"Me too. Could you imagine working in the flag loft and stitching all day?"

"I can't sew a straight line," Maggie said, grinning.

"I'll bet you can weld a straight line."

Maggie was betting on it too. She was so excited she put down her sandwich.

"Gonna eat that?" Holly asked, and Maggie handed it over. It went down in a single bite. My, but Holly was hungry. After swallowing and taking a drink of coffee, she admitted, "You know what I wanted to do? I wanted to fly planes."

Maggie's eyes went big. "Really! Like, really fly them? Not just make them?"

"Yes. I always loved planes, trains, and automobiles. I love that you can take a hunk of metal and add something combustible and whoosh! Off it goes! It's a miracle. I'm a very good driver. I'll drive you around someday, when I earn enough to buy my own car after the war is over." She gazed around the shipyard. Workers were already returning from their half-hour lunch. "The Women in National Defense Service was recruiting for female flyers last year, and my ma said no. Too dangerous. But now that I'm out of the house, maybe I will someday. But they're not recruiting anymore."

Out of the house? Maggie wondered if that was a euphemism for being kicked out. "I wish they made airplanes here," she said. "That would be even more exciting than ships."

"No, they only manufacture planes in Buffalo, Bethpage, Farmingdale, Tarrytown . . ." Holly ticked off her fingers until she noticed Maggie watching her.

"How do you know all that?"

"Oh." Holly shruggèd. "I just do." She looked into the distance, where the hammerhead crane was now lifting a load of sheet metal onto the enormous ship in Dry Dock 3. It occurred to Maggie that Holly hadn't really answered her question. But Holly continued talking as if Maggie weren't there anymore. Her tone changed, like she was speaking to someone else altogether. "All the flight schools are in the south, in Texas. I can't afford to go there. Ma would kill me. I'm all she has left now, now that—"

Somewhere, a whistle blew, signaling the end of lunch. Holly jumped up and seemed to shake herself out of her thoughts. She wiped her hand on her pants, then offered it to Maggie.

"Let's go."

After lunch, there was very little time to talk. Maggie was desperate to know what Holly had been about to say and why she'd gotten thrown out of her house. Maggie and her mother had never fought, not once, when she was a child; she felt nothing but despair at missing her.

But she and Holly had been separated into different groups by late afternoon, and when it came time to punch out, Holly was nowhere in sight. It was probably for the better. Even though there'd been no heavy lifting or labor, Maggie was bone tired. And once their in-service training was done in six weeks, she and Holly might be assigned to different shifts throughout the twenty-four-hour day. The Navy Yard couldn't afford to sleep a wink while the war raged.

By the time she was headed back to the Sands Street Gates, she'd regained some of her energy. She couldn't wait to tell Laurel about her first day of work. What would Laurel say? Perhaps, *You're a wonder, Maggie!* Surely this must be so different from her glamorous life. Maggie must go grocery shopping first, though, and make their mystery guest some corned beef hash and war cake with a bit of rationed sugar, followed by coffee.

A voice came from behind her, familiar enough that Maggie stopped in her tracks and turned her head.

"If you see her . . . please let me know."

It was Holly. She was speaking to their supervisor, who motioned to another building and said, "You could go to personnel, but they probably won't tell you anything. And they don't like people asking questions."

"Thanks. You're a doll," Holly said, grinning.

"I'm your boss," the supervisor snapped. "Don't call me that, Dreyer!"

Dreyer. Holly Dreyer. So that was her whole name. Of course, if Maggie had paid better attention, she would have learned that at roll call. She cursed herself. She needed to be more observant, smarter. Still, the question nagged at her nearly all the way home.

Who on earth was Holly looking for, on the first day of her job?

CHAPTER 5

When Will arrived home, he stood at the back stairs of the house for ten minutes before walking away.

He and Maggie both made a habit of entering from the back alley. The front inevitably had people milling about their stoops nearby, and Will couldn't afford to dodge too many questions about his work. Maggie preferred the back, too, as she was painfully shy at times. There was a freedom in coming and going without being watched.

Today, though, Will was uncomfortable no matter what door he used. He could already tell that Maggie was not yet home. He wondered what that meant about how her first day at the shipyards had gone. Part of him had expected to find her in the kitchen with a hot meal ready—a peace offering to make up for the disappointment of having been fired so quickly, or abandoning the job after a scant few hours.

Which meant: only the strange woman was home.

What had she been doing in there? Had she slept the day away? Had she already left? At the thought, he felt a pang that was surprising and wholly disagreeable.

"Food," he muttered. There was no food at home. Maggie might be too overwhelmed by her first day to remember to procure groceries.

Half an hour later, he stood yet again outside his back door, this time holding a small sack containing canned meat, vegetables, and flour. Prices were dear, but only sugar and gas were rationed so far, and Maggie had the stamps. Soon, more rations would come, like coffee and fat and milk.

Will's thoughts were a purposeful distraction; he still lacked the gumption to enter his own home.

"Stupid," he muttered to himself, then climbed the stairs. In the kitchen, he listened carefully for the woman.

A crash shattered the silence.

It had come from the washroom. Will dropped the groceries onto the counter and galloped into the hallway. The door to the washroom was open, and he heard running water.

Inside, the woman was on the floor. Her clothes had been removed, and a silk slip was falling off both shoulders, exposing her brassiere. Her auburn hair spilled in waves around her. One hand clutched the edge of the bathtub, and the other splayed on the tile floor.

Will turned the water off, then cradled her in one arm. "What happened?" he asked, searching her face. She had a red mark high on her cheekbone, and her eyes blinked in a daze.

"I don't know. I'm so sorry—I was getting a bath ready, and the steam—" She waved a trembling hand in front of her eyes. "I got dizzy."

"You should be back in bed."

"I was feeling better, and I thought—if I can just bathe, I'd feel human again."

"Maggie will be home soon. She'll help you."

He guided her up, and she sat on the edge of the bath. She gripped the rim and shook her head.

"I'm a big girl—I can bathe myself," she said, sounding slightly petulant.

"History proves you can't. You just fainted."

"If I don't take a bath, I'm going to crawl out of my own skin. I have to get him off of me."

Will went silent. *Him?*

But the woman didn't elaborate, only looked up imploringly. "Very well. I suppose I need a *little* help."

Will's face grew warm. "You should wait for Maggie."

Her eyes were large and unblinking. "I need help now."

"But—" Will stared at her. Her girdle stays marred the smooth wave of silk slip across her thighs. The pointed tips of her brassiere tented the front of her slip, and he could not look away.

There was something about this woman that compelled him to obey. With Maggie, he was always in charge. Always worrying after her, always making sure she was taken care of. Maggie didn't ask for it; she was so helpless it just had to be. With this lady, there was a vulnerability there, too; the bruises on her neck and thigh were starker in the light of the washroom. But that wasn't it.

This stranger had made her demand and not wavered. She held his gaze without looking bashfully away, and his body had flushed in response. When men acted in this manner, he knew exactly how to handle things. In this bathroom, with those unwavering eyes and that contralto voice, he had lost his bearings.

Despite whatever she'd been through, her words were an order, the same way someone might say, "Kill this bird" or "Steal that brooch," and there was truly no choice in the world. To refuse would be to accept fire and flame as an alternative.

"All right," he said.

He leaned over and turned the taps back on to fill the bathtub. The Ivory soap flakes were running low. He left for a brief minute, went into a trunk by the sofa where he kept some of his personal items, and pulled out a paper package. He unwrapped a bar of Cashmere Bouquet, a pricier soap that he was saving for Maggie's birthday, and went back to the washroom after grabbing a clean towel. He could always buy her another gift.

"Here." He put the soap and towel on the bathtub edge, and shoved his hands into his pockets. "You can use these."

"Thank you, Will." She smiled at him, a sun breaking through the clouds. "You are such a gentleman."

He nodded and put a hand on the washroom doorknob.

"One more thing." She stood unsteadily, turned her back to him. Her waist tipped in narrowly above her hips, and as she leaned against the sink, her shoulder blades elegantly pointed toward her spine. "I trust you. Can you undo my clasps? I can't reach them. I think I strained my shoulder somehow."

Will stepped back into the washroom, now humid from the water. For some reason, he feared that she would regret the request and snatch it away. Before he could think, he was standing behind her. He'd had just enough experience defrocking women that clasps did not confound him, but this woman did. In order to reach the clasp of her brassiere, he had to push the edge of her silk slip farther down, and in doing so, it fell completely off her shoulders and slithered around her ankles.

"I'm—oh," was all he could say. He saw the rectangle of smooth skin between her brassiere and the top of her girdle, which encased her hips in a parenthetical statement of femininity. There was a bluish bruise on her upper arm. Yet another one. What had happened to her? "I don't think I should—"

"Never mind that. Go ahead."

Will deftly undid the hook-and-eye clasps in the center of her back. Loosened, the brassiere slid a little off her arms, to the point where he could see the side of her ample left breast, curving softly against her rib cage.

"Thank you," she said, matter-of-factly, and held the brassiere to her chest as she looked over her shoulder. "I won't be long."

Will backed out of the room and shut the door too loudly. He was flummoxed, blazing hot under the collar, his erection straining against his trousers. Splashes of water could be heard from behind the washroom door, which meant that she was now naked and in the bathtub, with the slippery pink soap sliding between her fingers and . . .

To get his mind off things, he went back to the kitchen and doused his face and hands with cold tap water. He ought to cook something. With the groceries he'd bought, he made soda biscuits, brewed a kettle of tea, fried some canned ham, and warmed up a tin of green beans. It wasn't fancy, but he couldn't change everything for this one person. She'd be leaving soon, in any case.

Damn it. He was starting to get flushed again. He finished cooking, took the biscuits out of the oven, and set the table for two.

He went to knock on the washroom door. "You all right?"

"Yes, much better." She opened the door. Her hair was still dry and waved, but the short hairs around her forehead were damp. Her face was scrubbed clean, and she smelled deliciously of that perfumed soap. She had wrapped Maggie's old cotton robe around herself. He could tell by how the cloth draped that she wasn't wearing her lingerie either.

Jesus, calm down, Will, he told himself.

"You ought to drink something, and eat too. Get your strength up."

So you can leave were the words that were supposed to come at the end of that phrase, but they went unuttered.

He led her to the small table in the kitchen. Her hands were shaking a little. She smiled.

"My name is Laurel." She put the words out there like an offering, waiting.

Laurel. He'd never heard the name on a real person before. The word reminded him of a Greek myth he'd read in school. The story of Daphne and Apollo. The god had become obsessed with the dryad and chased her until Daphne begged her father, a river god, for help. She was transformed into a laurel tree, and Apollo used wreaths of laurel as a prize at his Pythian games. Will had never seen a laurel tree either.

"Laurel," he said, testing the name in his mouth. His tongue rested against his teeth. After a pause, he pushed the tea toward her. "Drink."

"Are you always so pushy?" she asked, picking up the chipped teacup.

"Eat something."

"My, you are a dictator!"

"Not compared to some. And that's nothing to joke about."

"Mm," she said, sipping the tea. She closed her eyes and exhaled. Her eyelids were satiny. "Hot bath, hot tea. I am in heaven."

"Are you still dizzy?"

"Yes. I feel like the human version of a Jell-O mold." She eyed the ham and biscuits, then picked up a biscuit, slathered it with jam, and crammed it into her mouth. Even the way she ate without decorum was fascinating.

"Easy now. Chew, for the love of God. I don't want to explain to the police why you choked to death in my house."

Laurel swallowed swiftly, raising her eyebrows. "Don't call the police."

"I was kidding."

"I wasn't." Laurel took a sip of tea and crinkled her nose. She was probably used to some fancier stuff.

Will narrowed his eyes. "Look. You've slept. You've washed up. And you're finally getting some food you need." He eyed her body. When was the last time she'd eaten? "So. What happened?"

She stabbed some ham with a fork, but after it slid off the tines, she abandoned the fork and just picked up a square with her manicured fingertips. She popped the ham into her mouth and groaned.

"Good God, I love pig."

"Did you grow up in a barn? Who taught you to eat without a fork?" He and Maggie might have been poor, and their mother distracted and deathly melancholy, but they had manners.

"You should try it sometimes. I think food tastes better when you eat it with your hands." And as if to send the message home, she pinched off a corner of biscuit, swiped it in the gravy, and offered it to Will.

"No," he said.

"No, *thank you*," Laurel corrected him. "What, did you grow up in a barn?"

Will actually cracked a smile. He couldn't remember the last time he'd laughed, or even smiled. Laurel's offering came closer, and he had the strangest sensation that if he ate the biscuit, dripping with gravy, off her fingers, the world might crack in half and he would fall, fall, fall forever. He shook his head, and she popped it into her own mouth, then licked her fingers.

Afterward, she inclined her head toward Will's cigarettes. "May I have one?" He lit it for her, trying not to be affected by the brief contact with her skin. She held the cigarette for a second while she touched the spatula sitting in the fry pan at Will's elbow.

"What is that? This shovel thing?"

Will was incredulous. "*A spatula?*"

"Oh. Food shovel. Spatula. Got it."

"Are you serious? You don't know what that is?"

Laurel shrugged. "I've never stepped into a kitchen my whole life." She pointed with her cigarette. "Except this one."

"Why are you here?" Will asked.

"You already asked me that."

"No, I asked what happened, and you dodged that question."

She exhaled a plume of smoke. "Speaking of dodging, why aren't you over in France, fighting?"

"I'm deaf in one ear." He crossed his arms. "I got punched in the head as a kid."

Laurel frowned. "Does it bother you a lot?"

"Only when people are trying to whisper," he admitted.

"Ah, so you'd be a terrible spy, wouldn't you?"

He froze. Joking about that kind of thing was never funny to Will. For the first time, he wondered if her arrival here wasn't an accident. Had Mrs. Rivers sent her, to test him?

"I'm sorry. I didn't mean to tease. And I'm sorry you got punched as a child."

"Not your fault. Have you been punched?" The other questions weren't working, so he might as well try a more direct approach.

"Yes, I have." Again, an exhalation of smoke. This time, she blew it slowly to cloud her face.

"Who was it?"

"None of your business."

"You're in my house. It's my business now. Or, you can leave." He gestured to the door.

"Your sister doesn't want me to leave."

"She doesn't make the rules here."

"I see." Laurel leaned in closer. The robe hung loose from her shoulders when she did that, and he could see her cleavage. Just a scant line of darkness, of flesh kissing flesh several inches below her collarbone.

"I need to be sure I'm safe. I need a few weeks." She puffed on her cigarette, making a soft kissing noise. "I won't say more. But I can promise you I'll pay you back for your hospitality someday. Starting with this." She took the ruby ring from her finger and slid it across the table. Will didn't touch it.

"Who is he?" Will asked.

"He who?"

"The guy who hit you."

"I can't tell you," she said.

"Laurel isn't really your name, is it?"

Her mouth dropped open. Not by much, only a millimeter or two. But it was enough, a tiny inkling of surprise that was as clear as a blinking Times Square sign. At least, before the dimouts, and the enormous Coca-Cola and Planters Peanuts signs went dark. She said so much and said so little at the same time. She was hiding. And clearly, she wasn't telling the truth—about her name, or possibly about anything.

She leaned closer. "My name is—"

Just at that moment, Maggie came bursting through the door, potatoes tumbling all over the floor along with her.

"Gosh darn it to heck!" she yelped.

"Watch that language, sister," Will said.

Maggie looked up, her face all astonishment. There was a long, awkward pause as she stared at them, studying them almost, before Will remembered she still had her hands and knees on the floor.

"Let me help you," he said, and jumped up. Laurel watched them through a haze of smoke.

"Hi! I got the groceries—oh—it looks like you did too!" Maggie looked so pathetic, grabbing dusty tubers from the corners of the kitchen. Will was embarrassed. He didn't want them to seem like country bumpkins, though why he felt the need to impress a sick and mendacious woman was not obviously clear to him.

"I'll get them." He leaned over and gently guided Maggie off the floor. "Wash up. I've made dinner."

"All right," she said. She froze, staring at Laurel, then wiped her hands on her pants and scurried into the washroom. She scurried right back out again, knitting her hands together. "Oh! Did you take a bath? You did, didn't you? How are you feeling? I'm so sorry, I didn't even ask. Do you need to lie down again?"

"Mags. She's fine. Wash up, come back, and let's have a talk."

Maggie nodded and disappeared again.

Laurel smiled in the direction of Maggie's exodus. "She is sweet. You're both so caring. I'm very lucky to have landed face down at your house."

"About that," Will began, but Maggie had already returned, flapping her barely dried hands in the air.

"All right. Where were we?"

"Sit," Will said. And then he realized they only had two chairs. And the table was only set for two. Maggie noticed, and her eyebrows constricted with hurt. He hadn't meant anything by it. But the truth was, he'd forgotten all about Maggie joining them. "One moment." He swiftly grabbed a chair from Maggie's bedroom and set out another plate of food. The table was crowded now, but Maggie seemed at home between the two of them.

Maggie hadn't taken a bite—she was simply staring artlessly at Laurel—when the color drained from the woman's face and she dropped her cigarette butt onto her plate. She grasped the edge of the table, and beads of sweat erupted over her forehead and upper lip.

"I think I'm going to be sick." She started to stand but listed to the left, her shoulder bumping the wall.

"Oh! Will, help her!" Maggie said, reaching to keep Laurel from falling to the floor.

Will didn't have to be asked twice. He came around and scooped Laurel into his arms, where she sagged with deadweight.

"She's out," he said. "How convenient for her. Just when I was ready to ask more questions."

"She's still exhausted. Put her back in my bed, Will. I'll look after her while you go to your classes."

Will nodded. He laid her on Maggie's bed, checked her pulse, and nodded again.

"Thready and weak. She needs more food, and more rest," he said. And more time away from whoever gave her those bruises, he thought. He shut the door. Maggie hovered a little too close.

"Maybe you should be a doctor, instead of a physicist," she said, elbowing him.

"Being a doctor or a nurse means dealing with blood, shit, and vomit. Blood, I can handle. It's the other two I've no interest in. Thank God she didn't vomit." He gently pushed Maggie away. "Leave her be."

She reluctantly followed him back into the kitchen. Together they put the groceries away, and Maggie began to eat.

Will had lost his appetite. For a long while, he said nothing, but the compass of his rationality had whizzed back to its true north. This is not what you need, Will thought. This is not in the plan.

This last year, he'd only ever planned on taking care of Maggie and figuring out exactly how to become indispensable to the MED's war effort. Now that he knew they were procuring uranium, refining and enrichment were the next steps. Will had to become a cog in a machine that wouldn't run without him. Somehow. If he succeeded, he and Maggie could get out of Gravesend. They could have a different, better life. The story of his father, mother, and stepfather predicted that Will, too, would die in obscurity. He refused to succumb to that inevitable history.

Maggie, and work. These two things already took all his focus. He had none to spare.

Especially for a distraction like Laurel.

"Look," Will said. "She's not well, and she wants help. I get that. But we need to find out what happened to her."

"Why?" Maggie asked, chewing.

"So she can go back."

"But she doesn't want to be found."

He sighed. "And yet, she can't stay here forever." He began cleaning the dishes off the table.

Maggie looked crestfallen. Was his sister's life so bereft of friends that she couldn't bear the thought of letting a stranger leave? Apparently it was, which made Will feel more guilty. Perhaps he should have been encouraging her to be more social instead of spending all her time doing blackout rounds or working on that bomb shelter.

"She really should go. She had a silly fight with someone, and now it's time to go back," Will said. "We'll talk about it later, I guess." It was a half-hearted concession. Usually with his size, and with enough authority in his voice, he could convince anybody of anything at all.

Being a man, a white man, made all the difference in the world when it came to getting his way.

But somewhere deep inside, he had a feeling—the way you know that a day is going to turn out rotten before you're even out the door—that a simple disagreement wasn't the reason Laurel had ended up here. There were the bruises, for one thing. Just like he knew, somehow, that Laurel was keenly aware of the effect she'd had on him when she'd undressed in the bath.

Laurel was dangerous, and a liar. And yet, Will was digging in his heels as if a precipice loomed ahead. Despite his better judgment, he was entirely unwilling to let her leave his world at the moment. Not yet.

CHAPTER 6

Ruby leaned against the doorframe and closed her eyes while she listened to Will and Maggie in the kitchen. She couldn't hear everything, but she heard enough to know they were far from trusting her. Eventually, her legs began to shake, and she sank gratefully onto the bed. She still felt odd. The medicine that Maggie had given her had left tendrils of effect in her veins, and her head swam. Or perhaps it was giddiness that was making her head swim.

How lucky that they had taken her in. Perfect. It was exactly what she needed, without knowing they were such a necessity. Maggie, with those pretty green eyes, so openhearted and eager to help. She had the loveliest thin pink lips Ruby had ever seen, with two little peaks in the middle. Anyone looking at her would see a mousy, brown-haired girl hiding in the shadows, but she simmered with intention. And she was working at the Navy Yard! A good girl, trying to do good things. Ruby had the feeling that if she asked for the world, Maggie would search for a platter large enough to serve it on.

And there was Will. He was so unlike Felix. Quiet, with a massive intelligence in those eyes, all housed in the body of Ares. Ruby had the feeling that he was used to having everything in his life orderly and under control, and Ruby was neither of those things. Will was a pot to stir, and she was looking forward to the ways she might wield the spoon.

Her survival meant watching them carefully. Listening when they weren't aware. Looking for whatever might help her cause.

Somehow, she would destroy Felix. She burned with fury at the thought of him.

Why had he had this address, in Gravesend of all places, amongst the papers on his desk? Fleeing here had been a flip of the fate coin. Will and Maggie were either hiding their involvement in his scheme, or they had no idea they were pawns in the making. Either way, they might be far more help to her than she'd expected.

A scritch-scratching noise emanated from nearby. She opened one eye to see a small gray mouse scurry across the floorboards. On the bedside table, a tiny spider crawled across the yellowed doily beneath the lamp. Ruby reached out a hand, and with her index finger, squashed the spider with a slight crunch, flicking the carcass to the floor. She narrowed her eyes at the mouse, who was sniffing at the far wall.

"I'll get you later," she said before yawning and snuggling luxuriously in the bed.

CHAPTER 7

Maggie was silently thrilled. Will hadn't said Laurel needed to leave immediately. That meant there was a tiny bit of room for negotiation. Book bag slung over his shoulder, Will headed for the back door, nearly shutting it before popping his head back in.

"I forgot to ask. How was your first day in the shipyard?"

"Oh! They didn't fire me." She wasn't ready to declare the new job an outright success. Not yet.

"Good, Mags. Keep it up." He shut the door and left.

Normally, Maggie would be satisfied by his brotherly quips and appropriate lack of enthusiasm for her little successes. And to be honest, her successes usually fizzled impotently before they had a chance to ignite. But today, she was annoyed that he had no confidence in her. She had more than survived one day of welding training at the shipyards, where her work might someday result in the launch of a ship just like the USS *Missouri*. Maybe she'd even be able to work on that very ship!

Living with Will was not a bad thing, in general. But increasingly, she felt that he inquired into her day not out of care for how she was navigating the grand journey of life, but out of worry that she would do something catastrophically stupid. With Will, there was no joking, no warmth, no embraces.

Love and affection were not the same thing. One, she had plenty of. The other, she was starving for.

Maggie washed her hands in the kitchen, then crept to her bedroom. She twisted the doorknob slowly, trying not to let the mechanism click too loudly. Inside, Laurel was lying on her side, her hip and shoulder forming rounded mountain heights that flanked the valley of her waist. Maggie's robe looked flawless on her. Laurel was muttering in her slumber, and Maggie craned her head forward to listen.

"Ich koche mit einem . . ."

She cocked her head. Was that German? It couldn't be. A fleeting worry entered her thoughts, that Will was right to be on guard against this stranger. A thrill quickened her pulse.

" . . . spatula."

Maggie nearly laughed. Must be dreamy gibberish. She appeared to be obsessed with spatulas. Definitely not a spy.

Maggie tiptoed to the washroom. In her haste earlier, she'd ignored the wet towel unceremoniously clumped on the floor next to Laurel's messy pile of clothes. She hung the towel, then ferreted through the fabric to make sure a lipstick wasn't tucked in a pocket that would accidentally dye the wash with streaks of pink. She returned to the bedroom, where she lifted Laurel's coat and brushed the streaks of dirt and bits of leaves from it. This time, she felt a bottle in the pocket.

Maggie pulled it out, looking at the label on the brown glass bottle. It was bigger than a pill bottle, and unlabeled. She opened it. It contained a snowy white powder. She leaned closer and sniffed it.

"Don't."

Maggie looked up. Laurel, groggy eyed, was reaching for her from the bed. "Don't touch it. It's not safe."

"I—I was just going to wash your things—"

"Maggie! Put it back. It'll kill you!" Her eyes were wide with panic.

Maggie capped the bottle. "What is it?"

"Zinc chloride. You eat that, and it'll burn a hole in your stomach, make you bleed from the inside out."

"Why do you have this?"

"It's a long story. I don't have the strength for it right now."

Maggie curled her fingers around the bottle, less afraid now of the poison, more afraid of it being close to Laurel. "Were you going to take this? Were you going to kill yourself?"

Laurel's eyes watered. "I don't want to talk about it. Please. Just . . . put it away. I won't touch it. And I wouldn't hurt you like that."

Maggie took a step closer to the doorway. "Of course! I never even considered—that is, I never thought . . .'"

Was she in danger? Why would Laurel bring that up so abruptly, that she wouldn't hurt Maggie?

"You should sleep," Maggie said, not knowing what else to say. "I'll put this away somewhere safe."

"Thank you. If it weren't for you and your brother, I'd probably be dead. You know that, right?"

Maggie nodded. Laurel slumped back into bed, her eyes heavy lidded.

"Sleep," Maggie said, still discomfited. "I'll check on you in a bit."

Laurel closed her eyes, and Maggie switched off the light. She went back into the kitchen with the bottle, not knowing where to put it. She and Will didn't really need to hide anything from each other. Anything Maggie did that was private was usually women's issues, so he didn't prod when she needed extra time in the washroom. She had no locked trunks or medicine cabinets. Where would she put the bottle?

After giving it some thought, she squatted beneath the kitchen sink and placed it behind a very old, very rusted can of floor wax. Someplace that Laurel would have to work to find. Whatever that chemical was, it was dangerous. There. That would do for now. She put on her coat, grabbed her purse, and left the house. There was laundry to do, but

Laurel's words—*If it weren't for you and your brother, I'd probably be dead*—had given her an idea. Surely there would still be some newspapers available at one of the shops on Avenue U. Usually newsboys were calling out the headlines, but it was nearly lights out, and most people were shuttering their stores for the evening.

It was cold outside. She wrapped a scarf around her neck. The back alley was quiet as usual, but on West Sixth Street, people were still out and about, and a few homes still had their lights shining.

"They ought to know by now that it's time to dim lights," Maggie muttered. She'd tell them on the way home. First, she skirted around to the front yard to check the hollow of the oak tree. Sometimes there were little gifts in there, like creatures that needed to be cared for—an injured bird, a wounded moth. She was always careful to make sure Will didn't see. But the oak was empty. She continued down the street to Salvatori's Grocery and found a few copies of the day's papers left. Ignoring *Collier's* and the *Saturday Evening Post*, she gathered a pile: the *Times*, the *Daily News*, the *Post*, the *Brooklyn Eagle*. And then for good measure, she bought the *New York Daily Mirror*, which was mostly gossip but, in this case, might be the most useful.

Mr. Salvatori, the owner, rang up her purchase.

"So many papers! You in the news? Saving clippings? What you looking for, eh?"

Drat. She should have bought papers at different places, so as not to draw attention to herself. "Oh, Will and I like to read certain ones. That's all."

"Hum." He made one of those clown frowns that labeled her as "peculiar." She hurried out with her purchases, tucking them under her arm. She couldn't wait to get home and look through them, but duty won out, so on the way, she knocked at several houses. "Lights out, Mrs. Kozinski!" she yelled, and "Dimout time! Thank you!" before they could open their doors and respond.

Down the street, one light in particular blazed bright as can be, a buttery, glowing window against the deepening darkness. Maggie realized the light was coming from her own parlor.

"Jiminy! What is she doing in there?" she said, running. She could have sworn she'd left the lights off and the blackout curtains drawn. She raced up the stairs, hid the papers beneath the sink, and went into the parlor. It was empty. The bedroom was empty too. A long S, in the shape of a sleeping woman, was still imprinted on her bedsheets. For a brief moment, she had the urge to lie down in the S and smell the sheets, but shook off the thought.

Where could she be?

Laurel's coat was still lying across the end of the bed, so she couldn't have left. Maggie ran around, until it dawned on her. She opened the door between the coat closet and the washroom and saw a tiny light shining down in the basement. The stairs were old and squeaky, and it sounded like the world was coming to an end when she galloped down them.

There, standing on the concrete floor next to the furnace, was Laurel. She was still in Maggie's robe, but the hazy light from the ceiling bulb spotlighted her. She was staring at a monstrosity of corrugated metal sidewalls, not quite fully concealed by stacked sandbags—the makings of a bomb shelter. There was a small doorway facing the stairs. Maggie knew what was inside: a case with first aid supplies, several cans of food, jugs of water, two narrow cots, and flashlights. Rope, an axe, and a shovel.

Laurel had her arms crossed under her breasts. "So. Planning on keeping me hostage in this thing?" she said. "If so, I would strongly recommend more pillows."

Maggie laughed, her voice hitting a much higher pitch than usual. "My goodness, no! It's a bomb shelter. In case of an air raid."

"In your basement?"

"Well, yes."

"What if the whole place goes down on your basement, like a house of cards?"

Maggie smiled with satisfaction. "We'd be alive."

Laurel hooted. "You'd be entombed! How would you get out under all the rubble? How would anyone hear you screaming?"

Maggie pushed out her lower lip. Oh. She hadn't thought of that. Well, Will had mentioned it. But when she went on and on about her plans, it was as if he'd tuned a radio to a different channel and didn't say more. With Laurel's commentary, true doubt set fire to her optimism. She had wanted the shelter to withstand a beating, and with several layers of sandbags (she was only half-done making and gathering them) it would have been able to stand up to an overhead explosion. Or at least she thought so.

Laurel tapped her chin thoughtfully. "You could set up a dead-ringer."

"A what?"

"A bell linked to a string in your shelter, so if you're buried alive, you can alert people. They used to have them in coffins, in case someone was accidentally buried alive. I should know. I think my great-great-great-great-grandmother or something was a grave robber."

"Really?" Maggie gaped.

"God, no. I was just joking. About the bell. Not about my ancestors."

Maggie shook her head, then gave up trying to reconcile her image of a grave robber with elegant Laurel. "Golly. I suppose I could rebuild it in the backyard."

"I could help you," Laurel said. She stooped by the entrance, her fingers passing over the boxes and cans. "Food. Bandages. Water. Can opener. Blankets. Everything you need to survive. All it's lacking is a flask of vodka and a jar of olives. I need a kit like this too." She seemed to be speaking more to herself than to Maggie. She snapped out of her reverie and looked up. "Like I said. I can help you."

"Really? You know how?"

Laurel stood. "I don't know a thing about it. Or about a lot of things, except dead-ringers, I suppose. But if you tell me what to do, I'll try. I need to learn."

She seemed less like a woman who was cowering after a lover's spat and more like a boxer standing up after a blow, ready for the next round.

"I would love your help." Then she added, "Any help at all. I would sure appreciate that." For some reason, Maggie was sure she was blushing, and she was grateful the dim light hid her cheeks.

"It's the least I could do." Laurel smiled. "I can't thank you enough for letting me stay here, even for two nights."

"You can stay as long as you like," Maggie blurted, even though it wasn't a promise she could keep.

Laurel laughed, a full-throated, luscious sound. "Be careful what you wish for! So. Can I ask you another question?"

"Of course," Maggie said, but she frowned. She never liked being interviewed about herself. About anything.

"What is that thing in the jar? In your bedroom?"

"Thing?" Maggie turned around. "Oh! The pupa! Someday, it'll be a moth, or a butterfly. I found it outside when it was going to freeze. I'm caring for it until I can put it back outside in the spring."

"Well, that's sweet of you." Laurel followed Maggie back upstairs and into the kitchen. "Did you eat?"

Maggie eyed the cabinet below the sink, where the newspapers were. She couldn't pull them out in front of Laurel. "I did."

"Well, that's a relief. Your brother fixed dinner. I certainly can't cook."

"You can't?" The more Laurel spoke, the more Maggie's suspicions solidified. She had to be an heiress of sorts. An heiress who, for some reason, carried poison in her pocket.

"No. Can't even make toast."

"Well, I can teach you." Maggie brightened. "You probably had dinner but not dessert. We'll make something."

She went to the icebox and pulled out an egg, then to the cupboard to get the sugar, spices, and a packet of raisins. "This is a cake Will or I make occasionally. It's got cinnamon and raisins, but you can use other fruit. I can make it in a jiffy."

Laurel sighed. "I never had a brother. I should have liked to have had one."

"What about your mother? Was she good in the kitchen?" As Maggie set the ingredients on the counter, Laurel picked up each one and examined it, the way you might examine a monkey skull in a curio shop. She tentatively licked her finger and, as a toddler might, tasted the cinnamon, then the ground cloves.

"My mother was always too busy," Laurel said, licking sugar crystals off her fingertip.

"Doing what?"

Her face went tense. "She has her own life."

"Does she know where you are?"

"No, and I'd like to keep it that way." This time, it was less irritation on her face, and more like worry. "I wouldn't want her to get involved in my scrapes. I'm a grown woman. It's not her business anymore."

"I would do anything to have my mother back in my life."

"Was she sick?"

Maggie shook her head but then nodded. "Yes. She was sick." She tried not to let her voice crack. There was no reason, really, to romanticize what had happened to her mother, or even keep it a secret. As for her own history, that was different. "My mother killed herself. Drowned by walking right into the water when I was twelve. Will was fifteen. He took care of me."

"Oh, Maggie. I'm so sorry."

Maggie turned around, shrugging. "It's all right." She cracked the egg into the bowl, stirred it hard with the other ingredients, and turned on the oven. "So what's your excuse for not knowing how to toast bread?"

"We employed a cook. And four maids. And a driver, and a riding instructor, and a tutor. I can't sew a button. I wouldn't know the first thing about how to boil an egg." Laurel crossed her arms—as if more irritated by the truth than harboring any feelings of inadequacy.

"You know an awful lot about zinc . . . whatever that is."

"That I do." Laurel watched Maggie carefully. "I have a thing for chemicals. Garden plants too."

"Plants?"

"Yes. Like hellebore, and snakeroot, and nightshades. Gorgeously complicated, they are."

"What were you doing with that powder?"

Laurel waved a hand, and turned away to pick at a piece of lint on the sleeve of the robe. "A work in progress. Insurance, so to speak. I'll tell you sometime."

Insurance? Maggie's understanding of insurance was that if you lost something, like your mother, or a house, the company would pay you back for what you lost. How on earth would poisoning someone bring something back to Laurel? What had she lost?

Strange. Maggie was learning more and more about her, but still felt like she knew so little.

"But as I was saying," Laurel continued, "I can make a good cocktail, but not much else. Not like you, Maggie."

Maggie flushed. "Oh. Surely, you can do more than that!" She poured the batter into a loaf pan.

"I can drink said cocktails," Laurel deadpanned. "I also have the uncanny ability to attract men who'd rather see me dead than speak my mind."

She went to the kitchen table and sat down unsteadily. Her face had gone a little greenish, and Maggie saw her shiver.

"Do you have a fever?" She shut the oven door and went to Laurel's side. She touched her soft cheek. "You're burning up. I'm so sorry. Here I am gabbing and you're still unwell. I wonder if you got the grippe from being out in the cold so long last night. Let's get you back in bed. I'll finish up here and come get you when it's done."

Laurel followed her orders without a word. As Maggie drew the bedclothes over her, she asked, "Would you like something to help you sleep?"

Laurel's eyes snapped open. "No. Don't ever give me that medicine you gave me. Never again."

Maggie dropped the edges of the sheets. She felt bitten. "I'm sorry. I was only trying to help."

"I've been given that medicine before. It makes you sleepy, makes your mind soft and cloudy. I hate it. It makes me feel like I'm dying."

"Oh." Maggie put her hand over her mouth. When she'd taken it, she'd felt different. Like she was just—absent. Free from worry, and nonexistent in a blanket of dark, empty unconsciousness.

"I know you're trying to help," Laurel said, grabbing Maggie's hand. Maggie squeezed back. "But that's not the help I need."

"What do you need?" Maggie asked.

"I need you to show me how to cook. How to clean. Shop. How to fend for myself." Laurel looked almost angry. Or determined. It was hard to tell which. "I need to know how to survive away from . . . where I've been."

"I can do that."

Laurel was quiet for a moment. "Maggie. Have you ever not wanted to be yourself? To slip into another existence? Wear someone else's clothes, drink their tea, look in the mirror and see different-colored eyes?"

Maggie scrunched up her face. "I get the feeling you've had everything you ever wanted." She paused. "Until now, that is."

"You're right, I have. But recently I've been given a bird's-eye view, and I don't like what I see."

Maggie nodded. "Yes. I know how that feels."

"I get the feeling that behind that quiet voice of yours, and these quiet clothes . . ." Here, Laurel reached out and let her tapered fingers touch Maggie's shoulder, tracing a soft trail down to her elbow and wrist. Maggie suppressed a shiver. "Behind all this, I bet you know exactly what you want."

Maggie didn't know what to say. She'd never thought of herself as being very ambitious. But perhaps she was, after all. With her one successful day at the Navy Yard, she already felt like she was forging a new identity for herself. Here in this bedroom, all she could do was nod. She was a little afraid she might agree to whatever Laurel suggested.

Laurel went on. "I need you to not tell anyone I'm here. I'll leave soon, I promise."

"No! You can stay as long as you like. I can talk to Will. He won't mind."

"You are my savior, Maggie Scripps."

Maggie's heart swelled. The little creatures she saved on a regular basis had no voice to thank her, but she didn't realize she craved it so much until Laurel spoke the words. Faintly, she wondered, had she told Laurel their last name? But before she could think more about it, Laurel was tugging hard on Maggie's hand, until Maggie was forced closer, leaning over the bed. Her other hand went to Maggie's face, tenderly. And then she kissed Maggie. It astonished her. This was how she'd wanted to be kissed her whole life but didn't know until that moment. Laurel's lips were soft, and she left the residue of cinnamon and a single granule of sugar on Maggie's mouth, so that when she left the room she tasted Laurel and sugar and spice and had to lean against the doorjamb in the kitchen so as not to swoon herself.

She shook her head. It was just a friendly kiss between two girls. Nothing more.

When she came to her senses, Maggie wiped down the counters. When she pulled the cake out of the oven, the scent of cinnamon and sugar and fruit rose into the air.

But Laurel was fast asleep.

Maggie was glad. She'd been uncomfortably distracted by nonstop thoughts of whether all Laurel's kisses would taste of cinnamon. And how wrong it was of her to even be thinking of a girl's kisses. But it was all innocent, of course.

She spent the next hour in a daze, absently touching her lips, lost in the memory of the kiss. She was putting away dishes and things when she opened up the cabinet beneath the sink and found the newspapers she'd stashed there.

Oh. Right. Maggie had planned to look for clues about Laurel's disappearance. The very existence of the newspapers felt like a betrayal on her part. She should read them before Will came home.

Reluctantly, she laid them out and began with the *New York Times*, then the *Daily News*. But it took a long time to read the headlines, scouring every page to the bottom to be sure that a little notation wouldn't be missed. Anything about missing young women, possibly heiresses being abducted or running away. There was no question Laurel was wealthy. Maids, and drivers, and not an inkling of how to cook! And as for where she came from, well. There was only so far a person *could* run away. Due to the war, there were no ships to Europe or London.

At some point, Maggie fell asleep on the newspapers. She was awoken just after eleven o'clock by a hand on her shoulder.

"Wha? Laurel?" Maggie murmured as she pushed herself up. A newspaper was stuck to her cheek.

"Hi, Mags. Smells like cake. What are all the papers for?"

"I wanted to see if there might be some information about Laurel running away," she said, yawning.

"I see. Good idea," Will said. He was clearly impressed—and surprised—with her forethought.

He plucked one from the bottom of the stack, the *New York Daily Mirror*. The gossipy one. The front page wasn't much more than a head-line: U.S. BOMBS GUADALCANAL! He scanned the headlines on the second page, then flipped the paper over. He dropped his canvas bag onto the floor and sat down across from her.

"Jesus," he muttered.

"What?" Maggie asked, suddenly awake.

Will flipped the newspaper and handed it to her. He pointed to an article at the bottom of the second page.

> Felix Cross III, Shipping Heir, POISONED!
>
> Barely Alive at Bellevue Hospital
>
> Fiancée Nowhere to Be Found

Maggie looked up at her brother, the same expression on his face.

Fiancée? It had to be Laurel. In their bones, they just knew it. And if it was true, then they had an almost-murderess in their home.

> Felix Cross III, Shipping Heir, POISONED!
>
> Barely Alive at Bellevue Hospital
>
> Fiancée Nowhere to Be Found
>
> Future Mother-in-Law Snappish
>
> Felix Cross III, 28 years old, has been hospitalized at Bellevue Hospital since yesterday evening. Sources in the hospital have said that the heir to the Lake Erie

shipping industry was stricken by an illness that closely resembled a poisoning.

"He was shaking and vomiting," said the source, who was outside the home on Park Avenue when the ambulance arrived at the Cross residence. "I wouldn't be surprised if he was dead by now. He looked half-dead when the ambulance got him." Cross was reportedly having a row with his fiancée, Ruby Fielding. A famed beauty and high-society socialite, Ruby Fielding is the daughter of Ernest Fielding, of the Fielding Bank fortune, and Dr. Allene Cutter Fielding, one of the only female physicians at Bellevue Hospital, where Cross is reportedly recovering.

Dr. Fielding refused to comment upon "private patient matters" when asked yesterday. She also refused to answer questions regarding whether this news reflects upon her own dramatic history and her father's ignoble death. Dr. Fielding added, "There is a war going on. Spend your time on more worthy subjects."

The hospital administration also refused to comment on the case.

"It is a case of patient privacy," Dr. Fielding told reporters. "The authorities are always involved, when it is necessary to involve them."

There are currently no reports from the 19th Precinct on the murder attempt or an active missing person case.

CHAPTER 8

Ruby Fielding.

Laurel had been wearing a ruby ring. It couldn't simply be a coincidence.

Will put the paper down. "Well, seems like quite a coincidence. Or not."

Maggie looked agog. "It could be her. She probably isn't using her real name."

"If this is who the paper is talking about, then yes, I doubt she'd use her real name."

Maggie touched the newsprint, her fingertip darkening slightly from the ink. "Ruby Fielding. Say, it says that her mother is a doctor. A doctor! And at Bellevue."

"That's what it says. Then again, the *Mirror* isn't exactly the most accurate paper in circulation. It doesn't all make sense, though. How could this Cross fellow beat up a woman and be on death's door at the same time?"

"Poison, that's how," Maggie muttered. Her hand went to her lips, as if she'd swallowed some herself. She looked slightly ashen.

"What?"

"It says he was poisoned. Laurel had a bottle in her pocket. Zinc . . . something. Zinc chloride. I don't know what that is, but she said it was poisonous." She glanced at Will, her face stricken. "She warned me not to touch it, or inhale it. Then she rattled off a list of plants I'd never heard of. It was odd. Why would she be carrying that bottle around, except to hurt someone?"

"Perhaps to protect herself," Will said. "Defense, not offense." He thought about the bruises, the faint purpling marring her skin. "Zinc chloride. It's used in paper processing. Pretty poisonous, and it's corrosive. But it's an odd choice if you were going to kill someone. It would taste terribly astringent, so it would tip off anyone. There are more clever ways. Arsenic, disguised as food poisoning, or cyanide. Where is the bottle now?"

"Here, under the sink. Should we throw it away?" Maggie asked.

"No. The second this was in your food, you'd know before you got seriously hurt. Anyway, we want her to trust us until we can figure out what to do."

"She said her life was in danger! I think we should find more information about her. Maybe ask around Bellevue. Surely there's more to the truth than what the paper is saying. We should help her. She's been hurt."

Will was ready to say no, they knew enough to be done with the stranger in their house, but truth be told, he was curious to know more. His mind said to throw her out, right now. She'd distracted him from his work, distracted him during classes. And her very proximity could bring unwanted attention. Especially from the MED. But his mind also thought of her as Laurel, who needed his help. Will's unspoken longing to have her stay—to see the soft edge of her shoulder blade beneath her clothing—it was addling his brain.

He found himself uttering, "Maybe."

"I wonder who tried to kill who first. Why would they, anyway? For money? He's some tony heir, and she's swimming in money too," Maggie noted.

"You think that money makes you civilized? Or less greedy? It makes it easier for a person to hide how barbaric they really are."

"How on earth do you know that, brother?" Maggie said.

"I spent enough time with rich boys at school. I know. Most were perfectly fine people. Really good men." He dropped the newspaper on the kitchen table, and went to the washroom to get ready for bed. "The others? Like I said. Monsters, wearing linen suits."

That night, asleep on the sofa, he dreamt that Laurel came to him, kneeling before him, begging him to let her stay.

Just a little while longer. Please.

And then she kissed him.

He remembered moist, warm lips on his, and his skin growing warm under her touch. Her delicate fingers searching below his waist, skimming the surface of his trousers for a response.

He woke up in a sweat. Heart thumping, he snuck a look at the sleeping Laurel. Maggie was sleeping right next to her, their legs a little too close for strangers. It was more like two girlfriends sharing a bed on a summer trip in the Adirondacks. As if Laurel wasn't capable of anything remotely nefarious.

Foolish Maggie.

Foolish Will.

He couldn't resist being generally paranoid about people trying to cozy up with the Scripps family. Especially with the type of work he'd been doing under General Groves. Tomorrow, he would put a stop to this. He'd go to Bellevue and gather what information he could. Laurel was either lying and could safely go home, or she was lying and an almost-murderess. Either way, he'd know how best to handle her.

By the time his day was over, everything would be back to normal.

But the morning was odd. Odder than odd.

Laurel had awoken early and curled her hair into serviceable victory rolls over her ears. She was rapt with attention in the kitchen as Maggie made breakfast. Maggie insisted Laurel stay seated since she was still weak.

"Let me show you how to cut the bread with a proper knife," Maggie said, demonstrating. "If you saw at it, it'll fall apart."

"I see," Laurel said. Will shook his head. They were making toast. She seemed anything but bored.

He stepped into the kitchen. "I'm off. I should be back around five." He looked at Laurel, whose tongue parted her lips briefly before she smiled. Her teeth were pearly. Like on a movie poster. His temperature rose, and he folded his hands to cover his crotch. He wanted to scream at his body to obey, to turn off like a light switch. "You should rest."

And then you need to leave.

But he couldn't bring himself to say it out loud. He would later. He wasn't looking forward to it.

"I will. Thank you, Will." Again, that husky voice. It never stopped being a glorious surprise.

Will cleared his throat. "Have a good day at the Navy Yard, Mags. Pay attention."

"I pay attention! I even made a friend. I forgot to tell you."

"Don't make friends, Mags. You're there to work, not attend a tea party."

As he was closing the door, Laurel called out.

"Will." He snapped his head toward her, and she winked. "Be careful out there," she said.

He slammed the door. Good God. What had she meant by that? It was almost a threat, but delivered as an invitation . . . to . . . what?

He left immediately. Will had to stop thinking about Laurel. He'd deal with her later. In the meantime, he had to focus. Today, he'd planned on scouting out at least two warehouses for Mrs. Rivers. *Mr.* Rivers. He couldn't help but feel like Mr. Rivers's wife was his boss, but that was another issue altogether. Will had promised to find storage space for the uranium concentrates in and around Manhattan. It wasn't so big a step from doing grunt work like this to making them realize that he could be even more valuable elsewhere. Like in the room where they were searching for the key: isolating enough uranium of the right kind to make an explosive the world had never seen.

And somewhere along the way today, he'd stop by Bellevue Hospital to speak to a certain Dr. Fielding, if she let him.

Will spent much of the day in Brooklyn, near the dockyards. He checked out some of the storehouses on Mr. Rivers's list, but they weren't quite right. One had windows that would be too easily broken into. Some were in areas that were too populated and might attract attention. Three of the storehouses were in active use for critical products like food or tool parts, and the managers were in no mood during wartime to discard their supplies and businesses, even for the government.

By three o'clock, the heels of his feet were sore from pounding the pavement. He jumped onto the BMT to cross the river, and switched lines to head uptown to First Avenue and Twenty-Seventh Street, where Bellevue and its surrounding buildings lived. Looking down Twenty-Seventh Street, he could barely see the East River and a barge passing by.

He hesitated before entering the hospital. What was the harm, really, in letting Laurel stay longer? What would asking questions about Laurel, or Felix Cross, really get him? *The knowledge of whether she was fond of poisoning people, for one.* But even as he thought it, a more powerful part of him wanted to remain in the sweet bliss of prolonged ignorance. Will clenched a fist.

"Get a grip, Will."

He smoothed down his shirt and brushed lint off his tie. He'd worn nicer clothes for his inquiries at the warehouse offices, but a part of him had been acutely conscious that he might meet Laurel's—or rather Ruby's—mother today. And that he'd helped her daughter get undressed for a bath. His nervousness was irrational; the doctor would never know. He was the one there to get information, after all. Yet he'd been less nervous challenging some of the world's most famed physicists on the Columbia campus about whether the graphite in their nuclear reactor pile was the right quality.

Will finally found the gumption to enter the main building, trying not to be intimidated by the imposing red brickwork and white lintels that dominated the avenue. There was an information desk in the rotunda, which was covered in freshly done murals with pastel paints. One depicted two men in white robes, one holding a rabbit while the other peered through a microscope. Another displayed antelopes and jungle plants twisting as if to escape the painting's borders. It was both welcoming and odd. He hadn't expected to see art in this place so famous for holding on to bridge jumpers and consumptives.

"May I help you?"

He knew better than to ask specifically for a patient. "I have an appointment with . . ." He looked at the torn article he'd stashed in his pocket. "Dr. Allene Fielding."

"Ah. She works on the Chest Service. Sign in here, please. The offices are up the elevator, to your right. Are you a patient? I believe she sees outpatients down the hall, though, in the next building."

"No. She asked for some research materials, and I was to meet with her today," he lied.

"Of course, sir." She pointed to the right, where he'd find the elevators. It was all too easy, slipping into buildings where he wasn't necessarily welcomed. Especially during wartime, when more, not less, discretion was warranted. Will could easily have found his way to the hospital kitchen services, distracted a few employees, and dropped cyanide into coffee pots and killed half the staff.

Far too easy.

Upstairs, the ward was busy, with patients lying in white-sheeted beds and nurses busily making notations on clipboards. Rattling coughs echoed in the hallways, punctuated by the clinking of glass and metal on trays. The Chest Service offices were close by, and he entered a wood-paneled door and asked a secretary in dark-rimmed glasses to direct him to Dr. Fielding.

"She's on the ward, rounding." She looked down at a large appointment book. "She isn't scheduled to meet with anyone right now."

"Excellent. She said she'd be able to fit me in. We have some research to discuss."

The secretary looked dubious, but stayed silent. She offered some blisteringly hot, bitter coffee, then went back to work organizing charts. It was at least twenty minutes before the door opened again, and a woman wearing a crisp white coat entered. Her hair was in a tidy bun at the back of her head, chestnut brown with gray strands silvering her temples, and a stethoscope draped over her neck. Her eyes were brown and piercing, and her mouth was slightly cocked, as if ready to tell a joke. But the resemblance to Laurel was there, in the curves of her cheek, the shape of the eyes. Will nearly coughed at seeing her.

"Dr. Fielding. A gentleman here to see you," the secretary said primly. "Not on your schedule."

Will stood up. He towered over her as he towered over most women.

"William Scripps. I'm sorry to bother you, but I have a few questions."

"Not sorry enough to ask, apparently," Dr. Fielding said, raising her eyebrows. She had a staccato way of speaking that was efficient and not welcoming to blather. "What can I help you with?"

"There was a gentleman you were . . . are . . . taking care of. Felix Cross? He's a friend." Will didn't consider himself a great liar, but he simply never showed much emotion, which was enough to convince most people.

"In my office, if you please," she said, indicating a room down a short hallway. The other doors were shut, or opened to reveal a physician scribbling on stacks of charts.

Inside the office, framed diplomas dotted the wall. Residency at New York University. Medical school. A Barnard College degree. Dr. Fielding sat at her desk, pushing aside a messy pile of paperwork. Will barely glimpsed a family photo at the edge of her desk that she knocked facedown in her haste. Dr. Fielding didn't bother to right it.

He wondered if that was a symptom of how she treated her family members. What was it like for Laurel to grow up in such a home? Perhaps she'd been coddled by her father, the bank magnate, while her mother worked here all day. Or perhaps they both ignored her. Will knew that feeling—his own mother had lavished all her affection on his stepfather, while his stepfather seemed to wish Will didn't exist.

"Tell me again—who are you?" Dr. Fielding asked. She seemed irritated by Will's presence.

"William Scripps."

"And you are friends with . . ."

"Felix Cross."

"Oh." She pushed back in her chair, her expression inscrutable. "Then you know what happened to him."

"Actually, I don't. That's why I'm here."

"We only speak to family. For privacy reasons."

"Well, he's like a brother."

Dr. Fielding smirked. For a second, he felt like Laurel herself was laughing at him. "Really."

"Yes." Will had a terrible premonition, not unlike a steamship captain who could see a U-boat in the distance, ready to launch a torpedo.

"So then you know all about what happened. His family must have informed you. Were you one of his Yale friends? Or from Exeter?"

"Yale, actually." Will's throat went dry. The lies were flying around like gnats on a cut peach. He could sense his pulse quickening.

"Felix Cross went to *Harvard*." She stood up. "You should leave my office now."

Will was sweating. He was unused to speaking to someone who could unravel him so easily. A line from the article he'd read yesterday flashed through his mind: *her own dramatic history and her father's ignoble death . . .*

This was the kind of person, he realized, he should have been more careful with. And yet, if Laurel was her daughter, he also hadn't gotten the impression that she was eager to turn her daughter in. Maybe she didn't even know what was going on. He decided to try truthfulness for a change.

"I'm sorry. I shouldn't have lied."

"No. You shouldn't have. It's not polite, and it's a waste of my valuable time. And also," she said, smirking, "you're an atrocious liar."

"Apparently."

Dr. Fielding went to the door, but Will held up a hand, pleading with her to give him some leeway. "Can you at least tell me—why did Felix become sick? I need to know because of a friend. A friend that I think . . . is involved with him somehow."

"A friend. Like Felix was supposed to be?" But as his question sunk in, Dr. Fielding's face, which was mildly ruddy from indignation, drained of color. Ah, that's the ticket, thought Will. He knew he'd hit a nerve, that she was thinking of Laurel. "What friend?" she asked.

"A lady friend, who, coincidentally, looks a lot like you. We are taking care of her right now. She's not well." He paused a long time, enough to watch her eyes widen and her eyebrows contract. It was a completely different feeling than the blustery, busy, irritated doctor she'd been moments ago. This was the look of someone who was watching their child being dangled over the precipice of the Grand Canyon, waiting to hear what the ransom would be. Will continued. "But we think she may have a connection to this Felix person. And we want to know if she's safe. Did Felix Cross ever hurt women? His fiancée? And did she really try to kill him?"

Dr. Fielding swallowed. Her voice, once acidic, had become a hoarse whisper. "What . . . what is the name of this lady friend?"

"I can't tell you. I don't think the name she gave us is real." He was giving away more than he'd planned on. "I found the article in the *Daily Mirror* about him. Was he really poisoned? With what?"

She tilted her head. "The way you ask that question makes it sound like you already know the answer."

Zinc chloride, he nearly blurted out. What was it about this doctor that made him want to tell her everything? The women in his life really were going to be the death of him.

"Is your daughter capable of killing someone like Cross?"

"I'm not answering that question."

"Everyone is capable of murder, under the right circumstances."

"Including you, Mr. Scripps. According to your logic," Dr. Fielding said.

Will sighed. This was like catching smoke with a butterfly net. Her evasiveness brought forth another thought. The coincidence of Laurel showing up, given Will's line of work, and Maggie's start at the Navy Yard. "Is your daughter patriotic?"

"Good God, are you asking if she's a spy?" Dr. Fielding looked incredulous.

"Most spies are good at hiding their true intentions from everyone around them."

She waved her hand dismissively. "Next question." Was she irritated, or had he pricked her conscience somehow? He decided to move on.

"Cross. What was he poisoned with?"

She waited, and when he stayed silent, she sighed. "We don't know. I have my suspicions, but the testing is not completed yet." She gestured. "Sit down."

Will did as he was told, and he heard the lock on the door turn before Dr. Fielding returned to her desk. She looked far less composed than at the start of their conversation.

"Will he recover?" Will asked.

She played a game of chicken, staring at him. Usually, Will won games like this. He loved seeing other people squirm under the oppression that silence brought. But this time, the eye contact was deeply disconcerting. She raised an eyebrow. Will took that as a yes. He finally used the excuse of clearing his throat to look away.

"In the article," he said, "it mentioned your daughter. She was engaged to Felix?"

"*Is* engaged to him," Dr. Fielding corrected him.

"And do you know where she is?"

"The official answer is, she's in San Francisco, hiding from the press." Her thin fingers spun her platinum wedding band, over and over. For a fleeting moment, he saw desperation in her eyes. "Tell me about your lady friend. Is she . . . a girlfriend?"

"Oh, no. Not at all." He looked down, hoping his face wasn't flushed. "She's a person that my sister befriended, really. She's—"

Will cleared his throat again. It was time to get his lying act in working order. "I don't actually know where she is at the moment. But she's intermittently in touch. And my sister is worried for her. She seems pretty scared."

"Your sister, or the girl?"

"Both." He leaned forward. "Should they have reason to be frightened?"

"There's a war. Everyone should be afraid. We're a heartbeat away from being blitzed into nonexistence."

"You know what I'm asking."

"Yes, you both should be. People who are afraid will do whatever it takes to protect themselves. And if this friend of yours is scared, then maybe she's been hurt." Dr. Fielding held his gaze.

"Did they fight a lot? Ruby and Felix?"

"Lately, yes."

"About what?"

"I don't know. People in our circle have seen them quarreling. And Ruby didn't tell me what it was about. She's always said she likes to clean up her own messes. Like her mother, I suppose."

Good God. Will wondered what other messes had happened in this family that landed them in the newspaper. He filed that question away for another day.

"Perhaps . . . you'd like to meet her," Will said. God, he had to drag the words out. Because that would mean Ruby would most certainly be out of their lives. Immediately.

Dr. Fielding half rose from her chair, and for a second, he thought she might leap across the desk to embrace him. But sat back down, composing herself.

"No," she said, frowning.

"No?"

"If your friend wanted to contact me or Felix, she would have. If she wanted to flee to Florida for all I know, she could have by now. She doesn't want me involved, that's clear."

Will watched her carefully. There was worry and anxiousness behind the mask of stoicism. Her hands were in her lap, but he'd bet a hundred dollars she was digging her own nails into her hands, trying not to swoop in and take Laurel back home herself. So this was what she had to do to protect her daughter—do nothing?

Dr. Fielding rose from her chair. "My patients are waiting. I'm sorry, but that's all the time I have today."

"I still have questions." Too many. Was Laurel in danger from the police? Or from Felix? Had she truly poisoned her fiancé? And if so, had she had a good reason?

"And I've answered them. Maybe not to your satisfaction, however. The police told me I shouldn't speak to anyone. Be thankful I made an exception."

"Thank you for your time." He went to the door and realized he couldn't open it. There was a keyhole. She'd locked the door with a key. How odd.

Dr. Fielding pulled a key ring from her pocket. She unlocked the door slowly, but didn't open it. She turned to him, her lips pressed together, moving as if trying to prevent words from coming forth. Finally she spoke.

"What about the money?"

"Pardon me?" Will cocked his head. What money?

"The large sum of money you're going to ask me for, as payment for not going to the police or the Cross family."

"I just wanted some information."

Dr. Fielding crossed her arms. "Despite your lack of financial ambition, I'll offer you this. If you keep this person safe and hidden, I'll reward you. Whatever you make in a year, I'll quadruple that."

Will shrugged. "That's very generous. But I didn't come here for money."

She stared at him for a long time, the way a person might appraise a new piece of cubist art they couldn't quite fathom. Finally, she sighed.

"I don't know what your true intentions are. I hope you tell her to be careful. I hope you stay safe as well." She opened the door, and a faint smell of bitter disinfectant wafted inward. Will felt like he was being sterilized and fumigated as he exited her small office. He thanked the secretary and left the Chest Service offices, heading toward the elevator.

As he hit the button to go down, Dr. Fielding's voice spoke from down the hall.

"Mr. Scripps."

He turned around and saw her standing in the middle of the hallway. No one else was nearby to hear her.

"Yes?"

"I hope . . . I hope you are a good man." Her eyes shone with moisture. "Be careful."

He nodded at her. But as he rode down in the elevator, all he could think of was how Laurel, and now her mother, had turned his life upside down. Dr. Fielding wanted her daughter to stay hidden, which meant the last thing he could do was turn her out on the street. It was a feeling of elation and a jail sentence, all in one. It was the last sort of complication he needed right now. And it was the one thing he also wanted—for Laurel to stay right where she was. But by helping them, by indulging his own uncertain desires, he was putting all his ambition at risk. Shakespeare's words rang in his head.

Cromwell, I charge thee, fling away ambition:
By that sin fell the angels . . .

Will was no angel. But he didn't have the gumption to say that to Dr. Fielding's face.

As he exited the Bellevue campus and headed back home to Brooklyn, he considered what he had learned today.

One, Ruby Fielding was most certainly the woman in his apartment.

Two, Dr. Fielding had expressed absolutely no warmth or concern regarding the stricken Felix Cross. Animosity? Possibly.

Three. Dr. Fielding was in no rush to swoop in and save her daughter. But even she didn't know why Ruby was choosing to keep her distance.

And four—Dr. Fielding wasn't entirely certain if her daughter was an attempted murderer. Only that if she was, she'd been pushed to do so. *Be careful,* were Dr. Fielding's last words. Though whether she was afraid of Will's heart being broken by her daughter, or that she might stop it cold, he wasn't sure.

As he made his way back home, a warmth filled his body, thudded up through his blood vessels, and lodged somewhere in his chest. He was eager to tell Maggie what he'd learned, but he was also relieved by what he'd gleaned about Laurel. Most likely, she feared for her life, and she was hiding for her own safety. And yet, these two items of information didn't extinguish the fact that he was anxious to return home, simply so he could see Laurel again.

He shook his head. No.

Ruby Fielding.

CHAPTER 9

"Hey!"

Holly snapped her fingers in Maggie's face. Maggie jerked to attention. She was at roll call at work, her second day. This morning's events had been replaying so incessantly in her mind she was hardly present. She had to focus.

She and Laurel had slept in her bed together, bodies cupped. Maggie had planned on sleeping in the chair again, but Laurel had patted the bed next to her.

"You're already doing so much. Please. There's plenty of room, and I won't bite you."

In the dark room, their closeness could be blamed on the unconscious acts of sleeping bodies. In reality, Laurel had snuggled closer in the middle of the night, and Maggie had allowed it.

"That was the most glorious night of sleep I've had in a long, long time," Laurel had said in the morning.

Then never go away, Maggie had nearly responded.

Making breakfast with Laurel—rapt with attention—was heaven. Maggie had decided that Laurel was still Laurel. Ruby was still not a solid person yet. There was no reason to face the truth until the truth slapped her back. They weren't 100 percent sure, after all.

"I can't thank you enough for letting me stay. I feel so safe here with you and Will," Laurel had said, her eyes brightening.

Maggie's heart had sunk just a little. She had briefly forgotten how she'd found Laurel and Will eating dinner together last evening, all cozy. When Will returned tonight, he might have more information about Laurel. Please, may it be something that means Laurel can stay longer, Maggie pleaded with God. Please.

Holly poked a finger hard into Maggie's arm. "Boy, are you acting dizzy today," she said. "Let's go."

The trainees were headed to pick up their equipment, and Maggie had still been standing there, staring at nothing, her mind full of Laurel. "Coming."

"Hi-de-ho! Nice to have you back!" Holly joked.

That morning, the novice group of women welders spent the morning reviewing the lessons from yesterday and watched several demonstrations of laying down a bead on a sheet of metal. By the afternoon, back in Building 4, Maggie was making her first attempt at using a stick welder, consisting of a pair of tongs that held a sticklike electrode. Her protective gear was smothering and heavy, and she was already sweating beneath her helmet, even though it was in the up position. Next to her, Holly grinned.

"I can't wait to do this."

"I can't believe I'm saying this, but me too." She grinned back.

"Say, that lipstick looks good," Holly said.

Maggie had put it on before she'd entered the Sands Street Gates. She normally didn't wear it, but something had changed her mind. When the guard had said, "Red suits you!" she'd responded with a wink. Maggie hardly recognized herself when she passed her reflection in a building window.

"Why the change? You got a beau or something?" Holly rubbed her nose, leaving a dark smudge behind. She looked like a black-eyed Susan now.

Maggie blushed. "No! I don't. Just a guest," she gushed without thinking.

"A guest?"

"A girl. She's staying over and it's . . . I don't know, it's nice to have company."

"A girl," Holly said. She suddenly frowned, as if she'd just recalled a bad dream. "Who is she?"

"Oh, I hardly know her, she's just . . ." Maggie's mind whirled. She'd said too much already. She thought of words to finish her sentence. A friend. A neighbor. A cousin. A stranger she'd just met. Nobody. But the longer her sentence went unfinished, the more suspicious she must have seemed. Finally, she thought of something to say. "She's someone from my neighborhood who needed a place to stay."

"What's she like?" Holly pressed.

Maggie lowered her helmet, and her muffled voice echoed around her ears. "Let's get to work."

Just then, the instructor—a great man with hands seemingly the size of dinner plates—towered over the two women as he asked them to strike their arcs and start making their beads.

Relief filled Maggie. She spent the next hours concentrating hard on welding together two flat pieces of metal. The tongs that held the welding rod were foreign to her hands and were tethered to a lead that ran to the "juice," or power supply. Each time she'd finish welding a few inches, she'd raise her helmet, and with goggles still on, scrape off the slag with a metal brush.

The instructor barked the first time he looked at her work. "Your arc is too long. Look at that spatter. You got no control over your pool. The weld is rough, see? And the base metal is undercut. Do it again."

Maggie did it again. The next time, she went too fast and her weld was small and irregular. If she used too much juice, she'd burn a hole through the metal. If she used too little, the rod would stick. Sometimes she went too slow and undercut her metal. But by the end of the afternoon, the instructor praised her bead. He gathered the class around to look at her last weld. Maggie nearly burst with pride. She was going to move on to vertical seams in no time. She imagined welding on a brand-new destroyer, knowing that her work could mean success or failure in a crucial battle. She was so proud.

When Maggie washed up and put away her equipment at the end of the day, she was shaky and tired. Holly waited for her at the gates. A boy was selling Wrigley's Doublemint and Juicy Fruit to workers spilling out from the entrance.

"You're a natural," Holly said, elbowing her.

"So are you. You're coming along just as well. I never was good at this sort of thing. Why are you so good at it?"

"I used to play around with my parents' cars in the garage. I knew more about them than our driver," she chuckled as their purses were checked at the gates by the guards.

Maggie looked at her curiously. "You had a driver?" Why would a rich girl be working in the shipyards?

Holly bit her lip, then shrugged. "We did. That was then. This is now."

Of course. The stock market crash in 1929. Sob stories were everywhere. Holly must be one of those girls who used to shop at Bergdorf's and now wore patchwork skirts.

"Say," Holly said. "Want to get a malted with me? I heard there's a shop on Flushing."

"I can't. I have to get home."

"To your guest!" Holly's eyebrows rose. "What a mystery! Can I come with you and meet her? I'll bet she's a spy!"

"Shhh!" Maggie said, eyes darting around her. "Don't joke about things like that!"

"It's patriotic to look for spies," Holly said, smirking.

"Well, I don't look for spies. I stay away from them. I do try to look for planes, though. Maybe you can help me do some plane spotting sometime. They're always recruiting. I'm to be a warden soon, if I keep up the work." Although she hadn't. The last two nights, she'd been so focused on Laurel that she'd ignored her volunteer work.

"You wouldn't rather spend your evenings cutting the rug with some GIs?"

"No," Maggie said bluntly. She wasn't one of those khaki-wacky girls.

"Ah. You'd rather go to a bond rally and collect scraps. Donate bacon grease. Of course." Holly fished out some coins to buy chewing gum.

"See you tomorrow, Holly." Maggie practically ran away. Talking to Holly was strangely exhausting, like she was always pushing away a tide of interest she didn't want or need. Or did she? If Laurel asked her questions, she'd answer them in a heartbeat. With Holly, it felt more like a pesky, sisterly intrusion. Still, it had been years since anyone cared enough to pester her.

There had been a boy once. He'd sold papers and always lingered at Maggie's house to chat if she was sitting on her stoop. One day, he asked for some lemonade, and she brought him inside for tea instead, since lemons were so dear. Their mother had died several years before, and at the tender age of sixteen, Maggie spent most of her days at school or home alone while Will worked.

When Maggie invited the paperboy in, she was achingly lonely but refusing to complain about it. The schoolgirls stayed away from her, awkward and shy as she was. She'd poured a glass of cold tea into a favorite cut glass decorated with flowers, and offered the boy a short-bread cookie. He was the same age as her, he'd said, but had had the route for nearly seven years. She'd watched him grow from a scrappy boy to a whiff of a man—taller, gangly, all arms and legs. His hair was brown, his eyes a muddy hazel with strikingly curled eyelashes; he had a Cupid's bow lip that she couldn't stop staring at.

After he'd eaten the cookie and drained the glass of sugary tea, he'd stared at her. Maggie shrugged. She said nothing when he came closer and kissed her cheek. Said nothing when he kissed her unresponsive mouth. She glanced at the clock—Will would not be home for at least three hours. His hands were on her knee, over the bodice of her dress, sliding up her thigh beneath her plaid skirt.

"What's your name?" she whispered when he pulled her to the sofa in the sitting room, the one that Will slept on at night.

"Sandy," he'd said with those doll's lips, unbuckling his belt.

Staring at those curled eyelashes, the feminine pink of his lips, she murmured the name—Sandy, Sandy, Sandy—as he fumbled his way under her cotton drawers and kneaded her flesh until she came with a convulsive gasp.

Sandy didn't last much longer, expelling his excitement before he'd even had a chance to consummate the tryst. He made a hasty goodbye, but showed up the next day for iced tea, and the next. It went on that way until Maggie could no longer ignore Sandy's masculinity. There was the time he took his shirt off, and the expanse of pectoral muscles disappointed her, like a planted flower seed that wouldn't bloom. Or the fact that his smell was undeniably masculine in nature—a combination of woodsy forest and dirty socks. She wished he smelled like jasmine and violets.

After a week, she no longer let him inside.

It had been years since those illicit liaisons at home, and Maggie thought of them often. She missed the hands on her body, never mind that they were always the wrong hands. But she'd been waiting patiently for another moment in time that would match that glimpse of heaven she'd had: those satiny lips, the slippery, pretty name, and the touch she hadn't felt in too long.

Once she arrived at the trolley stop in Gravesend, she practically ran home to Laurel. The sun was dropping in the sky, and Gravesend seemed dip-dyed in golds and elongated gray shadows. She scurried down Van Sicklen Street, which abutted the crossed square of streets in the center of the neighborhood, a remnant of its Dutch colonial beginnings. Maggie always marveled at how much history existed under her feet. Before the colonists, there were the Canarsee, who'd lived here and supposedly sold parts of today's New York City for less than twenty-five dollars' worth of shells, gunpowder, and guns. And before that, glaciers had bitten into the land, leaving behind a moraine that became Long Island itself. It had always made her feel small, and insignificant.

But today, Maggie's insignificance dropped away. Someone needed her. A mystery was unfolding. A job was being done well. None of the thousands of years of history before her mattered now.

She took the back steps to the house two at a time, and opened the door with excited hands.

Inside the kitchen, Laurel was leaning against the sink, her curved hip gently touching the edge. She held a burning cigarette in her fingertips, the minute red glow visible with her gentle inhalation. She puffed out smoke and smiled grandly. By God, she was like a movie star.

"Maggie!" she said.

Maggie put her purse down and ran her hands over her hair, whipped into messiness by a stiff October wind. She wanted to go to Laurel and embrace her, but that felt premature. Instead, she strode forward, trying not to grin too expansively.

"What have you been up to?" she asked. She noticed that Laurel was wearing an apron, one of Mother's old ones that Maggie didn't wear because she feared staining this relic of the past. If an apron could look magnificent on a person, it did on Laurel. She'd tied a crisp bow in the small of her back over her own nice dress.

"Gardening. Look." She gestured to the windowsill, and Maggie saw three teacups filled with ordinary soil, damp from a watering.

"Oh! A little window war garden! What did you plant? Where did you get seeds?"

"It's a secret. I'll tell you once they've grown a bit. In the meantime—" She winked at Maggie. "Don't touch."

Maggie's smile disappeared. She thought of the bottle of zinc beneath the sink. No, don't consider such things. Perhaps Laurel only wanted to surprise them with some parsley or thyme. Everyone planted war gardens, but since it was fall, most had died. But planting things also meant something else, something wonderful. Laurel intended them to grow, and growing plants took time.

Laurel was planning to stay awhile.

Wonderful!

"And also, your home needed a bit of cleaning, so I took the liberty to dust a bit."

"Oh!" Maggie was surprised again. Laurel was the type of person who probably had loads of maids. She hardly knew how to toast anything, or make coffee, after all. Dusting? Cleaning? Did she even know how?

"Look."

She pointed to the sink. In it, there was an inch of water. The plug was solidly in the drain. At first Maggie didn't see them, but then she did.

A dozen black spiders, floating on the surface. Their legs were curled in the way that dead spider legs always did, as if the living world now repelled them and they had turned inward in their death throes.

"It turns out boric acid is an excellent arachnicide."

Maggie reeled back. She had no love of spiders, but seeing the mass of them curled up brought bile up her throat. Some were still kicking in a last attempt to escape the acid bath they'd been placed in.

Seeing Maggie's stricken face, Laurel put her hand to her mouth. "Oh. I'm sorry. I should have washed them down the sink. But it's interesting to see what sort of toxicity they can handle. Every living being has a limit, you know?"

"That's very . . . scientific of you," Maggie said, her hand still to her mouth.

Laurel yanked the chain to the drain stopper, and the spiders swished down the vortex. Maggie's eyes watered.

"You're upset," Laurel said, her head hanging over the now empty sink.

"No! It's just . . . I don't like spiders, is all. Alive or dead."

Laurel looked up at her, eyebrows rising like the roof of a house. "I hope you don't mind. I don't know what I'm doing half the time. You know everything, Maggie. You should teach me more."

"I will." Maggie smiled, and Laurel's face blossomed. "I'll teach you whatever you need to learn. It's okay. I hardly knew how to cook or clean or do anything. Will did everything for so long. I'm a late bloomer, too, I guess."

"I'm so sorry," Laurel said. "Sometimes I think I've read too many books and not really lived in the world."

"But you had a man in your life, didn't you?" Maggie couldn't help but ask.

"Yes, I did. And he promised to open up my small world and make it bigger, but the opposite happened."

Maggie held her breath, waiting for more, but Laurel's face had gone cold.

"Well," Maggie said. "Er . . . maybe you can teach me something, and I can learn something from you too."

Laurel reached out and grabbed Maggie's hand. Her palms were so soft, so unlike Maggie's coarse skin that was untouched by perfumed lotions and creams. Laurel had the hands of a person who knew what it was to have a servant.

"You are truly a sweet girl. I couldn't be luckier." She tugged Maggie closer.

As Laurel leaned forward, Maggie turned her head to speak, and Laurel's lips found hers.

The kiss was only a peck, and Maggie pulled back in surprise. Laurel had kissed her before in the bedroom, but it must have been a mistake, or just a friendly gesture. Maggie was ready to apologize, to shake her hands in earnest protestation, when Laurel leaned in again and pressed her mouth to Maggie's.

This time, it was no mistake. Laurel's lips were soft and fit perfectly into Maggie's, better than keys in locks, closer than fingers in thimbles, more at home than clouds in the sky.

When they parted, Laurel laughed.

"You're a good kisser, Maggie." She turned around so quickly that Maggie had no idea if she was teasing or not. She walked to the pantry, slowly unknotting the apron at her waist. "When I was a child"—tug, tug—"I played at kissing with my friends, pretending we were to be married. Sometimes we'd kiss pillows! This was better." She hung up the apron and turned around. "I'm going to wash up and rest a little."

Maggie nodded dumbly. "Of course. Oh! If you need, I have extra clothes you can wear in the closet and dresser."

"You are a dear!" Laurel gave her a sweet smile and retreated to the bedroom.

When the kitchen was empty, Maggie looked to the windowsill and the three teacups of dirt, and the empty sink now devoid of spider carcasses.

Will came home soon after, and together they made dinner while Laurel rested. When he checked on her sleeping form on Maggie's bed, he seemed to watch her with a frightening intensity. He carefully shut the door.

"Mags. Walk me to the trolley stop?" He gathered his book bag for his evening classes.

They left Laurel behind. Maggie hoped she wouldn't do anything strange or odd while they were gone. Although she was bundled in her coat, the air felt colder than usual.

"I know who she is," Will said, warm plumes of breath clouding the air as they navigated the alley toward the MacDonald Avenue trolley stop.

"Who?"

"Ruby Fielding. She's most certainly the person mentioned in the article. I spoke to her mother, the doctor, at Bellevue. She didn't lie, exactly, but I just knew."

Ruby. Maggie let the name settle firmly in her mind, on her tongue. Ruby, a gem so precious, living in their very midst. If anything, knowing her true name made the stranger in their home more solid, more crystalline, as if Laurel had only ever been an idea in Maggie's imagination.

"So why is Ruby here? With us?" she asked.

"She's in some sort of trouble, but I can't tell if she's running away from trouble, or she *is* the trouble. If she tried to kill that Felix Cross fellow, I think there was a good reason for it."

Maggie told him about the teacups, and the spiders.

"That's bizarre," Will said, looking worried.

"Do you think she's dangerous?" Maggie asked.

Will nearly spoke, then held back. She wondered what his instinctual answer was, but he followed with a tepid, "I hadn't thought so, but now . . . I don't know. You should be careful with her. She does anything that shows she could hurt us, and we'll have her arrested so fast she won't know what happened."

"I think she needs us."

"I do too."

"She should stay with us. At least for a little while longer."

Will sighed. "Just not too long." He rubbed his forehead, like he had a headache. Maggie knew he was torn between getting rid of her and helping her.

"And anyway, I really don't think she wants to hurt us, do you?"

"I . . ." He shook his head, but he seemed hesitant. "You know, her mother offered us a reward to take care of her."

"Really? How much?"

"A lot."

"You could go to college full time instead of working," Maggie said.

"Maybe you could stop working at the Navy Yard, and concentrate on getting married, having kids."

"Maybe," Maggie said. Her response was far less enthusiastic. Rationally, it was what she was supposed to want, but Maggie had never really felt the earthbound pull of wanting children. She thought of the letters she addressed to her mother, how they helped clarify her intentions and observations of the world. But she had never dared write all of what she remembered about the past: How her mother had failed miserably at keeping her marriage happy and raising her kids. How the things she'd wanted—a husband that didn't die in the war; a husband that didn't seem to ignore her—had only inflicted damage on others. Maggie was supposed to do better. But it seemed like she was always failing. Until her new job at the Navy Yard—it made her feel different. She wasn't just a volunteer helping with the war effort, but a paid worker doing something valuable and appreciated.

At MacDonald Avenue, the electrified trolley lines hung above them, swinging lightly in the breeze. The trolley, with its trawler pole connected to the overhead wire, rolled to a stop, and before he boarded, Will pointed at Maggie's face, his hand like a gun.

"Be careful with her. For now, let's not let her know I spoke to her mother, or that we know her real name. Be nice, but not too nice. All right?"

"All right. I won't be too nice. Anyway, the reward money is a good reason to keep her," she said, tight lipped. She didn't actually care about the money. But she could also tell that Will didn't either. Lately, she was finding herself greedy. About her success at work, and about keeping Laurel—that is, Ruby—to herself somehow. Usually, Maggie's lies were quiet ones. A nod, to indicate she was happy to find a new job when Will pressed her, or that she was just fine when in truth she ached for her lost mother every day. After brushing off Holly about their new guest, and now with Will, she was finding it was easier to lie out loud lately.

"And one more thing." The trolley driver hollered at him to hurry up. Will replied in a calm, level voice that somehow felt like a razor-sharp scolding. "I'll get on when I'm damn well ready."

The passengers went quiet as Will turned back to Maggie.

"Someone has to talk to this Felix fellow."

"The man in the hospital?"

"Yes. So we really know what's going on. I figure a lady may have more luck getting information out of him. You have to talk to him somehow. Get as much information as you can. Pretend you're looking for donations or something. Don't give anything away."

"Okay. After work this week sometime."

"Good." He climbed into the trolley, paid the nickel fare.

Maggie exhaled in relief once he'd gone. She didn't cower around her brother like other people did. She knew he'd never touch her or hurt her in a million years, but she also knew that he could be indomitable in other ways. He wanted her to seek out Felix Cross, and she would, whether she liked it or not.

Before she went home, she pulled out a piece of paper, an envelope, and a pencil stub. She sat on an empty crate on Avenue U, in front of a closed superette advertising Dutch Masters cigars and 7UP.

Dear Mother, she wrote. *I've met a wonderful girl. Two, actually, but one more glorious than the other.*

Let me tell you all about them.

Once her full heart was emptied and she felt like she was more herself, she posted the letter, mind cleared and able to think without all the tangles that had clouded it. She went home, looked for any injured animals or insects around the house, then washed up and got ready for bed. Ruby was waiting for her in her tiny bedroom, already wearing the sleeping robe that was once her mother's. A negligee, they called it, with swaths of satin and edging in silk lace. It was the nicest thing her mother had owned and had been hanging uselessly in Maggie's closet. She had said Ruby could wear whatever she wanted, after all.

That night, when they lay side by side, Maggie touched the fading bruises on Ruby's neck. And Ruby asked Maggie if she could kiss her good night. Maggie nodded a simple yes. It felt like a first kiss somehow, as now this was Ruby, not Laurel anymore. Ruby, an heiress. Ruby, the woman who might have attempted to murder her fiancé. The woman in the papers, mysterious and hidden, who seemed to only want Maggie, right here and now. Perhaps tomorrow, and forever. Never mind that Maggie had promised to stealthily find out more information about Ruby, or that she would lie to Will tomorrow by pretending that nothing had happened in this bedroom aside from two girls sleeping soundly.

When Ruby tasted Maggie's tongue with her own and slid her hand onto Maggie's hip, Maggie only gripped the fabric of her robe, as if afraid Ruby would dissolve into the air at any moment.

The rest of the night, they continued to say nothing. Because speaking might somehow dissolve the fairy tale that was now growing right through them, the way an oak tree's roots would disregard the pavement and buckle it with a shrug.

CHAPTER 10

It was hard to believe that time could pass both so fast and so slowly. A new routine had emerged in the Scripps household, one that made Will both uncomfortable and oddly excited, as if there were a new version of Christmas morning every day.

Will would wake up to the sounds of Maggie and Ruby in the kitchen, chattering away where silence had previously reigned. Maggie had been teaching Ruby about the price of groceries, and how to shop for the best bargains—all without actually shopping, of course. Ruby was still too wary to leave the house, and still occasionally suffered from spells of dizziness. He watched them carefully, noting that Ruby's hand would sometimes casually rest on Maggie's shoulder a touch too long, or they'd lean into each other like the most intimate of friends who had known each other decades, not days.

At these moments, he found himself grimacing, eliciting concerned queries from Maggie about whether he needed some Bromo-Seltzer.

His work was suffering too. Dragging himself to his evening classes, he wondered what conversations were happening in the kitchen, or the bedroom. Wave and corpuscular theories of matter and the inner atomic workings of the universe seemed dull in comparison. He needed to turn in his report to Mr. and Mrs. Rivers in a few days, but his focus was elsewhere.

Some days, Will would come home to find Ruby in bed, resting, as whatever had sickened her the day she'd been found was still making its way out of her system. Other times, she'd be sitting at the kitchen table staring with controlled anxiety at seemingly nothing, as if something beyond the kitchen walls was ready to pounce on her. On more than one occasion, he'd found a cluster of dead mice in the kitchen garbage.

Some nights when he came home from classes, he quietly crept into the house and gently pushed open Maggie's bedroom door. The women were curled like two matching spoons nestled against each other. Jealousy would snag at his heart, but it stubbornly would not disappear. His eyes lingered where Ruby's bottom curved against Maggie's lower belly, and on how Maggie's hand rested almost proprietarily on the rise of Ruby's hip. Ruby was wearing a silky robe—where on earth did she get that from? It was knotted around her waist, but had sagged open over her chest, and the swell of her right breast bulged in a perfect crescent where it rested atop the mattress.

Refusing to touch himself, Will would take a cold bath and recite relativity equations in his head. This was how he put himself to sleep, with visions of warehouses, and the drumming of the laws of nature over and over again.

He started to leave the house before the girls awoke, and would scribble the same brief message on a pad in the kitchen.

Went to work. Be back at dinner.
Will.

It was more than what he usually wrote, which was nothing. He never bothered to tell Maggie where he was, or what he was doing. There was a quiet assumption that no matter what, he'd be back at a time that struck well before Maggie could worry about bodily harm to Will, or her abandonment.

The notes, really, were for Ruby.

Now it would be up to Maggie to find out more about Felix Cross and whether there was any claim to the possibility that Ruby was the danger, rather than vice versa. She had kept putting it off, citing that she was too tired, or too busy. But sooner or later, they needed to know the truth about Felix Cross and Ruby. That was all he really cared about.

No, that was a lie.

On this bright morning with November looming ahead, Will headed to Manhattan. This time, he would look at different areas of the island by the water. The warehouse the MED needed would have to be close to a port and far away from any busy areas where too many eyes would ask too many questions.

He spent the morning near the Brooklyn Bridge on the Manhattan side, visiting warehouse after warehouse. It was dull work, but something kept him on edge. Mrs. Rivers had told him he had limited time to find a place, but it wasn't that. It was this unrelenting feeling that he was not completely alone. Was it the constant thoughts about Ruby? Not that. It was a physical sensation. He found himself looking over his shoulder, catching eyes with this man, or that woman.

And sometimes, he could swear he would see a familiar face in the crowd, or a person just ducking into a coffee shop across the street. Not Maggie's face, but her eyes. Or her smile. Once, he swore he saw his dead father, whose body had been half burned to ashes after his infantry division fell under attack at Argonne. Will shook it off when he realized it was a man he'd never seen before. And yet, he could not disperse the feeling that he was never quite alone.

After visiting the fifth warehouse, he realized that nothing was adequate in this area. At noon, he made his way to the bland white Arthur Levitt building on lower Broadway. In the lobby, with its decorated plaster ceilings and marble walls, he showed his ID several times, then made his way up to Mr. Rivers's office.

The office area was fairly benign—drab grays and browns colored the walls and desks. Everything was right angles, with antiseptic surfaces that seemed allergic to anything remotely dusty. A woman was rolling a mimeograph machine in the corner, churning out a stack of copies.

Mrs. Rivers was one of many secretaries in a wide room, and she tipped her chin up when she saw Will. He sat down next to her desk, where she was typing out carbon copy notes from a pad of shorthand scribbles.

"And?" she said, as if they'd only just finished their conversation at the Staten Island warehouse half a minute ago, as if Ruby's presence had managed to alter time itself. At the thought of her, his insides twisted a little. He wished he could take another cold bath.

"Mr. Scripps?" Mrs. Rivers said. She raised her eyebrows, though her eyes were still on her steno pad. For a scant second, he'd forgotten where he was. He focused on those Victory Red lips.

"Yes. I scouted out the west side of Brooklyn, and the Lower East Side of Manhattan. Nothing. I think I'll turn up something on Manhattan's west side, though. Lots of warehouses. I know the businesses there, and they're more likely to have inventory that's dried up with the war effort."

"Excellent. I'm sure Mr. Rivers will be pleased to hear it." She went back to typing. The brisk clacking of the machine addled his brain.

Will stood. It was only two thirty; he could be home by three or so, and see Ruby. Alone.

"Mr. Scripps," Mrs. Rivers said, still typing. Still not looking at him. Will nearly jumped in place. "Are you well?"

"Excuse me?" He put his hands on his belly, as if to check that his organs hadn't moved recently.

"I asked if you are well. You seem distracted. Is there anything you need to tell me?"

Will shook his head. "No, ma'am."

"Good. Keep your eyes where they need to be. Mr. Rivers will want a foreman on this job when it's time to move material to the holding place, once it's vetted. We need it sooner than expected. In two days. Can you have a viable place by tomorrow?"

"I'll do my best."

Mrs. Rivers stood up. She pulled the finished documents out of the typewriter with a zing and smiled at him. Not a very nice smile.

"I'm quite sure that my husband expects better than that. General Groves too. You do realize that to have civilians working on our project is unusual. Your ability to focus is paramount. The last thing our country needs is wasted time, or complications. At any level."

"Of course," Will said, now slightly annoyed. He didn't need babysitting. Ruby would only be with them for a little while longer. Surely it couldn't be too much of a detriment to his work. Certainly nothing that would change the tide of a war. "You're welcome to tail me with one of your men, if it would make you feel better. I've nothing to hide."

"What makes you think we aren't already doing that?" she said, straight faced. And then, a brilliant smile. "I'm kidding. Be a waste of manpower, wouldn't it?"

The conversation was ridiculousness wrapped up in good manners. Will already knew he was followed half the time. But that was different than the feeling he'd had earlier today, when the ghost of his fallen father during the Great War seemed to be haunting him.

"Indeed. Have a good afternoon, Mrs. Rivers."

She nodded and turned, disappearing into the large office next to her desk. Will caught a glimpse of the interior—more drab colors, and a grand desk with a cigar resting in an ashtray belonging to some unseen smoker. Mrs. Rivers leaned over the desk, her derriere facing Will as the door closed its last few inches before clicking shut.

On the train home, Will wondered about the uranium in need of urgent storing. Uranium had several isotopes, some more stable than others. If they had wanted one that could sustain a chain reaction, as that Hungarian physicist Szilárd had talked about, they'd need an unstable one. His mind was so caught up in thinking through the possibilities that only belatedly did Mrs. Rivers's words came back to him—the implication that they'd assign him as foreman if he came through with a location. It was a lot of responsibility, and a step closer to his goals.

Still not close enough, though. He wanted to be at the nucleus, not somewhere circling the action, watching from far away.

But by the time the train crossed the bridge and drew closer to Gravesend, he was thinking less about uranium and more about Ruby. If he wanted to do his job better, he ought to make her leave.

That was the correct answer, of course—for so many reasons. But with Ruby, the answer always ended with the same confusing conclusion: he didn't want her to leave.

He put his fists to his temples as he rode the BMT back into Brooklyn, and found himself clenching his jaw as he exited the Avenue U station a few blocks from home. He ignored the store signs advertising popover dresses and the cream-colored flags in the windows of homes, stitched with blue stars for each enlisted family member. Normally those stars made him feel guilty, but he was full of other thoughts now. Thoughts of Ruby.

He unlocked the back door. "Hello?" he said, stepping into the kitchen.

It was empty. The kitchen countertops had been wiped clean. The dishes were all put away. The teacups with their soil still stood on the windowsill, the dirt almost black from being recently moistened. He listened—there was no sound of water running, no coughing, no crying.

"Hello?" he asked the void again. He went into the washroom, found the towels neatly hung on their rods, the toilet and bath looking old as usual, but clean. The pink bar of soap was still perched on the ledge of the sink, its milled edges smoothed with use. He imagined the soap sliding against Ruby's hip, and his breath came quicker.

Maggie's room was empty. Her bed was primly made, as if two feminine bodies had not slept cupped together all night long. The closet was closed; the bureau with its trinkets that all once belonged to their mother was recently dusted.

The parlor was devoid of life as well.

Where was Ruby?

She might have left or gone for a walk. The door to the basement was slightly ajar. He headed downstairs, where Maggie's air raid shelter was still a work in progress. The lower level was dark, and he turned a makeshift switch that lit a single bulb far down the stairs. The steps groaned under his weight. In the center of the dirty floor was the shelter, half-built. There were corrugated metal walls and part of some corrugated metal for the roof. He poked his head inside the dim space. Piles of supplies were sitting in neat rows.

No Ruby.

"Looking for something?" A woman's voice penetrated the darkness, and he stood up so fast his head bashed against the corrugated metal roof. The clang echoed in his head.

He grunted loudly, more in annoyance than pain. He withdrew from the tiny space, straightened, and turned toward the voice: Ruby, perched halfway down the stairs. He hadn't heard her come down or open the door, or the creaking of the upstairs floorboards. She was silent as smoke, and her presence astonished him despite the fact that his thoughts for the last hour had swirled around her.

"Are you all right?"

"I will be." It was hard to see her expression. She descended the stairs and stood before him. "Were you looking for something?" she said.

"You, actually."

"Well, you found me."

"Where were you?"

"I went out."

"But the door was locked."

"There are two doors, you know. It doesn't matter. I'm back now."

He grasped her upper arms. "You can't do that. You could get hurt." For a brief moment, he wished to say, *Or you could have hurt someone.* He blinked, wanting to thrust that latter thought into a bin and incinerate it.

"I feel invincible these days," Ruby said, approaching him a little too closely. He could feel the heat emanating from her body, rising up and warming his chin and neck. "You've made me feel safe. I can't thank you enough."

"You don't need to thank me." Or Maggie. Ugh. Don't think about Maggie right now. Don't.

"No. I do."

He was still gripping her arms, and it occurred to him he might bruise her if he clung to her for much longer. He let go, and her hands rose to cup his jaw. She went up onto her toes—she wasn't wearing shoes—and kissed him.

A chaste, brief kiss. But when they parted, she exhaled like she'd been waiting all day, all century even, for that kiss.

He should shake his head and sit her down at the kitchen table, grill her on everything she knew about Felix Cross's poisoning, about her mother. But he couldn't move.

Ruby didn't move either.

It would be three hours before Maggie came home.

"Your name isn't Laurel, is it?"

Ruby didn't say anything, but her eyes stayed fixed upon his. After what felt like a season passing by, she parted her lips.

"Let me be Laurel. For a little while longer."

And she kissed Will again. This time, she slid her palms up his chest, and the sensation of her warm hands drove away any last ability to keep his distance. His hand went to her back, pressing her forward, desperate to taste her mouth again.

They kissed for a long time before she pushed him away and stood there. Deftly, as if she'd practiced this for weeks, she unbuttoned her dress and let it fall to the floor. In her brassiere and slip, she smiled, the kind of smile that felt crafted for one person in the entire globe. She walked past him and disappeared into the air raid shelter.

Will removed his shirt and crawled in after her.

———

Who knew how much time had passed. Will was certain they hadn't much left before Maggie returned home, but for the moment, he couldn't move.

Ruby's head rested on his bicep, and they were skin to skin beneath a scratchy wool blanket. She'd switched on a small battery-powered lamp and had draped her brassiere over it with a giggle. The light shone through the bits of silk lace, and the corrugated roof a few feet above them was patterned like a moonlit sky with hazy tendrils of cloud passing by.

"She'll be home soon," Ruby said, her hand making lazy circles on his belly.

"I know." He continued to stare at the laced pattern of dark and light above him. "I need to ask you something."

A pause. "All right."

"Are you a spy?"

Ruby laughed. "God, no!"

The answer came so easily it sounded true. Then again, acting was a skill that could be honed like a fine blade.

"Did you . . . do something wrong? Is that why you're hiding?" He couldn't bring himself to say *attempt murder*.

This time, no spontaneous guffaw or exclamation. He listened to her breathing, which became shallow and light suddenly.

"Yes," she said. "And no." He could feel her blinking against his shoulder. She was crying. "I know I'm hurting my family right now. I didn't mean to."

Inwardly, he yelled at himself to ask her—just ask her if she tried to kill Felix Cross.

"Did you try to kill—" he began, but she flipped over, interrupting him. He could feel her breasts against his chest, and his body began to reawaken after its brief rest.

"Don't. Don't ask me. Not now. I'll tell you everything, but not now. Let's just have this for now. Please."

"Laurel," he said, but she quieted his protestations with her lips. He wasn't sure if he was asking a question, pleading for mercy, or commanding her to stop. But he allowed her to continue silencing him, even as she moved against his body, as familiar as if they'd done this a thousand times before.

After they'd finished, after her voice had cried out in pleasure in the darkness, there was no luxurious resting. They knew the clock was winding down, and wordlessly, they dressed and rearranged the air raid shelter as if nothing improper had ever happened there.

As they climbed the stairs, Ruby was already pinning her hair back into place, and Will reached out a hand.

"Laurel."

She paused and turned around. A hairpin was trapped in her lips, splayed and ready to capture a lock of hair. "Mm?"

"Where were you today? You never told me."

She took the pin out and stabbed a swell of hair above her ear. She wouldn't look at him.

"Laurel." Something about the tone of his voice made her freeze. "Whatever you do, for whatever reason . . . don't hurt Maggie. Please."

She exhaled. "Are we going to lie about what just happened?" she asked.

"I don't think I'll be able to hide anything when you're nearby."

"Well, then. I think it's too late not to hurt Maggie, isn't it?" she said lightly.

Will followed her up the stairs, his heart feeling shredded like old paper. Ruby escaped into the washroom to tidy up. As the setting sunlight hit his eyes, he realized that Ruby had never told him where she had gone.

CHAPTER 11

It had been a good day for Maggie. Even though a spark had hit her below her bib and burned a little hole in her shirt, straight through to her brassiere. But her asbestos gloves weren't feeling so utterly unwieldy anymore. She'd even gotten compliments on her last weld of the day, where she'd kept her bead nice and regular, not too deep, and minimized those spatter BBs that she'd have to scrape and chisel off later. This, of course, was after an entire day of ruined welds, but she was making progress. There were some girls who hadn't fared as well. One of them had forgotten to put her helmet on and was sent to the infirmary with arc eye—a flash burn to her cornea.

Holly was a natural, though—even more so than Maggie, who had to work at it. She had hands as steady as a surgeon's, and seemed to preternaturally know exactly the right distance to hold her electrode to make it do exactly what she wanted.

At the end of the day, as they exited the Sands Street Gates, Holly hooked Maggie's arm in her own. One of the men leaving hooted at them through cupped hands.

"Hey sugar! You rationed?"

Holly yelled back, "Not for a fathead like you!"

People nearby laughed, and Maggie put her head down and wished she was invisible.

"Hey, Mags," Holly said, grinning. It felt so comfortable being called that. It was what Will called her, after all. "How about you invite me to dinner, so I can meet that handsome brother of yours?"

Maggie nearly tripped over nothing. "What? Will? He's not so handsome," she said. She simply didn't see it. Anyway, Holly had never seen him, so she was obviously just guessing.

"Still. Hard to find a man these days. They're all overseas! And all he's got wrong is one bad ear. Not bad. If we were married, we'd get along swell because I'd only nag him on the bad side!" She laughed out loud. Several people nearby took notice at the trolley stop. Maggie shrank. She hated the attention, even the proximity of it.

"Aren't you going home?"

"It's so lonesome, Mags," she whined. "I'm boarding at this house full of other ship workers, and they won't talk to me."

"Why?"

She went quiet for a long while. "Promise me you won't tell?"

"Of course."

"They heard that one of my great-great-aunts, or a cousin a million times removed, or something, was Chinese. Or half-Chinese. I don't look it, of course, but they keep calling me 'Jap lover,' and they hate me now."

"Oh. Well, that seems silly," Maggie said. "Even if you were part Japanese, that doesn't mean you're unpatriotic." There was something about this sudden deluge of information that made her feel odd. But it was Holly's behavior, not her ancestry, that put Maggie on edge. Of all the girls in their welding unit, Holly always chose Maggie to befriend. Not any of the other girls. Not the vivacious and pretty ones who attracted attention like flies to a bitten peach. Only fuddy-duddy Maggie.

"Come on. I'll help you make dinner, and I'll even give you some of my sugar ration tickets to help."

It was too much. Maggie suddenly withdrew her arm from Holly's and stepped away. "Stop it. Why are you like this?"

Holly looked agog. "Like what?"

"So friendly. You've been all over me since the day I started here. I hardly asked for the attention."

"I'm just being friendly." Holly looked utterly confused. "Don't flip your wig. Is that a bad thing?"

"But why me?"

Holly's face changed from insulted, to confused, to querying. "I don't know." And then her eyes unfocused. "No, I do know." She looked back at Maggie. "I like your quietness. When I was growing up, there were always other people around who were louder than I was. Prettier. A brighter light in the room. Do you know what I mean?"

"Yes," Maggie said. Maggie was always the shadow. In school, on the street. She was hardly noticed. She'd come to find solace in the invisibility of herself, but sometimes it was heartbreaking to never be seen. "I understand that."

"It's nice, for a change, to be friends with someone where I'm the one who's confident. I'm the one who always has something witty to say." She shook her head. "I sound terrible, but it's the truth. I like who I am when I'm around you. I'm sorry if that's selfish."

"It's not selfish. Maybe I listen more. That's a good thing, right?"

"You bet it is. I can chew your ear off all day and you never complain. And you talk plenty too!"

Maggie smiled. "I guess I do." It was true. Holly kept Maggie talking all the time. She knew all about Will, and Columbia, that he'd worked for the physicists in Pupin Hall and that he was taking courses at Brooklyn College and she didn't really know what he did all day for work except that he wasn't allowed to talk about it. She knew Maggie's favorite color (purple), and her favorite food (schnitzel, which she could barely admit in a whisper, as it wasn't generally patriotic to admit you liked anything German right now). "Anyway, about dinner. Will is real particular about who comes over. Big brothers and all," she said, trying to sound cheerful. Holly picked up her arm, and they continued to walk together. "Maybe another time?"

"Oh, come off it. You're just going to run off to write one of your letters, aren't you?"

"What?" Maggie dropped Holly's arm. She felt the life drain out of her cheeks.

Holly put her hands on her sturdy hips. With her dungarees and thick boots, she had an obstinate look that demanded the truth. "Oh, you know! You're always scribbling things down when you think no one is watching. I saw you dropping them off after work two days in a row."

"Oh, those. I'm just writing to my aunt," she lied. She would die before she would tell anyone she wrote those letters.

"Ah. Okay."

The stress of Holly's inquisition was wearing on her. She wanted to go home to Ruby. She wanted to curl up into her arms and sleep. She wanted anything but this right now.

"I'm sorry. I tell you what. Some Sunday when we don't have to work, let's have a day out, you and me. We'll go uptown, have an adventure. And I'll tell you anything you want to know. Okay?"

Maggie smiled. Was this what friendship was like? You had your differences, but you made up quickly, and in the end it was a give-and-take of words and emotions. An ebb and flow that simply worked itself out.

"I'd like that," Maggie said. She thought of Ruby and decided maybe it was a good thing to have a friend. A friend was different from Ruby. Maggie could cultivate more than one living being in her life at a time, could she not? What was the harm in that? "I'd like that a lot."

"Okay, then." She hugged Maggie (who was stiff as a board—only in Ruby's presence did she actually like human contact) and waved goodbye.

As Maggie mounted the trolley, she thought of schnitzel, and her stomach grumbled. The thought of rich German food suddenly reminded Maggie that Ruby had been sleep talking German. Or maybe it had been incoherent mumbling? But there was more to figure out. She'd been dragging her feet all week about trying to get more information on Felix Cross, and it was Friday. Her heart sank. She didn't want to know more. She wanted to go home, back to the fairy tale that had started to take root in their very un-fairy-tale home. But she had promised Will.

It took nearly an hour, but she made it to the hospital before visiting hours were over. At the front desk, she signed her name and went to the Chest Ward. As soon as she stepped out of the elevator, she asked a nurse where to find him.

"Cross? Sorry, sweetie, you just missed him. He was discharged. Looks like you can visit him at home instead." She smiled and walked past Maggie.

Ugh. All that travel for nothing. But she had to talk to him. She could wait for her day off, but she'd rather spend it with Ruby. And come to think of it, she wasn't exactly looking forward to seeing Holly tomorrow at work anyway.

She'd call in sick, that's what she'd do. And then she'd find Felix Cross and get answers, and Will would be proud of her, and somehow she'd get the information she knew she'd find—that Ruby needed their help. Perhaps Will would then decide they ought to keep her in their home for months and months. Maggie could protect her from all that was unpleasant and evil in the world.

When she arrived in Gravesend, she stopped by the large oak tree on the front lawn. A dark bundle was lying inside the large hole in its trunk. A sparrow! Its foot looked crumpled, and it seemed half-frozen. She picked up the brown-feathered creature gingerly, checking it all over carefully, and cupped it in her hands. She breathed warm air, ruffling its feathers, and the bird shook itself. It was still alive. She walked to the back of the house, carrying the bird.

Approaching the steps going up to the kitchen, she halted. A dark mass was clumped on the lowest step. She peered closely and stifled a gag.

Four dead rats, all lined up in a row, as if waiting for their mass grave to be dug.

Surely it was Ruby again. What on earth compelled her to murder the little living things around her? Not that it mattered so much, as rats were troublesome vermin, but Ruby had a way of presenting her victims the way their old cat, Cassandra, had. Cassandra would dutifully drop a decapitated mouse or eviscerated rabbit on their back step every other day, mewing with pride. It was abhorrent. She didn't trust Ruby to be in the same house as the injured bird, so she dug out a handkerchief from her pocket, nestled the bird in it for warmth, and returned it to the knothole in the tree. Hopefully it would survive.

Maggie stepped over the rats on her way to the back door, letting her thoughts return to the beautiful stranger in her home. What new things would Ruby say and do tonight? She was impatient as a child waiting for an ice cream.

"I'm home!" she sang, entering the kitchen. She nearly dropped her key.

Will had his arms wrapped around Ruby's waist from behind, while Ruby wiped dishes in the sink. A bowlful of extravagant peaches was set on the table, next to a bowl with several peach pits. They were both grinning, and at the sound of the door opening, they didn't spring away from each other. This was no mishap, no accidental bumping into each other. Good God, they must have been feeding each other peaches all afternoon, and doing . . . other things too. Will smiled uncertainly, keeping his hands on Ruby's hips as he made firm eye contact with Maggie.

It was as if to say, *No, this isn't a mistake*, and *Yes, you will have to live with it. With us.*

Maggie's mind went abruptly to a memory, an echo of the present she couldn't escape.

Maggie had been eleven. She had been playing with her Raggedy Ann doll, a cast-off from a friend that had been resewn and patched to be serviceable enough for play. Mother had said, "Now she's a true rag doll, because she's been loved and used and loved again." Embracing the doll, Maggie had run into the kitchen to find her father with his arms wrapped around her mother, who was wiping dishes at the sink. One hand was on her belly, one on her left breast. His hands would grasp more if he could. He was whispering in her ear, and she was laughing softly, shaking her head.

"No, Norman," she had said. "The children will hear!"

"You're the only one that matters. I'd die without you," he whispered. When she didn't reply, he squeezed her breast. "Say it back."

She winced, closing her eyes. "I'd die without you, too, Norman." And then, as if reciting a line from a script, she added, "I'm only half-alive when you're in the other room."

Maggie could almost hear the unspoken words: *And I'm dead when we're in the same room. Together.*

Her mother and her father spoke as if she weren't there. Surely, Will didn't matter as much to them. Will's father had been dead for years, and Mother never mentioned him. Certainly not in front of Maggie's father. Sometimes Maggie was frustrated at Mother for not loving Father more. He would die for her. Wasn't that love? Mother seemed too meek in the face of so much devotion. That same meekness had imprinted on Maggie, like a permanent tattoo.

Maggie artlessly dropped her doll, and its button eyes clinked against the waxed floor. Her parents didn't uncouple, only looked placidly at Maggie before slowly separating.

"Don't ruin that doll," her mother warned, before going back to the dishes. "It's all you've got."

Here in her kitchen, as a grown woman, Maggie couldn't stop staring. Will finally released his hands from Ruby's hips. Ruby wiped her wet hands on a dishcloth and blinked several times, as if that could wash away the bad feeling that emanated from Maggie like a rotted tooth that couldn't contain its stink.

"How was your day?" Will said.

"Fine," Maggie said. She was tempted, so tempted, to be quiet. To say nothing, and just accept and swallow whatever was being thrust upon her. But she couldn't. Not this time. "I went to the hospital. He wasn't there," she said.

"Who wasn't there?" Ruby looked taken aback. "Why did you go to the hospital, Maggie? Aren't you well?"

Maggie didn't answer her, only kept staring at Will. "What's going on between you two?"

Will tilted his head ever so slightly, as if to say, *Must you make me say it out loud? You already know.*

Maggie wanted him to go through the degradation and shame of having to say it, but Will was immovable. Maggie could only muster one small rebellion by pointing to the bowl of fruit.

"You bought peaches. We can't afford those."

"A craving I had," Ruby said, smiling. "Will just bought a few. For us."

By *us* she meant only her and Will.

"Never mind that. Dinner is ready. Eat up," was all Will could say.

Nothing. No more words. As if she were a child too stupid to understand the ways of grown-ups.

Maggie stormed through the kitchen and into her room. Her eyes were blinded by tears as she gathered her field glasses and a blanket and changed her coat to an old, heavy one that had belonged to Will when he was two sizes smaller. She swallowed two aspirin for the pounding headache erupting in her temples, grabbed her plane-spotting armband with its red-and-white triangle in a blue circle insignia, and headed back outside.

"Where are you going?" Ruby asked.

"It's dimout time. Turn the lights off, or I'll call the police on you for being noncompliant," she snapped.

She slammed the kitchen door behind her. At the bottom step, she kicked the dead rats off the step with a wet thud, and their corpses flew in three directions and landed unceremoniously in the alleyway.

Maggie marched up her street, yelling at each neighbor to dim their lights. She angrily barked back at Mr. Winslow, who had yet to buy Permo blackout shades for his upstairs parlor. Tonight, gentle Maggie Scripps was not herself. Once the lights were completely out, she put her black silk armband on and climbed the side fire escape of a set of row houses next to theirs, whose tenants let her plane spot from their higher three-story building.

On the roof, there was a small flat area in the back, set up with an old rickety chair that faced the southwest horizon. She would scan the skies with her binoculars, and if anything suspicious should be seen, she'd run down the fire escape and report five blocks away to Peggy Bellini, the air raid zone warden who gathered all the information from the neighborhood and reported directly to the sector warden. Five months ago she had completed the training, and now there were over sixty thousand spotters like her around New York.

Maggie sat in her chair, covered her lap with the blanket, and started watching. She was lucky to have field glasses, which gave her better depth of field than a single handheld telescope. They had been given to her by their elderly neighbor who'd died a month ago. Maggie had sent him and his wife half a war cake every Friday while he was sick, and when the old man had died, his widow had given the binoculars to Maggie with a note.

He always appreciated how you looked after him. Now keep looking after America!

The couple was German, and they had a tendency to overdo the patriotic thing, for good reason. She'd pretended not to care why they had a pricey pair of field glasses in their modest home. Maggie understood their worry; technically, she was German on her father's side but made sure never to mention it in public during these times. As for the binoculars, she had scribbled her worry about the expensive gift in a letter to her mother, and then forgotten about it. It was so nice to let those letters be a repository for all her worries; they dissolved into the world and away from her. Anyway, the binoculars were very handy.

Maggie settled into a pattern, scanning the horizon from left to right, up and down in several sections of the sky. During the daytime, she'd see American red, blue, and yellow Cessnas and Luscombes flying around looking for U-boats, knowing they were safe from reporting. But at night, it was harder. After about an hour of this, her eyes grew blurry from the strain, and her stomach rumbled. She hadn't eaten any dinner. But at the thought of returning, she demurred. Already, she felt like a stranger in her own home.

She wished that she had invited Holly back with her. She wouldn't be alone now. Maybe she'd have the strength to say aloud what her heart was screaming. She couldn't tell who she was angrier at—Will or Ruby.

Oh, Ruby. The mirage that was Laurel had all but dissolved.

She didn't know she'd fallen asleep until she awoke with a start. Looking at the inky darkness about her, she knew it must be the middle of the night. Her back was stiff from being in one position so long, and she stood up to stretch. Her hands weren't cold, though. That's when she realized there was a second blanket on her and, next to her, a plate with a cheese sandwich sitting squarely in the center. There was a note beneath it.

You looked cold. I brought you something to eat. I can make sandwiches now! Are you not proud of me?

Please don't stay mad. A heart can swell to contain many kinds of loves.

Laurel

—◆—

Maggie frowned. What did she mean, many kinds of loves? Did Ruby think of her as a child, a platonic kind of convenient affection that fit nicely into a box somewhere on a shelf? She looked disdainfully at the sandwich, pushing it away with her booted toe. The sound of the ceramic plate scraping on the asphalt made her cringe.

After a full sixty seconds, she said to nobody, "Waste of a good sandwich." And then she proceeded to gobble it up.

It took a while to fall back asleep, so she watched the skies instead. But that left her mind open for all sort of thoughts. She wondered if Ruby and Will were downstairs together, enjoying their time alone and thankful that Maggie was out of the picture. Wondered if they were having relations, and where, and in what position. She actually slapped herself on the cheek then. What kind of a person had they forced her to become, having such carnal thoughts? But eventually, the boredom of watching the empty skies lulled her back to sleep.

When the sun had risen enough to brighten the eastern sky a deep blue, she went back down to her home. On the way, she remembered the injured bird she'd left in the tree. Inside, there was only her handkerchief and a smattering of bird down. A few more feathers were scattered at the base of the tree. Damn. A raccoon must have gotten it in the middle of the night. They often woke up out of their cold slumbers to search for food. Ruby was ruining everything.

Maggie opened the door to the kitchen. She was loath to intrude, but for now, it was still her home and she had to get ready for the day. She was going to look for Felix Cross, after all. The apartment was quiet. The washroom was open, and her bedroom door, too, but both were empty. She heard whispering in the parlor, and of course they must have spent an uncomfortable night on that lumpy sofa. Despite her disdain for it, she felt a pang of jealousy anyway. What she wouldn't do to spend a night on that old furniture, springs sticking into her back, if she could share it with another person.

Maggie went to get paper for a new letter for her mother, but didn't change. (She was still wearing her work clothes. Why bother?) She splashed her face with water and made for the door.

"Maggie."

She whirled around. Will was standing in the parlor doorway, as if shielding Ruby from her. She knew she must be there, though.

"Off to work?" he said.

A rustling issued behind him, and Ruby came into view. Without a word, Will moved aside. Ruby was dressed in one of Maggie's dresses, but it fit her too tightly. She really needed more clothes. Maybe they could shop for new ones. Get one of those McCardell popover dresses for seven dollars. Maggie imagined her closet being taken over by Ruby's new dresses, sleeping gowns, drawers filling with expensive, frilly lingerie. In her mind, Maggie hardly lived here anymore.

"Maggie!" Ruby came over and gave her a kiss on the cheek. Maggie didn't have the strength to dodge it. Ruby smelled like lilacs, which was somewhat impossible. They owned neither perfume nor toilet water. It was as if nectar oozed right out of her pores. "You spent all night up there! Don't do that again, you hear? Have a good day now. We'll see you tonight." Her finger trailed against Maggie's earlobe, and in response, Maggie's left knee wobbled.

"All right," Maggie replied. She turned away before she could inadvertently throw herself at Ruby or say something utterly stupid, like beg Will not to take Ruby away. "I'm off." She bolted through the door and was already in the alley when Will came out and shut the door behind him.

"Mags," he hollered.

She sighed and turned. "Yes?"

"Are you going to be okay with this?"

Maggie nodded firmly. "Of course. Why wouldn't I?"

"Well, it's just been the two of us for a long time."

"You're free to live your life any way you choose, Will. I'm not your mother."

He looked stung. "Of course you're not."

Perhaps it was good that she had the job at the Navy Yard. She would be making more money there than doing anything else. Perhaps she and Holly could find an apartment to live in together.

Perhaps, Ruby should leave.

Or maybe—Will should.

But now, Will would probably not let Ruby leave. Maggie needed ammunition. For what kind of war, she wasn't exactly sure. Something had to be done.

"Will," she said. "I went to Bellevue yesterday. Felix Cross was gone, already sent home. I'm going to see him today, actually. Find out what I can."

"Oh." Will seemed crestfallen. This was the plan, wasn't it? But Ruby had changed the plan. It was obvious he was already no longer in charge of his senses.

"I'm going to be late." She kicked a rock. It landed near one of the rat corpses. She wondered if Will had even seen them.

"Yes. Bye, Mags."

She turned and left without a parting goodbye. The conversation didn't deserve to have a neat ribbon tying it closed.

CHAPTER 12

Maggie was gone. But Will couldn't shake the uncomfortable feeling that he had utterly messed up everything. He reasoned with himself that Maggie was a grown woman; she should know that people had relationships, that things didn't stay static forever. He would speak to her more when she came home. Especially after she met with Felix Cross. Perhaps she would find out what he assumed to be the truth—that Ruby was a hurt woman trying to find a safe life. She was safe for now.

The question that itched the edge of his mind was, Are we safe from Ruby? But he brushed it aside when Ruby came up behind him at the doorway and slid a soft hand into his. Her right hand slipped around to rest at his belt buckle, while her lips enclosed his earlobe. It was warm, tickling, and rather infantile, but the message was sent, and he exhaled in response.

He had work to do, but first . . . he turned around and picked her up easily, the way one might pluck an apple off the table, and carried her to Maggie's bed.

They tested the limits of that good piece of furniture twice before Will washed up and got ready for work. The sound of the water splashing

couldn't rinse away the sound that played over and over again in his head—those moans and cries from Ruby, only minutes ago. He'd been both shocked and pleased when, after he'd rolled off her, she'd gently smacked his face.

"You're done, but I'm not," she'd said and had somehow managed to work him into yet another frenzy with her demands. "Be a gentleman, and finish the job."

Once she was satisfied, he was wide eyed and wondering. Who was this woman? What had just happened? He was nearly ready to ask that very question, when she slipped off him and left the room. He shook his head several times, as if to rid his mind of the cobwebs, that intoxicating blur that appeared whenever they were together.

Will had to work. Quickly, he washed and dressed. The water was running in the washroom once he'd downed his coffee and eaten a bite. He knocked on the door.

A plume of steam issued forth when Ruby opened it. She stuck her head through the narrow gap.

"I'm going to work," he said. "Please stay home. I need to know you're safe."

"The only way I'll be safe is if you're with me." She pouted slightly, and he felt a corresponding tug in his ribs.

"I can't stay home, love."

The last word slipped out before he could reel it back. But now it was out there, a word he almost never spoke.

"Then I'll go with you."

"I thought you were in hiding."

"I can hide behind you." She smiled. "I'll wear Maggie's clothes, and I'll cover my hair."

He shook his head. "I'm late," he said.

"And I'm ready." She stepped out of the washroom, fully dressed. She waved a kerchief and began to cover her hair. Her dress was indeed a bland beige from Maggie's wardrobe.

"Oh." He hadn't anticipated this. Then again, he hadn't anticipated most of what Ruby did to him. "I can't bring you with me," he said, even as his mind whirred with the possibility of how he could.

"Sure you can. I'll step out of the way and be quiet as a mouse whenever you need. And then you can keep an eye on me, and I'll feel safe."

"I don't know."

"Just this once! And we'll see how it goes. If it's a terrible idea, I'll stay home ever after. I get so bored here, and when I'm bored, I get in trouble." She lifted up a tiny gold compact. "I can even powder my nose on the way." She smiled. He liked her better like this, without her usual bright lipstick. The waxy, blood-colored cosmetic was just a barrier to her skin.

Had she just called this wreck of a place a *home*? Well, that was something. And then he thought, surely he could do this. Handle her, and handle his work. His mind must have the capaciousness for such tasks. He just had to ignore the needs of his body when necessary.

It was more a surprise to him than to Ruby when he found his mouth saying, "All right. Just this once."

He had succeeded all his life in keeping his goals in focus, to the point that he was ill equipped to wrangle emotion or desires stronger than he'd possessed before. It was foreign, this feeling of being lured irresistibly by all things illogical.

Ruby smiled for a moment, an evanescent glimpse of someone who'd been given exactly what she wanted. After they locked up, she hooked her arm in his, a message to the world that he was hers, and only hers. He liked it. He'd always seen couples walking on the street, sharing that negligible space between them. All the experiences he'd had with women (aside from his mother and Maggie) had been brief and heated and fulfilled one, and only one, purpose. He hardly remembered their faces. Not because he didn't care to, but because he'd care too much if he looked.

As they traveled by subway to the Lower West Side of Manhattan, Ruby said nothing. Sometimes she hummed to herself, and sometimes she just glanced at the buildings around her. Somehow, she seemed to know that he needed large acres of silence, and he was grateful for that. When they arrived at the Eighth Avenue subway station and began walking up the avenue, he stopped her.

"I have to check out some of these buildings. I may need to speak to some people, and I can't have anyone with me."

She nodded. He took out a pack of cigarettes and handed them to her. It would give her something to do.

At the first warehouse, he left Ruby across the street, which was within view of a park. He looked back over his shoulder. In her coat and bland dress, smoke issuing from her lips, she still managed to resemble a movie starlet, one that was hiding in plain sight. She held herself in a way that distinguished her from other women on the street, their war-appropriate clothes fancied up by victory corsages made of war stamps. But Ruby's personality had a way of declaring itself like a honking Klaxon.

Inside the first warehouse, metal parts were piled in discrete areas and destined for several wartime manufacturing plants. Another was full of paper products, but the manager would not budge with renting out the space. Will and Ruby went farther west and north, to Chelsea. On West Twentieth Street between Tenth Avenue and the West Side Express Highway, there were several candidate buildings that would work. They were only a short few blocks away from the docks—perfect. He eyed several warehouses, sandwiched between an office and a tenement building. All the same redbrick, and one with a tiered, almost pretty roof. It had a dearth of windows right down the center of the building, making it look somewhat stately. There was scant foot traffic here.

"Stay over there, on the far corner. I'll be back in a little while," he said to Ruby.

"Can I come this time? I'll be quiet as the grave."

"No."

"Please? I've been ever so good."

He sighed. "Let me check it out first. If it's clear for you to come in later, I'll fetch you."

She smiled. "Okay. In the meantime, I'll be fetching over there." She walked to the far corner, leaned against the building, and pulled out another cigarette. Her calf slipped out from her coat, and the curve of her leg was everything this street full of warehouses wasn't. Human, soft, full of intention. He looked away.

He knocked on the door next to the industrial-size sheet metal doors. The sign above was stamped **BAKER AND WILLIAMS**. An old man answered, holding a clipboard.

"We aren't expecting any shipments today," he said gruffly.

"I know. I'm working on behalf of a party looking for space. Your building is what, ten thousand square feet?"

"Why, yes. How did you know that?"

"I have eyes," Will said.

"Apparently you do. We're leasing all the buildings at the moment, including this one, and 513 to 519, as well as down the street at 529 to 535."

"You have half the block?"

"Yes. Vented, electrical, plumbing, all in good repair. What're your goods?" he asked, letting Will inside. There was a wide corridor for unloading shipments, ending in an industrial lift. A small office sat to the right, with a tiny light illuminating the space.

"I can't say. My boss is real particular with details. Suffice it to say, we'd need the entire building, and can provide an annual contract, with options for several years down the line. And access would need to be severely limited, for privacy reasons."

"Did you say . . . all the buildings?"

"Yes."

He eyeballed Will. Without an army uniform, he could be anybody. He added, for good measure, "It's all aboveboard, but confidentiality is of the utmost importance."

"I see."

"And I need an answer today, pending an inspection of the premises."

The old man peered at him from above the glasses perched on his nose. "I'll have to speak to my son—he owns the property—but I can get back to you in an hour. We've been looking for another company to work with, so timing is just right."

"I may be able to get you a contract by the end of the day."

"Very well. I'm going to drop by his office. You can take a look around the warehouse, if you'd like, while I'm gone."

"Are you sure?"

The old man laughed. He went into the office and secured a tweed cap on his head and grabbed his coat. "Ain't nothing to steal in here but some leftover paint, and I doubt you'd be able to haul away these couple of barrels by yourself. I trust you. You've got an honest look about your face."

He opened the door, and touched his cap. "One hour."

Will watched him walk down the street. The old man saw Ruby smoking on the corner and did a double take. His eyes went from her face to her legs, and then he walked on. She looked over, and Will motioned to her. She trotted over on her heels, careful not to trip on the cobblestones near the sidewalk.

"We can take a look. He'll be back in an hour, so you get one look, and I'm shooing you out after fifteen minutes."

"Fifteen minutes? That's all we get?" She smiled.

"None of that," he said. "This is business."

She looked disappointed. What kind of woman would be looking to tryst in public, and in such a place? It was a warehouse like all others—dirty in the corners, spacious, devoid of anything remotely romantic. They walked through the main floor, saw the small collection of paint barrels, then took a set of stairs to the next floor, and the next. They tested the industrial elevator, which clanked and whirred its way up and down, without groans or telltale screeches of infirmity. On the top floor, they peered through the windows, which were smoky and let in a dull, brownish light. They only opened a crack and would not allow anyone to crawl in or out.

"Well. I love what they've done with the place. I think they could have gone with the gilt moldings instead of the bare pipes, but it'll do."

Will smiled. "You think?"

"Mm-hmm." She started unbuttoning her coat. He watched her long fingers deftly moving from neck to waist. "What on earth are you going to do with all this space?"

"Store things." He figured vagueness wasn't a threat to national security.

"What kind of things?" She'd finished unbuttoning so that she could hug him, belly to belly, without the thick cashmere of her coat getting in the way.

"Stuff."

She squinted at him. "What do you do, exactly?"

"This and that."

"Boy, you are a thesaurus of all things cryptic."

He raised a single eyebrow. "It's why I'm good at what I do."

"It's not why you're good at this," she said, threading her fingers into the thick hair above the nape of his neck. She pulled him close for a long, warm, deep kiss. He put his hands on her shoulders and pushed her gently away.

"Not here, love. Not now."

"We're alone."

"And I'm exhausted."

She raised an eyebrow. "You don't look exhausted."

"That's just my face. It's not the part of my anatomy that's tired."

She leaned her head against his shoulder and laughed. "I'm sorry. I'm not usually like this. Honest to God. But there is something about you. I can't ever seem to quench my thirst."

Thirst was right. He'd never been with any woman more than once, so it was an alien experience to get to know a woman and her appetites. He didn't actually realize that women could have the same level of urges as men. Even so, this was only one part of her. He didn't know other things. Part of him didn't want to let her real life intrude.

Yet reality was coming. It was there on the horizon, like a tidal wave. But it had yet to arrive. There was plenty of time, surely. Inwardly, he laughed, knowing these were the thoughts of the foolish damned.

He pulled away. "It's been twenty minutes. Let's get you out of here."

"Very well. But you owe me. Bring me back sometime, and we'll have a moment. Right here, by the windows. No one will see. They're all frosted."

"You're really something." And he meant it. Never in his dreams did he think he'd play grab-ass inside an empty warehouse. But now that it was dangled before him, he realized he wanted everything she offered, no matter how odd, no matter how dangerous.

She kissed him one more time, and he let her. If he could, he would pin her down and kiss her for twenty-four straight hours, but that need was both frightening and exhilarating, and he had a job to do first. For the first time since he'd left Columbia, he wished that he lived alone. If only Maggie were independent or married or in another town, he could have the place to himself. So he could have Ruby to himself.

And then he thought about Maggie. How hurt she was. Bringing Ruby into their home had been her idea—her new project, now in her brother's arms. He thought about how the death of their mother had left her like a cicada shell hooked onto a branch, with Will the only living thing in reach, and if he took his eyes off her, she might blow away and be crushed underfoot at any moment.

As they walked to the entrance of the building, he promised himself he would make things right with Maggie. Give her and Ruby some time together without him. That would help, surely. That might fix everything.

Ruby was properly shooed away from the building and out of sight when the old man returned. Mr. Tom was his name, and he'd brought his son, a younger version of himself without all the tobacco-stained teeth, but with more worry, although it had yet to etch its lines into his face.

They discussed terms, and Mr. Tom slid the paperwork into a manila envelope. It happened very fast, but these weren't times to dawdle. Will's search was over. It was time to see Mr. Rivers and move on to storing the refined uranium ore and that precious isotope within it. The physicists at the MED and Columbia would now be working on extracting and enriching the isotope so they could create that desirable chain reaction. There was the step into which Will needed to insinuate himself. Being a foreman wouldn't be good enough. He needed to make himself an even more necessary part of the MED.

Will hailed a yellow cab heading downtown. "Two hundred seventy Broadway," he barked at the cabbie once they were inside. Thanks to his size, Will always felt squashed inside the back seat, but Ruby didn't seem to mind being crushed against him.

"What's at 270 Broadway?" she asked.

"Didn't I tell you that you could come but you couldn't ask questions?"

"Did I agree to that?" she said playfully.

"More or less."

She snuggled against him as the cab drove. Her closeness was starting to feel extremely familiar. Shockingly so.

"Did you grow up in New York?" Will asked. He figured he'd try.

She was quiet for a long minute. "Yes. But you already guessed that, didn't you?"

He shrugged. Still, he was satisfied that he'd gotten one kernel of information out.

"What did you do, before this job?" Ruby asked.

"This and that."

This time, they laughed a little together at how vague his answer was. He felt the need to tell her something real. Something concrete.

"I started college years ago, but quit. But I restarted again, at Brooklyn College." He was enrolled, so it wasn't really a secret.

"I see."

Will paused, but she didn't ask any more questions. Her silence was soothing. Most people filled the void, but with Ruby, it felt like she was in the void, waiting for him to meet her in the middle.

He started talking. "I was at Columbia, on the football team. I was studying physics."

Ruby chortled.

"I know, I got that a lot. Most football players were not physics majors. But it wasn't all physics. There was a core curriculum I had to take. Plato, Aristotle, Locke, Hobbes. And then . . ." He sighed. "Maggie was working alone in Brooklyn. I tried to come home as often as I could on the weekends, but I spent more and more time on campus to study and work." He looked at his knuckles as they rode steadily on. "She didn't do very well alone. I'd known that already. I'd postponed college for a couple of years before that, partly to save up money, but partly to be there for her. And then when it mattered, I wasn't around." He had a vision of Maggie in the emergency room at Coney Island Hospital, still soaked to the bone, sand crusting her wet clothes, with a nurse watching her warily. Still coughing up bay water, she cried when he came to her side. He grabbed her and held her in his arms, hating himself for not being able to prevent that terrible day from happening. And Maggie cried even harder, not because she was glad he was there. But because she was still alive.

"Growing out of childhood doesn't always mean you can survive adulthood," Ruby said.

"I know that now." He sighed. "When I was that age, I held down two jobs. Maggie couldn't handle one. She was so shy it was always getting her in trouble. You'd correct her for one fault, and she'd shatter for hours."

Ruby nodded. They passed Canal Street and a war bond rally on the corner. An elementary school was being let out somewhere, and children with little round Bakelite ID tags around their necks were flooding the sidewalk. Finally, the cab slowed to a stop in front of the MED building.

Will was glad of it. He was already heartsore from the little bit that he'd revealed. He told Ruby to wait on the street and handed her a dollar.

"Buy some candy or a paper. I'll be out soon."

"Meeting your other beautiful girlfriend, eh?" She winked.

What a disconcerting joke. It was as if Ruby knew he was meeting Mrs. Rivers, who happened to be rather a stunner herself. Will cleared his throat.

"Be back soon."

He checked in at the desk, took the elevator up with no fewer than three army personnel. They all got off on the eighteenth floor, but he headed solo to Mrs. Rivers's desk.

"Well?" she said, not looking him in the eye. She was reading a stack of paperwork in front of her, angling it so he couldn't see. She was licking her fingertip to turn the pages one by one. But the folder sagged under the weight, and Will briefly saw an image that looked like a diagram for a reactor pile, like the one at Columbia they'd made to create a nuclear chain reaction. Will remembered working on it. It seemed like a huge pile of blocks, not like the secrets that would overpower a country. He wondered if she even understood what any of the notes meant. When Mrs. Rivers realized he could see a bit of her paperwork, she closed the folder.

"Here." He handed her the contract. "Warehouses on West Twentieth Street. Right off the Express Highway, and with access to multiple piers. Perfect. Owners are ready to lease right now, and they can clear out their storage items within twenty-four hours once we sign. But it's already practically empty."

"Good." Mrs. Rivers took the envelope from him. Her eyes were slightly puffy, and she rubbed the bridge of her nose. "I'll have Mr. Rivers sign these after we do an inspection. You did tell them to expect that, right?"

"Yes."

"Did you do a survey of the surrounding area?"

"The docks are nearby, and there isn't much foot traffic."

"Does the building go to the other side of the block? Entrances and exits there we need to know about?"

"I didn't check." He cursed himself, feeling like a kid who forgot his homework. He couldn't even claim it had been eaten by a dog. "I will tomorrow. And I'll make sure they're ready immediately to receive shipments."

"Good." She stood up and reshuffled her sheaf of papers. "You're a little off today, Scripps. Not enough coffee?"

"Perhaps."

"Our country doesn't have the leeway for us to be off our game." She waited.

"If I could come to the meetings with you, I could stay on top of this better."

Mrs. Rivers laughed. "Are you serious? Those are high-level meetings. You don't have clearance for that." She hugged the files and the contract to her chest. "What you need to do is the job I give you."

"You mean the job that Mr. Rivers gives me."

She smiled. "Of course."

139

"I helped the physicists at Columbia design their pile, though my name will never show up in those academic papers. I can be more than a foreman. I could do more."

She leaned in a little closer and narrowed her eyes. "I'll see what Mr. Rivers says. Also, ditch the girlfriend. I thought that between your sister and me, you already had enough womenfolk complicating your life."

Will couldn't prevent his bottom lip from dropping.

She smiled. "Yes. We know about her."

Of course they did, but it was still a shock, nonetheless. Did they truly know everything, though? He didn't think so. If Ruby was so dangerous to him, or to them, surely they would have said something. Done something already. She couldn't be a spy, then. Or a potential murderess. Right?

"Come on, I'll walk you to the elevator." As they walked, he tried not to make eye contact with anyone else in the office, but he felt their gazes on him. Not an engineer, or physics professor, or military, Will was a curious anomaly. "You know, Will," she said as her legs matched his stride, "everything was so easy when all you did was work, went home, and went to your classes. Now you're visiting Bellevue and bringing lady friends along with you."

Will said nothing, but he could feel his armpits getting swampy.

"It's fine for you to have ambitions, but don't you think the physicists at Columbia already have that part of things covered? One of the reasons you're so valuable is you don't have to go through the bureaucracy of this government. You get things for us. Whatever we need. Up until now, discretion has been your asset. Don't lose it, or we'll have to find another Will."

Inwardly, he sighed. Whatever it was between him and Ruby, it should stop. It was endangering his future, and after he'd worked hard to become relatively indispensable. Next time, he'd just make her stay home. But how long would that last? He should probably get rid of her.

He didn't want to. Like a petulant child, he wanted to turn around and ignore his directive, and go on being in her tight orbit.

They'd arrived at the other side of the room. Mrs. Rivers seemed to be waiting for a response. He pressed the elevator button, then stepped inside alone.

"Will? Do you understand what I'm saying?" she said, eyebrows raised.

He felt as if he'd been spanked. In a near whisper, he said, "Yes, ma'am."

As the door closed between them, she smiled one last time.

"That's a good boy."

CHAPTER 13

Maggie's anger had simmered into a stew of overcooked jealousy, and by the time she'd left Brooklyn, all that remained was just a bad feeling. But her task lay before her, and it had to be done. She was going to find Felix Cross and have a word if it killed her.

She called in sick to work from a public phone inside Barratta's pharmacy, then headed for Manhattan to find Cross. It wasn't that difficult, actually. The Cross family was well known, and even as a child, she'd heard of their grand mansion on the Upper East Side. Her mother had noticed it one day when they had played in Central Park.

"It's in the Beaux-Arts style. See how flat the roof is, and the arched windows? And there, by the main doorway, the sculptures of the goddesses are so natural looking."

Maggie hadn't really understood what she was saying, except to notice that the house was enormous and intimidating. She couldn't imagine living there. Her mother had a love of architecture and would always point things out, like keystones in arches and Corinthian columns. Perhaps she focused on these solid things of beauty to offset the ephemeral things that occupied her life, including husbands.

Maggie arrived at the mansion and rang the doorbell. She was staring artlessly at the two goddesses above the doorway, their bare breasts so very bare, nipples in three-dimensional relief and making Maggie blush, when the door opened. It was a young maid in livery, but she had a sharp face and piercing dark eyes that immediately put Maggie on her guard.

"Shipments are to go to the service entrance on Seventy-Third, you know," the maid said crisply.

Maggie looked down. She was still wearing her dungarees and thick work boots and had her hair tied up beneath one of their old dishcloths. Even if she'd brought a change of clothes, it wouldn't have mattered. She didn't own anything nice enough to wear into such a house anyway.

"I'm here to see Mr. Cross."

"Mr. Cross?" The maid gave a vinegar-laden visual assessment of Maggie once again. "I'm afraid that's not possible."

"Please. I need to ask him about his fiancée. Laurel—" She shook her head. "I mean, Ruby Fielding."

The maid's countenance changed immediately. She looked fearful and glanced over her shoulder. Was someone there waiting behind her? She looked back at Maggie.

"What is your name, Miss?"

"Margaret Scripps."

The maid opened the door wider and stepped back. "Wait here," she said, gesturing to the grand foyer. She left Maggie behind gaping at the scarlet-and-gold carpeting, the carved and polished mahogany staircase, and the nearby oil paintings of fox chases. There was an oversize portrait of an old white man who looked like an angry, consumptive version of Santa Claus.

The maid returned promptly. "Mr. Cross states that he would be happy to host you for luncheon. Shall we?"

Maggie tried to hide her confusion. "It's only nine thirty."

"It'll take at least an hour and a half to get you ready," she said, exasperated. "You can't meet him like this. Per his instructions, I'm to take you upstairs and get you properly prepared. Otherwise, his parents might throw you out if they see you, and we never know when they'll come back. They are out calling on friends."

Maggie shrank in shame. "They would do that? Throw me out?"

"Oh yes. They would," she said knowingly. "Come now. We've some frocks that should fit you just fine."

Maggie was terrified. They wanted her to change? Into someone else's clothes, just to meet this man? What had she gotten into? She considered that this was some lurid device to prey upon her for some wholly unchristian plan, but she had no idea what that was.

"We haven't got all day. You have dirt caked under your fingernails. That alone will take half an hour to soak out."

Maggie curled her hands into fists, hiding her fingernails. She needed to find out more about Laurel. *Ruby.* This would be worth it. Maggie had initially wanted to find a reason to get rid of her, to banish her from the house. At the thought of Will canoodling with Ruby in the kitchen, Maggie went cold. But the truth was, Maggie was parched for information about Ruby. She wanted to know every detail about her, down to her bones and sinews.

"All right," Maggie said. She followed the maid up the grand staircase, her boots clunking clumsily on the waxed and polished steps. There was a hallway with several doors and more oil paintings, of ladies in stiff crinolines and landscapes from faraway places. Here and there, a polished table was choked full of extravagant white peonies that must have been from a greenhouse. There was so much carved wood on the walls and ceiling she couldn't keep her eyes from zooming left, right, up, and down, wanting to memorize every inch.

The maid ushered her into a room with a canopy bed, pink silk coverlet, and damask curtains. It was a bedroom fit for a princess.

"Whose room is this?" she asked as the maid disappeared through another doorway. She could hear water running from a tap. The maid reappeared.

"I hope you like French rose soap. The bath will be ready momentarily. This is a guest room, but Miss Fielding used to stay here on occasion."

"Miss Fielding?" Maggie felt the color drain from her face. "I don't think . . . are you sure this is all right?"

"Mr. Cross says so."

The maid went to an armoire near the window and opened it. Several dresses were hanging there—blue, lavender, rich red, of polished cotton and hard-to-find silk.

"You look about the same size."

"I don't think this is a good idea," Maggie said, wringing her hands. "Wearing his fiancée's dresses? A stranger?"

"He expressly told me to offer them," the maid said. "Are you going to refuse?"

"Oh! No, ma'am," Maggie said, retreating into her usual meekness.

"I'll lay out a dress." She clapped her hands, and pointed to the washroom. Maggie felt like a beagle. "Go bathe. You're not to have a speck of dirt on your person when you're done, or I'll scrub you down myself. It can't possibly be worse than washing the dog," she said, sniffing. "My name is Fiona, by the way. Call me if you need. I'll be right outside the door."

Maggie skedaddled to the washroom. It was all cream-colored tile, with shiny brass fixtures and polished mirrors. Steam issued from the claw-foot tub, and she turned the water off once it was three-quarters full. Timidly, as if she were not alone, she peeled off her kerchief, coat, dungarees, shirt, and underclothes.

The bath was unlike any she'd ever had. The water was frothy, and she felt like a confection rather than a human being. There was a nail-brush on a little table by the tub, a sea sponge on a stick, and a large bar of French milled soap. A sparkling new brass safety razor was nearby. By the time she was done, she had scrubbed herself raw, was nearly hairless where she ought to be, and felt new as a baby. In a fluffy velour bathrobe, she opened the door and found Fiona waiting for her. Maggie was bullied into sitting down, having her hair mercilessly towel dried and air fluffed, her nails buffed and filed into ovals, and rose lotion rubbed into her hands, face, and neck. Costly lilac perfume was dotted on the pulse points of her tender wrists, each side of her neck, and the crown of her head.

It was all heaven.

If I can live like this, she mused, I'll be Felix Cross's new fiancée. Except for the conundrum of having to actually marry Felix Cross, whom she still had yet to meet.

Fiona rolled her hair into waves, holding them in place with pins, and then Maggie got dressed. She decided to completely ignore the oddness and inappropriateness of wearing the silk undergarments that Fiona wordlessly handed to her. The brassiere didn't quite fit her across the chest, and it was distracting to think that it fit across someone else's breasts. And that someone was now with her brother, and he probably knew more about those breasts than she did.

And then Fiona was calling for her, clapping her hands again as if Maggie were a wayward sheep.

Fiona helped her into a stunning azure dress with a sweetheart neckline and gold piping around the wrists, waist, and hem. It was probably worth more than anything she and Will had ever owned. There were even a pair of silk stockings and a pair of matching silk heels. Maggie caught her reflection in the mahogany dressing mirror in the corner.

She nearly cried out in surprise. It was her mother, looking tall and lean, hair beautifully curled, with those uncertain eyes that never seemed to know if all was well, or all was a disaster. It was beauty on the cusp of shattering.

"You're ready. Pay attention. Mr. Cross is very particular about his guests. Don't speak until you're spoken to. Don't finish everything on your plate. Don't eat with your fingers; don't pick your teeth."

"I'm not an animal," Maggie said, her only defense of the whole day.

"Don't be ridiculous. We're all animals—it's how we act that sets us apart from the riffraff." Fiona paused, and pointed a finger to the sky. She leaned in and whispered conspiratorially, "Oh! And don't drink any spirits even if he offers. It's a test."

Maggie's eyes were wide with fear. She could only nod. But as the maid led her down the hallway and the staircase, Maggie whispered, "Thank you. You're being so nice to me."

"I'm paid to be nice when I ought to be nice and nasty when it's necessary," Fiona said, but then she paused in her march down the stairs. She turned, and for the first time since they'd met, her face softened to show an ounce of fear. "You seem like a nice girl. A simple girl."

Maggie tried not to wince at the backhanded compliment.

"People like the Crosses, and his fiancée, that Miss Fielding . . . they aren't like us. They play games with people's lives, and keep drinking their champagne after others are tossed away. You be careful, you hear?"

Maggie nodded. The warning did nothing to make her feel more prepared. If anything she felt like fleeing the mansion and running down Fifth Avenue all the way to Brooklyn, even if it meant blistering every inch of her feet. But she didn't. She was too curious about Felix Cross and Ruby Fielding, and what had happened between them.

Down the hallway, she caught glimpses of a grand library full of books on shelves so high they required their own metal ladders on wheels. There was a large parlor, another drawing room, and a dining room that could seat twenty people, but there were no place settings. There was no Felix Cross waiting for her.

"Fiona, where are we going?"

"The garden."

"Oh."

There was another fine drawing room at the rear of the house, with large french doors that opened up to a beautifully manicured ornamental garden, albeit with an autumn palette of muted greens and browns.

Boxwoods were trimmed into cones and spheres, and leafless espaliered trees were pruned and tied mercilessly against a stone wall, resembling a skeleton-like candelabrum more than anything organic. A small stone pond had browned lily pads, and Maggie saw flecks of gold and burnt orange from goldfish swimming beneath the surface.

Fiona stopped short and folded her hands together. "Miss Scripps, sir."

Where was he? Maggie looked about the garden and pond, and suddenly a figure stood up from behind a row of boxwoods. It was a gentleman wearing a heavy robe and a thick blanket, like a cape, overtop his shoulders. If not for the sparkle in his brown eyes, she'd have thought him an old man. His dark hair was slicked back with Brylcreem, and an expensive-looking paisley scarf was knotted at his neck. His fingers were long and elegant, or spidery, depending on one's perspective.

"Ah," he said. "Miss Scripps. I see you're ready for luncheon." His voice was warm and kind.

Maggie reached toward Fiona, as if looking for a hand to support her, but found that Fiona had silently backed away and was already within the house.

"Come. There's a small fire here, and a table set for us."

It was cold. Goose bumps erupted beneath the thin silk dress, making Maggie long to put her dungarees and heavy shirt and coat back on. But she refused to betray her discomfort.

There was a simple firepit crackling merrily with flames inside a ring of stones, next to a raised bed of various herbs and plants that was going dormant. A small table made of ornate iron, like one might find in a Parisian café, was set with two matching chairs. A thick coat of black sable was lying across one chair.

"For you. I realize the cold doesn't suit most people, and it would be a shame if you caught influenza or some such after your visit. The fresh air is helping me clear my illness away."

"Thank you," Maggie said. Mr. Cross helped her slip on the fur. She didn't like being so close to him. There was a medicinal smell to him—menthol, perhaps. He stepped away as if he, too, realized he was too close to her. Maggie noticed the rose soap scent rising from her skin. She wondered if she smelled like Ruby, and if it bothered him.

The lining of the coat was silk satin, and the fur hung on her heavily, hemmed as it was down to the ankles. She was grateful for the warmth, but was acutely aware that she wore the skins carved off dozens of adorable little animals. She shuddered.

"Still cold?"

"No, it's just . . ." She shook her head, the fur tickling her chin. "This is all so very strange. I came here to talk to you, and I've been washed within an inch of my life and put into a dress that isn't mine. And a fur coat. I feel like I'm in a dream."

"A good dream, I hope," Mr. Cross said. He lit a cigar, and the warm, brown smell issued comfortingly nearby. Along with the fire, it reminded her of Christmas.

"I'm not sure, to be honest," Maggie responded. "It's someone else's dream, I suppose."

"Well, you look like you belong in those clothes. I've been anxious to speak to you."

Maggie said, in nearly a whisper, "You could have spoken to me earlier, when I was wearing my own things."

"Ah, yes. I saw you from the window. I had a feeling you needed to be taken care of for a little while. You had the mien of a person who's been rather neglected of late."

Maggie's eyes watered. They had that habit when anyone guessed the innermost catastrophes within her heart. "How would you know that?" she asked.

"I guess my assumption was correct, then." He smiled. Not a nice smile. Maggie was annoyed at herself. Must she be so naive and give away all of herself? She was determined not to be so transparent.

Fiona had reappeared and set down a pot of piping hot tea and a basket covered with a tea towel. Steam escaped in curly tendrils from the edges. It smelled like sugar and oranges.

"Sit. Eat, and drink."

Maggie plunked down unceremoniously onto the chair. "I might as well. You had me go through this whole circus just to talk to you," she said.

"And wasn't it worth it? You don't look like a grubby ship worker anymore."

"How did you know that?" Maggie's attempt to hold her cards closer to her chest had already failed. She was too overwhelmed. "Why on earth do you know so much about me?"

Felix poured the tea, stirred in two lumps of sugar, and handed it to Maggie. He even knew how she took her tea. "I guessed, by your clothing. Also, Dr. Fielding was visited by your brother recently at the hospital. I suspect to find out about me."

"You mean your mother-in-law. She told you that?" Maggie asked.

He waved his hand, as if a fly had flown irritatingly too close to his face. "She didn't tell me. I bribed the hospital staff and saw who'd signed in to visit her. I never forget a name. As for my mother-in-law, well. It is rather convenient that she is particularly good at toxicology."

"Toxicology?"

"Yes. The study of poisons, and how they work, and how to save a person who's been poisoned."

Maggie hid half her face behind her cup. Ruby seemed to know something of the subject too. What was with this family? A woman doctor who was an expert in poisons, and a daughter intent on killing whatever vermin was in her way?

She put her cup down. "I read in the papers you were poisoned."

"I was."

"By who?"

"By *whom*."

Maggie was annoyed. "I don't need a grammar lesson."

"I apologize. It's the irrepressible snotty blue blood in me. Aren't I a monster?" He smiled grandly. Leaning forward, he unfolded the tea towel from the basket. There were half a dozen hot buns with satiny icing laced over their tops. Candied orange peel, encrusted with snowy sugar, formed a flower design. "Go on. It would be a tragedy to let these go to waste."

She hesitated.

"They aren't poisoned, for God's sake. The last thing I want to do is kill the person who might actually know something useful for a change."

It looked like fairy food. With the rationing and their tight budget, she didn't have access to such rich fare. Maggie reached over and plucked one gooey bun, then took a bite. The burst of sweet, buttery richness punctuated with the citrus perfume was beyond marvelous. She couldn't help closing her eyelids in ecstasy.

"Positively sinful, I know. I'd eat them, too, but I've no appetite. Still recovering."

Maggie ate one bun in three bites. Felix pushed the basket closer. "Waste is a crime in times like this. Go on."

A few minutes later, two more had disappeared into Maggie's stomach. Felix seemed to relish watching her eat and lick her fingers. It was disconcerting, but Maggie was too hungry to care. She sighed, gulped down the now tepid tea, and brushed the crumbs off her fur coat.

"Now that I've given you a show of gluttony, it's time for you to entertain me," she said, surprised by her own words. She didn't speak like that to anyone. But Felix seemed like the devil, and it brought her devilish side out. "Tell me about Ruby," she said, pushing her advantage.

"Ah, Ruby. The woman who broke my heart." He pulled out a silver case of cigarettes, lit one, and exhaled luxuriously through his nose. These weren't rolled cigarettes like the ones Will made, which meant they were expensive. "We met while she was in college and I was busy spending my inheritance."

"Inheritance? Fiona—the maid—said that your parents were out."

"Oh, they're alive all right. But they were disowned by my grandmother, who bequeathed all the money to me. They live under my auspices and good humor."

"Fiona said that they'd kick me out if I was dressed improperly."

Felix shrugged. "They like to feel important, scrambling to grasp what power they pretend to still have. I don't stop them, unless it gets in my way."

This man seemed so absurdly evil she wondered why anyone would ever find him attractive. And then she looked down at her fur coat, and the gorgeous garden, and the mansion. Oh. Silly Maggie.

"But Ruby is wealthy," Maggie said. "The article said so."

"Yes," Felix said, annoyance crinkling his nose. "She's got a mint of money. Her father is Ernest Fielding, of Fielding Bank, but you probably already know that."

Looking around her, Maggie was starting to have an inkling of what that life might be like. Whereas all her money was at home in a cigar box hidden under a floorboard.

"Recently, her father's been investing in other ventures. Mineral refining and ore mining in Africa and in the west."

"Refining?" Maggie blurted. "Why would a banker be interested in that?"

"You really don't know anything, do you? I love the simplicity of your mind!" He clapped. "Bankers don't just gather money and sit on it, my dear. They invest it. They look for ways to make it multiply faster than lusty rabbits on a rabbit farm."

Maggie blinked. Mineral refining and ores. She'd seen something about that, hadn't she? Ah, yes. It was in Will's textbook. He'd left it open in the parlor one morning, and she'd snuck a look. He was always so secretive about his work and studies. But the textbook had been about radioactive ores, the dangerous kinds. Was it a coincidence? It couldn't be.

Felix suddenly snapped his fingers. "Are you with us, dear girl? Paying attention, are we?"

"Don't snap your fingers at me. I'm not a dog," she responded tartly.

Felix's eyebrows rose appreciatively. "Looks like there was some ginger in those buns. Very good!" He sat back. "Well, you know, Ruby's mother is rather peculiar. Always was. Her father died in some tragic accident—burned to death in his bed—and a few months later, she declared she wanted to be a doctor. A woman doctor! They're a rare breed. Then again, her side of the family has a tendency to make waves." He leaned closer. "I know things about them."

Maggie leaned in closer. "What things?"

"They have a relative that used to dig up dead bodies and sell them."

Maggie gasped. So it was true, what Ruby had said.

"Yes! Also a woman! It was a long time ago, before the Civil War. Oh, and some yellow journalist woman too. The women in the family turn out a little odd, but by God, they aren't boring old drips." He leaned back and extinguished his cigarette in a crystal ashtray. He lit another. "There's an uncle, too, who's not an uncle. A chemist who seems oddly chummy with the family. Jasper Jones. His father and brother died before their time. Fascinating."

Maggie shut her gaping mouth.

"So," Felix waved his cigarette. "Your turn."

Maggie felt queasy from eating all the sweets. Was she really ready to tell him about Ruby? What if he'd given her those bruises? What if he planned to hurt her again?

But Ruby was hurting Maggie. And she could tell, by the countenance on Felix's thin face, that he would not reveal more without a payment of information.

"She showed up a few days ago," Maggie began. Felix sat up in his chair, his eyes bright and alert. "We found her under our stairs, unconscious. She seemed drunk, but we couldn't tell if it was from spirits or something else. Or both."

"Go on." He tented his fingers.

"She was dressed in nice clothes. We don't know how she got there. She had a ruby ring on."

"About this big? Set in gold? No side stones?" He indicated the size of a shooter marble between his finger and thumb.

Maggie nodded. "We almost turned her in to the police, but she woke up and begged us not to. Said she was in danger, and that someone was trying to hurt her." Maggie took a deep breath. "And she said her name was Laurel."

"Laurel." Felix blinked. He seemed a little confused at first; then understanding unfroze his features. He tipped his head back and laughed. "How perfect."

"What's perfect?"

"Do you read any Greek mythology?"

Maggie was getting very annoyed. He had this horrible habit of asking a question, knowing the askee knew nothing. He didn't wait for her answer, just went on.

"There's a Greek myth about a beautiful dryad named Daphne who was transformed into a laurel tree." He smiled, but not to Maggie. He almost seemed to have forgotten that she was there. "Ruby's middle name is Daphne. How perfect. And I'm her Apollo, chasing after like a crazed lover. She hates me, yes, but at least she admits I'm the god in this scenario."

Maggie looked at him, wondering. He didn't look like much of a god, thin and sick as he was. He more resembled the spider she'd thought of earlier.

"You hurt her. She told us she's in danger."

"Hurt her? Good God, no. I want to marry Ruby, not hurt her. We had a misunderstanding, and she's taken a completely dramatic turn and run away. Our kind of people, we don't *hurt* our women, not like that. We either have affairs and ignore them, or we divorce them."

Lord, Maggie thought. He's awful. But she still needed to know more. "So you really were poisoned?"

He took a pull on his cigarette. "I don't know. I fell ill suddenly, just after we quarreled. Given her little pet hobby of studying vegetal and mineral poisons, it makes sense."

Aha, thought Maggie. "She studies poisons?"

"Yes. She finished graduate school with a degree in toxicology. Testing which poisons kill what animals, in what amounts. She'd lay out carcasses of crickets and mice and rabbits in her spare time. So macabre."

Just like the rats and the spiders, Maggie thought. "And you chose her as a wife?" she said, aghast.

"Have you laid eyes on her?" he retorted. "She would be a crown jewel in any man's treasure chest. Also, the family fortune is so gloriously well endowed."

"Are you really sure Ruby tried to poison you?" Maggie said.

He smiled. "Are you defending her?"

"I just want to know the truth."

"All I know is, if she had nothing to be guilty about, she wouldn't hide from her family."

"You're not family," Maggie observed. "Not yet."

"And yet, she stays in my house whenever she has a squabble with her parents. That was her bedroom you were in before. Not just any guest room. I know this woman inside and out, for several years now." He gathered the thick blanket about his shoulders. "She's dangerous, and you should have nothing to do with her."

"Why would she hurt you?"

"Because I disagreed with her." Felix seemed bored with the conversation.

"About what?"

"About her duties as a married woman. As a new member of the Cross family." He raised his eyebrows. "Need I say more?"

Maggie was done. She knew what she needed to know, and it was enough to throw Ruby out of their home. She was a lady of means, and just as Will had conjectured when she first showed up, she'd had a quarrel with her friends and exaggerated the danger. It was time for her to go back.

She stood, and Felix rose too.

"It's time you were on your way," he said, as if Maggie hadn't first made the motion to leave. As if it were his idea. She got the feeling he liked to think he orchestrated everything himself, all the time. "I'm quite fatigued and need my afternoon nap."

Fiona was already waiting at the door to the house. Maggie walked ahead of Felix, but as soon as they were inside, he said, "I should like you to come back and visit me."

"Oh." Maggie had been relieved that the visit was finally over. "What for? I've told you everything I know."

"Oh, I doubt that." He leaned in closer. "I should like updates on what Ruby is doing."

"She's learning how to cook," Maggie said.

He clapped his hands together again. "Oh! Precious! Yes, more details! And I'd also like to know more about you."

"Me?" Maggie couldn't hide her surprise.

"Yes. She likes you; otherwise, she'd have left already. And I find you irresistible, in a way I can't quite put my finger on." He smiled. "I suspect you are far more brilliant than people give you credit for, and I should like to get to know you."

Maggie inwardly flushed. No one had ever said such a thing to her, and she secretly loved it.

"I suppose I could do that." She was nearly on the verge of saying, *Oh, but I was about to kick Ruby out.* But then again, Maggie wanted very much to return to Felix Cross's home. If Ruby left, there would be nothing to report on. She bit her lip and stayed quiet.

"So yes, bring me updates on Ruby. You can tell me more about how Margaret Scripps became this creature today. I shall provide funds for any lost wages, plus something more. Perhaps something from the jewelry collection Ruby left behind?"

Maggie flushed. Jewels? Money? Granted, it was probably just small change, considering his wealth, but still. All of that added up to a lot for a person like her. Maggie wasn't able to say no outright, so she just lightly nodded in agreement.

"Fiona will show you out. Toodles." Felix turned and went back to his chair in the middle of the fading garden.

Maggie pulled off the coat and handed it to Fiona. "Where are my clothes?" she asked.

"Here, Miss." Fiona handed her a large shopping bag with her clothes neatly folded inside, her boots at the bottom.

"And where may I change?"

Fiona waved her hand. "Oh. You're to keep the clothes. The coat too. Mr. Cross was very explicit."

Maggie's first reaction was, *Ohh, really? Wonderful!* But then she imagined herself walking through Gravesend in such a coat. The stares she would receive wearing a plush sable! And from neighbors who were scrimping and saving during these lean times. What would Ruby think, seeing her clothes on Maggie? "Oh no. I couldn't!"

"Well. At least take the clothes. You're already in them." Fiona reluctantly took the coat from her. As Maggie put on her old worn wool coat, she caught Fiona looking through the window by the door that opened to the back garden.

"It's a show, you know," Fiona said. "All that confidence."

"What?"

"Look," she said, pointing. Maggie stepped to the window and saw Felix Cross sitting in the garden alone, his arms around himself.

His expression had changed from haughty confidence into one of pure despair. When he thought no one was watching, he was a man stricken—a king in a dying garden.

Suddenly, Maggie didn't dislike him so much.

And suddenly, she wondered if anything he had told her was true.

CHAPTER 14

When Will exited the building, he had changed. It had seemed relatively harmless to bring Ruby along, but with Mrs. Rivers's stern warning and order, he felt like only half his body was paying attention. Part of him longed to keep Ruby close at all times. The other part—the remnants of habit that told him to stay away from sticky women and strangers—was adrift and alarmed.

He should tell Ruby to leave. Immediately. Everything he had done up until now was at risk. Running errands for Professor Fermi while he attended Columbia. Helping to run the enormous particle accelerator, the cyclotron, in Pupin Hall. Becoming a useful cog in the machinery under General Groves. Taking his classes so he could become more fluid in the language and understanding of atomic physics. Gravesend was full of people who worked for someone else, or were emperors of minute empires that didn't matter.

Matter. He laughed inwardly. Matter was what mattered in his life. The changing of it on a subatomic level, in a way that could alter history. Lives. Will could be more than what he was. Alchemists used to wish they could change the elements and unlock the secrets of the universe by turning lead into gold. Such a feat was akin to magic and historically impossible. But as uranium decayed and lived its half-life, it altered: uranium became thorium, then radium, radon, polonium, and eventually lead. Some steps took mere seconds; others took years. Will would help perform alchemy not only on elements, but he would also change the relative immutability of his life.

If he could just stay on task.

When he and Ruby had exited the subway in Brooklyn and began their way toward Lake Place, Ruby comfortably slipped her arm around Will's. He couldn't maintain his rigid posture anymore.

"You're not okay," she said simply, as they walked.

"No," he agreed.

"I'm sorry. I know I'm causing trouble."

His immediate reflex was to say no, it wasn't her fault, everything would be okay, don't worry. Why it was that she elicited such a reaction was beyond him. When Maggie made a mistake and apologized, he would say, "Don't be sorry—just don't do it again." Or he'd just grunt a reply. When Will made a mistake—coming home late on Maggie's birthday—he would say simply, "Won't happen again." Or some such. He was not about apologies, but fixing the problem.

With Ruby, he wasn't sure he wanted her to fix the problem.

His mind told him to wait. Not to be rash. Mrs. Rivers had said to get rid of her, because they were keeping an eye on him, whether he liked it or not. This was actually good news. Watching him meant that he was a risk, and thus valuable. He couldn't lose that value. Not now.

"How do you know you're causing trouble?" he asked.

"You've been different ever since you left that building. Something happened, and you've been cold toward me. I can read a body better than anybody. It's about me, isn't it?"

They were nearly home. They passed a grocer, and Ruby tugged on his arm. "Can we buy more peaches?" she asked.

"What? Aren't you sick of them? We ate half a dozen yesterday, and there are probably some still left." They weren't even in season. They were sad, wrinkled things that were overpriced, anyway.

"I ate them all."

Odd. He had money, and she needed to keep her strength up, so he relented and purchased another half dozen. Ruby sank her teeth into one, juice dripping down her chin. She laughed as she blotted it off with her hand. They passed a few people walking along the street, and Will noticed them watching. The world seemed to be watching.

"Let's go inside, have dinner. You've probably spoiled your appetite with that fruit."

"Not at all."

Ruby was washing up and Will was starting to fry some bacon and boil a pot of beans and greens when the back door opened. Ruby emerged from the washroom, flicking water droplets off her fingertips, ready to welcome Maggie home. When they saw her, Will almost dropped the entire pan of bacon onto the floor.

"Jesus Christ!" he exclaimed.

A pretty and gorgeously clad woman stood in the doorway. He thought it was their mother. Risen from the dead, from the very grave where they had laid her in the eastern edge of Green-Wood Cemetery. The same exact nervous expression, as if always ready to bolt away.

Maggie held a bulky shopping bag. She was still wearing her usual brown coat, but that was the only part of her that was immediately recognizable. Her hair had been curled into rolls over her ears, face dusted with powder and rouge. She wore a bright-pink lipstick, fine aubergine heels, and a blue silk dress that was a tad too loose. But it fit well enough for Will to be painfully reminded that his sister was not a child anymore, and hadn't been for some time.

His sister's hands started shaking, and he realized that she was staring at Ruby, whose expression was nothing short of livid.

"You," Ruby said in a half whisper, half growl, "are wearing *my* dress."

"What?" Will's head whipped between them. Ruby laughed, the kind of hollow laugh that might come from realizing that you just played roulette with a cheater who'd loaded the entire chamber with bullets.

"Where did you get it? Why are you wearing it?" she demanded. Maggie backed up until she was leaning against the shut door.

"I . . . spoke to Felix Cross today," she said. Her eyes dropped to the floor.

"And he made you get dressed in this outfit—in my clothes? Why did you see him? How did you know—"

Maggie lifted her chin and seemed to steel herself. "I think it's time for us to be asking the questions now," she said quietly. She shrugged her coat off, went over to the table and sat down. A waft of lilac perfume washed over Will. Maggie had never worn perfume before.

To him, she said, uncharacteristically, "I need a drink."

"I think we all do," he said, not knowing what else to say. "Dinner is ready anyway."

They took their seats warily, as if each were an exotic stinging insect species the others had never encountered. The first few minutes were filled with drinking whiskey and staring at their glasses. Finally, Will plunked his hand down on the table, and the silverware bounced. Maggie jerked, and Ruby sat back, arms crossed.

"Well?" Ruby asked.

"I went to speak to Felix Cross. After we found out about the article."

"What article?" Ruby asked.

Will sighed. "It was in the papers. About how Felix Cross was admitted to Bellevue Hospital after being poisoned by an unknown substance."

"What?" Ruby's face went red, then white. "Poisoned? By whom?"

"By whom," Maggie echoed, laughing. "Apparently your grammar doesn't need correcting."

Will and Ruby stared at her, agog. Will shook himself out of the moment.

"It didn't say, but the article did mention that his fiancée had suddenly disappeared. A fiancée named Ruby Fielding."

Ruby's bottom lip dropped open, but she couldn't seem to form any syllables, so Will continued.

"And Felix Cross was being cared for by a Dr. Allene Fielding."

Still no response from Ruby. But her fingers around her whiskey glass had started to tremble.

"Will went to speak to Dr. Fielding last week," Maggie said. She sounded apologetic. "We just wanted information. We wanted answers."

Ruby's hands went to cover her face. She spoke, voice muffled, through her fingers. "Why didn't you tell me? About the article."

"You didn't seem to want to be found," Maggie said.

They were all quiet a long time. When Ruby dropped her hands, she looked tired and grim. "And so you let my fiancé dress you up like some stupid—"

"You mean like you?" Maggie said, a bite of acid in her tone.

"Stop it, you two." Will poured more whiskey, but only into his own glass. "Everyone eat something, for God's sake."

Maggie ate mincingly of her meal, Ruby even less. His sister downed the last of her whiskey like bitter medicine, grimaced, and wiped her mouth with the back of her hand. Her lipstick was mostly faded now and barely left a mark on her hand. Even the nice clothes couldn't hide the Brooklyn girl beneath.

"Why did he make you dress up like that?" he asked.

Maggie sighed. "He didn't want his parents to kick me out if I looked improper." At that, Ruby shrugged and nodded slightly in confirmation. Maggie stared at Will, her hands sliding down the silk of her skirt. She didn't seem embarrassed about how she looked. She seemed proud.

The explanation didn't lessen Will's fury. Maggie was good enough, as she was, for anybody, never mind this hoity-toity family. He felt like he hardly knew this creature in front of him, with the curls and the rouge.

"You're never to go back there without me," he growled.

"Can I finish?" Maggie's sharp tone silenced him. His anger could wait for later, but he was surprised. It wasn't like her.

The rest came tumbling out. About Ruby's love of toxins and poisons, the premarital fight, Felix's mysterious illness. How Felix kept a room for Ruby in his house though they were not yet married, because she quarreled with her parents all the time. (Ruby had interjected: "I don't quarrel with them! That's a lie!" but Will had shushed her so Maggie could continue.) Maggie spoke about the Fielding family's odd past. And then she stopped.

Ruby's face had changed. Will, for the first time since she'd arrived, could not read her countenance at all. But perhaps that had been the fact all along, and all her emotions had been nothing but oil upon deeper, treacherous waters. "Ruby?" he said.

It was the first time he'd used her real name to address her. The stony countenance broke; she bent forward and covered her eyes, crying in earnest.

"Oh God. He found me," she said, between sobs.

CHAPTER 15

When she was a child, Ruby had ridden the Cyclone roller coaster at Coney Island. So many children she knew spoke of their trips to Coney Island. They talked excitedly of the parachute jump ride in Steeplechase Park, the carousel pavilion, the caramel corn and hot dogs at Nathan's. Her mother was busy working in the hospital, so it was her father who drove there, across the Brooklyn Bridge and down through the borough to Coney Island.

The Cyclone was a dizzying sight, a curved and twisted wooden structure that seemed terribly unnatural as it rose into the summer sky. The air had smelled of the briny ocean and that peculiar odor of rotting pier wood. The ride itself was an absolute fright. Ruby screamed the whole time. Every time they went over an apex, there was that moment that lasted far too long, before the cars plummeted downward. Every time, her head banged against the wooden back of her seat. It would throb for a full day afterward. A few times she was fairly sure she was airborne and would have flown off her seat if not for her belt and her father's hand grasping hers. For most kids, it was exhilarating. Pure emotion. For Ruby, that emotion without logic and thought was half-terrifying, half-incandescent happiness.

This was that feeling. Right now, right in this house. But it was the terrifying brand of pure feeling. Like there was hardly anything preventing Ruby from falling upward into space. Like gravity had failed and she had to grasp whatever she could to save herself, and all her reasoning held no sway against the forces at work.

Maggie had spent time with Felix, who had dressed her up like a mannequin. No doubt he'd buttered her up, too, with compliments. This was how Felix worked, after all. He'd done the same with Ruby. Despite her being an intelligent, educated woman, with a loving family and money to spare, Felix had managed to make himself essential in Ruby's life. Her parents had sought to keep her close to home, while Felix had promised explorations and second and third homes in Paris and Hong Kong. Ruby's mother tended toward pragmatic, well-tailored clothes, whereas Felix lavished pink satin shoes and amethyst gowns upon Ruby, a closet furnished with all the things she normally couldn't have. In retrospect, it was all so superficial, but he'd made her feel special. And who was immune to such overtures?

Maggie certainly wasn't, that was for sure. And now Felix knew where Ruby was. Right when Maggie had been showing signs that her heart was opening to Ruby, that damned Felix was stepping in to steer her away. And then there was Will. It was all too easy to keep him interested in her. Despite his quietness, he emanated strength, assurance, and a hidden warmth that he was surprisingly willing to share. On the surface, the Scripps siblings seemed to be self-contained, hardworking Brooklynites. Dig a little deeper, and they were both hungry, though for different things. Putty in Ruby's willing hands. Good God. What had she gotten herself into?

She could barely remember how she even got to Gravesend to begin with. The address of Maggie and Will's house had stayed stubbornly in her head, as if imprinted there in her delirious state. There was a connection between Felix and them. Ruby must find out what it was, and how to turn that information into an instrument to hurt him as much as he'd promised to harm her. But how?

Now that Felix knew she was here, what would his next move be? He might step in and drag Ruby back outright, after the fight that had led to Ruby refusing marriage and leaving him. But no—that wasn't his style. He didn't dirty himself up like that. Felix would force her hand by applying pressure around her. In this case, via Maggie. Maybe even Will.

But pressure could work both ways. She knew what she had to do.

Somewhere in the Scripps household—somewhere in their work, or what they loved, or what they hated—was a key to hurting Felix. She knew it. And right now, her presence here was blossoming, like a delicate oleander whose beauty held a startling lethality.

What about her family? No doubt with her disappearance, they were on their guard against Felix already. Ruby had to hope they were strong enough to brace themselves against the coming storm. She considered fleeing again, to protect her family. But she had no money—and she would not endanger her family by going home. She was already trying to learn how to take care of herself in a way she hadn't before.

That was the goal, after all. Survival. She had her part in this war—a part that could be small or enormous, if she played her cards correctly. The same way she'd studied poisons—figuring out which doses could kill, or maim; pushing those micrograms and drops and doses to the point of no return; or better yet, figuring out exactly how to make that point of no return disappear altogether—that was the game she played now.

How far would she go to win?

She wasn't sure. But she might have to die finding that out.

CHAPTER 16

Maggie knew her heart should be like stone. That she shouldn't be affected by Laurel's—by Ruby's—sobs.

She's an actress, Maggie said to herself, over and over again. But there was something about her weeping that seemed to pull on Maggie's rib bones, yank them free, so she felt just as injured as Ruby was. This is what Maggie had wanted, after all, after seeing Ruby and Will together.

She put out a hand to touch Ruby's shoulder, hovered there without touching.

Will shook his head as if to say, *No. That's what she wants.* Or perhaps, *No—she is mine to comfort, not yours.*

Maggie let gravity pull her hand to Ruby's shoulder. Her touch seemed to ease Ruby's crying. She blotted her face on the backs of her hands and looked up at the two of them.

"He's going to hurt you, too, Maggie." Her eyes were large and afraid. "I shouldn't have come here."

"Why *did* you come here?" Will asked, gently but firmly.

"I don't know. I don't remember what happened after I left Felix. We had a terrible argument. I told him I didn't want to marry him anymore."

"Why?" Maggie asked.

"He doesn't love me. He loves the idea of me. He seemed more concerned with parading me around town than being a future husband."

Will shook his head. "Why on earth did you want to marry him?"

"He offered me something I didn't have. Mother has her work at the hospital, and Father has his. He spends most of his free time worshipping her." She smiled faintly. "They're good parents, but I crave affection. Felix worshipped me, too, and I let him. And it wasn't just that. My parents always wanted me to stay here, in New York. Near was safe. But Felix was so worldly! He said we'd live half our lives overseas. New York is big, but it's still just a pond. Felix offered me the whole ocean. He promised that we'd be Mr. and Mrs. Fabulous, without boundaries."

Maggie was watching her carefully. "Why did you argue?"

"Once we were engaged, he demanded access to all my family's money. All our business connections. He said he would ruin us if I didn't provide it. It didn't take me long to realize that he never really loved me. He was just building his empire, and I was a decoration in his gilded house." Her lip shook as she spoke. "He said he would hurt us all."

Maggie frowned. Felix had mentioned how Ruby's father was dealing with mineral refining or some such. What was really going on? He'd also said they'd had an argument, and Ruby had taken a dramatic turn and left him. And Felix happened to get poisoned right at that time. Who was hurting whom?

Will asked, "So you poisoned him?" Good. Someone had to ask.

"I didn't!" She clasped her hands together. "You have to believe me!"

Maggie stared at her. "You keep killing things around the house. Rats. Spiders. You're growing herbs on the windowsill that aren't for cooking. What are they?"

"Foxglove, and anemone."

"Flowers?" Will asked. He wanted to laugh.

"Yes. Flowers." Ruby smiled a little.

Maggie narrowed her eyes. "By any chance . . . are any of these flowers poisonous?"

Ruby's eyes fell. "Yes."

"Why?" Will and Maggie asked simultaneously.

"Because they give me comfort," she said. "Because they are complex and beautiful and dangerous. I don't fully understand them, and I would like to. It's just an educational, academic thing. An escape. I promise. It's what I studied in school and worked on with my mother. It gives me order when I feel out of control. Something to focus on."

Her explanation made sense, but it was still hard to believe that she'd had nothing to do with Felix Cross's poisoning.

"And why did you come to this house, of all places?"

"Like I said, I don't know! After I fled Felix, I didn't know what I was doing. I can't remember what happened. Only waking up in your house, and knowing I couldn't go back. I thought of reaching out to my parents, but then I realized—if I stayed hidden, he had nothing to bargain with. No way to influence them."

"You were drunker than a boatload of sailors on New Year's Eve in port," Will said dryly.

"Maybe I drank that night. I don't remember," Ruby admitted. "I think he drugged me. It's not my nature to drink so much that I'd feel so strange for so many days. All I knew was that the angels must have been watching over me, because I ended up here, and here I've felt safe."

Will crossed his arms. He looked at Maggie and nodded. "Mags. Let's talk. Outside."

She and Will left the kitchen, walking into the cold fall evening. They hardly cared about the teeth-clenching chill.

"We should tell her to leave," Will said, sighing. "This is more than we bargained for. We said we'd take care of her for one night."

"But you're a couple now," Maggie said, almost in defiance.

"Yes, but you're more important, and she's putting us in the center of a drama we don't need to be in."

"I suppose she could pawn her ring and get funds for a hotel," Maggie added.

"Right. And I can go to Dr. Fielding, perhaps bring a letter written by Ruby, and procure more funds for her so she can live somewhere until things blow over."

Maggie thought of Felix, and the nice dress, and the iced buns with candied orange peel. She thought of how Felix would welcome her back—even pay her handsomely—if she had more information about Ruby and what she was up to. Maggie didn't want to go back to normal. There was too much yet to know—such a juicy story so close to home. How could she ignore it?

"No," Maggie said.

Her brother dropped his jaw. "What?"

"You two have something going, and I don't want to ruin that." She forced a smile. "This is the first time I've seen you happy, Will. In ages. I don't think we're in danger. I really don't. Let's let her stay one more week. Teach her more about how to care for herself, and then let her go."

"You really think that's safe?"

It was odd, having Will ask her advice for a change. Maggie relished it.

"I do."

She couldn't miss the light that sparked in Will's eyes, though it cut her inside. He knew Ruby wasn't good for them, but he didn't want to lose her either. "One week."

"One week," Maggie agreed.

They reentered the kitchen. Ruby sat waiting on the edge of her chair, hands clasped.

"What's my verdict?" she said, eyes expectant.

"You can stay one more week," Will said. "We've done a lot for you, but there's more going on than we're able to concern ourselves with."

The words that came out were like the kind Will would have said before he'd ever met Ruby. They were cold and logical. Ruby seemed to wilt.

"One week is a long time!" Maggie chirped. "Come on. It's time for bed."

Ruby looked dissatisfied, but not distraught. It was as if she were waiting for a marriage proposal to be answered and had received only an IOU instead. She stood up from the chair and went meekly into Maggie's bedroom. Will gave Maggie a look of surprise—they'd both expected she'd fall into Will's arms. He gave Maggie a resigned look as he headed toward the parlor.

"Aren't you going to school tonight?" she asked.

"I don't have the mind to. See you in the morning," he said and left the kitchen.

Ruby was shedding her clothes in the bedroom and putting on Maggie's mother's silk robe.

"I feel like I shouldn't be here at all," Ruby said.

"No, it's okay." Maggie tried to smile. "One week is a long time, like I said."

Ruby came up to her after knotting the robe about her waist. "I hardly recognize you, Maggie. In all these fine clothes."

"Well. I guess I should give them back to you."

"No. They suit you. You're so beautiful. I mean, you're beautiful without all the glitz and glamour."

"Am I?" Maggie asked artlessly.

"Of course!" Ruby smiled. "Here. Let me."

Wordlessly, Maggie let herself be undressed article by article. This was different from the way the maid had dressed her. Ruby took her time unbuttoning the silk dress until it slinked to the floor and Maggie stepped out of it. Her silk stockings were released from their garters and rolled off with excruciating gentleness. The lingerie was removed, until Maggie stood there naked. Ruby had seen all of her; she didn't mind.

She wasn't afraid, or embarrassed somehow. Perhaps it was knowing there was more out there for her than in this room. There were more meetings with Felix to anticipate. Her letters. She had a future opening up at the Navy Yard. No matter what happened within the walls of this house, Maggie would make her mark in this war.

Ruby handed her a flannel nightgown, and Maggie wriggled it over her head. Ruby didn't leave to return to Will's arms. Maggie's heart had already been extricating itself from Ruby with every day that she'd grown closer to Will. But as Ruby led her to bed, Maggie knew she'd been waiting for the door to reopen these last few days. They lay facing each other, a hand on each other's waists, and Maggie thought, Oh. The door never really closed. Maybe with people like Ruby, they stay open to so many rooms, with so many people. How odd. How wonderful, for me.

"This doesn't seem real," she whispered. "I feel like I'm dreaming half my days, ever since you came."

"Then let's play pretend," Ruby said, her eyes fathomless. "Like we're not ourselves. Like we're someone else. After all, the world is about massacres and sinking ships. If I can hide from the world a little longer, I will."

"I don't know," Maggie said, uncertainly, but Ruby's hand slid up Maggie's hip and rested on her ribcage, right below her breasts.

"I've lost you, haven't I?" Ruby murmured.

"Was I ever something worth losing?"

"Always," Ruby said.

"You hardly know me, Ruby," Maggie said. It was so odd, calling her by her real name. Ruby's hand was still on her side, inching ever upward.

"I know what I like."

"I find it hard to believe that I'm what you like," Maggie whispered.

"You're so different than everyone I know. I've always loved the kind of beauty you have to find, not the kind that announces itself to the world. And you know what you want. Working at the Navy Yard, and helping with the war effort. You do it quietly, without the fanfare. You're a marvel, Maggie."

Maggie smiled, and hoped her warm cheeks weren't too red. "You could probably describe Will that way too."

"Perhaps." Ruby frowned a little. "But he doesn't need me. I'm a complication to him. I can tell."

You're a complication for everyone you meet, Maggie thought. But all she could bring herself to say was, "Oh, Ruby."

Ruby sniffled and forced a smile. "I wish you would call me Laurel again. So much was possible when I was Laurel. Now that I'm back to my old self, I see my life stretched out before me. And the road isn't very long."

Maggie frowned. "Don't say that!"

"Then let's not speak. I have seven nights left here. Let's not waste it. Let's pretend every hour is worth a year or more. Every second can be broken down into infinite fractions of time. Let's live there for a while." She snuggled closer, and Maggie allowed it: the warmth of her body, the softness of her hand on her skin, and the feel of Ruby's proprietary arm on her body. When Ruby kissed her, she ignored who else had been kissing those lips. A voice inside her told her she was wrong, this was wrong, Ruby was wrong.

But another voice also said that this was all an illusion somehow. None of it real. Felix's attention. Ruby's lips. The beautiful dress she had just peeled off. It wasn't her. And Ruby would never be Maggie's. The world would not allow it. And then, of course, there was Will.

Seven days, Maggie thought. I can worry about the world and everything else in seven days.

For tonight, at least, I have Ruby.

Maggie dropped her boot in alarm.

"I'm sorry, what did you just say?" she asked, eyes wide.

Maggie was getting dressed in her heavy work clothing and was sitting on the edge of her bed, trying to lace up her boots. Ruby had propped herself up on her elbows, chestnut hair tousled in the most alluring way.

"I said, can I go with you to the Navy Yard?"

"Why would you want to do that?" Maggie said, hiding her shock.

Ruby sidled up to her, and her lips disturbed a few tendrils of hair by her ear. "I want to see what you do all day." God, that voice. Velvet on the rocks.

"No! That's not . . . no." Maggie shook her head. "You're not allowed in without an ID. It's not like a museum, where anybody can get a tour."

"Of course not! But I'll be so lonesome at home." Ruby squeezed her arm. "Tell you what. We'll go together, and I'll wait outside. All day for you. And then we can go home together."

Maggie's heart was thumping like a drumroll. Ruby would ruin her whole day if she came. Maggie had had a very clear plan in her mind when she woke up. She desperately wanted to see Felix again, to get more information. Why did he want to be so closely involved with Ruby's father? But the allure of being treated like a queen was also irresistibly tantalizing. She couldn't let Ruby know she wanted to go back to Felix's house. And she felt the urgent need to spill her thoughts into another letter to her mother. She hadn't had a chance to write one yesterday.

Maggie shook her head. "I'm sorry, no." Relief came to her in the form of an idea. "You need to stay here to be safe! Why don't you start making the new bomb shelter? Dig the foundation in the backyard?"

"Oh!" Ruby smiled, but it was the kind that shallowly hid disappointment. "Sure."

Will was already gone for the day, a plate of cold eggs and toast sitting on the kitchen table for them. Maggie smelled fresh coffee. Even in his absence, she could sense his melancholy. It was a familiar feeling; she'd felt it with her mother after her father had disappeared from their lives. The house seemed to feel lonelier, too, as if it knew that Ruby's time with them was ticking away.

Outside at the back of the house, Maggie handed Ruby a spade. Ruby looked at it as if it were as alien as a rhinoceros.

"The neighbors aren't too nosy, but just in case, try not to draw too much attention," Maggie added. "Five feet across, seven feet long."

Ruby nodded. She leaned closer, as if to give Maggie a kiss good-bye, but Maggie swayed away. In the light of morning and outdoors, it seemed terribly wrong for her to be so close. But also—there was something oddly pleasant about wanting to keep Ruby . . . wanting her. About not revealing all that she was.

Boarding her trolley, she briefly looked over her shoulder. She saw a flash of chestnut hair on a woman a block away, just like Ruby's. She looked again, but the woman had turned a corner. Ruby wouldn't follow her, would she? No. Surely not. Maggie shrugged off the worry and settled into her trolley seat. She took out a piece of paper and began to write.

<hr />

October 28, 1942

Dear Mama,

Work in the shipyard is going well. I can weld a bead as good as anybody, though I have yet to work on the ships. Right now, the USS Missouri is in the shipways, and there are at least three cruisers being fixed up and a big cruise ship that's being changed over to a troopship at Pier G. Ships go out every day, and new ones come in to replace them. The Navy Yard is its own city. There are workers on shifts so the building never stops, 24 hours a day. In no time, I'll be welding twin arcs with Holly on the Missouri!

As for Will, he's still going to his classes at Brooklyn College and working. I think I heard him speak about something regarding a warehouse. No idea why. He is healthy, as am I. But

Maggie paused here. Talking about their physical health rather than their happiness was easier, but it wasn't the truth. She sighed.

But we are upended by our visitor, Laurel. Actually, her name is Ruby Fielding, but she hid her identity from us because she was running from her fiancé, Felix Cross, a rich gentleman who already inherited his gobs of money. Can you believe it? She is safe with us for now. Apparently her father is a banker who is investing in some sort of ore refinery? I don't quite understand it, but I will soon. I think she will stay one more week. And in the meantime, we have grown very close to her.

Maggie paused again, and touched her lips. Only last night, her skin was warm against Ruby's. It was so wrong. Her mother in heaven would disapprove. She knew it.

She is beautiful and elegant. But she knows nothing about ordinary things. I am teaching her how to cook, and keep house. Oh, and I did meet her fiancé. He seems a sad, peculiar man and he and Ruby fought over her father's work.

Did you know, he dressed me up in Ruby's old clothes (I say old, but my goodness! They were magnificent!) and fed me sweets. I can't imagine there would be any harm in trying to persuade him to speak to me more about what he truly wants.

Yes?

Plus, he seems lonely. I would be helping Ruby. And Ruby needs my help. It would be the Christian thing to do.

I'd better go. I think I shall pay Felix Cross one more visit today.

Love,

Maggie

◆

The trolley had arrived a few blocks away from the Sands Street Gates. She slid the letter to her mother into the crumpled envelope, smoothed it flat, and exited the trolley, heading for the nearest mailbox. It wasn't much bigger than a shoebox and painted blue with a red top, attached to a wooden light pole. The envelope had a three-cent "Win the War" stamp on it with an eagle surrounded by thirteen white stars. So pretty.

She knew the letter would never make it to Mama. But her heart felt fuller, freer, every time she dropped a letter into a dark mailbox. She took a deep breath and turned on her heel.

"Who are you writing to?"

Maggie jumped in her skin. Holly was right there.

"Oh. Hello, Holly. Nobody," she lied.

Holly looked past her head for a moment, and her face darkened with worry. "Huh. I swear I just saw . . ."

"Who?" Maggie spun around, but there was nobody special except a steady stream of shipyard workers headed for the entrance.

"Thought I saw my Sunday school teacher. Ha. Anyways." Holly patted a paper bag under her arm. "I got a liverwurst sandwich for lunch from the shop on Flushing, and now I'm late. And there you are, writing away like a little scribe on the street corner! Who was it really for? I knew you had a beau!" Holly grinned.

"It's—no—I just . . . we should go in to work."

"Sure. Say, where were you yesterday?"

"Oh. I wasn't feeling well."

"You look fine to me," Holly said, eyeing her critically. They had their bags checked inside the gates, but Maggie stopped before they walked together to Building 4. "I thought maybe you'd donated blood, like they keep asking us in the *Shipworker*."

The Navy Yard newspaper encouraged it. You got a half day off afterward, and Maggie often saw lines of donors outside the drive building. It was the perfect excuse for today.

Maggie smiled. "Actually, that reminds me. I'm going to donate."

"After being sick for a day? I don't think that's a good idea."

"No, I wasn't sick. My brother was. I was looking after him." God, the lies just got easier and easier as time went on. "But I promised myself I'd donate blood at least once a month, and I told them I'd be by today."

"Oh. Okay. I'll tell the boss. Good thing you're ahead of most everyone in class. But you'd better show up for work tomorrow or you'll get canned."

"I will. Bye, Holly."

Maggie slid into the throng of workers who were leaving the shipyard at the end of their night shift, and made sure that a different guard checked her bag as she left.

She made her way to the subway station and rode the Brooklyn line into Manhattan, switching to an uptown train. She kept looking over her shoulder, watching for any signs of that telltale chestnut hair of Ruby's. She couldn't shake the feeling that she was being followed. So she purposely walked the streets on Park and Madison awhile, looked at window displays of flowers and books and war-appropriate dresses with buttonless and zipperless closures until she was sure no one was trailing her.

Finally, she found herself on Fifth Avenue, at the doorbell of Cross's huge house, in front of those naked statues above the front door, which didn't seem to bother her as much today.

Fiona answered the door. "Back again, are we?" she said. She didn't seem surprised at all.

"I had a few more questions for Mr. Cross."

"Very well. His parents are home this time. I'll be sure they don't see you until you are more properly attired." She opened the door farther and let Maggie inside.

"Don't you need to ask him if it's okay for me to be here?"

"Mr. Cross gave me explicit instructions to let you in if you visited again. It's almost lunch. They eat early. You can join him."

"With his parents?" Maggie said, gawping as Fiona led her upstairs to Ruby's old room.

"Yes. Don't worry, they are all bark, no bite."

But barking is bad, too, Maggie wanted to say. As she climbed the curving stairs to the richly decorated bedroom, she thought, What am I doing here, again?

And then she remembered: I'm here to get information from Mr. Cross. That's what.

But another voice inside her head said, Because you belong here, Maggie. You deserve to be cared for. You deserve this. Perhaps even more than Ruby ever did.

With that, Fiona swept her hand toward the open washroom, where the smell of lavender and rose invited Maggie inside.

"Shall we begin?" Fiona said. "You're not nearly as filthy as I anticipated."

"Sorry to disappoint, Fiona," Maggie said. "I'll try harder next time."

Fiona inadequately suppressed a laugh. Maggie was surprised at herself. She wasn't used to being such a tart.

They were able to get Maggie ready far quicker this time, as Maggie's hair still held much of the curl from the day before. Soon, she was descending the steps wearing a rose-colored dress with tight sleeves just below the elbow, and matching silk pumps. The neckline was low, but it set off Maggie's collarbones beautifully. Fiona had dusted some powder over her décolletage and cheeks. Her lips were cherry red from a brand-new bullet of lipstick.

"This way. The drawing room. You'll have a light cocktail and then luncheon."

She entered the drawing room—a vast space with vaulted ceilings, more paintings of hunting scenes, and furniture covered in satiny flower prints. Every surface was mirror polished.

Felix Cross stood at the hearth, smoking a cigarette over a warm and steady crackling fire. He turned to greet Maggie, a smile lighting his face.

"Ah! I'd hoped you'd come back soon." He walked to a table and began mixing drinks from a collection of crystal decanters. He held up a glass. "I'm more than happy to share this sidecar." He handed it to her. Maggie took a sip of the heady drink, the cognac immediately warming her belly.

"Thank you. Well, I have some questions," Maggie said. She put her other hand to her chest nervously. "I'm sorry to bother you."

"Looking like this, you would never be bothering me. You look marvelous." He cocked his head, eyeing her critically. "Something is missing, however. No matter. Come. Let's have some lunch."

He offered his arm, and Maggie took it, feeling odd being walked around like she was a debutante at a ball. She entered the dining room. At one end of the long table, two people were already seated. They looked up and stared at Maggie.

One was a lady who appeared to be Felix's mother. They had the same thin nose and piercing eyes. Her gray hair was done up in a neat chignon. Felix's father was mustachioed and portly, his hand holding a glass of wine. Almost stubbornly, he rose from his chair as they approached.

"Mother, Father. This is Miss Margaret Scripps. A friend of the Fielding family."

"Good afternoon," the elder Mr. Cross said. He looked severely annoyed. And Mrs. Cross was worse—she actually looked disgusted, as if someone had just served her a bowl of pudding made of dog excrement.

"Good afternoon," Maggie said. She performed a quick curtsy, not knowing if she should curtsy at all, or bow. Felix had her sit in a chair opposite Mrs. Cross, and he seated himself at the head of the table on her right.

"Oh!" Felix clapped his hands. "I know what's missing! Mother, hand over that pearl necklace of yours."

His mother looked livid. Her gnarled hand went to her throat, where she fingered a costly double-stranded necklace of graduated pearls. They stared each other down, until Felix rolled his eyes.

"Good God, Mother, they are *mine* after all. Hand them over."

She looked like she was going to cry. Maggie began to protest, but Felix gave her a severe glance that told her to remain quiet. The elder Mr. Cross whispered something to his wife, and her hands shakily removed the pearls from her neck. She handed them to Felix, who then stood up and draped them around Maggie's neck. Maggie blushed so hard she felt like blood might burst from her eyes. The pearls were still warm from being on Mrs. Cross's body. Surely, it was indecent to feel physical warmth emanating from a total stranger. Nausea churned in Maggie's stomach, and she attempted to look anywhere except at Felix's parents, who no doubt were glaring at the usurper before them.

Good God, she thought. No wonder Ruby ran away. Maggie was utterly regretting her decision to come back, but it was too late. She would have to glean whatever she could about Felix and Ruby in the next hour. It would be torture. She took a gulp of her sidecar. She needed every drop.

"Now we're ready for our luncheon," Felix said with an oily smile. The smile disappeared, and he barked, *"Where is the soup?"*

Yes. Torture, Maggie thought.

CHAPTER 17

Will had left home earlier than usual. He hadn't wanted to encounter Ruby or Maggie in the morning. Anyway, he couldn't sleep much. Just before dawn he awoke and quietly made breakfast. And then he left, heading for the west side of Manhattan. He had to get the warehouse ready to receive refined ore shipments.

As he rode the subway, he wasn't outwardly upset. They had decided Ruby could stay a week. It felt like the right thing to do. And when Ruby chose to go to Maggie's bedroom, it made sense. She needed some peace and separation from Will, and he from her. There was something volatile about having Ruby so close to him.

And so Ruby had preferred to stay with Maggie last night. The idea of the two together should be nothing disturbing. They'd be like friends, or sisters, curled up and whispering to each other. Maggie would be soothing Ruby's fears over leaving so soon, and Ruby would be weaving her spell over Maggie, as she was so good at doing.

But the truth was impossible to ignore, and he knew it in his depths. This was beyond friendly affection. He'd heard of women becoming romantic. The concept perplexed him; he didn't understand how the mechanics of lovemaking would occur, if at all. He tried to imagine what it would feel like to lust for a man, but it was a romantic and sexual affinity similar to how he felt about anything nonfemale.

One might as well ask if Will would like to date sauerkraut. He simply didn't like it (men, or sauerkraut). When he thought of Ruby, however, he could imagine anyone falling in love with her. Even mountains and planets would pledge themselves, if they could.

He exited the subway station at Fourteenth Street and walked uptown until he reached the Baker and Williams warehouse.

The father and son, the two Mr. Toms, greeted him inside. The younger held his hand out, and Will shook it.

"I signed the papers yesterday. It's all yours," he said.

Will smiled. "Excellent."

He spent the next few hours checking all the entrances, the foot traffic on the back side of the building, plus arranging for the incoming shipments next week. Mrs. Rivers actually came down to jot notes for her husband on the progress. She didn't like the claustrophobic small office by the front of the warehouse, so they spoke in one of the cavernous back rooms. She had a pencil and steno pad, and as she flipped a page, Will saw a number amid her otherwise illegible shorthand.

25.

He saw it twice. In his mind, he felt two cogs fitting together. But first, the warehouse.

"The shipments will be coming from multiple refineries, but the first from Port Hope arrives in three days. They can dock here on the west side, at Twentieth Street. We'll clear the dock ahead of time so it's only our people working and deliver the load after hours so we don't block traffic and invite scrutiny."

"This Port Hope shipment will need to be quality tested," Mrs. Rivers said, tapping her pencil on the pad. "We could assay them here, and build a lab so none of the product leaves the building."

"Sorry?"

"Oh." Mrs. Rivers tilted her head toward Will's good ear. Even she forgot sometimes. "I said we could assay them here, build a lab on site."

"That would duplicate existing labs. Wastes money and time. Just send samples to the chemists uptown and test for purity. It won't be a lot of moving around to raise suspicion. But that only gets you so far. Which enrichment method are you working on for the isotope you need?" Will asked.

Mrs. Rivers's red lips came together in a silent line, and she studied Will. Time and time again, Will would press for more details, and Mrs. Rivers would tell him "need to know" so that he could source the materials without understanding why.

Except that Will understood why.

He had been there when the cyclotron in the basement of Pupin Hall had spat forth various uranium isotopes to find there was one—a rare one—whose nucleus could be split, with its broken components causing an ongoing chain reaction. Nuclear fission.

"You don't need to know that," Mrs. Rivers said evenly.

"I need to know, so I can help you get as much 25 as you need."

"Be quiet!" Her voice rose to a pitch that was nearly shrill. "How do you know about 25? That is confidential."

"It's on your steno pad." He tilted his head toward the pad in her hands. Mrs. Rivers flipped the page and turned scarlet when she saw her own writing.

"What does 25 have to do with anything? It could be the price of a pair of shoes I intend to buy."

"I heard that number spoken by someone in the MED offices about a month ago—25 is close enough to uranium-235 that I figured out it was a nickname for the isotope. Because no one would ever actually call it 235, right? That's the isotope that'll sustain a chain reaction, the one that Fermi must still be working on uptown. I'm not clairvoyant. But it was mentioned a few times in a few physics journals before censors shut that down. Anyway, code words usually have some relationship with the truth."

"What else have you guessed?" She wasn't frowning now; in fact, she looked almost relieved.

"I know those physicists will try to get as much pure 25 as they can, and it can't be easy, or they'd have done it by now. Let me help."

"You don't even have a college degree!" she noted.

"You know I'm working on that. But right now, I don't need a degree to do more. I can see what's in front of me. You really think you can keep doing research in a tiny university lab building? You know they'll need more space."

Mrs. Rivers sighed. "We may move the project elsewhere."

"Probably to Tennessee, right? But the physicists uptown can't all go there. You don't want to concentrate all the best minds in one place. Too easy to kill them in one fell swoop if a spy infiltrated. You need another large lab here, in Manhattan." Will leaned against one of the cloudy windows.

"Not just another lab." She sighed. "Another building. One where we can house some pretty large machinery."

"For uranium enrichment."

She rolled her eyes, finally giving in. "Yes."

"Okay. I'll find you a building. On the island, somewhere closer to Columbia."

"Very well."

"And when I find it, I want to be working in the building. I want to be on the team."

God. He'd said it out loud. He held his breath, trying not to look like he was holding his breath.

Mrs. Rivers glanced down at her pad, erasing the 25s on her previous pages with her pencil. "Damn it."

"Look. You need people who can think sideways on this. I want this project to be a success as much as you do. I can do more than scout out buildings and source materials. You know this."

Once the 25s were all erased, she looked up. "Fine. Let me present the idea to Mr. Rivers. This is complicated."

As Will walked her out, he instinctively put his hand on the small of her back, guiding her around occasional debris on the warehouse floor. Mrs. Rivers allowed this.

As she was about to leave, she said, "Thank you, Will. You'll receive your usual payment." She hesitated.

"You need something else."

She smiled, just the littlest bit. Will was good at reading her needs. It was becoming a highly valued skill.

"I need a compressor."

"An air compressor?"

"Well, for gases. Something that can push a gas through a filter, or a chamber." She bit her lip.

"A gas. Uranium would be hard to get into a vapor state. It prefers to be a solid oxide, or carbide. Hmm. Unless . . . maybe you combined with a halide. Uranium . . . hexafluoride? Did they manage to make that? I don't think that exists naturally."

Mrs. Rivers closed her eyes and simultaneously raised her eyebrows in resignation. "God. Yes, that. How did you—never mind." She looked him straight in the eye. "Hex is extremely corrosive, so the compressor has to be corrosion resistant."

"Understood."

Will opened the door. The midday light was blinding for a moment. He squinted into the brightness as Mrs. Rivers turned around.

"Give Mr. Rivers my best," he said.

She chortled. There was a joke that she was squashing down. "Good day. It's nice to have you back, Mr. Scripps."

"Come again?"

"You haven't been yourself recently. You're back. Like you've been released from prison or something."

"I suppose so."

"Good. Let's keep it that way. You're far too valuable to me to lose right now."

"Valuable to Mr. Rivers, you mean. And General Groves."

She smiled. "Isn't that what I said?"

With that, she walked away from the warehouse. On the corner, a man stood by a waiting car. As she approached, he kissed her on the cheek. But it was not Mr. Rivers. Will had spoken to him in person only once. He was a man who seemed like he'd been bleached by life—pale, with cardboard-colored hair. He'd seemed so tired and wrought out, Will almost felt the need to ask him if he needed to sit down.

This gentleman had dark hair and dark eyes; he was thin and pale as well, but not Mr. Rivers. Mrs. Rivers threw her head back to laugh as she ducked into the car. The man looked over at Will, staring for longer than a stranger ought. He smiled—grinned, almost, like a skeleton laughs at the grim reaper for being too late.

"Felix!"

Or so Will thought he heard.

It couldn't be Felix Cross, could it? He shook his head. Couldn't be.

Will withdrew into the darkness of the warehouse, his retinas seared by the sun.

⊷

Will was shaking cobwebs from his head as he boarded the subway to head home to Brooklyn. Had it been Felix Cross outside the warehouse with Mrs. Rivers? He didn't know what Cross looked like, but he must look like an ill man, given he'd been in the hospital so very recently. Will closed his eyes, thinking harder. The sun's glare hid so much detail, but he remembered a spare man, tall, who seemed to be sharply alert and finely dressed. He easily could have been sicker than the average person without it being obvious.

Inwardly, he cursed Cross for ruining a glorious moment for him. Mrs. Rivers would raise it with the higher-ups, maybe even Groves, about having Will work on the gaseous diffusion method of uranium enrichment. This was the opening he'd been waiting for, and she hadn't said no. He thought about celebrating, and then he immediately thought about celebrating with Ruby, despite the fact that she was the last distraction he needed at this point in his life.

"Hey!"

Will looked up. The subway car was crowded with commuters, and a man was staring at another gentleman who was walking away, farther down the car.

"He knocked my hat off, the dolt!" the man said, groping for his hat amongst the legs of the people around him. At the sound of the loud complaint, the other man turned around for a quick glance.

Will's heart thudded in his chest. It was the face of his stepfather. He knew this because Maggie's eyes were identical—the same light green that made it look like they were lamplit in a fog. But it was an aged version of his deceased stepfather. It couldn't be him. And just as Will stood up to get a better view, the man walked into the next car and was gone.

Will rubbed his eyes. Once, he thought he'd seen his dead father. Now he was seeing his stepfather. He was going silly from worry, no doubt. His stepfather was dead. He remembered the day he came home from playing outside for hours with Maggie, their chatter suddenly hushed at the sight of their mother standing in the kitchen over an overflowing pot of boiling soup.

"He's gone," she'd said. She was staring at the wallpaper above the stove.

"Who? Who's gone where?" Will had asked.

"Your father. Dead."

In his head, Will corrected her: my stepfather. Maggie's father. Never mine, really. He did this all the time, this internal editing. It made it easier for him to tolerate the occasional slaps and shoves whenever Will displeased his stepfather. He always suspected that Norman Scripps was bothered by the fact that Will nearly 100 percent resembled his own father and was a reminder of the love that their mother had lost in the Great War. Norman had only been a shallow replacement. Will's mother felt differently, and that was all that prevented him from rebelling more.

But replacement or no, Norman Scripps had died. It had been Labor Day, 1932. Norman had been arguing with Will's mother over working on a holiday. With ninety-nine other men, many of them iron workers like him, he boarded a steamboat at an East River dock to work on a project at Riker's Island. The boat hadn't even left the berth when it exploded. Will and Maggie had heard the bang from a distance but hadn't thought much of it that morning as they played kick the can in the street. Apparently, body parts had been flung into the air, even landing on distant rooftops. Norman had apparently been standing right above the engine. His body had been shredded and charred to unrecoverable bits.

Will's mother, so meek, had doled out all her adoration for Norman Scripps as he'd demanded. And when he left their world, left her, she obeyed to the very end, until her nose and mouth filled with water from Lower Bay and her heart stopped beating beneath the icy coldness. Because without him, why bother living for anyone left behind?

So no, that couldn't have been Will's stepfather. He was gone, and even if he was a ghost, if Will believed in such things, his stepfather had cared so little about Will that he wouldn't even be worth haunting.

"I need more sleep," Will muttered to himself as he went back to staring at the floor of the subway.

He arrived home far earlier than usual. He could start dinner before Maggie got home, enjoy some hours alone with Ruby. But he wasn't sure how she'd react to him, now that her identity had been confirmed and she'd chosen to sleep in Maggie's bedroom last night.

As he rounded the corner on Lake Place and walked the back alley toward their home, he was met with a sight he didn't expect.

It was Ruby, her caramel hair bundled under a kerchief, wearing an old pair of Maggie's trousers and a plain blouse, digging a hole in the small lot behind their kitchen door. Digging! A hole! And what was more, there was a rectangular plot of ground that had been turned and tilled, and several plants he didn't recognize were situated neatly in it. Nearby, a low pile of deadwood was burning.

"Will!" Ruby said, putting her spade to the side and smiling widely. She looked happy—genuinely happy—not like the expression that so often hid other feelings. All those faces she'd been wearing since she'd arrived. The only expressions he'd truly ever trusted were real were the ones she wore when they were in the throes of lovemaking. And even those, he suspected, were sometimes more exaggerated than natural.

"What's going on here?" he said, shoving his hands into his pockets. They were safer there. Otherwise, he'd be tempted to reach out and grab Ruby's waist and bring her closer.

"Maggie asked me to start working on a better bomb shelter. My hands are so sore, but I did some of it!"

Will looked at the ground. True, she had meticulously outlined a rectangular footprint and had already dug about one foot deep along the edges.

"And this?" He pointed to the plants.

"Oh. I took a walk and found some things to grow here. I walked to the park by the ocean. What's it called? Something Offerman? There's a playground there. And I found these, and these."

She pointed to plants that looked like jack-in-the-pulpit, though they were browned and decaying from the cold. There were plants with purplish stalks and pointed oval leaves. "Pokeweed."

"It's not very pretty," Will remarked.

"Its beauty is on the inside," she said, winking.

"I recognize these," he said, pointing to some small bushes that he often saw near the front doors of houses that cared enough about planting decorative things.

"Yes. Rhododendron, and hydrangea." She lowered her voice to a whisper. "I stole those from a house that looked abandoned. That's not too much of a crime, is it? The one next to them is called monkshood. And the other one there is snakeroot. It has a pretty flower in the summer."

"Strange time to be planting things, before winter comes."

"They're helpful," she said, crossing her arms. Her hands were filthy with mud and dirt. It was oddly attractive, seeing such beautiful hands dirtied up.

"For a war garden?" he said.

"For war." She looked at him with an even glance. "They're not for the supper table."

"What do they do?"

She pointed to the hydrangea. "The flower buds contain a cyanide compound. The rhododendron has poisonous leaves that can stop the heart and cause nausea and tingling. Oh, and honey made from the flowers is poisonous too."

She walked over to the one that looked like a delphinium. "Monkshood. Aconitine is the poison found throughout the plant. Causes heart palpitations, salivation, vomiting. And finally, snakeroot. It can cause nausea, vomiting . . . and death. White hellebore. A plain-looking plant, isn't it? You eat enough of this one, you'll fall into a coma and die. Abraham Lincoln's mother died of snakeroot poisoning. Very potent."

"You know, you're not exactly inspiring confidence with this garden."

"You have to find truth any way you can, Will. When Francesco Redi did his first experiments in the seventeenth century, people didn't believe him when he said that venom was why vipers could kill. They used to think it was from evil spirits formed by the snake." She sighed.

"Redi?"

"Yes. Some say he was the founder of toxicology."

He smiled. "I thought you'd be more entertained by Errol Flynn."

"Errol Flynn isn't nearly as interesting as scorpions and cyanide."

"This conversation isn't making me feel safe right now."

Ruby turned to him. "I would never hurt you. Or Maggie. But I have to protect myself."

"Guns and knives usually do the job faster," he commented.

"That kind of violence doesn't always help a woman. We have to protect ourselves in ways that work for us."

"Are you planning on killing Felix Cross?" he asked. "Or did you try? With that zinc chloride we found in your coat pocket?"

"Hush. Let's go inside."

She parked the shovel by the back door. In the washroom, she scrubbed the soil off her hands, cleaning under her fingernails. The scent of soap reminded Will of images from before, and he tried to keep his body from reacting as he leaned against the door. A sickly sweet fruit odor emanated from the sink. He looked and found the fruit of all the peaches he'd bought lately browning in a lump. Ruby scooped up the pulp and dropped it into the wastebasket.

"I thought you were going to eat those," he pointed out.

"I need the pits."

Will went quiet. Peach pits had cyanide in them. He remembered that from chemistry class. Apparently, there was cyanide in apple seeds too. If you ate too many, you could die.

"What are you using the pits for?" he asked, trying to keep his voice measured.

"Why, to donate to the war cause," Ruby said brightly. "They use them for making gas masks."

Will decided it was easier to believe the fiction. "Ah, yes. Of course. Expensive way to help, though. You'd be better off donating blood, or saving those dollars for buying war bonds."

"Maybe." Ruby seemed distracted.

"So. Are you?" Will asked again. "Planning on killing your ex-fiancé?"

She met his gaze. "If I have to, yes."

"With the zinc chloride?"

"No, no. I told you," she said, her voice agitated. "I didn't poison him when I left. I think it was the other way around. I was intoxicated, yes—but not by my own hand. I think he poisoned himself, to point a finger at me."

Will raised an eyebrow.

"Will. I'm telling you the truth. I think he's the one who poisoned me." She blotted her hands and went into the kitchen. Will sat down, and instead of taking the seat across from him, Ruby sat on his lap and casually draped her arm around his shoulder. "I've been fascinated by medicinal plants since I was a child. I got a terrible rash from some stinging nettle and begged my mother to tell me why the plant bit me." She laughed, and her free hand played with his hair. Will had trouble breathing.

"So you like plants that kill."

"They heal too. It all depends on the plant, and the dose. They're like people. They aren't always just good or bad. We all have hands that could pick up a knife and kill someone viciously. Does it mean we're bad?"

"No," he said. He couldn't stay still anymore. His hands found their way to her waist and hips. Even under the trousers and the old blouse she wore, he could feel her curves. He started to unbuckle the belt that held up her baggy pants.

"When is Maggie coming home?" she whispered into his hair.

"I don't know. I don't care," he said, pulling her blouse free. His hands slid up her stomach.

Ruby's eyes closed. "She'll be jealous."

"I'm jealous, and Maggie isn't even here."

She pushed him away and stood to let her trousers drop to the floor. She kicked them away and sat back down on his lap.

"I am ruining you both," she said, her lips on his ear. Which always drove him mad.

"I don't care."

And he didn't. There were moments in a person's life when logic and thoughtful decisions were the rule. And there were other times when senses, not sensibility, reigned.

Will knew he was lost, even as Ruby kissed him, even as his thoughts still held flashes of warning—seeing a man who looked like Felix Cross outside the warehouse; the vision of his stepfather on the train. He could nearly hear Mrs. Rivers's voice: *Will. I thought you were going to help me win this war.*

Go away, Will thought. There's only room for Ruby right now.

CHAPTER 18

The soup course was a nightmare. Maggie had slurped the creamy oyster soup and elicited stares from the Crosses at her faux pas. Mr. Cross had asked Maggie questions about her parentage ("dead") and her place of abode ("Brooklyn") and how they were managing during the war ("I'm a welder"). Each answer made it seem more and more as if they'd invited an absolute ruffian into their midst.

Felix wasn't bothered, however. He hardly ate, but instead leaned back in his chair, clearly amused.

When the fresh lobster salad and scalloped potatoes were served, Maggie watched him eat mincing bites and wondered why she was here.

"Miss Scripps, tell me more about your new guest," Felix said as he nibbled on a lettuce leaf. "I understand she's quite skilled in botany. Or is it . . . vermin extermination?" He suppressed a laugh.

"She's growing flowers," Maggie said.

"Flowers," Felix said, eyes lit. "You mean poisonous ones!"

"Yes."

"Be careful when you drink your tea. You might wake up dead," he said, waving a fork.

"Are you speaking about Ruby Fielding?" the elder Mr. Cross boomed from across the table. "Is she staying with you? She's a murderess! She ought to be in jail!"

"Oh, Father, do shut up," Felix said. His father did just that, looking like a balloon that had been squeezed until it was going to pop. "I'm not dead, so she's not a *murderer*. She's an attempted murderer."

"She was drugged or drunk when we found her," Maggie said. She ate a bit of potato, buttery and spiced from the chives. For some reason, the more upset her lunch companions got, the calmer she became. "Perhaps *you* poisoned *her*, Mr. Cross."

"Stuff and nonsense!" Mrs. Cross said. She banged down a fork. For such a lofty mansion and people, their behavior at this table was atrocious. "My son would never!"

Felix rolled his eyes. "Please. We're responsible for the death of this crustacean, and these potatoes, and the squab we ate last night. We're not so innocent."

"A woman and a lobster are not to be compared!" Mrs. Cross's face was redder than her rouge.

"I'm tired of you." Felix planted his elbow on the table and pointed his fork at his mother. "You too," he said, nodding to his father. "Go away."

They stared at him.

"I said: Go. Away. I'd like a meal in peace with Miss Scripps, and you are both behaving like infants."

Red faced, they stood.

"Come, Shirley. We'll go eat with the cook. At least she treats us with respect," Mr. Cross said, his napkin still tucked into his cravat. "Perhaps she still has some charlotte russe left from yesterday."

Maggie waited until both elder Crosses were gone and their footsteps could no longer be heard clicking on the polished hallway floor.

As soon as it was safe, Maggie let out an inaudible sigh of relief. Felix was not as polite. He slumped in his chair, exhaling so loudly it came out sounding like a sick bassoon.

"Are you all right?" Maggie said.

"No. Yes. I don't know," Felix said. He rubbed his eyes and temples for a long time. Finally, he looked up at Maggie and said, "You must think I'm a monster."

"Are you?" Maggie asked.

"Probably." He laughed ruefully. "I may have sole ownership of our family's money, but I can't turn my parents out. I do what I can to make my presence unpleasant, so they spend as little time with me as possible."

"Why?" Maggie's appetite had picked up again. She started eating the lobster salad with gusto.

"All my life, they've been cruel to me. Starved me if they thought I was getting too fat. Whipped me when I turned out left handed. And I confess, I'm a petty man. I can't forgive them. After all, they've never apologized."

"You're still not eating," Maggie noticed.

"A by-product of old habits. They like me to cut a fine figure. I don't exactly have a friendly relationship with food anymore. That being said, don't let me prevent you from eating. Please."

A fresh-fruit bowl, coffee, and petit fours soon followed. Felix filled her cup himself, asked if she was warm, or cool, enough. Asked if her clothes were agreeable. After Maggie was filled to the chin, she thanked him.

"You're very kind to me, Mr. Cross."

"Do call me Felix. Please." He lit a cigarette and offered one to Maggie, who declined.

"Tell me more about Ruby," she said.

"Ah. The gem in our life. Yes." He looked sad again. "I would never have hurt her. Never. But she hurt me. She lied to me incessantly, but it took a long time before I realized what was happening."

"Lied about what?"

"Me, for one thing. She never loved me. She loved my money."

Maggie frowned. "But her family is wealthy!"

"Ah, but her mother doesn't like fuss and feathers, and kept her drab as a mouse. Ruby is a hedonist at heart. Loved it when I dressed her up." He sighed. "She also had an affair right in front of me, and I didn't see it because I couldn't even fathom that she would do such a thing. And with such a person."

"Who was it?" Maggie asked.

"With whom did she have an affair?" Felix corrected her. "I apologize. Old habits, again." He inhaled from his cigarette and exhaled a plume to the side so it wouldn't puff into Maggie's face. "She had an affair with her maid."

"Her *maid*?" Maggie tried not to open her mouth as wide as she wanted.

Felix leaned in close, as if conspiring with her. He lowered his voice. "A woman! Can you believe it? Sappho would approve, no doubt," he said, sitting back and inhaling again. "Still, that it was a woman bothered me less than her perfidious nature. And she was more upset about having to stop the affair than my disappointment!" Here, he smiled. "Like I said, she's an absolute gem. Forged in this earth and unlike any I've ever met. And now she won't have anything to do with me."

He was so good at making Maggie feel sorry for him. But she doubted he was truly heartbroken. She was tempted to make him angry and see what happened.

"She said you were going to kill her," Maggie said. "That you wanted control of her family's fortune, and information on her father's business. She said you were furious when she resisted."

"Of course I was! Her father and I are in the same line of work, you know. How could I not want her to keep me close to her family? Our businesses would be united. She's the heiress to the family fortune. If your father were a bricklayer, and your future husband were a mason, should they not discuss their trade?"

It made sense. "What about her interest in poison? It's so odd. Why do you think she poisoned you?"

"Oho! Well, this is precious. She's been interested in plants ever since she had a bad run-in with a nettle bush. Her whole life, she wanted to understand what chemicals in plants could hurt people. It was a kind of power. But here's the thing—I think there is something bigger at play. Much bigger."

"What do you mean?"

"Come." Felix stood. "It's getting late, and you need to be on your way or your brother and Ruby will be worried."

Maggie's eyes flew to the clock on the mantelpiece. It was early afternoon. She should try to make it to the Navy Yard to get in an afternoon shift. "Oh! I had no idea it was so late."

"Let me drive you. We have enough gas ration for the trip."

Felix rang a bell, and Fiona showed up to pin a matching rose-colored hat, embellished with silk flowers, to Maggie's hair. Once again, she was given her work clothes in a bag. She followed Felix to the sleek black Rolls-Royce waiting outside. A sticker with the letter *A* was in the windshield, designating their regular citizen's gasoline ration. The driver looked at Maggie curiously when he opened the door but of course said nothing. She nestled into the back seat with Felix. It was nice to sit in a car like this.

"Tell me," Maggie said. "You were going to say something. Something important."

"I will. Only if you'll make me a promise."

Maggie only nodded. She was impressed at how focused she was on Felix's earnest expression, not even pausing to regard the rich leather upholstery. Central Park whizzed by. There were few cars on the streets.

"Ruby is dangerous. She didn't just end up on your front step by accident. She meant to be there. She wanted you to find her."

"How do you know this?" Maggie said.

"I just do, and I can't reveal why I know. Look. You work in the Navy Yard—the largest Navy Yard in the country. And with all the ships it's birthing, it's a target for sabotage and spies."

Maggie went cold. Ruby had asked to come with her to the Navy Yard just that morning. "What are you saying?"

"Do you know what your brother does?"

"Yes. He does odd jobs. He mentioned General Groves, but I'm not sure what he's doing, exactly. And he's taking classes at night, of course."

"He's working for the government, you poor, naive child. How can you be so blind?"

Maggie's skin prickled. She didn't know, because Will told her nothing. And it made her feel like she didn't know him at all. Why wouldn't he trust her? Did he think her too much of a simpleton—too emotionally fragile after her near drowning to handle such information?

"How do you hear about all this?" Maggie asked.

But Felix stayed silent for a minute or two, relishing holding back the information. Maggie felt sick to her stomach. Everything he was saying made sense. Her meal of lobster salad and rich potatoes was rising up in her throat. She looked out the window and tried to take a deep breath. Times Square passed by, quiet without its usual dizzying light displays. Even the *New York Times* news zipper, announcing the news in a continuous electronically lit ribbon, had gone dark months ago after a final message: "The New York Times Bids You Good Night." Maggie felt unmoored and directionless.

"Tell me, Felix," Maggie begged.

"Very well. After you showed up on my door and I realized Ruby was living with you, I did my own research. It didn't take long to find out what I could about you both. And it was so very obvious, as bright as day. You're both perfect targets for a spy to cozy up with, and manipulate, and ruin everything for our country in the process."

"No," Maggie muttered. "No, no. She can't be a spy. She's just . . . she's rich! And she doesn't talk about the war at all, or seem to care."

"Oh, she cares all right. Just not about the right side. All that interest in plant toxins is not because she's an odd girl with an odd interest. She's developing poisons and handing her information to the German government. Gas is one thing, but poison can be wielded like a fine scalpel, and she knows it."

Maggie had visions of dead rats lined up on her stairs. She felt ill.

Felix went on. "When she was young, her mother introduced her to a prominent German chemist. No doubt with political ties to his homeland. Has she ever asked to go to work with your brother?"

"I don't know. I just assumed she stayed home all these days."

"Has she ever gone missing?"

"Not that I know of," Maggie said, but the truth was, she had no idea.

Felix raised his eyebrows. He looked like a young boy when he did that. "Did you know she speaks fluent German? Don't you think that's odd?"

Maggie remembered the time she'd heard Ruby speak in German while she was dreaming. She hadn't been sure then; she was sure now.

"Still, I can't believe she'd be involved that way," Maggie said. "She's different, that's a fact. But she also seems so ordinary. I think she's lonely. Like you," she said. When she heard her own words, her hand flew to cover her mouth.

Felix smiled sadly. "No, don't apologize. I *am* lonely. And I'm not even very good at hiding it, though my parents have no idea. But they care less about my heart and more about their bank account. But yes. I'm lonely. Very much so."

Maggie wasn't sure what to say. They rode in silence for a long time. Felix seemed to appreciate the companionship without the words. As the car drove south, the bumps in the road occasionally knocked their shoulders together, and Maggie allowed it. On the car's leather seat, their hands nearly touched.

After a long while, the Brooklyn Bridge loomed ahead. A couple walked on the sidewalk, leaving a restaurant. The man was in his army uniform and had a patched eye. The woman clung to his arm, like he might fly away like a lost balloon if she let go.

Suddenly, Maggie blurted, "I'm lonely too." As soon as she said it, she regretted it. But Felix didn't laugh at her.

"Even with the illustrious Ruby Fielding to keep you company?"

"Yes." Maggie's eyes watered. She was deathly afraid of getting tearstains on the lovely rose-tinted dress, so she blotted her eyes with her gloved fingertip, smudging cake mascara onto them. "When Ruby is with me, it feels like . . . like a dream. The kind where you know you'll wake up soon, so you're frantic to make the dream last longer, but the whole fear of it disappearing makes everything worse."

"Yes. It's as if you never know if she'll be there when you wake up. Or blink," Felix said.

Maggie turned to him. "Exactly."

"It's because she can't love completely. Her heart is not in America, Maggie. It's in Germany."

"I can't believe this," she said, passing a hand before her eyes as if smoke had gotten in the way of her vision. "There are days when I feel like I'm dreaming my way through the hours."

"That's the war too," Felix said. "It's ruining everyone, little by little. But we'll get through. Together. I'm so glad you came to my house again."

The car crossed over the bridge and into Brooklyn, turning south. Maggie was wishing that the ride could go on longer. With Felix, she felt like she had a value with no limit—at least for now. At home, Ruby could choose to stay with Will tonight and Maggie would feel utterly empty again.

When the car finally stopped in front of their home, Maggie realized with a start that she forgot to tell the driver to go to the Navy Yard. At this point, there was no time to travel to work so late in the day.

The driver did not automatically get out to open his door. He was waiting for Felix. And Felix didn't seem to want her to go either.

The afternoon light was weakening a little. Somewhere, a neighbor—Mrs. Polanski, perhaps—had her window open to the cool air and was listening to *The Green Hornet*, but otherwise, the street was quiet. A few lights were on, but not many. Even without Maggie to remind everyone on her street to switch their lights off, it had turned into a habit. The blackout drill scheduled in a few days' time would go well.

"I don't want to go in," Maggie said. "I don't even feel like I belong in my own home."

"Not looking like this. Like the great lady that you are, and they don't know you can be," Felix said. He gently took her hand and kissed it. "Don't forget your worth, Maggie Scripps."

"What will I do when I tell them we spent the last hours together?" She could feel her face morphing into an expression of panic. "They'll be furious with me."

"Tell them you're learning more about me, which is true. And arm yourself with this: I've told you what I know about Ruby. It's your turn to find out your own truth. Follow her. Listen to her. Can you do that?"

"I can."

Maggie reached for the car door, but Felix held his hand up. Of course—the driver was supposed to get the door for her. She was still so disoriented by this way of life. The driver rounded the car, and she stepped out carefully so as not to muss her dress. Felix handed her the bag of work clothes.

"Thank you," she said politely. She'd only gone a few steps when Felix called to her. He'd rolled down the window.

"One more thing. The room in my house—the one that Ruby used to keep? It's yours. I'm going to change out all the clothes and put in new ones. Fiona knows your measurements. She's clever that way. She'll be thrilled to have a young lady to look after once in a while."

"I . . . I don't know what to say. I have a home, Felix." But she couldn't suppress a thrill. Her, living on Fifth Avenue? With a closet full of silk dresses? A maid, and a gentleman to take care of her who didn't hail from Canarsie or Sheepshead? "Oh, Felix. I hardly know you. And I can't just leave my brother."

"Is that true? Or is it that he can't leave you?"

Maggie truly didn't know what to say. Because she didn't know the answer to that question anymore.

"You know, I've heard a rumor that your brother may lose his job because he's been too distracted by Ruby. He can't take care of you, but I could."

Maggie said nothing, but her mind was whirling faster than a merry-go-round, and she felt nearly as dizzy as a rider on one.

"You have more freedom that you think," Felix said. "I'm at your service. Consider it. Keep a lonely gentleman from being lonely. It would be my pleasure, and I would be a gentleman. A friend."

"I don't know, Felix." Her hand went to her throat at the thought, and her fingers found the double pearl necklace still hanging there. Pearls were funny, like a living thing. They had warmed to match her body's temperature, and she hardly noticed them anymore, as if they'd become part of her being. "Oh," she said, stepping back toward the car. "I must return these. Thank you for lending them to me."

She felt for the clasp behind her neck, and Felix reached out of the car to lay a staying hand on her wrist.

"No, don't. Take them. Mother has more than enough jewels to keep her company. They suit you so. So handsome on that pretty little neck of yours."

"I can't! These are worth more than everything I own, and then some."

"They belong on you. I refuse to take them back. Think of it as a gift, in exchange for you considering my offer."

"All right, Felix," she said. She couldn't help grinning. Really smiling, dimple to dimple. When was the last time she'd smiled so widely that the satisfaction took up her whole being? It was an incandescent feeling. She went up the front steps of the house and unlocked the door with a key fished out from her bag of clothes.

When she opened the door, Will and Ruby were waiting for her.

One with hands on hips.

One with arms crossed.

Both with expressions of deep disappointment on their faces.

CHAPTER 19

Will heard the car pull up and lifted the curtain to see who it was. Ruby followed.

"Who is it?"

Peering through the window behind the shades, he saw a grand Rolls-Royce idling in front of the house.

Ruby visibly stiffened. She backed away from the window.

"It's him, it's him," she muttered.

Will recognized a person on the verge of fleeing—he'd prevented twelve-year-old Maggie from running away in panic when she'd heard that her father had died. And later, when she awoke from nightmares. The same terror was in Ruby's eyes. He reached out and snatched her wrist.

"No. You'll be okay."

She pulled against his grip, but when they saw Maggie emerging alone from the car, the tenseness in her body altered. Her terror morphed into abject disgust.

Maggie swung the door open, wiggling the key out of the lock. This time, she was wearing a dress of rich rose, with matching silk heels and hat. White gloves covered her hands, and a costly double string of pearls hung around her neck. Once again, that lilac perfume wafted forward, expanding the space in which Maggie existed.

Felix Cross was turning his sister into a puppet. When Maggie had first entered the parlor, her face was pink from the smile on her face. The smile deteriorated into a frown the second she saw Will and Ruby.

"You look absolutely ridiculous," Will said, disgusted. "Go change and take those things off. Return them immediately. I won't have you go to that house anymore."

"I can so go to his house! He treats me nice."

"He threatened to kill my family, Maggie," Ruby reminded her, practically growling. "Please. Do as your brother says. Felix Cross isn't being kind out of the goodness of his heart. He's using you."

Maggie dropped her bag of belongings. She put the keys on the table, and both hands went to her neck, fingering the pearls.

"You're jealous," Maggie said. "You're both acting like my parents, but I'm old enough to make my own decisions."

"You can make your own decisions when they make common sense, Mags. You're acting like a fool, a pawn."

Maggie, still touching her pearls, swept past them into the kitchen. Ruby and Will followed. She filled a glass with water from the tap and drank it, leaning against the countertop. With her hair styled like a lady's instead of her usual messy bun or braids, and in the elegant dress and heels, Will found her somewhat intimidating. He wondered if it was his imagination, or if her outfit actually conferred powers heretofore unknown to her.

She turned around and gently removed her hat, primping her hair. She lifted her chin up and stared at them both.

"He's not using me. He needs me."

Ruby threw her head back and hooted a loud "Ha!" at the ceiling. "Maggie. That's what he does! He made me feel like I was a veritable

American princess, like Britain's royal family. He does that. And then hooks you in, and then takes everything from you. Everything."

"He said things about you," Maggie said, staring at Ruby. Boy, no one ever taught this girl to play poker, Will thought. She showed her hand right away. "I know things about you." She looked at Will. "We have to be careful around her."

"Says the girl who is cavorting with a strange man who's dumping jewelry in her lap. Those pearls aren't yours. I expect you to give them back," Will said.

"Why? Because another man gave them to me? Why can't I keep them? They're a gift!"

"It's blood money."

"You're just jealous," Maggie said, her eyes alight with fire. "Both of you are."

"That's enough." But Will's voice sounded like defeat. He could hear it. "Let's all go to bed and get some sleep. I've a long day tomorrow, as do you. Speaking of which . . . did you miss work today? Are you going to lose this job too?"

Maggie looked like she would burst. She stormed into her room and slammed the door.

The tension in the kitchen didn't go away, but followed Will back to the parlor, where he sat on the sofa, leaning forward with his head in his hands. Ruby sat next to him.

"She'll come to her senses."

"I don't know. I can't compete with what he's giving her."

"You're not supposed to compete," Ruby said, rubbing his back. "You're her brother. Not her lover."

Will looked up, startled. He turned to Ruby. "Do you think . . . that they're . . ."

"I don't know. But I wouldn't put it past him. He's a prize manipulator, Will. I should know."

"Did he teach you everything you know?" Will said.

He didn't mean to be cruel. It just came out. Ruby had been a slippery prize that he could never truly get a fix on. She was always shadow and fog, even while she sat next to him.

"Perhaps," she said lightly. "I won't lie. He did teach me how to protect myself. And sometimes lying is a great way to protect yourself."

It was one of the most truthful things she'd ever said. She looked terrified for a moment, before putting her usual face back on—the one he could never read.

Ruby got up to leave.

"Are you staying with her again tonight?" Will asked without looking at her. He couldn't bear it. He craved her closeness so badly that three feet away might as well be a mile. He stared at the faded carpet flowers, waiting for her answer.

"If you even have to ask, then I think you don't know me at all," Ruby said.

And she left.

All night long, Will was restless on the sofa. His stomach churned, echoing his heart's discomfort. Maggie was angry with him, for no worthy reason. And Ruby wasn't with him. He reviewed the things he ought to focus on, to make himself remember his purpose.

The MED would need a new building to work on uranium enrichment. Someplace out of the way, and someplace that was already set up for industrial work. And he needed to find a company that could make an air compressor that could handle corrosive gases.

Should be easy.

He laughed at himself. Not easy at all, but he enjoyed the challenge. Actually, he'd enjoyed the look on Mrs. Rivers's face when he'd delivered precisely what the MED needed. What no one else could acquire as quickly and efficiently as he could. He knew the city so well. Since he was fifteen, he'd run errands for any company that would hire him, and gotten to know the web of businesses in the city, how the longshoremen worked, where the goods were being bought aboveboard and off the backs of trucks. Never did he think such knowledge would help him do wartime work. It could transform his life and thrust him into a whole different atmosphere, if he was careful. If his life didn't churn out more chaos than it already had.

When he woke up, he was stiff from the sofa and the horrendous night's sleep. He felt like he had the flu. He shuffled toward the washroom, careful not to awaken Ruby and Maggie. He paused outside the bedroom door and heard nothing. His heart sank at the thought of two nights away from Ruby now. Somehow, he discounted the fact that she'd been in his lap only yesterday afternoon, doing things that civilized folk ought not to be doing in a kitchen.

Still, to have lain with a woman wasn't the same as sharing an entire night with one. It was the difference between getting shot with a pebble and handing someone a grenade. One was far more likely to cause permanent damage.

He pushed open the door to the washroom, ready to relieve his full bladder, when he nearly yelled out loud in surprise.

Ruby was curled up in the bathtub, her coat balled under her head. Her bent knees leaned against the side of the tub and her arms were crossed, as if judging the ceiling while she slept.

Will gently knocked the side of the tub with his foot. Ruby awoke with a start, looking confused for a moment before remembering her surroundings. She sat up and stretched, yawning.

"Morning," Will said. He couldn't help but smile—he was soothed by the fact that she hadn't stayed with Maggie. The realization was somewhat upsetting. To think he was competing with his own sister for this woman's affection was too much to consider, so he tried not to.

"Morning, handsome," she said, yawning again. She stood up. "I'll be out of here in a second, so you can get ready."

Will nodded, and backed out the door. Before he could close it, Ruby reached for his collar, pulled him back in, and kissed his cheek.

"Missed you last night. I'd rather lie on you than in this old tub."

Will only smiled a little before pushing her back into the tub and shutting the door. But he was glad.

When he was able to, he readied himself for work. Maggie was already in the kitchen. She had brushed out her curls and tucked them under a kerchief. In her work clothes and with a face scrubbed of makeup, she was the old familiar Maggie.

Ruby was sitting in her robe at the table. She took a sip of coffee, but pushed it away, trying not to make a face of disgust. Ruby was used to her upper-class coffee and tea, that was for sure.

"Here," Maggie said, smiling. She handed Will a big mug. The brew was dark and black, strong enough to give an elephant palpitations, the way he liked it. He drank it down, and Maggie seemed satisfied by things being somewhat back to normal.

"What will you do today?" she asked Ruby.

"Dig in the backyard. I can keep working on the shelter. I got a good amount done yesterday, and my hands aren't that sore."

"Good," Maggie said, sipping. She looked away.

"Or, I could go to work with you again, Will," Ruby said.

Maggie abruptly stopped drinking. "Again?" She looked at Will. "She went to work with you? When?"

"Just once," he admitted. "There wasn't much to see."

"You've never invited me to work," Maggie said, hurt suffusing her face.

"Because it's boring, and you've got a job now."

"I didn't have a job before," Maggie said.

"That's enough, Maggie. It's irrelevant now. Ruby, you can't come to work with me anymore."

Ruby smiled, but her disappointment was clear. "I understand." She put her cup down and lifted her shoulders. "I'd better go change. I have a lot of digging to do!" She disappeared into the bedroom.

Will looked at Maggie. "I'm sorry. That won't happen again."

"It's not safe, Will. I don't know what you do, but you never talk about it, which probably means that you shouldn't talk to Ruby about it either. You were right when we decided to only give her a week. She ought to go."

"That's a quick change of heart. You were the one who wanted her to stay so badly."

Maggie shrugged. She finished her coffee and got up. "See you."

She left, shutting the door behind her. Will stood up and followed her outside, down the stairs, next to the shallow trench that Ruby had dug yesterday. His foot nudged something; he looked down and saw two dead rats lying next to each other on the lowest step. God, was Ruby still trying to murder things around the house? Maybe she hadn't spent the whole night in the washroom after all. He looked up. Maggie was a house away now.

"Mags," he called.

She turned around as if waiting for his lecture.

He caught up to her. "Listen. I don't know what this Felix fellow wants with you, but I can tell you whatever it is, it isn't real. None of it is. The dresses, the shoes, the jewelry. And the attention. I know people like him. They'll use the people around them and spit them out. This isn't real love."

"Who said it was love?" But Maggie's defensiveness itself was an indication that he'd poured vinegar into a fresh wound.

"I'm just saying. Be careful. And don't meet him again. Not without me."

Maggie shrank a little. Just like she used to when Will spoke with authority, like the only parent she'd ever had. Even when their mother was alive, she'd hardly parented Maggie. She'd treated her more like a little friend, and only when her father wasn't around absorbing all their mother's affection. Their mother had never been one to dole out lessons on how brutally hard true life really was.

Maggie seemed to shrug off her milquetoast skin and lifted her chin again.

"You know I love you, Will. I always will. But you're not my father." She turned and left.

Will knew what his job was today. He was already thinking of some large factories that had emptied out because of the war, farther uptown and closer to Columbia, that might suit the MED's needs. The air compressor search could happen later.

But first, he had a visit to make. The subway today was agonizingly slow, and his lack of good sleep was already showing. His head ached, and he fell asleep with his head leaning against the subway car's window. The chugging movement with every acceleration and deceleration made him queasy.

By the time he got off at the Sixty-Eighth Street station, he felt like vomiting. But the cool air revived him as he walked to Fifth Avenue. He knocked on the front door of the Cross residence, noting the disgusting display of wealth on the carved statuettes outside the front door. The entire building likely belonged to the one family and was big enough to house half a dozen families.

A maid in a black uniform answered.

"I'm here to see Mr. Cross," Will said, towering over her.

"My, but you're a wall of muscle. Mr. Cross is waiting for you."

"He's—what?"

The maid pointed past him to the sidewalk. A polished Rolls-Royce Phantom III was idling, and the driver stepped out to open the rear door. He touched his hat and motioned that Will was to step inside. Vaguely, Will saw a thin hand holding a cigarette in the darkness of the back seat.

He didn't have to get any closer to know that he already despised Felix Cross. No matter that he was on death's door a few days ago. The fact that he was constantly throwing Will off balance from afar was enough to stoke his fury.

"Thanks," Will said to the maid as he stepped away from the door.

"I was only obeying orders," she said.

"I'm sorry, what?" He turned back to her. "Did you say something?"

She went tight lipped, and though she never broke eye contact, the closing of the massive front door did the job.

The car was not the same one that had dropped off Maggie last night. Its engine purred more quietly than any engine that rolled by in Gravesend. Even before ducking inside the back seat, Will smelled the essence of fine tobacco and beeswax. And another thing—lilac perfume. It smelled of Maggie.

He had one foot in the car and one foot on the pavement when he froze.

A man who must be Felix Cross was waiting for him. But there was a woman next to him.

Mrs. Rivers.

Trying not to show his shock, Will smoothly slid in beside her. The car was large enough to sit all three, even considering Will's size.

He didn't know what to say. Mrs. Rivers didn't either. Theirs was the kind of work that meant ignoring each other's existence in the normal world. When the car had pulled away from the curb, Will broke the silence. "I suppose introductions are in order."

"I suppose so," the man said. "Felix Cross. I believe you were asking about me in the hospital recently." He didn't offer his hand to shake. Will would have refused anyway, but he was irritated that he wasn't given the option to refuse.

"I was," Will said. "I assume you already know who I am."

"William Scripps. Half brother to Margaret Scripps, who is a recent acquaintance," Felix said with an oily smile.

"I'd call you more than acquaintances," Will said. "You've been throwing clothes and jewelry at her."

Felix lit a cigarette. "And I assume you know Mrs. Rivers." He held out his silver cigarette case to each of them.

"I don't really want to speak to either of you right now, so please do drop me off at 270 Broadway," Mrs. Rivers said, looking straight ahead. Her hands grasped her purse tightly, as if she were trying to strangle the strap. Will had never seen her so discombobulated.

"Of course, my dear," Felix said.

Mrs. Rivers's voice could cut steel: "Do not call me dear. That's highly inappropriate." In another time and place, Will imagined she would have slapped him.

"Yes. Of course." Felix looked absolutely tickled by her irritation.

"And how do you two know each other?" Will said.

"Ah." Felix smiled. "We all have the same goal here. To win the war. Is that not correct?"

Will and Mrs. Rivers were silent.

"And I believe I know how we could get by. To win, we must make a machine. And that machine has cogs. We believe you have access to one of the most important cogs, Mr. Scripps."

Will wasn't sure what Felix Cross was talking about, exactly. Or rather, he was worried that Cross was just trying to get the two of them to reveal more than was appropriate.

The car drove by Central Park South, where vendors of hot corn and roasted chestnut called out to people.

"Look at you two," Felix chortled. "Butter wouldn't melt in your mouths! Oh, come now. My driver is deaf except to the sound of honking horns before an imminent crash. Let's talk plainly."

"About what?" Will said.

"You do a good job of looking like a meat-headed Columbia football player recruited to crush Princeton quarterbacks like little balls of foil. But no, the ruse is up. I know all about you. I heard about how your classmates treated you like a janitor. Left a toilet plunger at your lab seat in chemistry class every week. You barely acknowledged it and received the top grade in your Contemporary Civilizations class."

Will's expression didn't change. The truth was, they'd done worse. Big boys, with big mouths, and too much money. Some were perfectly nice, of course. Like the ones who apologized about the plunger and put it away half the time, yelling at the others to leave him alone. Some of them, he wanted to tear to pieces. Once he overheard a few in his literature class smoking outside Hamilton Hall, bragging about a conquest. There had been a drunken woman at an Upper West Side party, and they'd each raped her. They'd just laughed about it, like it was nothing more than sporting entertainment. He'd informed the dean, and then the police. They didn't even get a slap on the wrists.

Felix yawned rudely, before continuing. "I know you're an intelligent fellow, so please stop demurring."

Mrs. Rivers gave Will a warning glance. One of her hands slid to her thigh, her red nails indenting the gray fabric of her dress.

"Very well, I'll start," Felix said. "I believe it was Niels Bohr who heard the news about Otto Hahn in Berlin. Hahn had split an atom by bombarding it with neutrons, had he not?"

"Fermi did it first," Will said, too stubborn to stay quiet.

"Ah, yes. You worked with Enrico Fermi at Columbia."

"Not really. I ran some errands for him," Will said warily, although he hated to downplay his experience in front of Mrs. Rivers. He'd been far more than an errand boy. There were days when Fermi would emerge from behind a cloud of sulfuric acid fumes asking Will to fetch him a piece of equipment. Will was the one who joked that Fermi was in his "London Fog."

Felix waved his hand. "Oh, you may have lugged materials into the basement of Pupin Hall. But that was where the first nuclear fission happened on American soil."

Will tried not to panic. He knew about the cyclotron? About the nuclear piles? How? The details of these were being squashed by censorship. Who was telling him? Mrs. Rivers?

Mrs. Rivers leaned toward Felix. Until this moment, she'd been immutable, like stone. But now a flicker of alarm showed in her face. "Now, Felix, this isn't good conversational material. Let's talk about something else. You know Gene Kelly and Judy Garland just released a movie? *For Me and My Gal.* That will be lovely."

"Why bother?" Felix shook his head. "There is a far more interesting twenty-yard dash happening right now between the greatest countries of the world. Wouldn't you say, William?" He laughed. "When a neutron hits uranium-235 and it undergoes fission—" He winked at Mrs. Rivers here. "Fission is quite a word, isn't it? So biological. Like fornication!"

Mrs. Rivers looked like she was suppressing a scream. If Will could have reached him, he'd have smacked Felix himself.

"When the atom undergoes nuclear fission, more neutrons are emitted, causing fission in more uranium atoms, and a chain reaction occurs. Enormous amounts of energy. A weapon that the world has never seen before. A force like God himself."

"Or the devil," Will said.

"Oh! You have a sense of humor!" Felix said, clapping like a child.

Not a sense of humor. None of this was clap-worthy or happy making. Both Mrs. Rivers and Will knew this. As did Felix. He was trying to get a rise out of them. Why, Will wasn't sure.

"And now you just need enough uranium-235 to make a few kilos' worth to keep that chain reaction going, enough to fell a city. Or a leader, at least. But there's so little 235 in those tons of refined uranium ores you're going to store in the Baker and Williams warehouse that you and all your smart little men can't figure out how to extract enough to make a bomb." He tsked at both of them.

Will could stand it no longer. "What do you want, Felix?"

"I want to drop off Mrs. Rivers at her place of work. And look, here we are! Two hundred seventy Broadway. I'll see you soon, my dear."

Mrs. Rivers inhaled deeply, her nostrils flaring, as if she smelled horse manure.

"If you call me dear one more time, I'll have you castrated," she said calmly. "With a rusty knife."

Felix half smiled, half frowned, as if he was unsure her words were completely in jest.

The Rolls-Royce stopped at the curb in front of the Arthur Levitt building. Pedestrians walked by, a few gawking at the fancy automobile in their midst. The driver opened the door on Felix's side, and he exited to give Mrs. Rivers room to leave.

She gave Will one glance of warning, and whispered, "We'll talk. You have some explaining to do."

"As do you," Will whispered back, his face nearly as livid as hers.

She slid out the door and walked calmly to the building. Even in her simple clothes and brown pumps, men's heads turned her way. After only a few steps, she turned, as if remembering something.

"Will."

"Yes?"

"Are you feeling all right?"

What an odd question. Especially since he wasn't, today. Nothing awful, but just a little off. But the question was a non sequitur. Did he look that bad?

"I'm fine," he lied.

She nodded, turned on her heel, and strode inside.

"Come," Felix said, ducking his head into the car. "Walk with me."

Will had had enough. "I can't. Got to go to work."

"This *is* work. You'll see. The air is fresh, and I'm headed just down the street to the Woolworth Building." Felix paused for effect. He knew Will would respond to the destination.

"The Woolworth Building," Will repeated. He exited the car, and Felix curled a finger toward him, enticing him to walk the few blocks southward.

"The whole eleventh floor is taken over by Kellex, but you knew that."

Kellex. The chemical engineering company that was working closely with New York–area engineers on the Manhattan Project. He'd done a job for Kellex, thanks to Mrs. Rivers, only a month ago.

"There's a weekly meeting there," Felix went on, "with the people from the MED, General Groves, and the physicists at Columbia. And your special friends, Mr. and Mrs. Rivers. I could get you an invitation, if you'd like."

Will found himself walking alongside Felix Cross, hating himself for being there, and unable to know what Felix was going to say next. It was usually Will who was ready to surprise Maggie, or Mrs. Rivers, or his professors. His professors were weary of saying things like "Yes, Mr. Scripps, gamma radiation has theoretical practical applications, but the rest of the class needs to learn the basics of what it *is*, first." He was always the one who upended the conversation, tilted the world, reversed gravity. Even when he quit Columbia, his advisor and Fermi himself had begged him—a mere sophomore—to reconsider.

The sun was bright that day. Felix squinted into the sun, but Will did not. He could feel his pupils constrict to pinpoints, a pinching sensation within his eyes that was uncomfortable. But he would not shield himself when so close to a man like Cross, the type who took joy in bringing down intrepid men.

"I'll tell you what I'd like," Will said. "I'd like for you to leave my sister alone."

"Is she only to have room for one man in her life? That's very selfish of you."

"I didn't say that," Will said.

"Just because I give her some fine dresses, pretty baubles, and attention doesn't mean that I'm out to ruin her. Maggie is special. And she deserves to be treated as such. You have her running off and working in a shipyard. A gentle, shy little woman like that, in a shipyard of all places! Welding metal!"

Will bit his tongue. He had a dozen barbs to throw at Felix, but what he said was true. Will couldn't provide the satin-lined lifestyle that Maggie might desire, or even the warm affection that he had never really been capable of with anyone. She did deserve better than what he was able to give her.

He looked west, and stared at the pyramid top of the US courthouse nearby. Usually covered in gold, it had been painted a sobering black, so as not to reflect moonlight for passing U-boats to see. Maggie would have approved.

"You came to seek me out," Felix said. "Is that what you came to tell me? To leave your sister be?"

Will turned to him. He wasn't sure. He'd come out of anger. Perhaps he was hoping that his sheer presence would be enough to intimidate Felix into staying away from Maggie. But he knew there had been another reason. He realized that Felix was acting as if Will had something precious, and Felix wanted it back. As if Will were in a position of power.

And then Will realized: Ruby.

He had Ruby. No matter how tenuous their affair was, it was theirs, and Felix had lost that place in her world.

Ah. Felix Cross still needed Ruby to get to her father, and to do that, he now needed Will too.

Change the footing. Tilt the wheel. Keep them off balance.

Will said slowly, "You're right. Maggie is a grown woman who deserves better. Maggie is all yours. You're welcome to have each other. You've my blessing." He glanced very slightly in Cross's direction, and saw the tiniest drop of the corners of his mouth.

There. Now he knew. Felix didn't want Maggie. He just wanted the upper hand.

"As for Ruby, I've no power over her. Nor does Maggie. I wouldn't be surprised if she disappeared, even today. I just thought you should know. I don't think she cares for me, or for Maggie, in any profound way."

That was only somewhat true. He didn't actually know the contents of Ruby's heart. But lately, he felt as if he held less sway in that sphere. He felt Ruby slipping away from him as rapidly as she had slipped into his being.

You win some, you lose some. Though the losing part felt rather rotten, now that he truly considered it.

"I think your assessment is worth less than an enormous load of horse dung." Felix crossed his arms. "I wondered why she picked you two. Neither of you seem particularly useful, in the grand scheme of things."

Will bristled. He was used to hearing things like this from the likes of people like Felix, but it still irked him.

"In truth, though, you're both quite valuable, and even I have underestimated your worth."

They were now in front of the Woolworth Building, on Park Place and Broadway. The green-hued copper crown and the terra cotta and limestone facade always struck Will as beautiful. The observatory was off limits, he knew. It was too close to the Brooklyn Navy Yard, and they didn't need anyone up there with binoculars, gathering information.

Will would have liked to go up to the eleventh floor and listen in on the conversations that the Kellex company had about the project.

But there were other ways to get there, and he was already working on it. The last thing he wanted was to be beholden to a person like Felix.

Will looked up. "Nice building. It was the highest building in the world, until 1930. There's always something bigger and better coming along. Keeps you grounded, doesn't it?" He shoved his hands into his coat pockets. "Well, good luck, Cross," he said, and walked away.

He could feel Felix's eyes on his back, boring into him, wishing that bullets could do the same.

"William!" he called out.

Will's foot touched the curb. He turned around, making sure he had the same bland expression on his face as always. The kind that could be read as stupidity, or anger, or concentration, or fury. You never knew.

"What?" Will said.

Felix marched up to him so he could keep his voice low. "Ruby will ruin you, and ruin this country. I know this."

Will shrugged. Everyone was capable of being accused of being a spy. What else was new?

"Maggie knows this, but I'm telling you now," Felix said. "Ruby is targeting you and Maggie because of what you do. To get more information. Nowhere else in this city can a person glean so much detail about the making of bombs and the sinking of American ships."

"The quicker she leaves us, the better, then. Anyway, you seem to know plenty about how the world works with regard to this war, and yet she left you," Will said. "And you seem pretty cozy with Mrs. Rivers."

"Hannah Rivers. Yes. She's a friend. We've known each other for years. Our families are quite close."

"And you work with her?"

"Work? Oh no. I just guess about what she does. It's quite delicious, watching her squirm." He clapped. "But she knows I have access to something she wants. And I haven't budged."

"You mean Ruby. Ruby is the 'something' that Rivers wants."

Felix scrunched his nose and looked up at the sky. "Mmm. Not quite." He seemed to balance on his heels, wondering if he should show the card he held to his chest. "Her father, actually."

Will shrugged. "Her father is a banker."

"Not just a banker. He just bought a company that Groves is quite interested in. And Mr. Fielding is not committed to working with him yet."

"Why not?"

"Because Ruby is still technically missing." Felix's face lost the jovial, mischievous expression he'd held from the moment Will had gotten into his Rolls-Royce. "Ernest Fielding is considering turning over this company to Groves. A vanadium mine."

Vanadium. It tended to live with deposits of uranium ore, but Will didn't know there were any mines on American soil. Apparently, Felix and Mr. Fielding did.

Felix went on. "I can tell by that Neanderthal look you're giving me that you know why vanadium is synonymous with uranium. See? I'm getting better at reading that stony face of yours! Mr. Fielding can choose to hand over his company to Groves for the vast quantities of uranium he needs. But he can choose not to. And his worry over his daughter has brought everything to a standstill. If she were to tell him she was fine, and to go ahead with the deal, all would be well. His decision could push the MED work forward, or set it back."

"So Ruby could show up out of the blue, say, and tell him not to work with Groves. And Fielding would listen to her."

"In theory, yes."

"Surely, there are other mines," Will said.

"Yes, but this is by far the largest one. Without it, the supply of uranium will be bottlenecked. The whole project would be at a standstill."

Will tried not to show his surprise, but Felix's words chilled him. All Will was ever thinking about was the next step. He knew the MED had a current supply of uranium ore—it was what he'd been moving onto barges, and arranging storage for after it was refined. So the scientists could then enrich the scant amount of fissile uranium-235.

But he'd never realized that moving forward, that supply wouldn't be enough. He'd been looking ahead in the process of making a bomb, not backward to basic source supplies.

"Every day, every week counts in this war. Every step along the way. As I understand it, they need five kilos of the 25. Maybe twelve. Enough for a chain reaction, and enough to destroy a city. If we fall back in the supply stage by mere months or weeks, then someone else moves forward faster. And we've lost."

"You care that much about losing?" Will asked.

"I'm in the business of coming out on the right side, for the sake of keeping the Cross fortune afloat. We all must do what we need to survive and succeed in the world, do we not? And if it makes me more comfortable in the process, even better."

Will stared at Felix, who seemed irritated that he had been forced to make such an admission. The one thing Will knew about the wealthy was they didn't like to actually speak of wealth itself—it was vulgar. But it was clear that Felix liked money more than his country, and he was betting on his own country to win simply because it was the faster thoroughbred in the race. Disgusting.

"What do you want from me, Cross?" Will asked. "And tell me straight. I have no problems knocking out a gentleman in the middle of the day, right here in front of this fine building."

"I need you to bring me Ruby," Felix said.

Will laughed, a rarity for him. "Go get her yourself."

"I can't. She'll bolt. I'm shocked she didn't when I dropped off Maggie last night."

"What do you want me to do?"

"Bring her somewhere I can get her. No police. Something tells me you wouldn't want the extra attention anyway. Let me handle her.

I'll take her home to her parents, and if she wants to leave after that, she can."

"Fine. I'll take her to her parents right now."

"You know that won't work. She'll run. But you're right. I'll bring her parents straightaway so she knows they're involved."

Will wasn't sure. "Then it's best her parents are there, and not you."

"Perhaps. But I want the satisfaction of seeing her face. Of letting her know she didn't hurt me as much as she thought. If you do this, William, I'll put in a good word for you with Mr. Rivers. You know he has a direct line to General Groves. Think of the war. Think of your career."

Will wanted to roll his eyes. He was always thinking about his career. But sourcing the uranium was important. It was bigger than Ruby, bigger than Will. He'd spent sleepless nights imagining what would happen if the Axis powers won. But most importantly, he thought of Maggie. He'd been failing her of late as her only family left in the world. It was time to remedy that failure.

"All right, fine. And Maggie?" Will said.

Felix swelled his breath. "If you do this, then I'll leave Maggie alone. She'll never hear from me again, and the doors to my home will be shut to her. And she'll go back to her small ways, in her small world."

He had a way of twisting an insult into a favor. "Very well," Will said. "I'll find a way." He stepped off the curb and began crossing the street.

"When?" Felix yelled. "Where?"

"Two days," Will shouted, and traversed the road. He didn't need to dodge the cars or buses; they simply stopped for him.

It was done. Ruby would be brought back to her family, and Maggie would be brought back to hers. They had promised Ruby time to recover, and the time had run out.

It was a perfect scheme.

Except that Will felt as if he'd just shaken hands with the devil, and he had a strange premonition that something precious would be lost forever in the transaction. Perhaps Ruby's love, perhaps Maggie's. But to Will, it felt like he was somehow forfeiting his whole life.

It was still worth it.

CHAPTER 20

Maggie hadn't gotten far after she left for work that morning. She'd departed in a hurry, but when she arrived at the subway station, she paused.

Her vision was blurry with tears as she found a bench on Avenue U and pulled out paper and a pencil from her purse. Curious passersby looked at her in her coarse clothing, kerchief, and reddened eyes as she feverishly wrote.

> *Mama.*
>
> *What should I do? Felix Cross promises me the world, and he has only known me a short while. But I know his loneliness. I have it too. He would treat me well, I know it. I wouldn't be like Ruby Fielding. I would take care of him, and nurture his wounded heart, and we could be merry most of our days. I don't feel romantic towards him, but other things are more important. That's a good plan, don't you think?*
>
> *I know I should do my duty. I know I should keep working at the Navy Yard, and be a good sister to Will. But I want more. Ruby has warmed to me. And yet she loves Will too. Don't be angry. It's nothing, really. But*

surely Providence must have a hand in why love just happens in the most inconvenient ways sometimes. God is testing me.

Ruby has more power in how this battle plays out. Not just in the walls of our house, but across oceans. I think you know what I mean.

In my heart, I know what the right thing is. I only need the strength to do it.

Maggie signed the letter, sealed it, and carefully tore and affixed the stamp. She stuffed it into the mailbox attached to the light pole nearby. She sighed. Writing the letters always exhausted her. What her mother actually thought of her, looking down from heaven—if such a place existed—was a mystery to her. Ruby was a mystery too. Perhaps everything she was doing was an exercise in futility.

As she made her way to the subway entrance, something caught her eye. She turned around and could have sworn that a person ducked behind a newspaper stand. Maggie waited and watched to see if the person peeped their head out. But nothing happened.

She needed to go to work. Missing two days this week was entirely too much. Three would mean she would be fired. She thought about the importance of her job, and how it thrilled her to make progress in her welding. How important she was in the war effort. And then she thought of Ruby, and how much Ruby mattered.

Like an irresistible itch she had to claw at, she found herself turning away from the subway station and going back home. It would mean the end of her job, but she could beg to have it back. Surely her skills already proved she was worth it.

She would go home and spend time with Ruby, what little they had left. How had Ruby fared with her digging? She wanted to wrap her arms around her. She wanted forgiveness for seeing Felix, and to be told that she, too, deserved affection. When she turned the corner and went to the back of the house, there was the plot of freshly dug earth, a little deeper in one corner. The row of plants had been freshly watered—Ruby seemed to care for her plants like people cared for babies. There was a scorched patch of earth where Ruby had burned something. She saw a tin in the ashes and gently kicked it with her steel-toed boot. Maggie pried the top off, but inside, there was nothing but more sooty, granular ash.

The spade was stabbed into the center of the dirt, as if the digger had gone inside for a quick drink of water. Maggie looked up at the house and down the back alley. At the far end, someone was about to turn the corner. Someone in a familiar brown dress, coat, and heels.

Ruby.

Where was she going?

Maggie wished she hadn't sent her letter—there would be more to write today. It was a waste of a stamp. She ran down the alley, so as not to lose sight of Ruby, who walked very fast, wearing the fancy pink heels that Maggie had just removed last night. It was an odd combination, those pink sling-back wedge pumps and the plain brown dress. Somehow, on Ruby, the combination fit. No matter how plain she tried to be, there was something about Ruby that always stood out.

She followed Ruby all the way to the subway stop, careful to keep her head down. At a newspaper stand in the station, she purchased a newspaper. The salesman, an old gentleman with a ratty, patched hat, handed back her change.

"I'll give you a quarter for your hat," she said quietly.

The salesman raised his bushy white eyebrows, blinked twice, and handed over his hat. It smelled like a sweaty armpit and was probably only worth half a penny. But it would do. She plunked it over her kerchief-covered hair—a dead giveaway that she was a woman despite her manly work clothes.

Ruby took the subway over to Manhattan. Maggie's heart pounded the closer they got to the Sixty-Eighth Street station. This was where they'd have to get off to go to Felix's home. But Ruby didn't get off. She kept going until Eighty-Sixth Street. Maggie followed her out of the station and into the bright sunlight. Ruby headed east to Eighty-Seventh Street and First Avenue, deep into the heart of Yorkville.

As soon as Maggie realized where they were, she froze. Will had always told her to stay away from Yorkville, especially while the war was going on. It was a German enclave, full of people whose relatives had immigrated years ago, as well as those who had recently fled Germany. But she remembered Will telling her that a pro-Nazi group met here regularly. Its leader, Fritz Julius Kuhn, had been in Sing-Sing since 1939 after embezzling money for his mistress. And then there was the Duquesne Spy Ring. Herman Lang would meet spies in Yorkville at the Little Casino Restaurant.

But German New Yorkers were enthusiastic about showing their American loyalty. "Our country, first, last, and all the time" was a slogan one of the German societies had pledged, and there were plenty of signs in the windows for upcoming war bond rallies and blood drives. War gardens, with their dying fall vegetation, were present in countless patches of yards, abutting the sidewalks in every space. But still. You never knew who was in cahoots with whom.

But Maggie had to know. She trotted to make up for the lost distance while she battled with herself. And then, on Eighty-Seventh Street, Ruby stepped into Glaser's Bake Shop.

Maggie hung back. She couldn't help but salivate at the buttery pastries and cakes in the window. They were expensive nowadays. She hid around the corner, checking once in a while to see if Ruby had left. She wished she could go inside but worried about being seen. Maggie opened up her newspaper and leaned against the brick wall, pretending to read, as if she were waiting for a friend. She watched who entered, kept her hat low, and glanced inside once in a while, where she could see Ruby in line to buy a pastry.

Why on earth did she come all the way up here just to buy dessert? It was so odd.

It reminded Maggie of herself, actually, and Will. About how willing they were to upend their lives for a woman. To risk what was truly dear to them. Maggie snapped her newspaper crisply, which had been sagging from neglect. She needed to pay attention. Just as she was dipping her head back between the pages, a woman passed by and swept into the shop, the bell on the door ringing merrily. Maggie looked up.

It was Holly.

Maggie stifled an utterance of surprise. What was Holly doing here? Shouldn't she be at work? Maggie nearly laughed. Maggie needed to be at work too. Her heart pounded hard and fast. Was she being followed? But when she turned slightly to the window, she saw that Holly hadn't seemed to notice the grubby little man reading the newspaper outside the shop.

What she did do was make a beeline for Ruby.

Maggie's blood pounded so hard that she heard a swishing sound in her ears. She felt faint. Ruby and Holly were standing right next to each other, but they hardly seemed to acknowledge each other's presence. And yet, it was clear they were together. The cashier packaged up the pastries into a little box tied with red and white string, and Holly and Ruby headed for the door. They exited and turned the corner.

Maggie carefully folded her paper, and inched past the door and planted herself against the wall, careful not to block patrons from entering or exiting the shop. She cautiously peeped around the corner. Ruby and Holly were leaning against the wall, the box of treats open in Holly's hands. Ruby picked one out.

"Good God, I miss sugar," she said.

"Me too. There's none to be found at the Navy Yard."

"Shh. We shouldn't."

There were sounds of chewing. They started talking again, but quietly. Maggie inched closer. She heard Holly speak.

"Weiß er, wo du bist?"

"Ja," Ruby said.

"Wirst du wieder weglaufen?"

Ruby paused, then: "Ich denke ich muss bald gehen. Aber ich mag die Leute, mit denen ich zusammen bin." Then another pause. "Aber ich vertraue dem Mann nicht. Er ist jetzt so kalt."

"And the girl?" Holly said. She seemed to have forgotten they were speaking in German.

"So sweet!" Ruby said. "But she's growing colder. I don't know what to do. I don't know where to go, or how to finish this."

"You have to get out."

"I can't. Not yet."

Their conversation devolved into more German, but this time, it sounded far less friendly. Holly's voice rose, and Ruby started to respond with "Nein!" repeated in a staccato of anger.

"You know about the letters?" Holly said, her voice so loud now that it was clear Holly had lost her patience.

Maggie's skin erupted in gooseflesh. Letters? What letters? Could Holly mean hers? Before Holly or Ruby could say more, a group of people approached, their shoes clacking on the pavement. Happy chatter grew louder. Knowing they would be a distraction, Maggie peered around the corner. Holly and Ruby looked at each other, concern marring their faces. The group paused near the girls. It looked like they were waiting for more people to join them. Holly closed the box of pastries.

"Don't be angry with me."

Ruby said nothing, only looked at the ground.

Holly wrapped her arms around Ruby. "I love you. So much. When will I see you again?"

Ruby pushed her away, wiped a tear from her face. She shook her head.

"You're scaring me. What are you planning, Ruby? Ich werde dich beobachten, wenn ich muss."

"Don't," Ruby said, and she walked away. Holly, too, walked away in the opposite direction, but clearly wasn't upset enough to neglect eating the leftover pastries one by one as she crossed the street.

What on earth had they been speaking about? How did they know each other? Holly had always seemed so different from Ruby. The two never fully occupied the same space in Maggie's mind. Ruby, elegant, rich, and sheltered. Holly, the girl who wanted to fly airplanes, never wore a stitch of makeup, and took no issue with gobbling up Maggie's leftover sandwiches like a hungry puppy. Were they lovers? Ruby had certainly shown her penchant for people quite unlike herself, like Will and Maggie, who were as different as night and day.

Maggie scurried back to the subway, hoping not to run into Holly. Tonight, she should tell Will everything she had seen. He'd be disappointed that she missed half a day of work. Actually, he'd be more than disappointed. She couldn't do that to him. She was so sick and tired of Will living the consequences of her failures.

She wouldn't tell him. Maybe just wait a day or so. Surely that wouldn't matter. And anyway, her conscience would be sated by writing another letter. Yes, that was what she would do.

She was back at the Navy Yard by late morning. Her instructor gave her a long lecture on what a privilege it was to be serving her country, and warned her not to miss any more days.

"You're going to be a stellar welder, Scripps, if you just stay the course."

"Yes, sir."

"So I can count on you to be here first thing tomorrow morning?"

"Yes," Maggie lied.

Holly never showed up.

CHAPTER 21

Will was exhausted.

After an afternoon of scouring manufacturing sites on the Upper East Side, he was spent. His exhaustion seemed to trickle into every sinew of his body. Even his skin ached.

The nausea he'd been feeling before only grew worse after his decision to turn Ruby over to Felix Cross. It served him right. Will had never been terribly demonstrative, and now even his emotions and guilt refused to manifest with tears or anxiety—instead, he had belly cramps and his stomach seemed to rebel against the very idea of food.

When he arrived home that night, it appeared that Ruby had dug another several inches deep in the footprint of the backyard bomb shelter. Soon, they'd be able to put in the corrugated metal siding and start putting a roof on the top. He eyed a pile of ashes next to the hole. Why had she been burning things? He vaguely remembered a little woodpile there yesterday, but he hadn't asked. People burned leaves now and again. But with Ruby, he ought to have been more observant.

Ruby was in the kitchen. A meatloaf, speckled with burned spots, rested on a plate with boiled potatoes. The table was set for three.

At the sound of his entrance, she turned abruptly from the sink, where she was washing dishes. Her face looked almost ashen with surprise.

"I made dinner," she said hurriedly.

"You did," Will said. He sniffed the air. A burnt smell seemed to linger. "Is that . . ."

"Yes. I burned it. Well, the outside scorched, but the inside was still raw, so I had to cut off the black parts and then keep cooking it at a lower temperature. I found the recipe in a cookbook on the shelf, but I messed up anyway."

"That's all right." Will's stomach lurched again. How could he even look her in the eye, after what he had agreed to? "Excuse me," he said, and bolted to the washroom. He retched and vomited bile into the toilet. He hadn't eaten anything since breakfast.

There was a knock on the door. "Are you okay?" Ruby called.

"Fine."

He washed his sweaty face and calmed himself. Maggie came home shortly thereafter. She looked tired, and sad. She looked like Will felt.

"Say, maybe we can eat at a restaurant, instead of at home," Will suggested.

Ruby laughed lightly. "I understand. It doesn't smell good, and I'm a terrible cook."

"It's a waste of money," Maggie said quietly and plunked down in a kitchen chair. He wanted to tell her not to eat the food, that it was a risk given Ruby's odd hobby of growing toxic plants in the yard. But Maggie seemed bent on eating. Ruby cut herself a slice and made faces every time she took a bite, but it was impressive that she tried. Will hardly ate anything, just stuck to water and ice tea. Later, he ate a handful of crackers from an unopened box and felt better.

That evening, Ruby once again did not seek out Will's sofa. Will didn't have the heart or focus to attend his classes at Brooklyn College. Like all good things in his life, school would have to be put on hold or stopped permanently. But he felt heartened that changes were coming that would be better for Maggie. Things must be done for her sake. If he could thank Felix for one positive that had come of their meeting today, it was the reminder that he had a duty to care for his little sister. No matter what.

The next morning, the kitchen and washroom were empty. Someone had been up, though, as there was hot coffee in the percolator. The bedroom door was shut, and he put his ear to the door and heard Ruby speaking in a low voice to Maggie. It sounded sweet and tender, and Will had to stop himself from bursting in to put a stop to the lovey-dovey talk.

As he was pouring coffee, the bedroom door opened and the two girls emerged in their nightgowns, looking sated and sleepy, as if they'd dined on cake, wine, and each other, all night long.

"Time to go to work," Will said, and he left the house without another word. But he waited across the street from the trolley stop, inside a store that sold cigarettes and candy, and pretended to glance over the day's papers. When he saw Maggie board the trolley for the Navy Yard, he went back home.

Ruby was already in the backyard, wearing a pair of old pants belonging to Maggie. She was knee deep in the rectangular trench and holding the spade. When she saw Will, her eyes lit up.

"Will! Why are you back so soon?"

"I thought you might like to come to work with me."

"Really?" Ruby thrust the spade into the ground with a good amount of force. It surprised him. He didn't think her capable of any labor, let alone handling a shovel. "I'd love to. There's nobody to talk to but myself, and I might go batty if that happens for much longer." She smiled. "I'll get dressed in something more appropriate."

He felt a little parched, so he went into the kitchen for a drink of water. Pulling a clean glass from the cupboard, he remembered something. Ducking beneath the kitchen sink, he searched for the brown bottle of poisonous zinc chloride that Maggie had stashed when she'd found it in Ruby's pocket shortly after her arrival. Pushing aside tins of shoe polish and floor wax, he saw it. He grabbed it and unscrewed the top.

Empty.

Will stood up and went to the backyard, looking at the new plants dotting the landscape around the freshly dug soil. He remembered what Ruby had said.

Rhododendron.

Hydrangea.

White hellebore.

Monkshood.

All poisonous. And yet she had said, *I would never hurt you, Will. Or Maggie. But I have to protect myself.*

"Ready?" Ruby was standing in the doorway. She'd borrowed some of Maggie's clothes—a brown plaid skirt and cardigan. Her shoes were the bright-blue ones from her own closet that Maggie had worn home the first time she'd gone to Felix's house.

Will nodded. "Let's go."

They headed to catch the subway this time. Their destination was the Northside section of Brooklyn, one mile east of the East River.

"Where are we going?"

"To find a good air compressor."

"Why?"

"You don't need to know. But I'd appreciate the company," Will said. He was still so tired from yesterday and didn't have the energy to lie. When they exited the subway at Metropolitan Avenue and began walking north on Union Avenue, she wound her arm in his, and he lacked the fortitude to push her away.

They were here. The Beach-Russ Company, located within a flat redbrick building. He approached the clerk at the front desk.

"I need to speak to your manager."

"Do you have an appointment?" she asked.

"No. But it's important. And confidential." He said nothing else. Luckily, it was enough. She stood and went into a back area, then waved him in. Dropping in unannounced wasn't one of his favorite things to do, but usually once people saw that Will was serious, well spoken, and knowledgeable, they pushed aside their wariness to talk.

He left Ruby waiting with the secretary. By the time two hours had passed, Will was back with the answers he needed. The company was able to make compressors that would meet the standards that the MED and the physicists at Columbia needed. They only needed to test some first, and Will had arranged for a delivery to Pupin Hall tomorrow. If all went well, a large order would go in by the end of the year once they had secured a place to do the gaseous uranium enrichment.

When he returned to the lobby, Ruby had fallen asleep. Her head was leaning against the wall, her arms crossed, legs crossed, and lips closed. She looked so angelic and so at peace that even the secretary put a finger to her lips and smiled when Will appeared. As if she wanted to babysit Ruby for just another few precious minutes.

He tapped Ruby's shoulder, and she blinked languidly up at him.

"Done?" she asked before yawning like a drowsy kitten.

"Yes, done. For the day, actually. I've some more appointments, but they aren't until later next week."

Truth was, he wanted to hear from Mrs. Rivers about whether his job of seeking and finding equipment and warehouses was over, so he could work directly with the physicists. But even thinking of that prospect seemed to exhaust him.

"Oh, good. Then I have you all to myself." She stood up and stretched like a cat, then leaned hard on his shoulder as they walked out. "What shall we do? Dig more of the shelter?"

"No. Let's go to the water. I've felt landlocked lately."

"The beach? We could go to Coney Island!"

"That sounds great. But . . ." His mind whirled. Coney Island would be a perfect excuse to get her away later, to meet Felix. "Not right now. Maybe another time when we could go with Maggie. Maybe even tonight."

Will's mind turned. Yes, tonight would be best. Like a wound that needed cauterizing, it was best to do this quickly, painful as it might be.

"Tonight! That would be lovely. How about we just walk near the East River right now?"

He nodded. They strolled down Union Avenue, over to Havemeyer Street, and zigzagged their way toward the Williamsburg Bridge, which loomed ahead with its angular steel towers and rows of suspension cables.

"That was the longest suspension bridge, until 1923," Ruby said, still hugging Will's arm. "A few men died making that bridge."

"Men die all the time, building great things," Will remarked. "Around twenty men perished while building the Brooklyn Bridge. One of the designers got a foot crushed against a piling and died of tetanus. Others died of caisson disease, falling debris . . ." He trailed off. Why was death always on his mind when he was around Ruby?

They were quiet as they made their way around a needle factory and a shuttered distillery, through half-dying shrubbery and neglected portions of cracked sidewalk. Will was glad of their silence; walking was tiring. It was an odd feeling. The nausea he'd felt yesterday had come back with a vengeance, and he struggled to keep his mind from being diverted by queasiness.

In his heart, he suspected his illness had to do with Ruby. It was beyond obvious. But it wasn't so bad. He could handle it awhile longer. When she was gone, his symptoms would be too. He knew it, the same way he knew the sun would rise tomorrow. It was an incontrovertible fact.

Beneath the bridge itself, the area was peaceful, and dirty. Bottles were strewn here and there, as well as some pieces of clothing that looked like they'd been left ages ago, matted into nubs of dirty gray fabric embedded onto the cement.

The bridge was beautiful—all steel lines, angles, and curving cables that came together in a modern, inverted version of a classical arch.

They were alone beneath the bridge, and Will wondered if Ruby would take advantage of the privacy for intimacy's sake.

She did, turning him toward her, propping herself up on her toes to reach his face. She kissed him chastely, and instead of taking the simple kiss further, she turned around and wrapped his arms around her middle. Slowly, they sank down to the cold ground, listening to the water lapping at the edge of the concrete shore, watching a few brown finches land nearby, pecking for food.

As they sat there in silence, Ruby pulled his arms tighter around herself, as if afraid he might pull away.

"This feels like a goodbye," she whispered.

"You'll be leaving next week," Will said, maintaining the lie. Though he usually welcomed silence, he wasn't satisfied by it now. This might be the last time he got any answers from her.

"Do you love Maggie?" he asked.

Ruby nodded.

"Would you leave me to be with her?"

Again, a nod. And then, "Maggie needs me in a way that you never could. A girl likes to be needed, Will."

This time, he settled back into the silence that felt like home. Ruby had said enough for a lifetime. They sat there for another hour, neither speaking a word.

Once or twice, the silence was broken by a quick sniff from Ruby. She was crying.

He declined to ask why.

⟞⟝

Will dropped Ruby off at home. He went inside to the kitchen without comment, for a moment resting his head against the frame of the kitchen door. Everything about this house right now was a disaster.

He went to the front of the house and checked the mailbox. There was one envelope addressed to him, with no stamp or return address. Inside, a folded note.

7:00 PM, Rivers.

Will sighed. Mrs. Rivers and her husband wanted an update. Will often showed up as soon as he had one to give, but it was unusual for them to contact him this way. He knew it was about Felix Cross, and that god-awful car meeting yesterday.

Fine. Afterward, he would hand off Ruby to Cross at Coney Island. The sooner, the better, before he had time to change his mind. He checked the clock. It was eleven-thirty in the morning. He would have to tell Maggie to bring Ruby. He wouldn't say why. She didn't need to know.

Will didn't say goodbye to Ruby. As he stepped onto the sidewalk along Sixth Street, he heard the faint clangs of the shovel hitting dirt and rocks, and little grunts from Ruby as she dug. She was not quite the helpless rich lady he had found under their steps only a little while ago. She was a known entity to him, and yet . . . Ruby still managed to always leave a thin layer of the unknown between them. Like a piece of film negative that only let some of the light through.

He shook his head and steadied himself as he went to Barratta's drugstore on Avenue U to make a phone call to Felix Cross.

"Nine p.m. Tonight. Coney Island Wax Museum."

He hung up and went to catch the trolley to the Navy Yard. He might be able to find Maggie at her lunch break.

CHAPTER 22

That morning, she did her new morning ritual. Woke up (with Ruby); washed up and dressed; had a small breakfast. Waved goodbye to Ruby, digging in the backyard. Stopped by the oak tree in the front of the house to look for little creatures.

Today, there was something in the knothole that surprised her. She looked in and saw a curl of white paper. She picked it up, but there was no writing on it. Anybody passing by might think it was a corner of a newspaper that had torn off and had blown into the hole.

It's not a coincidence, Maggie thought. Today, she would change her fate.

Instead of going to the Navy Yard, she rode the subway into Manhattan, to Felix's house. Perhaps he wouldn't make her dress up, and would say hello just for a second. She thought of how Felix was so generous with the pearls. Those glowing, opalescent gems had been tucked into her dresser drawer, wrapped in a silk scarf that once belonged to her mother.

At the house on Fifth Avenue, she rang the doorbell. It already was feeling like a second home to her. She smiled. Yes, things were changing.

Fiona answered. She did not seem pleased at all.

"You're not expected," she said. She seemed irritated, or frightened. It wasn't clear.

"I was in the neighborhood and wanted to say hello to Felix. I mean, Mr. Cross."

"He's busy, unfortunately, and stated that he would not be taking visitors today."

Maggie frowned. "Is it because I'm not wearing the right clothes? That never was a problem before." She added, "Please! I have something important to tell him. About Ruby Fielding. I only just found out this morning."

Fiona stepped back. "Very well. But I don't believe there will be time to get you tidied up for a visit. You'll have to wait over here in the parlor."

As they walked inside, Maggie whispered, "Are his parents here?"

"Thankfully, no." Fiona opened the double doors to the parlor. There was a small fire in the hearth. Maggie didn't want to dirty up the beautiful silk-covered chairs, so she stood by the fire and clasped her hands together as if praying. Fiona nodded and closed the doors.

At first, Maggie enjoyed looking over all the rich things in the room, from the cloche-covered clock, to the oil paintings (the hunting dogs always looked like they were doing balletic leaps). But as the minutes ticked by, she grew unsatisfied. Would Felix make her wait here all day? Did he not remember that only last night he practically invited her to share his life with him?

Maggie hadn't ever been truly interested in marriage. At the shipyards, she watched the marrieds talk about their children or overseas husbands with indifference. With Felix, she wasn't so much interested in marriage as she was fascinated with what came with it. Like iced orange sweet rolls and nice dresses.

"I could be mistress of this whole house," Maggie muttered to herself. "And I'm being treated like a nobody right now."

She went to the double doors and cracked them open. Fiona was nowhere to be seen. Maggie hadn't even been offered tea or cookies!

The stairs to the second floor were only ten feet away, and down the hallway were several other doors. Perhaps Felix's study was there. Surely it would do no harm to peek through the doors, give a friendly wave. Perhaps he'd mistakenly thought she would take a whole hour to get ready this time. She had to get over to the Navy Yard soon.

She crept down the hallway, quiet as could be. Her boots were well worn in, not a squeak to be had, and the muddy dust in the treads made for a quiet step. Sure enough, Felix's study was next door. There was an enormous desk with a glossy black telephone upon it. Shelves on two walls were laden with leather-bound books, and there was a large painting of a distinguished-looking man on a rearing horse holding up a sword. It looked vaguely like an older version of Felix, an angrier one at that.

The desk itself was a messy array of papers in various piles. A ledger was open to money amounts going to and from people and organizations she didn't recognize. Under a stack of untidy bank papers was the corner of a photograph. Curious, Maggie tugged it out. In the process, several sheets of paper fell onto the floor.

The photograph was torn in half. It was of Ruby's family, or at least part of it. A middle-aged woman, who Maggie assumed was Dr. Fielding, sat in a chair wearing a beautiful but simple gown. Standing behind her must have been her husband, a blond, meek-looking fellow in a costly and impeccable suit, though half the image was missing. Ruby stood to his right side, wearing a gorgeous dress bejeweled with rhinestones and lace, perfectly balanced on a pair of pumps. Her hand rested on her mother's right shoulder. Maggie wondered what had happened to the other half of the photograph. Somewhere in the hallway, a door shut crisply.

"Miss Scripps?" Fiona called.

Maggie panicked. She shoved the photograph haphazardly back into a stack of papers on the desk and stooped to grab the ones that had spilled to the floor. She'd gathered them to slide them back from where they'd come, when a few lines of writing, circled with a red pencil, caught her eye.

215 West 6th Street Gravesend

It was her address. Where she and Will lived.

There were several other addresses on the sheet. Some in Manhattan, some in Queens, and several in Brooklyn. No names attached to them.

Of course, by now Felix knew where Maggie and Will lived. But why would he have her address on a list of others? And circled?

"Maggie!"

The doors of the study had opened, and Felix Cross stood there, looking irritated and surprised.

"I came to visit you again," Maggie said. She still held the paper in her hand.

"And you thought nothing of coming into my study and rifling through my papers?"

"Oh no! I was just . . . I was waiting ever so long in the parlor, so I came to look for you. I thought you'd forgotten about me." Saying those words made her eyes smart. "And I came in here, and I knocked some papers off your desk. I'm so clumsy! This was one of them." She handed it to him.

Felix came forward and snatched the leaf of paper out of her hand. His eyes narrowed, and then his expression went completely blank before he smiled congenially. The blank expression was a mere fraction of a second, hardly noticeable, except that Maggie was staring hard at him when it happened. The paper had spooked him, somehow.

He folded the paper. "Party invitations. Going out shortly, as a matter of fact. I thought I'd have a little bond-selling soirée for the war effort next week."

It was so obviously a lie. She decided to test him.

"Are Ruby and Will invited?"

"Of course not. Ruby will probably not even be there when it arrives. She wants to leave New York, you know. With Will."

"What?" Maggie blurted, before she could think.

"Yes. I spoke to your brother. He's incredibly incensed that I've taken a liking to you. Jealous, to be honest, that I can do what a brother could not. I can take care of you. He mentioned that he is shortly going to tell you that he and Ruby are going off together. To California."

Maggie went silent. She stared at the gold scrolls in the carpet, and finally looked up.

"I don't believe you. Will would never leave me."

"Ah, but you are ever so ready to leave him. Are you not? He's a grown man, with a man's appetites. Ruby is taken with him."

"I don't know about that," Maggie said, biting off the words that threatened to follow. Only last night, Ruby was in Maggie's arms. By choice. And not with Will.

"I think you're not looking with your eyes wide open." Felix rounded the corner of the desk and sat down. He didn't look at Maggie—a gift, really. Tears were forming in her eyes, and she would have been mortified if he saw her this way.

"Maybe not," she admitted. Her tears tumbled over her lower eyelids and onto the very fine carpet. *Plop, plop.*

"Well, you'll be happy to hear that I have managed to convince your brother to let Ruby reunite with her family shortly, to obtain their blessing first. He'll talk to you about that. I'm to help. It's the only way they'll find true happiness. Don't worry about them, Maggie. Worry about yourself. And your own future."

Misery stole away any conviction she'd had when she'd arrived. "I should get back to the Navy Yard," she whispered.

"Yes, you should. I'm afraid my driver can't bring you today. We've used up our gas ration for the time being. The subway would likely be faster, anyway." He stood up and swept his arm toward the door of the study.

He wanted her to leave? Maggie thought he would say, *No, don't go to work! I'll provide for you. You don't need to get your little old self all grubby in that place. It's beneath your station. Your new station in life.*

But he did not.

"I'm quite proud that you're doing such work at the Navy Yard. Keeping our ships afloat! We ought to have dinner, just the two of us, next week. I want to hear all about how you so cleverly weld bits of metal together and keep our ships from sinking!"

"Yes," was all Maggie could say.

"Are there any ships launching soon?" he asked casually.

The hair on Maggie's neck bristled in warning. "No. But they usually announce a citywide blackout on the nights the big ones launch. Likely you could figure that out yourself."

"Ah, but when you know so much, why rely on newspapers that are censored to the point where you can't trust anything they say? You, I trust." He hooked his arm in hers and led her to the front door. He seemed to be rushing her out of his life. "Next week. Dinner!" he chirped.

"And the party," Maggie reminded him.

"What?" Felix's face went blank again.

"The party. For the war fundraiser? You said the invites would go out soon."

"Yes, yes! Of course!"

Maggie stepped out into the bright day, and Felix reached for the great door.

"Toodles!" he called out, before it shut firmly and Maggie heard the click of the lock tumbler being turned.

She walked over to the Third Avenue subway line, feeling bewildered. What, exactly, had just happened? Had anything from the past weeks been real?

CHAPTER 23

Maggie arrived in Brooklyn with only ten minutes left of the midday lunch break. It was quite possible that her supervisor would turn her around and show her the gates—a permanent exit. She didn't know. But she did want to see Holly. To confront her, and ask about Yorkville. Pieces of a puzzle were settling around her, but she still had to fit them together by hand.

As soon as she exited the station, the bright fall sunlight blinded her. The end-of-lunch whistle blew. She blinked hard, took a breath, and began running toward Sands Street. The gates were within view, with workers lining up to be let back in after the break.

"Maggie!"

She skidded to a stop and whirled around. Will was standing half a block away. He looked somewhat shrunken, with a yellowish pallor.

"Will! What are you doing here?" She was out of breath, more from surprise than exertion. It was so odd to see Will here of all places.

"Listen. I'd like to do something special for you, and for Ruby, tonight. A night out. We can go to Coney Island and ride the Cyclone, and get some good food for a change. The ocean air will be good for us."

What an odd request. First of all, Will never really liked to go out after hours. He was always shuttling between home and the Brooklyn College campus. And Coney Island, of all places? Will was the kind of man who would grind his teeth with irritation around jolly, jostling crowds like those at Coney Island. The only time he'd ever gone was when their mother had enough money to spare for the ice cream and games on a rare summer day. Even as a child, Will didn't enjoy it. He'd begged to be excused and ended up waiting beneath the pier in the darkness. Alone.

"Why tonight?" Maggie asked.

"Ruby is leaving soon. We said by next week, and she agreed. This would be the best time to finally have an enjoyable night, before we have a few quiet ones and she goes."

"I didn't think you like Coney Island."

"Ruby would, though. She said so. I thought it would be a nice treat for the both of you."

Maggie planted her feet. "You're not telling me the truth, Will."

He looked surprised. He certainly wasn't used to her pushing back.

"You're right. I'm sorry." He stepped closer and spoke low. "I met with Felix Cross yesterday."

Maggie almost wanted to peep, *I met with him too! And he hardly seemed to care for me!*

"About what?" she asked.

"About Ruby. He thinks she'll reconcile with her family, but she'll bolt if we let her. So he arranged for us to bring her to a meeting place, and Cross and Ruby's family will be there waiting. With all of us there, she'll be more reasonable about going back home. Where it's safe."

"Why does Felix have to be there?"

"He's masterminding it all. I think he wants to let Ruby know he's still alive and kicking. Old lovers' spat, I guess. But I think he's harmless. I'll make sure he stays in the background."

"I don't know," Maggie said. "She ran away. To us."

"But she's not meant to stay with us, and you know it. By next week, she'll probably come up with a new excuse and still not leave."

Will looked at his watch. "After work, we can all go together. We have to be at the Wax Museum by nine p.m."

He looked sad, and exhausted. He wasn't lying this time. And if he had planned on staying with Ruby and kicking Maggie out, or running away with Ruby, this clearly didn't fit the plan. He must be telling the truth.

"All right." Maggie looked nervously down Sands Street. Workers were becoming scanter as the seconds ticked by. "I'll do it. I'll be ready to go by eight tonight." She looked away again. "I have to go."

"Where were you?"

"Oh. I . . . took a lunch break with a friend at a place near her house." She shrugged, trying to make it seem all natural. She should tell Will that she followed Ruby, and that her best friend at the Naval Yard turned out to know Ruby intimately. None of it made sense. She just wasn't sure what to do with the information yet. And she didn't want to tell Will. Not yet.

"Where is she?" Will asked.

"Who?"

"Your friend. The one you had lunch with."

"Oh. She's coming later." Maggie tried to shrug again, but it more closely resembled a shiver. "Listen, I have to go before I'm late."

Will nodded and began to walk away.

"Will," Maggie called.

He turned around.

"Are you okay?"

"Right as rain," he said. But his pants hung on his hips, and his shoulders seemed to sag beneath an invisible weight.

Will was lying again. She knew it. But about what, she wasn't sure. Maybe he was just sad. He was going to say goodbye to someone tonight, someone that he cared for immensely.

Maggie entered the Sands Street Gates, had her pockets checked, and went to Building 4 to explain her absence yet again. For once, she wasn't overtly nervous, nail biting, and frightened. There were bigger things at hand that needed her attention.

"Scripps. You have some nerve, coming in here again after missing a half day of training. Pack up. I don't want to see your face again in this shipyard."

Maggie would have cried, or trembled, but she was too busy noticing that Holly wasn't there. Where was she?

"Scripps! Do you hear me? Have you no sense of duty?"

"I do," Maggie said. "More than ever. Goodbye."

She left her fellow trainees and supervisor, jaws hanging open, as she walked calmly out of Building 4, punched her card for the last time, and left. Fine, so she wouldn't make a stellar career for herself at the shipyards. But she had Felix—no matter if he was feeling moody that day. And there was tonight—a night to end all nights. She sighed heavily, and after exiting the Sands Street Gates, boarded a trolley and found a seat alone by herself.

She took out a piece of paper, the last one in her pocket. It took the whole trip to conjure the strength to write what she needed to. In the end, she wrote the note right outside of her home, by the large oak tree where she'd found the scrap of white paper this morning. It was devoid of injured sparrows and pupae and sick little rodents.

In that gaping hole, there remained hope, and possibility, and a plan. Maggie steadied herself.

Dear Mama, she wrote.

I have to do the unimaginable tonight. And I don't have the strength to do it.

And then she dropped the pencil to the ground, her eyes filling with tears. Her shoulders hunched over, as if to shield her body from everything apart from herself. But she managed to take the letter, fold it with shaking hands, and stick it into the knothole of the tree. This time the regular mail would not do. Sometimes when you needed to speak to a higher power, you had to change the rules.

This letter won't fix anything, she thought. My life as I know it is going to be over when Ruby leaves.

I can't do this.

I can't.

⟢

When Maggie rounded the corner to the back side of her home, she found Ruby sitting on the stairs, wiping sweat from her brow. Soil smudged her forehead, and her hands were filthy with dirt. The perspiration made her complexion glow with satiny pink cheeks. Even covered in dirt, Ruby was glorious to behold.

It felt like years since they'd found her insensate beneath their stairs. It was all to end, tonight.

Maggie felt like a piece of straw about to blow away.

Give me strength, she thought. Just for one night.

"Maggie!" Ruby said, standing up and wiping her hands on her dirty trousers. "Look at all the work I did today! The foundation is all done. I made it a good three feet deep. With the roof, it'll be about five feet high inside. All we have to do is start adding the roof. Look at that mountain of dirt I collected! It'll cover the top nicely, and you can plant grass on top in the spring, if this terrible war is still going on."

Maggie's chin wobbled. She walked faster and faster toward the house.

"Maggie! What's wrong?" Ruby exclaimed, extending her arms.

Maggie fell into those arms, a wave of sobs issuing from deep within her. She could hide a lot of things, but she would never be able to hide this.

Not from Ruby. Not ever again.

CHAPTER 24

Will stayed away from the house all afternoon, spending a bit of time brooding at a corner table in a Horn & Hardart automat. His french-drip coffee had long grown cold, but he managed to force down some mashed potatoes and gravy over the course of a few hours. He walked around lower Manhattan as the sunlight dwindled, disregarded the chill, and finally made his way to 270 Broadway a little early. The streets were getting pretty quiet. When he walked into the empty lobby and showed his ID at the guard's desk, the guard held up a hand.

"Kind of late for an appointment, isn't it?"

"That's my boss's choice, not mine."

"I have to call upstairs."

"Why? You never had to call up before." He didn't want this to take all night. He had to meet Maggie and Ruby and get to Coney Island after this meeting was over.

"New policy," the guard said. He looked at Will like he'd never seen him before, even though the same guard had been letting him upstairs for months now. Will put a hand on his stomach as nausea churned hard, working its way up his esophagus like a reverse tornado.

"I'll be right back," Will said, and he turned and left the building, only to vomit on the pavement outside the double doors. It was the potatoes and coffee, and what appeared to be a cupful of coffee grounds straight out of the percolator. Damn. He'd kept everything down all afternoon, and then this. He wiped his mouth with a handkerchief and gathered himself. His hands were shaking.

He wouldn't go back inside until he knew his stomach was settled. It wouldn't do to pitch stomach acid all over Mrs. Rivers's desk. It was a good thing he'd come early. After at least fifteen minutes of time squandered as he begged his body to calm down, he reentered the lobby, and the guard looked at him suspiciously.

"Are you okay?"

"Fine. Peptic ulcer," he said.

"Mrs. Rivers says you can come up."

Will went to the elevators and clenched and unclenched his fists, trying to get them to stop trembling. On the eighteenth floor, the rows and rows of secretary desks were unattended. Only a quarter of the ceiling lights were on. Most of the world was enjoying a hot dinner with family, and here he was—one of probably a handful of people in a building that encased the decisions that would change the world.

Maybe.

When he walked down the office aisle, Mrs. Rivers and her desk at the far end of the room were out of focus. He rubbed his eyes. Only then did he see her leaning against Mr. Rivers's door, hand on the doorknob.

"Will," she said, eyeing him critically. "You look awful."

"I've had better days."

"You seem . . . pickled."

"I ate a bad oyster," he said.

Her ability to tell the truth from lies was like a finely tuned Geiger-Muller counter, but the falsehood didn't seem to bother her.

"Well, come in." She opened the door to Mr. Rivers's large office. It was empty and dark, save for a single lamp illuminating a circle around the desk.

"Where is Mr. Rivers? Are we having a meeting?"

"Yes. Just you and me, I'm afraid. Today was packed with meetings that couldn't be postponed, so I apologize for this being so late. But we also needed a little more privacy this time. With Mr. Rivers's permission, we can use his office." She sat in the chair behind the desk and folded her hands on the surface. The angle of the lamp made it so that her face was still in shadow. Will sank into one of the two chairs thankfully. His knees were a little wobbly.

"I went to visit Beach-Russ today," he began. "A very good meeting. They're going to send sample compressors to Columbia tomorrow, as well as some of their component samples so they can be tested for corrosion. But I have a good feeling we've got a match. They use nickel plating and nickel alloys. Excellent for corrosion resistance, if we're talking about sending uranium hexafluoride through these. They're willing to forgo a portion of their output to make what we need, if it's suitable."

"Excellent." She stared at him, filling the silence with nothing but that stare.

Will coughed, and proceeded. "And I think I have a good idea for what kind of industrial space you'll be needing uptown. I have a few places to visit, but I made a few calls. I think the Nash Garage would work. On 3280 Broadway."

"Hmm. We'd need to make a lot of changes to the infrastructure of that building. But we don't want to use federal money to buy it. It'll raise flags," she said.

"Make Columbia buy it. They own much of the property around the campus anyway. People won't bat an eyelash."

"Of course."

She went silent again. She didn't even reach for, or offer, a cigarette. Smoking was the best way to kill an uncomfortable moment like this that seemed to stretch into a year. Finally, he spoke again. Whatever chess game they were playing, Will was losing horribly. All his usual tricks weren't working anymore. He seemed to be falling apart, in too many ways.

"I was surprised to see you in that car yesterday," he said.

"As was I. What is your relationship with Mr. Cross?"

"We'd only just met right then and there."

Mrs. Rivers smiled. She was pretty when she smiled, but it also reminded him of when a lioness yawns at the zoo and shows off its enormous canines in the process. Cute, but damned scary as hell too.

She leaned forward a bit. "You aren't really answering my question, so I'll ask it one more time. What is your relationship with Mr. Cross?"

Will sighed. After spending time with Ruby today, he had no energy to try harder. His strength was gone, leaked out as if he were nothing but a tin can punched with nail holes.

"My sister seems to think he's her beau. I don't like it. I went to tell him to stop filling her head with nonsense. To break it off with her."

"I see. And how did your sister meet him?"

Will shrugged. "How do you know him?"

Mrs. Rivers's smile had long since disappeared. She studied him a long while before she finally spoke.

"I'm going to say this because I trust you, Will. But let me be clear—you've messed up. To the point where I'm not sure if you can work for the MED anymore. This project is worth more than you, or me, or a million Wills or Hannahs put together."

It was so odd to hear her refer to herself as Hannah. As if speaking her name had conjured up a memory that she wasn't an automaton for the government, she suddenly hunched over the desk and rubbed her temples.

"This isn't a game, Will. If we make one mistake, the other side wins. And by wins, I mean we lose everything. *Everything.* Lives, yes, but also our way of living. All the power, all the standing, and the advancements we won in the Great War will dissipate. All those deaths, and the deaths we're incurring now, will be for naught." She looked up and suddenly appeared ten years older. "My brother is over there, fighting. My father died in the Great War. We cannot lose, Will."

"My father died in the war too. I understand." Will heaved a heavy sigh and rested his head in his hand. He didn't realize until he leaned into his palm that his head was throbbing. "Felix Cross is the fiancé of the woman who's staying with us. They have a complicated history. And she's—"

"Having an affair with you," Mrs. Rivers completed his thought.

"Not anymore. And she's leaving."

"I see."

"And how do you know Cross?" he asked again.

"Family friend, but I'm sure he's already told you that. Not that that matters. He claims he has access to Ernest Fielding and his company, Monticello Vanadium Corp."

"I know," Will said. "And I should have told you about Ruby Fielding before." He sighed. Apologies were exhausting and uncomfortable. "Are you trying to get to Fielding through Cross?"

Mrs. Rivers leaned back in the chair. "Yes. I am."

"And Cross is trying to get to Fielding through his fiancée, who currently wants nothing to do with him."

Mrs. Rivers finally reached for a cigarette in the drawer, and lit two at once. She handed one to Will, who didn't mind the lipstick on the thin cigarette against his lips. It smelled like roses. She exhaled a plume. "Cross tells me it's all but a done deal in the next few days. He's going to arrange a meeting between us and Fielding by Monday."

Today was Friday. And tonight was the night he'd planned to turn Ruby over to Felix. He glanced at the clock on the wall to their right. It was already 7:30 p.m. He'd barely make it home in time.

"Are you in a hurry?" Mrs. Rivers asked.

"No." He looked away from the clock. "No," he repeated, as if to reassure himself that all was fine. "So why not just talk to Fielding yourself? Or even have Groves give him a visit? Tell him how important this is, and it's his patriotic duty. He can't say no to that."

"We tried. He refuses to speak to anyone since his daughter disappeared."

"You try his wife, Dr. Fielding?" Will asked.

"You do know a lot about this family, don't you? We tried her as well. She gave us an earful." She shook her head. "We even tried a close family friend. A chemist named Jasper Jones, at Columbia. You know him?"

"I think I may have taken his gen chem course. But no, not really."

"Well, he was a dead end too. About as helpful as a car with no engine."

"What do you want me to do?"

"Return Ruby Fielding to her family, and let Cross speak to her and to her father. I think he can actually settle this."

"I don't trust Cross," Will said, before puffing deeply on his cigarette. The smoke soothed his nerves. Now he was pickled and smoked. He would have laughed if he'd had a gram of humor left in him.

"Nor do I, but I don't need him to run the country. I just need him to set me up with a meeting. I care less about the family dramas going on there. I just want you out of the mix, and I want her back home, so her father will speak to us."

"I'll see what I can do."

"If you play this right, then what I said before—about helping you work directly with the physicists within the MED—I won't just ask, I'll make it happen."

For the first time in days, there was clarity in Will's brain. She would do this for him? This is what he'd wanted all this time, after all. Mrs. Rivers had known this. She was simply deciding when and if she might clear the obstacles for him. It was really happening.

He stood up.

"Consider it done," he said.

Mrs. Rivers smiled. This time, it was a genuine smile that showed a true glow of appreciation. She didn't get out of the chair as he strode to the door. As Will opened it, he stopped and looked about the office. There were framed maps and pictures of all the standard patriotic icons, like the Statue of Liberty and the Liberty Bell.

There was nothing more personal whatsoever. But looking about the office, the truth arrived to him in such a plain and simple way that he felt idiotic for not realizing it before.

He faced the desk.

"There is no Mr. Rivers, is there?"

"Of course there is. He's my husband."

"No. I mean, you aren't his secretary. He's not your boss. You're the boss. You've been calling the shots all this time, haven't you?"

Mrs. Rivers said nothing at first. Her lack of shock or amusement said everything. Finally, she said, "I don't know what you're talking about, Mr. Scripps."

"Today you said 'I' over and over again. Not 'Mr. Rivers says' or some such. You sat at his desk like you owned it. You're no secretary."

"Mr. Rivers expects an update by Monday," she said nonchalantly, shuffling some paperwork on the desk into a neat pile. "And you'll report through me, as usual."

"You're really something, you know that?"

Mrs. Rivers smiled back. "Have a good day, Mr. Scripps."

He left and shut the door. It made sense. No normal man would comfortably report to a woman in this situation, or for a project of this magnitude. But as a so-called assistant to her husband, they would. They would find her charming, accessible, efficient, and beautiful to boot. As he left the building and signed out, he wondered if she would be okay with the fact that history would likely erase her out of the books completely. Even Mr. Rivers might not have the glory of being a footnote alongside names that would dominate history books, like Groves, Oppenheimer, and Fermi.

That being said, he knew she was ambitious. The job wasn't only about status. It was about winning for the country. Always, winning.

And now, it was Will's turn to make a personal sacrifice for the sake of the war effort. If he did everything right tonight, Ruby would be gone. Maggie would be safe. Will's future would be brighter than anything the Columbia physicists could cook up in their basement experiments.

He looked at the clock as he left.

It was time to excise Ruby Fielding from their lives.

CHAPTER 25

When Maggie's crying paused, Ruby had led her into the kitchen. Now, she clung to Ruby as they stood there. Underneath her arms and fingertips, she could feel Ruby's flesh molding to her. The warm, satiny skin of her neck, her hips and belly pressed against Maggie's own.

Ruby crooned gently, swaying a little left and right the way a mother does to soothe her child, magically turning the inconsolable into the sated. One of Ruby's hands rested against her back, while the other stroked her tenderly.

"It's okay," Ruby crooned. "It's all good. The shelter is nearly finished. I cooked us a meal—a meal!—even if it was a lousy one. We've accomplished so much together." They parted and crumpled to the floor, holding hands. "But you know. I have to go. The sooner, the better. Maybe even tonight."

Maggie looked up in shock. "Tonight?" Did she know something? Had she guessed? Maggie had relished the idea that they'd have a little more time. A few more hours.

"You know, I haven't been truthful with you or Will. It wasn't entirely an accident that I landed here. Felix had your address. I truly don't know why. But I did think for a while that I might learn something about you and Will—about your jobs, maybe—and it might give me the keys to take him down. Injure him enough to keep him from hurting me again, or my family."

"It's why you wanted to come to work with me," Maggie said faintly.

"Yes. But I've realized something. He won't stop until he gets what he wants, which is me. And I'm sorry to say, I do believe he's just trying to get to me through you, Maggie. So the best way for me to force his hand is . . . to leave you. Both." Ruby's eyes reddened. "Stay or go, either way, I lose the game."

Maggie squeezed Ruby's hands tighter. She shook her head and said nothing. Her tears left a damp patch on her lap.

"I wish we had more time," Maggie said. "Everything is so complicated." She knew what she had to do. What her duty was. She'd set her conviction down in the note she'd left in the tree earlier. But there was a part of her that wished she could turn back time. Not even to those intoxicating few days after she'd first met Ruby, but earlier than that. She felt like her decisions hadn't been her own for a long time.

Ruby stood and wiped her eyes. "I should go now. Even if I can't say goodbye to Will."

Ugh. Ruby was always thinking of Will. Even now, alone together, her thoughts of him intruded. This was what Ruby did. She never gave all of herself. Even when she was right in front of you. Anger stirred in her chest, but she tried to stay calm.

"Where will you go?" Maggie said, stalling.

"I don't know. I can't go back to my family. I'll figure something out. I can take care of myself better than I did when I landed under your stairs." She tried to smile. "I'll get my coat."

Did she want Maggie to chase after her? Perhaps. It worked; Maggie wanted to throw her arms around her, pin her down, and refuse to let her leave. But then she thought of Ruby meeting Holly in secret. Of all the lies.

"Wait." Maggie touched her shoulder. "Let me at least get you something to eat and drink before you go. Just a few more minutes."

Maggie must have looked atrociously pathetic, with her nose congested and runny, because Ruby seemed to relent, and sat down at the kitchen table.

"Very well, just a few more minutes."

"And anyway, it's only fair to say that I have something to confess too." Maggie took out some bread to toast. Her hand with the bread knife was shaking. "There was a plan. Will and Felix . . . they made a deal. We were all supposed to meet them at the Wax Museum on Stillwell Avenue. At Coney Island. Tonight."

Ruby froze in her chair. "It doesn't matter. I won't go. Not back to Felix. Never."

Maggie wiped her face with her sleeves. "I know. I knew you'd never go back. I wasn't supposed to tell you."

"I trusted Will. Why would he do this?"

Maggie thought, I trusted Will too. And look what he did. He was almost a father to her. But he'd never be like her real father. She reached for the tin of ground coffee in the cupboard.

"He thinks it's best. For the both of us. And for the war effort."

Ruby cocked her head and laughed. "Why would it help the war if Felix Cross kept me under lock and key again? Which is what he did, you know. He locked me in that bedroom in his house for almost a day. No food, no water."

"He did?" Maggie felt hollow. Mechanically, she put water in the coffee percolator, spooned coffee into the metal basket at the top.

"Yes. I won't go back. Next time, it'll be worse. So there won't be a next time." Ruby looked around the kitchen, as if it were contracting closer with every passing second. "I have to leave."

"You played with us both, you know," Maggie said. Her hands stayed on the coffeepot, unwilling to embrace Ruby again. She put it on the stove to boil, turning knobs, glad to have something to occupy her. She needed to hear what Ruby had to say for herself. It would make everything easier.

"That's not true. I can't control what I want. It happens. And yes, it happens that I fell for both of you. My heart can be . . . messy." She pulled away and covered her face. "I was never trying to hurt you. I swear it."

"You speak German," Maggie said, turning around and nearly spitting out the words. "Explain that. Explain why you and Holly were speaking German together."

Ruby uncovered her face, an expression of surprise replacing her regret. "Holly?"

"I followed you. I saw you outside the bakery in Yorkville. Yorkville is full of Nazi sympathizers! Why were you there with her?"

Ruby looked like she couldn't breathe. She grasped the edges of the table.

"God, I've been so clumsy."

"So you admit it?"

Ruby looked up. "Holly is my aunt."

"What?" Maggie laughed. "Your *aunt*? She's our age! That's impossible." By God, Ruby couldn't even lie properly.

"It's true. She's not quite our age, though. Holly is about five years older than I am. She's my mother's half sister. They share the same father—my grandfather—and Holly's mother was an old friend of my mother's. She was incredibly young when she gave birth. If I do the math correctly, Holly's mother was only thirteen when she was born."

Ruby paused there, allowing Maggie to fully understand the implications of what she was saying. Ruby's grandfather had relations with a child? Who gave birth? It was disgusting. The shame on Ruby's face reflected the recoil and disgust within Maggie.

"That's awful. How . . ."

"I don't know why, or what he was thinking. I'd prefer not to think about it. He died a terrible death. Burned alive in his bed. Holly's mother died the same night, in the bedroom down the hall. We think it wasn't an accident. But none of it is Holly's fault. We grew up like sisters, and that's what she is to me. That's all that matters."

"It's an awful big leap for you to make me believe that you being here in our house, and Holly working at my side at the Navy Yard, is coincidence." Maggie clutched her hands together. "You've both been spying on me."

"It seems like that, I know. But it's not the case! Holly told me that the Navy Yard is the biggest employer of women in New York right now. I hear it's like a little city. I didn't know you were working there. I didn't know you'd both be training in welding together, but then again—it has the best pay in the yard, doesn't it? Holly always loved cars and airplanes. She had been planning to work there before I ever disappeared. I left her a note to tell her to leave home, to be safe, so Felix couldn't use her against me somehow. I knew she could take care of herself, and all the while, she kept looking for me. Hoping I'd turn up at the Navy Yard asking for her. She ended up following you home once when you said you had a mysterious lady guest in your house. She had a hunch, and looked through the window and saw me, and left me a note to meet her in Yorkville."

Maggie looked at Ruby, who had tears on her face, but wasn't sobbing. It was as if despair was simply leaking out where it could no longer be contained.

The percolator was boiling now. Maggie was eager to turn away from Ruby and busy herself with pouring the coffee. It gave her a moment to think.

She handed a cup to Ruby, who watched the steam rise from the brown liquid.

"Oh. You'll want sugar," Maggie said and took the cup back. In the cupboard, there was a small crock of precious sugar. In the corner, hidden inside a tin of stale tea, was a tiny brown dropper bottle. She pinched a dropperful into the cup and stirred. If Ruby gave her a hard time about what had to happen tonight, this would help keep her quiet. Extra insurance, on top of the coffee itself. She handed the cup back to Ruby, who eyed it suspiciously.

Maggie went back to the sink, where a dirty pot from yesterday's dinner still hadn't been scrubbed. She started washing it. Behind her, she could hear Ruby sipping.

"This tastes odd," Ruby said.

"The coffee is cheap where we buy it. Not like your fancy coffee uptown. Ours is probably mixed with wood chips, for all I know. I can add more sugar." Maggie didn't want Ruby to see her face, in case she gave something away. Her heart was beating fast. She turned to the sink and started scrubbing a cooking pot with a soapy dish towel. It would hide her trembling hands.

"No. It's not just bitter. It tastes different."

Maggie turned around. Ruby had stood from the kitchen table and was holding the cup of coffee.

"Let me see the coffee you used to make this."

"Of course." Maggie reached a soapy hand into the cabinet for the canister and handed it to her.

Ruby didn't take the canister. She looked at it, then at Maggie, then at the cupboard. She put the coffee down and walked to the cupboard, opening it wide.

"Wait, Ruby—"

"That's not the canister you used. You used this one." She reached into the cupboard and pulled out a tin in the back and opened it. She sniffed it, and looked up at Ruby. "What the hell is this?"

"It's coffee," Maggie said, her heart pummeling her chest.

"No. There are green flakes in here. A lot of them. You put some sort of herb in here." Ruby withdrew a fragment of a leaf. "This is rhododendron. Maggie, you tried to poison me."

"No," Maggie said, alarm prickling her neck. "I haven't. You're the one who poisons people. Not me. I saw those rats."

"Did you check on the rats recently?"

"No."

"Because they got up and walked away. Haven't you noticed that they aren't still rotting on the steps when you leave every day?"

"What?" Maggie couldn't believe it. "I don't understand. I thought you were trying to kill them. I saw them twice—"

"I've been poisoning them *every day*. You don't see them all the time, because they get up and leave. I'm trying to save them. Well, I mean, after I give them poison. Trying to test amounts, and how to stop the poison from working. I would never do such a thing to you or Will! I never have."

"But the spiders!"

Ruby shook her head. "Well, I hate spiders. That's beside the point." She looked deeper into the cupboard and pulled out another tin. "What is this?" She grabbed the brown dropper bottle, holding it up, her eyes accusatory. Maggie had been so hasty using it that she hadn't hidden it behind the canned beans. "Maggie! Answer me!" Ruby said, taking a menacing step toward Maggie, who backed away, the soapy pot still in her hand.

"I don't know," Maggie lied.

Ruby halted, staring at her with a revulsion that Maggie had never seen before. All the love, all the concern and care for Maggie, all the tenderness, had all disappeared in a fraction of a second, replaced with this. A look of pure disgust.

"I'm leaving," Ruby announced, and dropped the canister on the kitchen floor; it clanked noisily as ground coffee and rhododendron leaf bits dashed everywhere.

Maggie watched her as she went for her coat hanging by the door. She quietly strode forward, and using her newfound muscles from all her welding work, swung the pot with both hands and struck Ruby on the side of her head. The almost bell-like sound reverberated in Maggie's ears.

Ruby said nothing, only staggered a step before falling to her knees and hands. She held her head with one hand, dazed and unsure of what had happened. Blood stained her fingertips, and she looked at them with awe before glancing up at Maggie, still holding the pot like a baseball bat.

"Maggie?" she said, bewildered.

Maggie gripped the pot afresh, and this time hit Ruby so hard she fell unconscious to the kitchen floor.

CHAPTER 26

It was after rush hour, so the trip home from Mrs. Rivers's office went more quickly than Will anticipated. He exited the subway and hurried down Avenue U to their home. Despite the darkness, people chatted comfortably on their front stoops, and a few men were outside the R & R Saloon smoking cigarettes in their thick coats. Somewhere inside, a nickel jukebox was playing Jimmy Dorsey's "Amapola." Down Sixth Street, the war gardens in people's front yards were dark and decayed. The lights were off in most of the houses.

Their house, too, was dark, even though the blackout curtains weren't drawn. Ruby and Maggie must be waiting for him in the dark. It had been a while since his sister had done her rounds, encouraging their neighbors to shut their lights off.

And then he remembered. There was a blackout drill tonight. Maggie had mentioned it a while ago, well before Ruby had ever arrived. The usual evening dimout would go a step further. Lights at all stores and buildings would turn off. Even the Liberty torch, already low lit with two-hundred-watt bulbs, would go dark, lighting the way for no souls.

He'd hardly noticed the blackout after he'd left Mrs. Rivers. Will had been too queasy to notice, and the moon was at three-quarters, so he'd been able to navigate okay. It occurred to him that many of the shops and places on the boardwalk and Mermaid Avenue would be darkened. Ruby might get suspicious that they were planning an outing on such a night. Of course, all Coney Island would be dark, and any restaurants would have shuttered early. Too late now to change the plan. Cross had set the time and date. It was already done.

The moon cast slight shadows as he approached the backyard. The shovel was gone, and the haphazard piles of dug-up sod and dirt had mostly been removed. Will smiled ruefully; Ruby had been working hard, all for nothing. It was sad that she would leave before seeing it through, and feeling a sense of accomplishment outside of her highbrow ways. She had settled down to earth in many ways since she'd arrived.

But that was the past. Will was already getting sentimental, which was loathsome to him, as sentiment usually brought nothing more than regrets and acid-stinging memories.

He opened the door to the kitchen and paused, letting his eyes adjust to the darkness. Ruby and Maggie weren't there at the table, waiting for him as he'd expected. He thought they'd have a single candle lit, sharing a little time together before their inevitable separation.

"Mags?" Will called out.

Nothing.

"Ruby?"

Still nothing.

Maggie's work boots were by the door, and crumbs of soil had been scattered and smeared on the kitchen floor. He went to the bedroom, where Maggie's bed was neatly made, including the embroidered pillows from their mother, more than a decade old and starting to fray. A faint movement caught his eye, and he stiffened before he realized what it was. On the dresser was the glass jar with the stick and pupa that Maggie had rescued. The pupa had cracked open and dried to a crisp. At the bottom of the jar was a magnificent moth with spotted brown-and-gray coloration. Its legs were curled up in the paroxysm that heralded death, and the wings flapped just once more—a last, instinctive effort to escape.

Will stared at the creature. Maggie had forgotten all about that pupa and had missed the chance to set it free. But it occurred to him that such a creature would never have survived a Brooklyn winter. And then he realized—the pupa was probably supposed to overwinter outdoors naturally, wherever it was, and hatch in the spring. Maggie hadn't saved it. She'd sealed its doom by bringing it into the warmth of their home. God, what a terrible joke.

He continued his search. The washroom was empty too. It was then that Will went back to the kitchen and saw a piece of paper glowing almost luminously on the tiny kitchen table. He turned on the kitchen light to read it, his eyes smarting from the brightness.

Will—

We went to Coney Island early without you to walk on the beach a little. See you at 9, but I don't have a watch, so we may be late.
    Maggie

That explained it. Though he was irritated with Maggie for upsetting the plan. If he'd known they were going early, he would have just gone straight to the boardwalk.

Will drank some water, and forced down some days-old war cake from the bread box. A few coffee grounds were spilled on the counter; a scattering of tea leaves were on the floor. Sometimes Maggie was so messy.

He drank a little more. Will felt even shakier than he'd been before he'd seen Mrs. Rivers, and he hadn't had time to buy medicine at the druggist. Come to think of it, he'd hardly had a chance to rest well for days now. Everything was catching up to him, and not in a good way.

After tonight, he would rest. For a long time.

He considered walking down to the beach from Gravesend, but he was so tired that he climbed back onto the subway just to take it two stops. When he exited on Stillwell Avenue, it was even darker. He looked southward and heard the waves on the beach, but even with the glow from the moon, it was impossible to see if there were people walking there. The streets were nearly empty. Everyone seemed to know tonight was a planned blackout.

For many children growing up in Gravesend, Coney Island was an easy escape. But Luna Park and its fading paint depressed him; the Thunderbolt and Cyclone left him with headaches after his head would slam backward after the precipitous dips and turns. In 1932, the same year his mother died, the boardwalk caught fire. His mother had told him about a blaze that took Dreamland Park, as well as stories of the elephant that was electrocuted to death in 1902. The garish booths and amusements had always made him feel on guard, not entertained.

He walked past Nathan's, which advertised its five-cent frankfurters no less than six times on each facade of the building. The store was closing, with a single light on in the entrance. A few lucky people had walked away with hot dogs in hand, heading inland to go home. Across and down the street in the Henderson Building, the lights of the waxworks were off.

Normally, someone stood in the podium at the front, waving people forward to buy tickets. People would lurk about the entrance, staring at the placards boasting of the oddities and atrocities inside. Will remembered one with vivid disgust—the murder of a child by Hickman the Fox, detailed in wax and fake blood, complete with the bathtub where the child had been violently slaughtered. It still haunted his dreams.

He looked around the corner, down to where the Chinese American restaurant was, but no one was waiting for him. No Ruby, no Maggie.

A car was idling across the street. Not a Rolls-Royce, but an Oldsmobile with a dent in the fender. The driver in the front seat did not look like the driver that Felix had employed the other day, and it appeared as if no one was riding in the back seat. Will looked elsewhere, only seeing a few more shivering people here and there, hurrying to their destinations and to escape the cold.

Will considered walking to the boardwalk to see if Ruby and Maggie were idling there, unaware of the time. Perhaps stealing time—that was the more appropriate term for what they were doing. Will wasn't exactly eager for this handover to occur either.

Another car drove up, headlights shining through black-papered slits, and stopped in front of Will. The door opened, and Felix Cross emerged, cigarette in hand.

"Where's Ruby?" he asked, irritated.

"Maggie is supposed to bring her here. They're on the beach. I'm sure they'll be here any minute. Where are her parents?"

Felix sighed. "They refused to come. Said to bring her to their home afterward. Said that if she wanted to come home, she could, but they wouldn't force her hand."

Will looked at him suspiciously. Had he really spoken to them? He couldn't tell. Meanwhile, that Rolls-Royce was so conspicuous. If Ruby saw it—in fact, if she saw Felix—she'd be less likely to approach. It wasn't a good idea for Felix to show up until the last minute.

"You should have your driver park elsewhere."

"I suppose so."

Felix leaned over to speak to the chauffeur, who drove the car around the block. Felix backed into the recesses of the World in Wax Musee's entrance, behind the podium.

Across the street, the Oldsmobile's engine turned off, and the driver came out. He walked toward the Musee, and Will assumed that he was hoping for one of the last hot dogs at Nathan's. But he stopped in front of Will.

"Tickets are ten cents, right?" he asked. He had a slight accent, something like a British accent that was being faked, or southern accent that was being squashed down. Not Brooklynese.

Will bristled. "They're closed. I don't work here."

"Still, I think we should go inside. Don't you?"

Felix emerged from behind the podium.

"Who is that?" he blurted. Not subtle, was he.

"I don't know." Will turned to the stranger. He had curiously pale blue eyes, so light they almost seemed to glow in the gloomy light. His hair was a sandy shade that matched his coat, and he had a peaked nose like a raptor. He was the same height as Will, but not the same breadth. Despite being thinner, the man certainly looked healthier than Will did at the moment. Even so, old habits kicked in. Will took a deep breath, which made his chest deeper and his shoulders wider. "Look. We're meeting friends. Get on your way. The place is closed."

"No, I think we should go inside," the man said, and took out a revolver. "Don't be foolish."

Will backed away, his hands out. "Hey. We don't want trouble. Cross, what's going on? You plan this?"

"No!" Felix said, his voice rising. "We don't want trouble," he added, repeating Will's words. Will could sense his panic. This was most certainly not as planned. What a night to be robbed! Though this man seemed too well dressed and well coiffed to be an ordinary Brooklyn mugger. Will hoped Maggie and Ruby kept to the beach, but now it was so late, they surely must be coming soon. He had to defuse the situation, as soon as possible.

If only he didn't feel like throwing up a bucketful of blood right now.

"The door is open. Go in," the stranger said. Felix turned to the front door of the Musee, and found the door was indeed unlocked. "Keep the lights out. Sit down inside with your hands on your head."

Will looked up and down the street. There was no one anywhere. And Felix's driver was around the corner, out of sight.

"Listen. There are two other fellas coming to meet us here. Any second. I have some money. Just take it. It's all I got. This fellow probably has more," Will said, tossing his head in Felix's direction.

"*Will!*" Felix hissed.

"Well, you do. Give him your watch. Your billfold. Now."

"Inside, we'll talk," the man said, almost coaxing.

There wasn't much of a point in fighting. Even without the gun, Will was in no shape to fight, and Felix looked like he'd piss his pants before he could even make a fist.

Inside the Musee, the entranceway was crammed with figurines, stuffed monkeys, and more signage. **THIS WAY TO THE LINA MEDINA, MOTHER AT AGE FIVE! SNYDER-GRAY ELECTROCUTION AND BEDROOM MURDER.** The place smelled musty and suspect, like the aroma from rotting piers nearby had concentrated amongst the macabre oddities.

Felix looked at the dirty floor, and cringed at sitting down. The man waved his gun.

"Here," Felix said, digging into his pockets and removing his billfold. Felix's hands were shaking. He took off his watch and held them out. "Take them." The man didn't make a move to reach out to them. "I said take them!" Felix cried out almost shrilly.

Will, his hands on his head, studied the man. He actually seemed to be considering the watch and the money, then shrugged and pulled the trigger.

It went off with a sound that startled Will, and he immediately recoiled, his one good ear ringing. Felix Cross grimaced, his shoulders curling inward, and he fell to his knees. A slow bloom of dark, syrupy blood appeared on the front of his white shirt. A faint reflection from the dim moonlight outside showed a shining crimson color for a second.

"William!" he cried out, and fell over, clutching his belly.

The gunman swung toward Will, who moved without thinking. Will swiftly struck the hands holding the revolver as it went off with another bang. Something shattered behind him to the left. The gunman staggered back, pulling his arms in to shoot again, and Will tackled him from below as he shot the gun again. Instantly, there was searing pain at the top of Will's left shoulder.

They landed hard on top of a basket full of rolled-up flags. The impact knocked the gun out of the man's hand, and Will heard it slide beneath a cabinet of curios against the wall. There was a scrabble of legs and arms, and the man wrestled Will until he straddled him, hands on his neck, squeezing.

Will had wrestled enough kids in Brooklyn to be able to get out of most fights. He shoved his hands through the man's wrists and parted them, breaking his hold, then clapped his hands over the man's ears, boxing them. He howled, and Will punched his left jaw.

It wasn't a powerful blow, given he was beneath him, but he was able to kick the man off. Just as Will was pushing himself to a standing position, the man grabbed at something and thrust his hand toward Will.

There was a sharp pain in his side. Will took a step back, clutching his waist and feeling a warm, sticky wetness. The man held a knife, and there was a dark liquid glimmering on its tip. In this small space, in his condition, there was no way Will would win this fight. Panting, he took inventory of his body. He was exhausted. He could barely catch his breath. He'd most certainly been shot in the shoulder, but not through the joint. As for the stab wound, it was hard to tell how bad it was. But stab wounds were never good news.

Will would not be able to muster the strength to keep fighting for much longer. He knew it, and the attacker smiled a little, his teeth glinting pearly white in the dim light. The man knew this too.

Felix was now motionless on the floor. The girls would be here any second. Will couldn't allow them to get hurt. But nothing was going his way. What had happened? How had he utterly lost control of everything, so fast? He had all these plans to work hard, stay out of sight of people so he could do something in the world that mattered outside of Gravesend. He'd wanted to protect Maggie, and he'd failed at that.

He'd wanted Ruby out of her life, his life, and that strategy tonight had gone belly up.

The man touched his jaw where Will had punched him, and the movement left a dark, crimson smear behind. The man's left eye was starting to swell shut.

"What do you want?" Will said, letting go of his wound and balling his fists, ready for the next round.

The man smiled. Blood stained his teeth, outlining them like a carved Jack-o-lantern's. His face was so pale he vaguely resembled the wax figurines of the museum itself.

"I need you to be dead," the man said simply. "You were waiting for them, were you not?"

"What?" Will said.

The smile was still there. The man clucked condescendingly. "The girls. They're not coming. They were never coming."

Will's fists dropped a few inches as his mind raced. It must have been nearly half an hour after their meeting time, and they still hadn't arrived. What had happened to Ruby and Maggie? How did this man know they wouldn't be here? Had they been taken before Will and Felix had even arrived?

Surely the man could see the sheer confusion forming in Will's face. The energy draining rapidly away. He started toward Will, knife out.

Something prevented him. He looked down.

Felix Cross had reached out a hand and was grasping the attacker's ankle, tethering it to him. The man pulled, but couldn't release his leg. He reached down and sliced at Felix's wrist.

Felix screamed, but Will had already taken the opportunity that Felix had given him. He bent his head down and ran full force into the man, tackling him hard and ramming him into the curio cabinet. It hadn't been that long since Will had been a football player, and the move was all muscle memory. Shattered glass rained down, and the man's head hit the cabinet hard, stunning him.

Will grabbed the hand holding the knife, and he whacked it against the shards of the broken cabinet. The knife fell, and Will grabbed the man's neck, squeezing.

Weakened as he was, Will concentrated and forced every scrap of energy left in his body to tighten his grip. The man's eyes bulged. He exhaled, spattering blood all over Will's face. His legs began to push, pull, kick, his hands pummeling Will's chest and arms. But Will was taller, bigger, and he leaned into the hold. The man's eyes went dull but stayed half-open. All the while, Will squeezed, squeezed, squeezed.

His hands weren't even that tired three minutes later when he finally let go and the man collapsed to the floor. Will felt for a pulse and found none. For good measure, he picked up the knife and slit the artery in the man's neck open, a pool of blood gushing onto the Musee's floor. It didn't spurt in rhythmic gushes. His heart had stopped.

Will went to Felix's side. He shook him gently.

"Cross," he said. "Felix."

Felix opened his eyes, which seemed to be the only movement he could manage.

"William," he said, barely audible.

"What just happened?" Will said. He felt Felix's pulse. It was barely there. The front of his shirt was almost entirely blackened crimson. Felix was already pale, but now he looked an unearthly color, like gray putty.

"I don't know." He smiled vaguely, and breathed shallowly between every few words. "I thought . . . it was a good plan . . . I thought she was . . . coming back . . . to me."

"Ruby."

He nodded. "Tell Maggie . . . I'm sorry." He smiled again, but it turned into a frown. "She's . . . danger."

"She's in danger?" Will repeated for him.

Felix took another shallow breath, ready to speak again. But the few seconds waiting extended into more.

Will realized Felix wasn't breathing anymore.

He stood for a second, dazed, unable to think. He leaned over to throw up, mostly acid and saliva. He had to find Maggie and Ruby. Where could they be now?

Will rifled through the stranger's coat. He found the keys to his car, then staggered out of the Musee into the empty street, now glossy with a light sheen of rain. The car was completely devoid of anything that might help Will understand what had just happened. There were no papers, no notes, no stack of money paid for a grisly deed.

He didn't know where to go. But there was only one place that would have any clues about what had just happened.

He drove as quickly as he could back to Gravesend, but as the engine of the car started, he was already feeling like his dash home was an effort in futility. He'd already been there, and it was empty.

"Ruby," Will said aloud. "What have you done?"

CHAPTER 27

Memories feel like dreams, sometimes.

Unreal, forgotten, not quite forgotten. They are a different kind of unconsciousness, covered by layers of time and fissured by trauma. Sometimes, it is the pain that brings them back; an illumination that arrives without asking.

Felix and I were in his house. He had locked me in my room. I had pounded on the door, hoping his parents would hear, but it wouldn't matter. The Crosses were utterly afraid of him. He possessed full control of the estate, every pat of butter they consumed, and so they were as weak as water around him. No matter that their future daughter-in-law was locked in her veritable princess's turret in the Cross castle on Fifth Avenue.

"Let me out!" I screamed and pleaded. "Fiona! Please. Let me out!"

They had somehow turned the valves off to the washroom taps and toilet. I'd had no water to drink for twenty-four hours now. My parents would not know I was missing. They thought Felix and I were on a three-day trip to Long Island, and I was not due back until tomorrow. We'd been arguing so fiercely that we'd never made it out of the house.

My throat was parched. I was hungrier than I'd ever been in my whole life.

Yesterday, our arguments had escalated.

"If we are to be married, then you will obey me. They are sacred vows. And you'll obey now, as my right."

"You've no right!" I said. "No right to tell me what to do."

Felix and I were in the dining room, having breakfast before our outing. Fiona was in the hallway, but oddly, all the other house servants were gone "for personal reasons" today. I thought it strange that the butler, driver, cook, and his other five servants all had family affairs to attend to at once, but I let it go. Servants needed time to tend to their lives. Mama and Papa were always so generous with the people who worked in the house. They treated them more as if they were lucky to have the servants there, not the other way around. More than once, my mother had taken in a sick servant or their child for weeks at a time, so she could care for them directly under her own roof.

Felix had gotten up from the table and rounded it to meet me at the end.

"You will tell your father that he is to work with me directly. That it is your heart's wish that I be an essential part of his dealings with his companies. That is what families do when they unite."

"Are you to step into the wards of Bellevue Hospital and dictate how my mother should care for her patients too?" I said, unable to hide the disdain in my voice.

"If I wish it, yes."

"That's absurd, Felix."

"You owe this to me. Have I not treated you well? Have I not fetched you everything you wanted?"

I thought for a second. I knew I was sometimes a silly girl who fully enjoyed all the flourishes of courtship that Felix had brought. He'd lavished me with gifts like the new ruby engagement ring, the diamond drop earrings last month, and a new wardrobe of dresses that was exorbitantly expensive, given the difficulty obtaining silk during wartime. They were far more extravagant than what my parents had provided.

Mama had admonished me for accepting such gifts. She was too busy with the household and her work at Bellevue for such "fuss and feathers" as she put it. *What you do is more important than what you look like*, she'd tell me. I, who was too busy peacocking at my dresser mirror with my new diamonds. I liked fine, glittery things, like a crow. It is one of my worst weaknesses, I suppose.

Felix had furnished a room in his home for me—packed with silk, lace, a wardrobe of clothes, pricey hats made at John-Frederics and Sally Victor. A brand-new washroom full of French bath salts and perfume and all the rouge and lipstick that I adored, and my mother disliked. A princess's little empire. I was used to being pampered and spoiled by my father. On my tenth birthday, Mother gave me German chemistry textbooks wrapped in a ribbon decorated with a test tube. Father gave me five dresses and a pearl bracelet. I adored all the gifts, especially Uncle Jasper's intensive weekend lessons of German so I could understand those chemistry textbooks. *If you are to love chemistry the way your mother always has, and I do, you must learn German. All the best textbooks are in German*, he'd say, and Mama and Papa would look on fondly as he quizzed me all those hours.

Felix went an additional route to secure my affection. He'd ordered a new glass greenhouse built on my family's grounds where I could grow and study poison plants with Mama. He was overly kind to Holly, who was also terribly spoiled by my parents. Her parentage mattered not. Felix bought Holly her own car, which was unheard of—a woman driving a car that belonged all to herself. Holly adored it. Which made me love him even more.

He seemed to really know me. Marriage made so much sense.

But now this?

"I can't tell my father what to do with his business," I argued.

"He would bend over backward for you. You know it. Look how he treats Holly. She isn't even his blood! You know he thinks of you as the most priceless gift on earth."

I stood up. "I won't. I won't manipulate my father in such a way."

"You will, or there will be consequences." Felix crooked a finger. "Let me show you."

He led me to my room, as if to show me something, then turned around and slammed the door. I was locked in for twelve hours.

The windows were fixed shut. There was no food, no water. I pounded on the door for so many hours I grew tired and fell asleep against the door, before waking up and pounding again.

By sunset, I was parched, terrified, and worried that I would die in the room. And then it opened.

Felix stood there as if nothing untoward had happened. "Are you ready to speak to me in a reasonable manner?"

I stepped out of the room, feeling a little woozy but too angry to care.

"How dare you, Felix! I'm going home right now."

"Not yet. Not until we've settled our disagreement."

"You call this a disagreement? I call it torture!"

He tsked me. One hand was behind his back. He drew it forward to show a glass goblet of water, only a quarter full. I grabbed it greedily, drinking the small amount down so fast that I started coughing.

"My, how unladylike."

"I need more water."

"When you agree with my proposal. Or else back in the room you go. No water until tomorrow."

I glowered at him. I was weak and tired, and I knew that between the two of us, he could overpower me and force me back inside.

I reluctantly followed him into his office, a beautifully furnished space full of paintings and old books (which Felix never read—he just thought they looked marvelous and imposing). Inside the room he stood behind his desk. He had closed the double doors of his office behind us, as if worried Fiona—wherever she was—was listening.

"I know about you and your romantic past."

I crossed my arms and said nothing. What could he possibly know?

"It's quite extensive, given you are barely twenty-four. I know you have an unwomanly appetite for lovers. For both sexes. Imagine if I were to let everyone know in the society pages of the Daily Mirror?"

I bit my lip. How had he found out? I had indeed taken several lovers in college. It was far too easy for me to find a beautiful mind and tender character attractive. No matter which type of body housed that mind and character. There was an irresistible beauty in all forms that God made.

"Go ahead," I said, my voice raspy from my thirst. "It'll only embarrass you. I'll just move to France for a while. The papers will call me European and artistic and eclectic. I can live with that."

"It would hurt your parents. Scar their good standing forever."

"Felix." I raised my eyebrows knowingly. "My mother is a doctor, for God's sake. She and my father love Holly without any regrets, and everyone knows her parentage. The Fieldings and Cutters have always been in questionable social standing in New York. But they have enough money that this means very little. Everyone has a misbehaving child that embarrasses them."

"Well. I thought that might not work. So I have this." He opened a drawer in his desk and pulled out a bottle.

"What's that?" I asked, wary.

"It's aconite."

"Why on earth do you have aconite?" I wanted to laugh. Felix didn't think much of my hobby of obsessing over all things poisonous in the plant world. True, the glass greenhouse was thoughtful, but he'd actually chided me for the hobby. I had tried to explain to him how fascinating it was that the family of nightshades could produce delicious eggplants and tomatoes, but also the mandrake, which could cause hallucinations and make unicorns appear in your bedroom. He wasn't interested that cassava, a starchy root eaten elsewhere in the Americas, contained cyanide toxins that could poison unless the root was properly prepared.

Learning more about why poisons worked meant finding ways to make them help, instead. Or, as my mother found fascinating, finding better antidotes.

"Aconite. I know about this, thanks to you," Felix said, tossing the bottle up in the air. "From blue rocket. Monkshood. Devil's Helmet. Wolfsbane.

It causes nausea, vomiting, and diarrhea. Possibly may stop my heart, too, if I take too much."

"If you take too much?" I said, aghast. "Why would you do that?"

"I'll say you poisoned me. And you'll be sent to jail, where I do believe the food is quite atrocious. For the rest of your life. Unless they fry you in the electric chair like that horrible Ruth Snyder."

"You wouldn't dare!"

"Stop yelling. It hurts my delicate ears," Felix said. "So. Do we have a deal?"

"Good God, Felix. No. After what you've done to me? The engagement is off. I'm leaving. Go kill yourself. I don't care much."

But I did. I had thought Felix loved me the way I had always wanted to be loved. The way my father loved Mama—she with her quirk of wanting to be a physician, of always being curious about the plants we talked about, about the chemicals that danced an intricate waltz within their stems and flowers. There was order in the natural world, even order in the chaos, she would say. And my father adored her, despite the fact that she was so very different from the other mothers in their sphere—the ones who wore gloves whenever possible, who vacationed in their enormous houses in Rhode Island and Sag Harbor. I thought Felix loved me the same way.

"Fine. Then I'll kill Holly. And then your mother." He grimaced, or smiled. It was hard to tell the difference. "You will do as I say, or you'll be ruined, in every way that a man can ruin a woman."

I was wrong.

The idea of Felix hurting Holly made me want to strangle him. I had to leave, or else I'd commit a crime that would hurt everyone. I was wishing I had poured an entire tincture of hemlock into his breakfast coffee.

I had started for the doors to the office when Felix grabbed my arm. He swung me around and slapped me hard across my face. The sting was nothing I'd ever felt before. My parents had never struck me.

"Stop!" I yelled, gasping.

He swung me away from the door, and pushed me so hard that my body struck the desk. I could feel the bruises already forming on my thighs. His neat stacks of papers and ledgers scattered. I felt fingers slither into my hair, gather it, and pull against my scalp. I screamed.

"You will do as I say. As a wife ought to do."

He slammed my head down onto the desk. I thought he would beat me more, but the hand left my throbbing scalp. I cowered to the floor, balled up to protect myself from further blows. I heard the door open and the sound of Felix patting down his mussed clothing.

"Put yourself together. I can't stand it when you look anything but perfect," he said, and the doors to the office closed.

I was dizzy, the skin of my face throbbing. My eyes were filled with tears, my ears ringing. He would take everything away, unless I agreed. I thought carefully for a second. I could succumb to his orders. Marry him. Plead with my father to work with him. And why my father of all people? Felix was wealthy in his own right, and didn't need help from my father to keep himself afloat.

But the idea of him hurting Holly . . . hurting Mama. It made me want to scream so loud I'd tear my heart right open. My hands grasped the papers on the floor, crinkling them beneath my face as I cried.

"Miss Fielding."

Fiona's voice was nearby. She sounded kind, almost pitying.

"Let me help you get ready."

I was too embarrassed to let even Fiona see me like this.

"Give me a . . . minute," I said, hiccuping.

The doors closed, and I tried to sit up. My fists were still grasping a few leaflets of paper that had spilled from Felix's desk. I let go of one as it fluttered to my lap.

It was a list of addresses. At the top, it said only one word, underlined in red:

High.

Beneath it were other papers, marked "Medium" and one that had more words: "Low Priority—No direct contact."

One address on the paper marked "Low Priority" had a word on it that caught my eye.

215 W. 6th Street

Gravesend

I'd never heard of the place, but it sounded like the end of the world. In some odd way, it gave me comfort. Surely whoever lived at this address could not be suffering the way I was at this moment. I would do anything to be away from here.

I looked at another page. It read, "Manhattan Proj. Employees/check" with more addresses. What did it mean? Felix seemed to be trying to track down addresses of employees of a company. I smoothed the wrinkles gently, and looked back at the first page.

215 W. 6th Street

Gravesend

Low priority, it had said. It wasn't a place he'd look anymore, surely. I repeated the address in my mind, closing my eyes. For some reason, my mind latched on to the place—Gravesend. A place to rest. A place at the end of the world.

"Miss Fielding!"

I dropped the page and sat up, wiping my face.

"Come. Let's get you cleaned up. I've a cup of tea for you that'll soothe your nerves. Or a little absinthe if you'd like. Your favorite cocktail!"

I dragged myself up from the carpet and followed Fiona like a child. Up the curving mahogany steps, ignoring the stares from Felix's ancestors in their golden frames. I could never be one of them. I'd rather be anywhere else right now.

Like Gravesend—215 West Sixth Street, to be exact.

Fiona opened the door to my little gilded cage. She'd set out a crisp poplin dress, a new one, stitched richly with pink roses. There was a matching hat and silk shoes. Water was running in the washroom, reminding me of how horribly thirsty I was, and how Fiona must be aware of how to turn off the valves to keep me unquenched.

A cup of steaming tea sat on a tiny table inlaid with mother-of-pearl, and next to it, a glass full of foggy absinthe probably just the way I liked it—extra sugar, and extra cold, the louche from the water already making it nice and cloudy. I could even smell the faint licorice flavor from afar. Mother had mentioned once that her father abhorred the drink for some mysterious reason, and it had attracted my attention, especially after I'd found it might have a poisonous intoxicant. It was outlawed, for one thing, but I liked Pernod and licorice, so Felix had found an illicit bottle from 1910 that he'd given to me as one of his many gifts. It shone like liquid emeralds in the bottle.

"Go on, drink up," Fiona said, patting my back. She started combing my messy hair back into place.

The tea was hot but not scalding, and I drank it down in three gulps. Still thirsty, I gulped down the absinthe as well. It was delicious, but having it after my fight with Felix soured the taste. I would refuse it forever after, I decided.

"More tea?" Fiona asked sweetly.

"Yes, please."

She poured another cup, and yet another, as I drank thirstily. She dabbed my swollen eyes and pink cheeks with rosewater, and powdered my neck where Felix had grabbed me, to downplay the redness. Before long, I was dressed, looking perfect, makeup in place.

"You look like a doll," Fiona said, smiling.

"How approp—pro—propriate," I said, my speech slightly slurred. I swayed where I stood, feeling like I was bobbing in water. What was going on?

"Are you all right?" Fiona said, though her face didn't look much like she actually cared. More like she was watching me, the way a cat would observe a mouse before it bit its head off.

Something was wrong. I felt almost drunk, but different. As if my reality had slipped crookedly and everything was askew. Fiona's face warped and looked like it was made of melting wax. I tried not to scream. But something deep in my mind told me not to succumb, not to let her know I was feeling unwell.

And then I thought . . . oh. I've been drugged. Or poisoned. The tea. The absinthe. Absinthe wasn't truly hallucinogenic. I'd had it a number of times. But this was pharmacologic, whatever was happening to me.

I laughed out loud. Felix had beaten me at my own game. What had he used? Opiates? Jimsonweed?

But this wasn't helpful. I tried to focus on what I must. The address kept flashing in my mind, a drumbeat that brought tiny, regular pulsations of focus.

215 West 6th Street

Gravesend

215 West 6th Street

Gravesend

"Fiona. May I use the telephone?"

"No, ma'am. Mr. Cross said under no circumstances. As you know, due to the war we are not to tie up the lines."

"Please, Fiona," I pleaded. Her face warped again, her eye seemingly dripping closer to her nose. I tried to keep my mind lucid. "Let me call them, let them know I won't be home for a few days more than what I told them. They won't panic if they know it's coming from me." I put my hand on the bedpost, steadying myself, my eyes shutting against my will. "I'm in no condition to go back home for a while. Please."

Fiona bit her lip, and I was struck with a fear that she might bite me too. I wanted to flee—a correct emotion, but not yet. I steadied myself.

215 West 6th Street

Gravesend

"All right. One quick call. Mr. Cross gave me explicit instructions to keep you here."

Drugged, I thought. Quiet. As a good fiancée should be.

Fiona led me downstairs to the study that was still messy with the papers I'd accidentally strewn on the floor. I couldn't get my fingers into the rotary dial, so she did it for me. I grasped the smooth black receiver against my face. The coolness of the Bakelite woke me up a little.

Holly answered.

"It's me. Ruby."

"Well hello! I'm so glad you called! I just found out about flight school—and Mama won't speak to me about it, because none of them are in New York! Papa looks like he's going to cry every time I bring it up. But anyway—since that didn't work out, guess what! I actually passed my civil service exam at the Navy Yard. I can start training soon!"

I could barely keep my eyes open.

"Holly. Stop. Listen, I'm with Felix."

"Oh. Did you get the zinc chloride I left in your pocket? I wanted to surprise you. It took forever to get that. Now you can try your experiment with the charcoal, like you wanted."

"Holly! Listen, please!" I snapped. "I bla—can—won't be home tomorrow." It was hard to string my words together, but my slurred speech could come in handy.

"Why not? You sound drunk. Are you all right?"

I shut my eyes, because the room was starting to swirl like a merry-go-round.

"Our trip is . . . out—outside, verstecken . . . going to take longer. The weather isn't ideal. I'll be fine. Brooklyn will be nicer."

"What are you talking about?"

"Oh, yes. You should work on it," I said. "The ships. Holly. Verstecken," I said again, hoping she'd understand. The German word for "hide."

She could work at the Navy Yard now, and hide amongst the thousands of workers there. It would be perfect. She had been wanting to work there for some time but had put it off because she hoped to go to flight school instead. But Mama had firmly said no to flight school; as for the Navy Yard, Papa had thought it too much rough work, and we didn't need the money. But

Holly had already put in her application days ago. I hadn't told Felix about it, because I knew he'd disapprove—his own soon-to-be family, being a ship worker? He'd find it outlandish. The Navy Yard had only just opened up a slew of jobs for women, and Holly had wanted to do something for the war effort. The timing was just right. She could hide amongst the thousands of women there. She could be safe, and take care of herself.

Without me for Felix to bargain with, Papa would be safe. And Mama always knew how to take care of herself. I was the least worried about her.

"Holly . . . Du must weglaufen. We'll go verstecken, on that walk next week instead. Gefährlich . . ." I coughed, to mangle my German words.

Hide.

You must run away.

Danger.

Holly would understand. And when I didn't show up soon, she'd fully fathom how urgent my hidden words were.

Fiona came up to me. Her hand paused over the switch hook to end the call.

"Bye, Holly," I said. "See you later."

I didn't know if I'd ever see her again. I started to feel my throat spasm, and I was nearly ready to call out to her in agony when Fiona's finger dropped on the switch hook.

The call went dead.

"You're to wait in your room."

I nodded, but the world was still spinning when I stood. I couldn't hear Felix in the house—he didn't like seeing me when I wasn't perfectly put together, and Fiona would keep me away until l was presentable. At this rate, he might not expect to see me until tomorrow. Fiona should have just put me in a nightgown instead of this dress.

I had trouble walking to the stairs. I leaned heavily on Fiona, who was staggering under my added weight. I could see the front door only twenty feet away. I was still lucid. Cotton headed, but lucid. Felix was nowhere to be seen, and all the other servants who might otherwise stop me were out of the house.

I was taller than Fiona. Perhaps not stronger, but the several inches of height could be enough. I didn't want to do this, but there was no choice. I rested my weight heavily on her, so she pushed back to shoulder the pressure.

And then I abruptly pulled back.

Fiona found herself scrambling backward as I yanked hard on her arm.

"Oof—Miss—watch it—"

But it was too late. As best as I could with my rubbery legs, I kicked at the back of her knee and let go. Fiona buckled and cried out in pain, falling to the polished marble floor.

I galloped down the hallway to the door.

"Ruby!" Felix roared. I twisted my head to see him at the top of the stairs, coming down to stop me. Fiona was rolling on the floor, clutching her knee. I wrested the door open. The freezing cold air hit hard, and brought me a second of clearheadedness. My coat. Wherever I was going, I might freeze to death without it. The coat closet was right there, and I wrenched it open and grabbed my new cream wool coat, and ran out into the bright daylight.

CHAPTER 28

It was the pain that woke Ruby. The side of her head throbbed, and she felt wretched. She lifted her arm to touch the tender area, but her arm would not move.

As unconsciousness peeled away in gradual layers, she opened her eyes and tried to remember where she was. Who she was.

Her wrists were tightly bound behind her with something scratchy, like rope. She was lying on her side, her hipbone sore from being pressed against the floor. Her ankles were tied together too. She wriggled and moaned. Something thick was tied around her mouth, muffling her sounds.

It was dark, wherever she was, and it was damp. The air smelled of something metallic—blood, perhaps. Come to think of it, her upper lip was sore and also throbbed. She must have hit her lip on something and bled.

It was then that she remembered. Maggie coming home. Embracing her. And then there was the coffee.

Maggie had been adulterating the coffee. She'd been preparing it for Will regularly, but lately Ruby hadn't drunk any of it. Maggie and Will always made it so strong and bitter, and it wasn't to her liking.

She'd confronted Maggie. Maggie must have watched what she had been doing with the lethal plants lately. It was a good thing she'd used up the zinc chloride. That would have scorched her insides like hell if Maggie had used it. Instead, Maggie had taken mental notes and had tried to poison Ruby.

"*Mmf*," was all Ruby could say through the cloth tightly bound around her mouth.

"She's awake," a voice said.

A man's voice. Deep, and slow. Not Will's. Not Felix's.

The voice was matter of fact, devoid of anything aside from stating the obvious. It was so dark. Stiff as she was, Ruby tried to turn her neck in the direction of the voice.

Maggie spoke next. "Let me check on her."

"She's fine. Leave her be, Margaret."

Margaret. How odd to hear Maggie's full name spoken. The man's voice was commanding, without being much more than a low whisper. Ruby's skin had puckered with goose bumps when he spoke.

A small light switched on. At first, it seemed so bright that Ruby's eyes smarted. She squinted and blinked, and blinked again before adjusting to the flood of light.

She was inside what felt like a small cave. She lay upon an old blanket atop a dirt floor. The walls were made of bricks of earth, like one of those old dugouts from the pioneer days. It absorbed sound, making even her breathing nearly soundless to her own ears.

How had she ended up like this? She remembered why she had first shown up at the Scripps house. The address in Felix's office. She never knew why it was there, only that it had given her solace for a time, a place to run to. She wasn't meant to stay here for long. Only enough to get her bearings before she could leave and hide elsewhere. But Maggie had been so inviting. Her skin so soft, and those eyes so pure. And Will had been as ravenous for her as she had been for him. And for a time, she thought that maybe Felix was using them for some scheme. She should have left a long time ago.

It was too late now.

Maggie was sitting on a low stool nearby. Something overhead obscured Ruby's view so that she could only see Maggie's lower legs and booted feet. But it was her. Knees together, sitting primly and nervously as she often did. The man was somewhere farther back, beyond the circle of yellow light. His shoes were old ones, the leather worn into creases that threatened to crack after one more bad New York winter.

"I should check on her," Maggie said again, almost a whine. "She's no good to you dead."

The man grunted. Ruby saw Maggie's legs stand and approach her. She kneeled down, and Ruby could finally see her.

Maggie's face, smudged with dirt, was one of concern. She looked eternally tired, with redness at her lash line that revealed she'd been crying. Ruby struggled and wriggled, but Maggie shushed her.

"No point. You'll just hurt yourself," Maggie said, her voice firm. Her fingers brushed against Ruby's temple. It was sore there, and Ruby recoiled from her touch. There was a bowl of water nearby that she saw for the first time, and Maggie dipped a cloth in and dabbed Ruby's head. It stung; she must have gotten a cut. The cloth came away pink tinged. "This will get better. You just got knocked out, is all. You'll be fine."

Ruby tried to yell at her. "You hit me! *I'm not going to be fine!*" But it only came out as strangled, muffled grunts.

"Shhh," Maggie said.

Ruby started to hyperventilate, and the cloth against her mouth was so claustrophobia inducing she only breathed faster. Her nose became congested as tears formed at the edges of her eyes, and she truly thought she was going to suffocate. She bucked and kicked, until finally the man's voice intoned, "Shut her up, Margaret."

"If I take this off, will you promise to be quiet? You'll breathe easier. Anyway, no one can hear you here."

Ruby nodded, her nostrils flaring, trying to get more air into her lungs. Maggie tugged at the knot behind her head and removed the cloth.

Ruby gasped for a while. She could finally breathe. Her eyes teared, not from sadness or fear but infuriation. She would have screamed, but she knew it meant that the gag would go back on, and she couldn't be smothered like that again. When she caught her breath, Maggie tried to sit her up. Their heads almost reached the roof of whatever small cave she was in. Maggie offered a little cup of lukewarm water that tasted of dust, and Ruby drank it down thirstily. Maybe it was poisoned, too, but her instinct to drink was too strong. Finally, after coughing and catching her breath some more, she glared at Maggie.

"What have you done?" she said, quiet but with fury still making each of her words sound like they were forged in steel. "Where am I?"

"You're in the bomb shelter. The new one."

"What are you talking about? I only just dug that out in the backyard. It's not finished."

"No, I mean the one in the basement. I fixed it up."

Ruby's eyes adjusted to the darkness. It *was* the bomb shelter in the basement of Will and Maggie's home. The corrugated tin walls had been replaced with sod ones. The comforting blankets and boxes of supplies were gone. All the while, Ruby had been digging like a dolt, for a person she thought was a naive sweetheart. She thought she'd been lucky enough to fall into their lives by accident.

Only, not really by accident.

"I thought the whole point was to rebuild it outside."

"Oh, it's not a bomb shelter anymore!" Maggie said brightly. "See, after you went unconscious—"

"You mean after you attacked me," Ruby corrected her.

Maggie waved Ruby's words away. "I took all the sod you'd dug up outside and built up the walls here, and a roof with some leftover wood scraps, and more sod. It was a lot of work, but luckily you were unconscious a good while." She patted the walls.

Ruby blinked, not understanding.

"So no one can hear you scream," Maggie added helpfully.

Ruby felt the blood drain out of her face. "What?"

"You know, New York can't be bombed by the Germans in airplanes, so a bomb shelter is useless."

"Then why have you been plane spotting all this time?" Ruby said.

"I have to be patriotic, don't I? Anyway, forget bombs falling from the sky. The Blitz didn't work in England. And the Luftwaffe could never manage a surprise strike in New York. We're too far away. It will take years to create an airplane that can make the round trip and carry a payload of bombs."

Ruby's skin prickled. "How do you know this, Maggie?"

"Never mind that. Anyway, we have other ways to affect the outcome of the war. And you're one of them."

"We? What do you mean, we?" she asked. Oh God. All this time, what had Maggie been up to?

The man made a hissing noise. "Margaret, be quiet. You speak too much."

"But she has no one else to talk to, Papa."

"She's not here to be your friend. She never was."

Ruby coughed from surprise. "*Papa?* Your father? Maggie, you said your father was dead! There was an explosion."

Maggie smiled sadly. "No. Not dead. But I thought so. Back then. He never boarded that boat for work. He'd left us. And then . . . he came back."

"Does Will know?"

"No. And he won't, now," the man said.

Maggie's face spasmed, and a shadow of grief passed over it. What did that mean? Where was Will? The man stood up and walked toward the shelter. Maggie shrank away from Ruby and scuttled like a crab out of the entrance. The man grabbed a nearby chair and sat down.

He didn't look much like Maggie at all. Around fifty or so, with a head of hair that was half-gray, shorn closely around the sides. His eyes were green like Maggie's but lacked their warmth. Without an expression on his face, the lines around his mouth and nose were carved in such a way that he looked like he was frowning deeply. A pair of parallel lines were embedded between his eyebrows, making him appear silently furious.

He leaned in closer, and Ruby opened her mouth to protest.

"If you scream, I'll strangle you before you even have a chance to say 'help,'" he said calmly. He threaded his fingers together, belonging to hands that were thick and beefy. They looked like they could take down a gorilla. Ruby closed her mouth.

"Better," he said. "Women these days, they don't shut their mouths like they're told, the way they used to." He leaned back a little and kept staring at Ruby in a way that made her feel like he was peeling her skin off little by little. The gaze hurt. She looked away and stared at the dirt floor instead.

"I know all about you," he said. "Maggie told me everything. Good for nothing, unnatural abomination. Well, you'll be good for something now. You'll do as I say, and you'll live, and your family will live. You disobey me, and they'll all be dead."

"You're working with Felix." Felix had said exactly the same thing.

"No. Just stealing what's his. Your father was considering handing over Monticello Vanadium Corp to General Groves to mine and purify more uranium. Felix Cross was going to broker that deal. But you will once and for all put a stop to that."

"I won't." Ruby clenched her teeth together. "Go find another company to manipulate. This won't work. They don't even know I'm alive! They'll think you're lying."

"Of course they know you're alive. Will told them as much." He leaned in closer and casually slipped his hand to her throat. Ruby pulled back at his touch, but he pinned her neck to the floor of the shelter. He squeezed just enough to make it impossible to breathe. Ruby's head felt like it was going to explode. She kicked and struggled, but she couldn't fight back. She started to see stars. "There's no one to rescue you. Not Will, not Felix, not your family. Not until we get what we want."

Ruby couldn't even gasp. She kicked harder as his palm compressed her trachea. When blood pulsated like a waterfall in her ears, just as she started to truly panic—*I am going to die, right now, right here*—he suddenly let go.

She gasped and coughed. When she was able to catch her breath, she rasped one question. "Where is Will?"

"He's dead. Along with Felix Cross." He stood back and looked to Maggie. Her face was contorted in despair.

"You said you wouldn't hurt Will!"

"Enough. Go upstairs," he commanded. Maggie swayed where she stood, but her resistance seemed to last only a few seconds. She turned toward the stairs, unspeaking and ready to walk upstairs to the kitchen. Her father placed the gag back on Ruby's mouth.

"Shut up. And you might live."

In the corner of the basement was a pile of sandbags. Maggie's father hauled a few over and piled them to bar entry to the shelter, making a low wall. A few more bags, and it would completely block all light and sound. Even if she could scream, like Maggie said, there was no one who could hear her.

She wriggled, but there was no escaping the rope that was digging so hard into her wrists that she could feel the sting of tiny cuts.

Ruby sagged against the floor, letting gravity pull her down. There was no hope. She began to cry, mourning for the loss of her family, for Holly. For herself.

A puff of dust landed on Ruby as Maggie's father dropped another sandbag.

A shout issued from somewhere far away.

Maggie's father straightened to listen.

The shout came again.

Thumps across the ceiling shook the very floor on which Ruby lay.

Please, she prayed. *Please be Will. Please don't be dead.*

She heard a door open, and another shout.

"What the hell is going on here?"

It was Will.

CHAPTER 29

The entire block was quiet as a graveyard, and dark. The blackout drill was in full effect, and people were complying with the rules. It had to be after ten o'clock, well past the curfew for the beaches. The moonlight was the only brightness anywhere now. Houses had shut off lights, and store lights had already winked out. There were almost no cars or taxis out now. New York was blindfolded and gagged.

Will stood outside the back of the house, listening. He heard a vague murmur within, then nothing. The rectangular hole for the new bomb shelter looked like a large grave, and he shivered.

His vision was already a little cloudy from feeling so damn sick. The wound to his shoulder had clotted (he thought), but the stab wound in his abdomen was still bleeding. It couldn't be too bad, or else he'd already be dead. Maybe he had another hour to live without help, maybe another few days. Who knew. But all he needed was a few minutes.

Will had stopped believing in God years ago after his mother walked into the Lower New York Bay and gave up on the world, strangled by despair. But right now he'd take the help he could get. Supernatural or not.

"Please, God," was all he said. It encapsulated everything he needed right now. For Ruby to have some sense to make this all end. For Maggie to be alive. For himself to survive, somehow, though he wasn't sure what he was surviving for. Himself, or his country. Which came first, these days? It didn't matter.

He forced himself to forget the pain and the sheer exhaustion that cloaked him like a thousand pounds. Just one step at a time. All he had to do was talk some sense into Ruby and whoever she was working with. To make sure Maggie was safe. They might have to leave Gravesend. Where to? He had no idea. For a man whose life had always been about planning and preparing, caring for his sister and their ultimate survival, he was doing pretty poorly.

The door to the kitchen was locked. He still had his keys in his pocket, but after unlocking it, he found it was jammed shut. He'd taught Maggie this: block the door with a propped-up chair and wedge the bottom with a doorstop or a rubber glove. It would stop an ordinary intruder who tried to enter with brute force.

Why would she bar the door? Surely Ruby didn't do this. Ruby had no idea about Coney Island. Maggie did. Were they attacked at home, before they even got to Coney Island?

Will had to get in. He wasn't any ordinary intruder, after all. And Maggie probably forgot two key things—the door needed to be wedged along a particular groove on the floor, and she always forgot about the rubber glove whenever he quizzed her about it.

Will pushed and pulled against the door in tiny rocking motions that would loosen the dig of the chair against the floor. The door moved infinitesimal amounts with every minute push and pull, until he heard the chair slide to the floor with a hard slap.

He opened the door, shoving the chair away, and stepped inside. It was dark and quiet, just as it had been when he'd checked in before Coney Island. But then, steps issued from the basement, and the door opened.

Maggie emerged, looking shaken and spooked. She shut the door, and jerked in surprise.

Will almost cried out. "Maggie! You're all right!"

Maggie's eyes were wide. "Will! You're . . . you're . . ." She clapped her hand over her mouth. Her expression said everything.

"You thought I was dead," Will said simply. He switched the light on in the kitchen, and the bright yellow made both of them squint for a second. Maggie marched over to the switch and turned it back off.

"Oh! That's silly! I thought you were in class, is all." It was hard to see her face now in the darkness. "Why are you holding yourself like that?"

"Oh, let's see. Because I was stabbed and shot at. And by the way, your new beau Felix Cross is dead."

Maggie didn't react. For someone who seemed to want to spend her life with Felix Cross, this was an interesting response. The whole trip back here, he'd worried that Ruby was turning the wheels in whatever scheme had just left two men dead.

But Maggie knew. And she wasn't surprised.

"Where's Ruby?" he asked.

"Ruby left," Maggie said. She went to the kitchen sink and started rinsing off a coffee mug. "Would you like something to drink? You look so tired, Will."

There was something about how she reached for the tin from the cupboard that made Will see that which was previously hidden. She'd always made the coffee nervously—counting the spoonfuls, measuring the water just so in the percolator. But now she seemed almost nonchalant about how she spooned the ground coffee beans into the percolator jug. More than was needed.

Will went to her side and seized the tin from her hands. Maggie froze. He dumped the contents into the sink and saw the tiny fractured bits of leaf. Some sort of herb.

God. The sickness. The vomiting and stomach pain. The constant feeling like his body was a foreign territory he didn't know, growing weaker by the day. She'd been poisoning him. It explained why he felt so goddamned awful lately. Not a peptic ulcer, like he'd thought, but death slowly but inevitably creeping up and seizing his body.

He looked at Maggie, then glanced back at the door to the basement, where Maggie had emerged moments ago. Will marched over to the door and twisted the knob.

"No, Will, don't!" Maggie said, reaching for his arm.

He threw her hand off him and glared at her. Maggie only covered her mouth again, as if afraid that the truth would spill forth like a tidal wave that would kill them both.

What the hell was going on down there? He opened the door and went down the stairs. The single light bulb cast a warm honey glow over the unfinished corners of the space.

A man stood there in the dim light, next to what used to be Maggie's shoddy bomb shelter. Now, it looked like a small mausoleum from a bygone era and peoples. It was a little earth structure with a door of piled sandbags. The wall of sandbags wasn't complete, though, and there was a scuffling, muffled sound coming from behind it.

The man stared at Will, a look of faint amusement playing on his wrinkled features. He was Will's height, wearing clothes just as unfussy and worn. But he was not like Will in other ways. The man stood as if the world owed him something. Will knew his face as well as he knew his own reflection, though he had not seen him in ten years.

"Well, this is a surprise," the man said.

"You're supposed to be dead, Norman," Will said. He'd never called his stepfather Dad, or Papa, or Father. That was the title for a man who actually cared about his children.

"You're supposed to be dead too." Norman took a cigarette out of a pack and struck a match against a box in his palm. "As usual, you're a pathetic mess."

Norman had a way of delivering pronouncements akin to a sharp stone buried in a tossed snowball. Of course Will looked horrible. Norman was also talking about his life, and how he'd bungled it up.

"You sent that man to find us, didn't you?" Will said. He heard Maggie behind him. She had sat on the top step and was now covering her face in her hands.

"Ah, you're a bright one."

Another sting. He knew Will prided himself on his intellect. Will curled his fingers into fists, but Norman saw and smiled. He was getting to him, and they'd only been speaking for less than a minute.

"Well, he's dead now."

"I see," Norman said. "And he did a poor job. Only fifty percent done, I believe. I'd ask for a refund of my money, but too late for that, eh?" He puffed on his cigarette. He held it between his thumb and third finger. Will had always associated bastards with that cigarette hold.

Will tried to stand straight, not show the physical pain that racked his sinews. He could feel warm blood dripping down his belly. "That's typical. You always leave your work to someone else. Or rather, you just leave."

"Oho! Looks like you finally grew a backbone. That was my doing, you know. Can't live a life coddled all the time."

"You left us," Will spat out.

"Oh, you think I did. You didn't see me, because I didn't want you to see me. But I've been around. Me and the leftover Bundsmen, we've been keeping an eye on things."

Bundsmen. Did he mean the German American Bund? Weren't they forced to disband because of all their rhetoric about Jewish influence on FDR and their demand for a gentile-controlled America?

Will stared at his stepfather, who stared back with emotionless eyes. The last few weeks, he'd felt eyes on him amongst the sea of strangers on his daily commutes. He'd thought he was imagining things, but he wasn't. It was Norman's eyes, following him. How many times had he followed Will right to the MED, or to the piles of uranium under the Bayonne Bridge?

"You know, Will," Norman said. "I made you stronger by leaving. You know it. And anyway, there was more important work at hand."

"You as good as murdered our mother."

He heard Maggie sniffle behind him, and he ignored it. Norman shrugged. "She was weak. Only weak people kill themselves."

"That's a load of tripe. She was sick. And you made her sicker. You made yourself the center of her world, and then left. What did you expect?"

"Ah, but you. You almost drowned your sister."

Will gasped. "What?" What was he talking about?

"When Maggie tried to follow in her mother's footsteps. You think she just luckily washed back onto shore? *I* found her in the water. *I* saved her." He jabbed a thumb at himself to underscore his point. "Because you couldn't do your job of taking care of her. I did more for both of you when I was dead than you could alive." Norman bared his teeth. "Your sister. Aimless. Lifeless. So I stepped in and gave her a purpose. And look what you did because I left. You stopped being weak. You became a man. Though not man enough, I suppose."

"We don't need you anymore." Will's knees were in danger of trembling. He was growing dizzy again. The only thing he wanted more than Norman disappearing like magic was to sit down on these stairs and rest.

"Oh, Will," Norman said, and clucked condescendingly. "I didn't swoop in to mollycoddle you. No, no, no, boy."

"You came to kill me," Will said, finishing his thought.

"Very amusing. No. Your sister took care of that. With those plants that whore planted on your land, like a witch. Put in your coffee and your food, just like I told her."

"I didn't want to," Maggie whispered. She looked up, her palms shiny with tears and her eyes reddened and wet. "He told me to. I wrote to him. He gave me so much comfort, Will. He knew what to do."

"What are you talking about?" Will said.

"I had to keep it secret! I pretended to myself I was writing to Mama because I was afraid I'd give it away, even though it was him all along. And he would write back. In the tree, out front. It was where he usually left me sick animals to rescue, and always—there was a hidden note from him tucked nearby."

"'Find' sick animals?" Norman laughed. "Sure."

Maggie looked aghast. "Didn't you . . . find them?"

"Sure I did. I'd catch 'em, then break their legs and deliver them to you."

Maggie looked like she was going to be sick.

"Will!" a voice, gasping, from somewhere in the basement suddenly called out.

"Ruby!" Will bolted forward to the bomb shelter. Norman backed a few steps away and let him pull the sandbags away from the opening. He found Ruby tied up, with a gag that had fallen to her chin. At first he thought it was stained with blood, but it looked like only lipstick. She was wearing the pants and old shirt from working in the backyard. He felt a twinge in his heart, knowing she'd worn lipstick while digging in the dirt. How like Ruby that was!

She wasn't whimpering or afraid, the way she'd been after they'd found her under their stairs those weeks ago. Ruby looked furious. And strong.

"Are you hurt?"

"I'm all right. Watch your back, Will."

Will stood up. Norman was holding a gun, pointed at Will's chest. Will showed his hands.

"Just go. Take Maggie. Leave us here, and we'll be out of your lives." Will held his breath, waiting.

"Oh, you'll be out of our lives. But we need her," he said, slightly nudging the revolver down to where Ruby lay seething.

"Father. Don't. It'll be too loud, like you said. The neighbors will hear," Maggie said.

Norman inhaled, his eyelids fluttering ever so slightly to show his annoyance. He clearly knew she was right—it would be too noisy. But she'd revealed a truth that prevented Norman from outright killing Will right then and there. Will allowed himself to exhale.

"Fine. I'll use it if I have to. But have it your way. Make him a drink, Mags. Be a good girl," Norman said.

"Don't!" Ruby said. "He's already so sick, Maggie."

Will touched Ruby's shoulder and shook his head. It didn't matter what Ruby said. She'd only get hurt if she spoke too much.

"And make it strong this time," Norman said. "Go."

Maggie disappeared back to the kitchen.

"It'll kill him," Ruby said.

"That's the plan," Norman said. He yawned. "You didn't think you were digging a hole in the backyard for a bomb shelter, did you?"

Ruby said nothing, only trembled and dropped her head to the floor. She was trying not to cry.

Will was so tired. So very tired. He had been stooping near Ruby, but couldn't hold himself up anymore. He plopped down, his legs out in front of him. He hardly had the strength to sit up. He closed his eyes.

"You made this too easy, Will. I'm not as afraid as Maggie is about using this gun. You know I'd do it, and not have a single speck of regret."

Norman walked up the stairs, and soon they were alone. It was a testament to his confidence that Will was completely unable to defend himself or escape that he left without much care.

"Loosen these ropes, will you?" Ruby said, struggling.

Will tried. But his fingertips felt oddly numb, and he just didn't have the strength to tug at them. He was short of breath just trying, and he leaned against the doorway of the shelter, catching his breath.

"I can't. I'm done, Ruby."

"You can't be done. Will! Wake up!"

Will opened his eyes, not realizing they'd been closed. It seemed like an hour had passed, when really it was only a few minutes later that Maggie descended the stairs with a tray holding a single mug. They heard the door to the basement locking.

Maggie put the tray down in front of Will, then sat on a chair a few feet away. Her face looked haggard. In the dim light, the dark circles under her eyes were magnified, and she was a ghoulish version of her usual self.

"Go on. Drink," Maggie said in her small voice.

"Why are you doing this?" Ruby asked.

"What do you expect me to say?" Maggie replied. "That I'm doing this because I was jealous of you two? That I'm tired of being treated like a little girl who can't take care of herself?"

"Is that really how you feel?" Will asked, his voice a weak whisper.

"Oh, Will. There you go again. You don't know what I want. You never have. Father has always been there for me. He told me what mattered—that I was part of something so much bigger than just me, or you."

"What are you talking about?" Will said.

"This war. It has to end. And it has to end the right way. Germany will win. And Father and I will be on the right side of history when that happens."

"What? Have you lost your mind, Maggie?"

"Oh, Will!" Maggie cut him off, leaning forward and baring her teeth. "You don't get it. You're unable to see what's in front of you. The bomb shelter was for show. I mean, it ended up being useful for keeping Ruby here for a little while." She smirked. "But the plane spotting? The blackout drills? They work both ways. I've told Father everything about what I've done, to prove a different kind of patriotism. You know I'm not terribly good at sewing or keeping a job. Why would I get a job at the Navy Yard? I keep an eye on which ships come in, and leave. How their welding is done, where the weaknesses are. Did you know I was the best in my training class? I could have made a career of it." She looked wistful for a second, then remembered herself. "It was Father's idea, not mine. He always knows what to do."

"God. So you're one of them," Ruby said faintly.

"I tried as hard as I could to get more information from Will about his job. But he was always so tight lipped." She shrugged. "Felix told me that they were thinking of firing you because you'd been so infatuated with Ruby." She laughed. "You were a good distraction. But you've stopped being useful, Ruby."

"You're a liar," Ruby said, her voice rising. "You felt something. I know you did. That wasn't a lie."

Maggie's face seemed to shimmer with panic before she regained her composure. "That's all past. That wasn't real. That was acting."

"I know a lie when I see it," Ruby said, glaring. Maggie looked away.

"This is what you want?" Will said, motioning to the mug. "You're my only family. I tried . . . I thought I was taking care of you."

Maggie turned back to him, venom in her expression. "You treated me like a child!"

"You're telling me that was an act. What was I supposed to do? That man you call your father hit our mother every day for a month before he left, and she killed herself. Why would your loyalty be to a monstrosity like him? Why, Maggie?"

"He loves me!" Maggie said as forcefully as she could without shouting.

"He's using you!"

"No. We want the same things. That's the difference between me and Mama. She wanted him, but she never helped him. I help him. We want the same things."

"You are not his wife, Maggie."

Maggie looked away again. "He needs me. The way you don't. Ruby never did either."

311

"Oh, Maggie," Ruby said. "That's not true! I thought we needed each other."

Maggie frowned. "You should be ashamed! I don't know what you're talking about."

Ruby looked like she'd been slapped. "Maggie!"

For a long while, no one spoke. Will finally reached for the mug and looked at the dark, greenish liquid inside. It smelled like grass and dirt, mixed together.

"Would this really make you happy? This is what you want?" he asked.

Because he would do anything for his sister. He'd given up his life in so many ways for her. In some ways, Maggie was like a broken part of his mother, still roaming the world unsatisfied. Eternally needing something beyond his ability to deliver.

But maybe this would finally give her what she wanted.

"Yes," Maggie said stiffly. Her lip was trembling, but the word was spoken with clarity.

Ruby shook her head, a faint *Don't* coming from her lips, or perhaps wordlessly from her heart, he didn't know. His body was already almost spent, and his heart was so broken. What was left? Nothing. He thought of the work with the MED, with Mrs. Rivers, and all those endless hours studying for a college degree that would never happen. It seemed like a silly game, in the end. He was losing that game too.

And to think that the impossible—the creation of vast amounts of energy through the splitting of an unseeable atomic nucleus—was something Will once believed to be a beautiful feat of human creation. Clarity shook him with a ferocity that made him want to weep. He could see it now for what it was. The splitting of a whole. The breaking of a world.

Humans are already so goddamn fragile, and broken, and imperfect, he thought. And yet we do everything in our power to break each other, and call it something else.

Patriotism.

Love.

Family.

And in the process, it destroys and destroys, in outward circles of perfect annihilation. The gods of our own fate and failure.

He lifted the mug. It was a small gift from a brother whose love was an arrow that hadn't hit the target but boomeranged back and hit himself. He had caused this, and he would fix it.

Will drank it down entirely as Ruby sobbed beside him, and Maggie watched with tears of triumph rolling down her face.

CHAPTER 30

Will drank the decoction of snakeroot obediently. It was a shock to Maggie, and yet she was so relieved that he was making it easier on her. Any resistance would have scratched and tugged at the edges of her angry mind, reminding her of what she should or shouldn't do.

Will was being a good brother. Even during his self-immolation.

"Good," Maggie said, and she picked up the empty cup with a gloved hand that trembled ever so slightly.

"Maggie. Please. You can do whatever you want with me. But whatever else—you have to stop."

"The wheels are already in motion. I've made my choice," Maggie said, without turning around. She didn't want to look Ruby in the eye. It would be good having Father here to help her now. He would deal with Ruby with an adamant resolve. Whereas Ruby's very voice made Maggie sway with indecision. Even knowing what she ought to be doing, Ruby's presence made her feel as unsettled as a recently shaken snow globe.

As she climbed the steps, she heard a groan from Will. Her eyes spasmed in fear, and she forced herself to iron out the worry lines on her face before Norman let her into the kitchen.

Her father was smoking at the kitchen table, light on, and looking relieved. The way one might after chloroforming a litter of nuisance

kittens. So he'd really hurt all those animals for her to save. Her conscience felt bruised, but she would get over it. Eventually.

"Good girl," he said. As Maggie went to put the cup in the sink,
he pinched her bottom, and she winced. "You filled out nicely after all
these years." He mashed out his cigarette on a plate and waved her over.
"You were such a string bean before. Come have a seat. Let's talk." He
patted his lap.

Maggie hesitated. She'd longed for—no, she'd practically ached for
her father's touch, the comfort of a man holding her and telling her that
all would be all right. It wasn't the same when Will told her these things.
He was not demonstrative or physically affectionate, and she didn't wish
it from him. But looking at her father's wizened face, Maggie was aware
that she was no longer a child. She would barely fit on that lap of his.
It didn't seem right.

"Listen to your father." He patted his lap again.

Maggie opened her mouth, ready to say something, anything that
would defer his attention. Though he'd entered her life the day she'd
tried to kill herself, and they had written ever since, he'd only really
been back in her life in the flesh for a few hours. Still, she was devoted
to him. He had disappeared from her life once, and her world had gone
to flames.

Her father commanded her. "Come here."

Maggie had begun to walk toward him in defeat when there was a
loud yell outside the front door. And then, a loud rapping. Five knocks,
in quick succession.

"Maggie?" a voice yelled on the other side.

"Who the devil is that?" Norman growled.

"I don't know. We're not expecting anybody." Despite the intrusion, Maggie was relieved. She jumped to the wall and switched off
the light.

"Get rid of them," he demanded.

Maggie went to the front door. She pushed aside the curtain, but it was so dark out that she couldn't make out who it was. There was more than one person.

"Maggie!" a woman called. "Maggie! Are you all right?"

Maggie jerked back in surprise. It was Holly! Why was she here? Had Ruby told her to come?

What should she do? She wanted to do nothing. Wait until Holly went away, and whoever was with her. She stood a little bit away from the window. Damn it. Maggie had forgotten to draw the blackout curtains closed. Holly had probably seen the faint glow of the kitchen light. It was off now, but maybe too late.

"I know you're home," Holly said, her voice loud. Behind her, in the darkness near the sidewalk, someone stepped forward and walked up the stairs.

"Maggie! It's Mrs. Polanski, from down the street. Are you all right?" Maggie put her hand to her mouth as Mrs. Polanski spoke again. "We're worried about you. You haven't been doing your dimout rounds lately. And tonight—for the blackout drill—when you didn't show up, we got scared for you, dear. Even Mrs. Brandeis says you haven't sent any reports of your plane-spotting work for days. She asked us to check on you too."

Maggie froze. God, the blackout tonight! She'd completely forgotten. All the things she had done as a cloak to hide behind—they weren't helping to keep her hidden now when she needed it the most. The door between her and Holly and the neighbors felt paper thin, as if Maggie's own panicked breath could blow it down.

"We're not leaving, Maggie," Holly said. "Or we're calling the police."

Her father's footsteps sounded behind her.

"Get rid of them, Maggie," he hissed.

"Yes, Father."

His steps withdrew, and Maggie unlocked the door. She stepped outside and shut it quietly behind her.

"Shhh!" Maggie put fingers to her lips. "Lower your voices!" she whispered, as loud as she could without actually using a normal speaking voice. "You should all be inside for the drill."

"Where have you been?" Mrs. Polanski asked, wringing her hands. Her hair was wrapped up in a scarf. "We hadn't seen you at all. I saw Will the other day, looking sick. I thought something had happened to you too."

Maggie was surprised. She'd always thought herself more of a nuisance when she begged her neighbors to turn out their lights. It reminded her about how Americans had no idea what they really wanted, or cared for. She'd thought she could practically hear their eyes rolling behind the windows and shades. But perhaps those were all her own imaginings. They'd appreciated her, and cared. They cared now. Or at least were just busybodies who were looking for gossip. Yes, that must be it.

And now, she must say something. She had to make them all go away.

"Oh, I only had a cold." She waved her hand. "Will insisted I rest, so I did. He's recovering from a cold too."

"And where is Will now?" Holly asked.

"You don't even know who he is, Holly," Maggie said, trying to make her sound like she had no idea what she was talking about. "He's at his night classes, as usual."

"But I saw him come home early, only half an hour ago! Looked a fright, like he'd had a brawl," Mrs. Polanski said.

"Oh, yes. That's right, he's, ah, staying home tonight. It's nothing. And we ought not to be talking like this! It's a blackout. Really. We should all be home. I'll be back to my rounds in a few days. I promise."

When no one moved, she smiled brightly. "Come now. Let's do our duty. Lights out, quiet as lambs. Off you go. I'll be seeing you soon."

The neighbors looked at each other, and seemed satisfied. One by one, they dispersed—all but Holly.

"Go away, Holly. Or is that even your real name—Holly Dreyer?" she said nastily. She opened the door and stepped back inside.

Holly slapped the door, preventing Maggie from shutting it. "It's Holly Dreyer Fielding. Where is my niece? *Where is Ruby?*"

"I don't know who that is. Go away, or I'll call the police."

Maggie shoved the door hard and shut it in Holly's face. From the internal darkness of the sitting room, she watched as Holly's shoulders fell. Holly raised her hand as if ready to knock again, but then dropped her fist.

She left.

Maggie sighed, but only a portion was due to relief. She had enjoyed Holly's friendship, precious and limited as it was.

"Gone?" Her father's voice issued from the kitchen.

"Yes."

"Tonight is a good night to get rid of the body."

The body?

Oh. He meant Will.

"Yes."

"It'll be dark, and I can be quiet. I saw some clouds in the sky, so when the moon gets low, we can do it. But first, we have to move that whore out of this house."

"Move? Ruby? Why?" She went into the dark kitchen.

"We can't have people snooping here anymore. I'll bring her to my place."

"Which is where?" Maggie asked.

"That's not your concern. I'll arrange messages with her father. I'll make sure he doesn't turn over that refining operation of his to General Groves. I'm confident of that."

"But Ruby—"

"Is not your concern, Margaret." He stood, towering over her. "I've been too distant for too many years. It was necessary. But I know you can't be a good, obedient daughter through words alone. You've needed a stronger man in your life to make decisions."

Maggie hardly heard what he was saying. Everything would change. Yes, it would be a good thing, but . . . Ruby. Maggie was aware of how childish her words were, even as they left her mouth.

"I want Ruby to stay here. Please, Papa."

His gaze bored into her. She tried not to cower in the darkness.

"Is she a plaything? Grow up, Margaret. Whatever she did to make you feel like you needed a companion was a ruse. She was using you, just as you used her." He started to move past her to the basement door. He took a deep breath, and Maggie thought that maybe, just maybe, he was relenting. "After she's gone, we'll need to find you a husband. Good stock, someone loyal to our cause. You'll be less nervous once you have a busy household full of children. Boys, hopefully."

"I thought I could try to get my shipyard job back again. After all, I was doing so well in my training class."

"I've thought of that. But I think your time is better spent giving me grandchildren."

"But—"

"Margaret. Don't start getting ideas in your head. The shipyard job was good while it lasted, but having you around so many other independent women was a mistake. It's over. We'll get someone else from our people to work there instead. A man, doing real men's work on those ships. Someone who can cause real havoc, if we need."

He went down the stairs.

Maggie's hands went directly to her lower abdomen, as if already sensing the children that would come and immerse her, drown her future. He was taking Ruby away. And any hope of returning to the shipyards. There was nothing she could do about it.

She had done so well as a welder, even for such a short time. Her work could have been more consequential than he realized. Regret began to burn within her, but she shook it off. No, she'd made her choice.

Maggie heard a muffled sound, and some distant banging down in the basement. Her father's heavy footsteps came plodding louder and louder, the sound of his more than two hundred pounds thumping heavily with the burden of another hundred pounds.

Her father squeezed through the doorway with Ruby thrown over his shoulder. Her left cheek was freshly red where he had struck her. Tears wetted her eyelashes and cheeks. Her arms were still tied together behind her back, and though she wriggled, there was little she could do to escape. But her defiance made her weight more of a burden, so Norman took a fist and hit her on the side of the head. Ruby yelped, her pain muffled by the cloth over her mouth.

"You want your parents to live? Stop moving."

Ruby whimpered and shook her head. For a single second, her gaze met Maggie's. Ruby's eyes had such a look of fury and despair, Maggie's heart caught. Oh, Maggie thought, if only those tears were for me! But she knew they were for Will, lifeless downstairs. With a single expression, Maggie tried to show Ruby everything. That she was sorry, but she'd had to do it. That she had cared, but not cared enough. That she'd wanted Ruby to stay in the quiet, impossible moments they'd had together, hoped they might last forever. That what had happened had mattered. That it was all a glorious fiction that could never be allowed in the real world.

But Ruby turned her face away.

Her father grunted as he lumbered to the front door. Maggie looked out the window. It was black, so dark that she couldn't even make out the neighbors' parked cars or the houses across the street. The entire neighborhood was blanketed in smothering, lightless night.

Father grasped the keys from a table by the door, and turned the doorknob. Silently, he carried Ruby to the curb. He unlocked the back door of his car and tossed her inside, though Maggie could hardly see in the darkness. Her father had disabled the lights within the car, as well as the headlights.

Maggie shut the door. It was the end of an era in her life. She thought of Will, and Ruby, and everything else she had lost, all for this bloody war. She had showed her true patriotism.

It was worth it, wasn't it?

CHAPTER 31

Ruby was shoved face first into the back seat of the darkened car. Norman pushed her legs in, bending them so that her knees rammed against the front seats. She wanted to kick but knew better. It would accomplish nothing but fan his ire, and her ears were still ringing from that punch to the side of her head.

Ruby's lip was swollen, and she tasted blood from a cut where her cheek had encountered her own teeth. Her eyes were puffed from crying, wrists stinging painfully from their bonds. How, how had she gotten here? She might have done better dealing with Felix, but everything had gone so awry, gasoline poured on the mess, and the entire lot lit with a fire. Her family was in danger, and her father would no doubt do whatever this monster asked. It would slow down the work on the side of the American scientists. The Germans would have enough precious months to surge ahead. Everything would change.

Norman shut the door quietly and got in the front seat.

"You stay down, and you stay quiet. I can shut you up in a thousand ways you don't want to know about."

Ruby was terrified to make a sound. But she was still facedown on the leather seat and had to move so she could breathe. As the leather squeaked a tiny bit, her elbow hit something stored in the leg space. It felt lumpy, and strange. Not hard, and not soft. It felt like a body.

Oh no. Who had Norman killed and stashed in the car? It didn't smell like anything rotting, so whoever or whatever it was, it must be freshly dead. So much so that when Ruby's elbow touched the lump again, it felt faintly warm.

Nausea flooded her.

She heard a jingle of metal as he slid the car key into the ignition. But instead of an engine starting, there was an empty clicking sound.

"God dammit," Norman muttered.

He fiddled with the key, trying again and again, pumping the gas pedal.

Ruby felt something moving under her elbow. She was about to scream, when a pair of eyes appeared from beneath a blanket, only inches away. Brown eyes. Familiar, kind eyes.

It was Holly.

Holly pulled the blanket lower, put a finger to her lips. Ruby froze, unable to breathe, while Norman swore under his breath. Of course. Holly must have done something to the car to disable it. She knew a car's anatomy as well as her mother knew a human body's. As Norman reached for the car door, perhaps to check under the hood for something he could fix, Holly sprang from hiding. She held a rope between her fists, and pitched herself forward to loop the rope around Norman's neck.

"Christ!" Norman yelled, and his fists went to the rope tightening under his chin. Holly dug her knees into the back seat and pulled the ends taut behind his head. Norman kicked and thrashed as he struggled to wrest himself from the stranglehold. Holly grunted and pulled, but Norman was falling over on the front seat, kicking the door open, gasping and clawing at his unseen assailant.

Holly kept pulling, but Norman had gotten his fingers around one side of the rope and twisted his fist, pulling the rope forward and giving his throat the scant centimeter he needed to gasp for breath.

Holly threw herself back to pull tighter, but Norman already had momentum moving forward. The rope went with him, and Holly howled as it tore through her palms. Norman took advantage of the slack to yank the rope over his head. The rope fell onto Ruby's body.

Norman scrambled out of the car, and before Holly could even touch the door handle, he had exited the car and pulled it open, reaching in to grab her by a booted ankle. He pulled so hard that she slid right out of the car, her head banging hard upon the edge of the door, then slamming right onto the road.

"Get off me!" she roared. Holly was never a screamer.

"Shut up!" Norman hissed, his hands immediately going to her neck and squeezing. "I know who you are. The bitch bastard sister to this whore here. Good. Now you can go to hell where you belong."

"I'm her bitch . . . bastard . . . *aunt!*" Holly grunted and yelled, trying to wrest his hands away.

Somewhere down the block, Mrs. Polanski yelled, "Hey! Who's making that racket? Be quiet, or I'll call the police!"

"Do it! Call the police!" Holly yelled back.

Ruby tried to scream through her gag, but decided that the more people could see and hear, the better. She wriggled like an inchworm out of the car, legs first, and ended up falling right atop Holly, displacing Norman's squeezing hands. Norman kicked her off Holly and resumed his attack. But the rope had also tumbled out of the car, and the end fell right into Ruby's hand.

Not that she could do anything with it. But she held on to it as if it mattered, and thrashed her bound legs toward Norman as he continued his assault on Holly. Holly was strong, though. She punched back and kicked, bit deeply into Norman's hand when he tried to press it against her mouth to stifle her yells. At one point, Norman howled too. Holly spat something into the air, and blood spattered her lips.

"Bitch!" he yelled again. "You bit my fucking finger off!"

Holly's grin was bloody. She raised a knee hard into his groin as he rolled off her.

Right onto the rope.

Holly grabbed the other end, pulling it over his neck to make a loop while he writhed, giving her the few precious moments she needed.

"Pull, Ruby!" Holly gasped as she straddled Norman's chest and arms. She pulled on one end of the rope and Ruby held fast to her end. Norman gurgled and choked as the rope grew tauter. In this position, Holly could pull with more force, bending her back and using all her muscle.

Even in the darkness, Ruby could see Norman's eyes bulging, his face turning a shade that boded his coming asphyxiation. He couldn't lift his arms from beneath Holly's body weight, and his kicks became weaker as the minutes wore on.

The kicking stopped.

"Don't let go!" Holly said.

Ruby held fast, so much that the muscles of her hands and forearms were screaming with exhaustion for her to relent. Her fingers cramped, but still she held on. She saw the resolve in Holly's contorted, sweating face as she pulled hard.

Norman's expression, once grimacing, slackened until it was puffy and staring vacantly. Finally, Holly gasped.

"He's gone," she said, panting. She let go, and Ruby released her end of the rope. Her hands and arms ached from the effort. Holly scrambled off Norman's body and went to Ruby, carefully pulling down the gag. Ruby inhaled hard to catch her breath as Holly untied the bindings around her wrists and ankles. She was too out of breath to ask questions, but Holly answered her anyway, knowing what she wanted to know.

"I followed you. And I saw Will come home, injured."

"Why didn't you call the police?"

"I was afraid Maggie might kill you both outright. And then one of the neighbors saw me skulking and asked if I knew anything about Maggie. I asked them, and a few more, to come knock on the door so I wouldn't be alone. I had to be sure you were still alive."

"How did you know?"

"Maggie was so intent on getting rid of us when she opened the door. I just knew. I've spent enough time with her to know when she's hiding something. Which is to say, almost all the time. But when she tells the truth, it's bright as day. I knew you were in there and that they wouldn't keep you there for long if the neighbors were always on the lookout."

"My smart Holly! And the car—you did that?"

"Pshaw. Easy as pie. I just removed the coil wire." She pulled a length of wire from her pocket. "Disabled the ignition. Although, I thought of cutting the cable to the battery—"

"Wait." Holly was pulling her away from the house. Ruby pulled back. "Will's in there. We have to help him."

"Let him and his sister rot. They deserve it."

"No! Will has nothing to do with it. He's been poisoned."

"Is he dead?"

"Maybe. But if he's still alive, I can help him. We have to go back in there."

Mrs. Polanski had craned her neck out of her front door, peering at them in the gloom.

"Girls!" she whispered. "Are you all right? I called the police!"

"Good!" Holly yelled. "We were attacked by this man. Someone keep an eye on him. We have to help Will Scripps. He's been attacked."

The woman's eyes went wide. Ruby and Holly limped back toward the house. They saw the curtains flutter within. Maggie. Holly reached for the doorknob, but it was locked. Luckily it was not for nothing that Holly had worn her steel-toed shipyard boots.

"Stand back," she said. She took a few steps back, lifted a foot, and slammed it into the door with all her might. The sound was like a thunderclap. She aimed three heavy kicks, all her force hitting the door at the knob. It only took four kicks before the door broke wide open and the darkness of the Scripps household yawned before them.

Ruby sensed movement nearby and jumped away just in time. Maggie was swinging a wooden chair by the legs, her face strained with panic. She came forward, but Holly lunged for her as soon as she'd swung the chair to the side. She tackled Maggie like a Giants linebacker, shoulder first. They went down together, the air leaving Maggie's chest in a squeal as Holly scrambled to grab her shirt and punch her squarely in the face. Ruby had seen Holly get into enough scrapes at school to know that she was a good fighter, quick and tidy. She never needed to fight dirty. Three punches later, Maggie's mouth was lolling open and her eyes were half-lidded with coming unconsciousness.

Ruby ran past her.

"Where are you going?" Holly asked, between heavy breaths. She was sitting on Maggie's chest. "I need something to tie her up with."

"Will. There still may be time."

Ruby raced to the door that led to the basement. She slapped at the switch to turn the light on, running so fast she nearly fell down the last few steps.

Will was lying facedown in front of the cave-like shelter. With great difficulty, she pushed him over to his side. His face was pale, his mouth slack.

"Oh God. Will!" She slapped his face, but it was clammy to the touch. His breathing was shallow and fast. But he was breathing. She felt his pulse. It was slow. Too slow.

She knew what to do. There was only one thing she could try. Ruby ran upstairs, where several people—neighbors, most likely—were talking heatedly in the parlor. They surrounded a tied-up Maggie on the floor, who was wailing for her father.

Ruby went to a cupboard in the kitchen—one she knew was rarely used by Maggie or Will—and took out a canister. It held a fine dark powder. It had taken days to make. She'd heated the peach pits in a tin, buried in the fire outside until they turned to charcoal, then crushed it into a fine dust and mixed it with zinc chloride. She'd rinsed it with water and dried it. All while Will and Maggie had been at work. The resulting concoction had managed to reverse the poisoning of several rats. Now, it had to work on Will. There was no other option.

She dumped the lot of the sooty, black substance into a glass. Mixed with water, it looked like ink. She hurried downstairs, trying not to spill it.

"Will," she said, setting the glass down on the floor. "Come. Drink this. It'll make you better."

Will was insensate. She tugged to make him sit up, and cradled him in her arms. He had lost at least ten pounds, maybe more, in only the last few days, and she could feel the difference. She slapped his face, hard. Will moaned, and his eyes fluttered.

"Drink this. Come now, Will." She put the glass to his lips, and at first, he drank, almost thirstily. But at the taste, he grimaced and turned away. "No, Will. This will make you better. Please."

Bit by bit, he drank more and more. The black liquid dribbled out the side of his mouth and over his lips, until he looked like a vampire who'd feasted on some black-blooded victim. The charcoal smeared against Ruby's face and hands as she pushed her hair out of the way, forcing his mouth open to drink more. She managed to get him to drink nearly the whole glass of activated charcoal.

Exhausted, she gently lay Will down on the floor and curled her body against him.

"Don't go to sleep. Will, stay awake. You need to give this time to work. It'll adsorb the poison. Come on."

But Will's eyes stayed shut this time. His breathing, short and shallow, lengthened and slowed. She felt his pulse, which was slow as ever but skipping beats, as if time were pulling away at the last threads of his being that kept him together. Distantly, she heard loud voices as people approached. Will would go to the hospital. He might die, and he might live. But no matter what, nothing would be the same.

Ruby gripped him harder. She had done all she could. She had either saved him or, by entering his life that fateful night, killed him. Either way, she wondered if there was any mercy left in the world. If she deserved it. If Will did. She thought about the wickedness of her human race. Perhaps this was part of the punishment. Realizing, all too late, that with all your good deeds and all your sins, nothing really matters.

Heartache comes to all.

CHAPTER 32

Maggie's wrists were bound behind her back, but she did not struggle. Her cheek lay pressed against the parlor room carpet, the smell musty, of long-ago baked goods. The smell of home. She despised the odor, but it would not be in her life for much longer.

What was home? Was it this place? No, not with these people swirling about her, throwing glances of abject horror and disgust. Not with the siren growing louder in the distance, her fate coming closer and closer to cinch itself about her body and pull her down inevitably to its impenetrable depths.

It was over now. Everything she had done . . . was it worth it? Her father was dead. She'd heard the officer say so, only minutes ago. It was an unfathomable fact, even after he had already left her life once. That fateful day when the explosion happened on the dock as he'd boarded it for work on Riker's Island. But it hadn't killed her father. He had simply gifted himself with a new life.

After living with her mother, Maggie, and Will, her father had come to realize his life was larger than the one he'd had. She didn't know this, of course, until later. After Maggie had decided to trade in her life for one of oblivion. It had been nearly a decade after her mother walked into the Lower Bay with no plans to ever return—and succeeded. Will had gone to Columbia to start his new life, studying atoms and attractions and forces, things that would somehow change the world but that in Maggie's mind seemed ever so far away and abstract. Her world had contracted painfully, and the heaviness and terrible feeling that outright consciousness brought was a torture that pressed upon her until she could no longer breathe, no longer function. The only way to breathe was . . . to not to.

And so she had followed in her mother's footsteps, walking into the cold water on Brighton Beach that dark, rainy Monday, when no one would be there and no one would care. But it was a typical Maggie decision, to think of the outcome and not so much the means. Getting caught in a riptide, she was swept out to the depths of the icy cold water, as she kept frustratingly bobbing up with the waves. She'd finally swallowed enough water and exhausted herself to the point where she could feel numb exhaustion obliterating her body, when something grabbed her hard. A hand on her wrist. Yanking, tugging, just like her father used to when she stepped off the curb in Gravesend without noticing that a car was about to decimate her.

She fought, but there was no fight left—and instead of being pulled beneath the waves, she was instead pulled against them and back to the beach, where sand clogged her hair and she vomited water, gasping for air, spitting, replete with disappointment.

God, Maggie, you fail in everything, even this, she thought.

And then God spoke.

"It's not your time, Margaret. It's not your time."

She'd looked at the owner of the hand that had dragged her back to the beach. Drenched in water and with a face that had aged half a century since she last saw him, her father knelt beside her, panting.

He was alive.

Not just alive—he had been watching her.

Lydia Kang

The explosion that day was his doing, in order to leave his life. There had been people after him for money, he explained. And he couldn't fathom living with Will and her mother anymore. They were holding him back from a greater cause. A cause that Maggie needed to join.

"You're not done yet," he said. "This is my fault for leaving you. I won't leave you again."

People began walking toward them, noticing the spectacle that they'd brought to the rainy beach. A girl, drowned! Or nearly drowned. It was worth a closer look. Under the steely, weeping sky, the world was drawing closer.

Her father stood. He put a crumpled piece of paper in her hand.

"Margaret. I'll be watching you. I saved your life, and it's worth more than you think. It can be useful."

He walked away, just as others arrived to throw their warm coats on her, call for more help, ask who she was, and who she belonged to.

My father. I belong to him. But she didn't say it aloud. She didn't open her hand until much later. It had an address on it, with no name. She knew without asking that she was not to address letters to him, for fear that he might be found. It was all too easy to substitute her mother. In more ways than one.

But now, here, with the police roughly pulling her off the carpet and cramming her into their vehicle, with the neighbors watching with horrified eyes, Maggie realized that in that conversation on the beach, her father had only ever referred to Maggie and her life as "it."

It's worth more than you think.

It can be useful.

Like she was a cog in a machine, a screw to be turned. And turn she did. The machine would go on functioning, but for how long? Had she made a difference? Would they win the war, and show that her German roots through her father ran purer, stronger than everyone else's? She

332

didn't know. All she knew was that for her, it was over. She thought of the bright flashes of feeling she'd had with Ruby, the warmth of the adulation from Felix, the unspoken brotherly care that she had always found inferior to her father's missives.

Her life was over. And she wondered . . . was it really ever hers at all?

EPILOGUE

The November air was cold, but there was no wind inside the greenhouse. Ruby wore a muslin smock over her dress. Clippers in hand, she tended to a beautiful oleander tree that was in bloom. The five-petaled pink flowers were lush against the pointed green leaves.

"Are you wearing your gloves?" Holly asked. She was sitting on a small wooden stool nearby, a newspaper on her lap. Holly must have been tinkering with one of the family cars earlier. She was wearing dirty trousers and a pink blouse—an odd combination that Ruby had given up on chiding her about. Holly was eating a ham sandwich out of one hand. The other hand was fiddling with a little brass thing. Holly had told her, but she'd already forgotten what it was. A bullet end connector? Something like that. Who knew what it was for. All she knew was it belonged in a car engine somewhere.

"Of course." Ruby snipped off a few branches and put them in a glass vase. She admired the bouquet, tilting her head left and right. "And what did I tell you about eating in my poison garden? You really are flirting with disaster."

Holly's cheeks were bulging, and a few crumbs spewed out as she protested. "It's not like I'm putting your plants in here like lettuce!"

Ruby shook her head. "So. What does the news say?"

"Maggie is going to trial in a month."

Ruby said nothing. And for a long while, neither did Holly. Any time Maggie's name came up in the news—as "The Brooklyn Spy Girl" or "The Navy Yard's Near Miss"—Ruby's eyes smarted. She would not quickly recover from what had happened. None of them would. But it was a particular sting that came from a wound that was being carefully torn open every day. Every week.

She had given herself to Maggie. Some would say she was too generous with her heart. That she believed that there was good in everyone, before she had a chance to really judge if they deserved her heart or attention. She had given those things to Maggie, and Maggie had at first returned the offer with gentleness and sweet embraces. Ruby had not known until too late that Maggie was also dousing her with untruths. But Ruby knew, as Holly did, that sometimes Maggie was a first-class liar, and sometimes she was a terrible one. They had shared something that much of the rest of the world would call an atrocity, but for those moments, it had been a new bloom, full of everything beautiful and right.

Maggie had never felt the freedom that Ruby did in loving whomever she wanted. When Ruby had first told her mother that she had a romantic inclination for a female college friend, Dr. Fielding had said, "Huh. Interesting." And that was it. But what of Maggie? Pity flooded Ruby. Not for Maggie's dangerous choices, but for Maggie's eternally broken heart.

"You okay?" Holly said. She had finished her sandwich and was now standing behind Ruby. She placed a hand on her shoulder, warm and strong. Ruby had frozen, her clippers in the air, arrested until her thoughts loosed her from her prison. She leaned against Holly's steady hand.

"Oh. Yes. I guess I'm just hungry."

"Liar."

"Are we ever going to recover from this?" Ruby asked quietly.

"Yes, and no. We'll remember it forever. But we can't let it keep us from living. We survived, Ruby. Like all the women in our family who have endured more than their share of pain."

They were quiet for a moment. After talking thoroughly with the police, they vowed never to speak to anyone, or each other, about what had happened that night. How they had extinguished a life, how they had invited death in to take a man who would have destroyed them both without any hesitation. Ruby could still see his death grimace in her nightmares.

The police had dismissed the Fielding women's case as self-defense, and that was that. It gave Ruby some relief, but it didn't make the bad dreams go away.

Holly kissed her niece's cheek and patted her back. "Come now. I know just where those horrible flowers should go."

Ruby put on a smile. It was like adding a fresh coat of lipstick. Armor. Didn't always change how she felt inside, which lately was wretched and heartsick and frightened of the world, but it helped.

We fight, because there's no other choice.

"Let's go," Ruby said, putting her clippers down and grasping the vase of flowers. At the entrance to the greenhouse, she hung up her smock, then washed her hands in a special sink with a powerful detergent that effectively removed plant gum and residues from her hands.

The backyard of the house was smallish. Gone were many of those vast mansions that took up a whole block. The Fielding house had a view of Central Park, and the small green garden that was relatively wild, though Ruby would say that she'd "curated" it to work with the natural elements within it. Papa didn't seem to notice, and Mama was always so busy with the hospital that she left Ruby to care for the garden, her very own playroom since she was a little girl.

Now it had the greenhouse in the center containing not flowers, but a large array of poisonous plants. Hellebore, belladonna, hemlock, tobacco, snakeroot, and more. Ivy snaked up metal trellises, and bright red-and-black rosary pea seeds popped out of their brown husks. She loved the pink and purple spires of the foxglove and the gorgeous five-petaled pink oleander. All beautiful, all powerful and dangerous— if used as such. Through the moisture beading on the glass, the green inside looked ready to burst out and grab someone who walked by, unsuspecting of the death that lay within.

Ruby clutched the vase as she followed Holly through the house's french doors into the large and sprawling sitting room. Inside, her mother was leaning over a figure on the sofa. Ruby placed the vase of flowers on a table. Holly hovered nearby.

"Oh, Ruby," her mother said, taking her stethoscope from her ears and coiling it in her hand as she straightened. "Must you bring those inside?"

"They're pretty!" Ruby said, smiling. "I thought they might brighten this otherwise dull room."

Will looked up from where he lay on the sofa. A thick striped blanket was draped over him, and his eyes were large in his face. He smiled. God, that smile. It was warm and gentle. Something else too. Forgiving.

"Are you calling me dull?" Will said.

"Well, she'd better not be talking about me," Ruby's mother said, raising her eyebrows.

"Never! I meant how dark it gets in here, now that winter is nearly upon us."

"Mm-hmm. Well, don't tire him out with all your chatter, Ruby. I have a guest coming by, and I won't want Will to be unconscious when he arrives."

Ruby nodded. She sat on the chair nearby and clucked at an uneaten bowl of broth and some tea. "You need to drink more," she said to Will.

"You need to nag me less," Will said.

"Remember. When I say you should drink something because it's good for you, I mean it."

But he sighed, pushed himself up, and reached for the tea anyway. His large hands nearly made the mug disappear in his hands. Even in his illness, his presence was like having an immovable boulder in the room. Though this boulder had nearly died and had been in a coma at Bellevue for two weeks before he woke up.

"Tastes better than that charcoal slurry you made me drink."

Ruby wrinkled her nose. "Do you remember that?"

"Vaguely. It tasted about as good as it looked. But it did the trick. I was on the razor's edge of life and death. The charcoal pushed me to the right side of things." He put the mug down. "I'm still sorry I doubted you."

"I wasn't being very forthcoming, as you know. You had reasons to doubt me."

"I suppose so. You were growing lethal plants in my backyard, after all," Will said. "And poisoning rats by the dozen."

"Well, yes. I was. But I was also trying to figure out how to save them!"

"And now, she and Mother are going to try their activated charcoal on other toxins. It's very exciting," Holly said proudly. "Will, they're going to write up your case in a toxicology journal. It'll save more lives. If not in this war, in other ways."

Will looked up at Holly, and his eyes twinkled. Ruby looked pointedly from Will to Holly, and back to Will again. They seemed to have forgotten that Ruby was there. Funny, Will's eyes never twinkled when he used to look at me, Ruby thought. Hmm.

Ruby cleared her throat, and they snapped their attention back to her. "Yes, well. Our family has a legacy of being entangled with chemistry and poisons, unfortunately," Ruby said. "It's nice to change the association to one that's positive, I suppose."

"It is." Will smiled but looked weary. He passed his hand over his eyes and rubbed his temple. "It's all very . . . strange. After everything . . . one wonders if anything I thought was real was truly . . . real."

Holly and Ruby looked at each other, concern mirrored in each other's faces. Ruby put her hand on Will's hand.

"Hey. Maggie did love you, you know," she said. "But she loved other things more."

By *things*, of course, she meant Maggie's father. And those horrible Nazis.

"I don't know what that was. Not love."

Ruby squeezed his hand. There were answers that she could not provide. The whys and what-ifs. Will was a good man. Deep down, his compass was true. But love blinded him, just like every fallible human with a soul that ever walked the earth.

"Can I ask . . . ," Will began.

Ruby looked uncertain. "Anything."

"Did you really not know how to cook anything? Was that all a ruse?"

"Oh. God, no. I wasn't faking one whit. I didn't know how to boil an egg, or make coffee." She blushed. "I'm so embarrassed at how helpless and dependent I'd become, living this life. Felix made it even worse. He put my privilege on an even higher pedestal, and it was turning me a little rotten in my core. You both did help me there. The cooks are pretty flummoxed when they see me in there, making my own breakfast now. I can make Betty Grable's gashouse eggs beautifully."

"I'll bet," Will said, grinning.

There was a knock from the hallway. Holly excused herself and walked to the foyer. After a few minutes, both of Ruby's parents and another gentleman entered along with Holly. Holly had her arm around the visitor behind Papa.

Ruby's mother smiled. "William Scripps. This is—"

"Uncle Jasper!" Ruby ran over and threw her arms around her uncle. Holly strode forward and took the seat that Ruby had left, eyeing Will furtively. She fiddled even more with the little brass connector thing in her hands.

"An honorary uncle," the man said. He was Mama and Papa's age, slim and handsome, with brown hair and a crooked smile. "Sorry to bother you during your convalescence. Jasper Jones. Good to meet you."

"I took your gen chem class in college," Will said. They shook hands. "Though I doubt you remember me amongst that sea of freshmen. Didn't you write that paper on alternative methods of synthesizing ascorbic acid?"

"Yes. Working on other vitamins as well. Pyridoxine, or vitamin B6. We're looking at it as an antidote to hydrazine poisoning."

"Really!" Will seemed to wake up out of a fog he'd been in for the last few days. "Fascinating. I guess the whole family is in the business of antidotes."

"I suppose so."

"Are you feeling better, Mr. Scripps?" Ruby's father stepped forward. Despite his age, Papa still managed to look like a nervous boy sometimes. Always so eager to please. "If there's anything you need, let me know."

"I'm much better. I can't thank you enough for you and your family taking care of me while I recover."

"It's the least we could do. You're practically family now," he said, winking at Ruby. Will went a little white and looked distinctly uncomfortable. Holly looked downright mad.

"Papa!" Ruby rolled her eyes. "Will is wonderful, but we are only ever going to be good friends." She widened her eyes and gave Holly a knowing look.

"I see." Her father looked confused, and her mother whispered in his ear. "Oh. *Oh!*" His eyes went to Holly, sitting rather close to Will.

Papa was always a little slow on seeing the obvious, but he was smart in other ways, and had a heart the size of Manhattan. It wasn't a surprise that he hadn't seen it coming. True, Holly and Will hadn't even known of each other's existence much before that fateful night in Gravesend. But while he recovered, Holly had spent hours reading aloud books on automobiles and airplanes, enough to dull anyone's senses into a good daily slumber, when something clicked.

Perhaps it was Holly's straightforwardness, and lack of shyness. Perhaps it was Will's being in a particularly vulnerable position. They seemed to recognize a similar element within each other. But Ruby had caught them talking for hours about astrophysics, about the news, about cars, about carburetors. Somehow, an affection formed, and growing strong as steel every day. Holly was never far away from Will. And Will looked not just happy, but relieved. As if he'd been missing something he didn't realize until he found it.

Meanwhile, Ruby and Will distanced themselves until what had happened before seemed more like a strange dream than anything real. The truth was that for a time, they were hungry, and they'd had each other. But now they hungered for other things. There had been that infatuation that had faded. It was a page they had seemed to be equally eager to turn over, fold, and put away.

"Ruby and Holly told me that you'll be looking for a new job when you're better," Jasper said.

"I will. It's pretty clear that my work with the MED is over now. To be honest, I'm glad of it."

"Perhaps," Mr. Fielding said. "I received this for you." He took a letter out of his pocket and handed it to Will.

Will opened it, scanned it, and handed it to Ruby and Holly, who read it together.

> *Dear Will,*
> *It was good to know you. I wish you well.*
> *HR*

That was it.

"Your old boss?" Ruby said. "Mrs. Rivers?"

"Yes," Will said. "I'm surprised she even bothered to write anything. She played her part well."

"You say that like this is a dramatic play, rather than a war," Holly said.

Will shook his head. "We're all bit actors in the grand scheme. Ones that won't be counted in history."

"We may not be remembered, but we count. Never forget that, Will," Dr. Fielding said.

"You'll be happy to know," Ruby's father said, "that my company is full steam ahead with the uranium mining and refining for the MED. We haven't lost a step in our path forward."

"And . . . that's probably all you should say, dear," her mother said, patting his arm.

A silence hung in the air, something heavy with intention. The project would move, inevitably, to some conclusion. Success? Failure? Will had explained what he could to Holly and Ruby about how the physics of it all worked. So Ruby knew—as did her mother (there was something in her eyes that spoke of it)—that success would be a terrible thing as well. The first law of thermodynamics said so.

Energy can be changed from one form to another, but it cannot be created or destroyed. The total amount of energy and matter in the universe remains constant, merely changing from one form to another.

There would be a horrific consequence of letting that energy out into the world. For that reason, Ruby was relieved that Will wasn't such a direct part of it anymore. At some point, the project would no longer be theory, but truth. And that truth could be too terrible for Will to claim any penny of ownership. That trajectory of inevitability would continue without him.

Jasper sat down in front of Will. Ruby looked at her uncle fondly. Though he was really starting to look like a distinguished gentleman of middling years with those silver temples, his rakish handsomeness had not disappeared. Mama had hinted that he'd broken hearts when he was young, but now he was fairly married to his chemistry research. And he'd practically adopted Ruby and Holly as if they were his own flesh-and-blood nieces.

"What would you think about working with me? In my lab, at Columbia."

"I don't have a degree yet," Will said.

"Finish it. Do your graduate studies in my lab." He smiled. "I understand you had your heart set on atomic physics."

"Ah. It seems to have lost its luster for me lately."

Jasper shrugged. "I had my heart set on being a doctor. A forensic pathologist, actually. And look what happened."

Papa jabbed his finger at his wife. "She was the one who was going to be a chemist."

"He wanted to be a banker," Ruby's mother said, looking at Papa. "Oh wait. He still is!"

Everyone laughed.

"Not everyone's first love can be their last," Papa said, and he gave his wife's hand a squeeze. "Right, Miss Cutter?"

"Oh God, not in front of me, you don't," Ruby said. Papa called her mother by her maiden name when he was being sugary sweet.

"Anyway! Now that everyone is fully uncomfortable," Holly said, smirking, "we should let Will get some rest."

They all nodded. Will and Jasper shook hands again, and Will thanked him for his generous offer. Ruby left Holly to fuss over Will as they walked Uncle Jasper to the door. As her parents murmured to each other, Jasper took her arm in his.

"And how is one of my favorite nieces getting along these days, being in the newspaper and famous?"

"Infamous, perhaps?"

"The heiress who went missing, and turns up defending herself and her family member, while uncovering a spy plot that could have turned the tide of the war for the worse?"

"Well, when you put it that way." Ruby smiled, but it was the false one she'd been wearing for some time. Her parents waved to Jasper from the front door as Ruby walked him to his car outside. When they reached it, Jasper turned to her, and his smile disappeared.

"You don't fool me for a second."

"Don't I?" Ruby said lightly.

"You will get over this. It was a lot. More than a lifetime's worth of violence, and pain."

Ruby said nothing for a while.

"When you're ready, I'd like to introduce you to someone."

"Oh?" Ruby said, not really listening.

"She's an anthropology grad student. Sumi Park. I think you might get along swimmingly."

What a beautiful name, Ruby thought. Then she sighed. "I don't know," she said. "Maybe I'm not ready yet. I just feel like—I don't know who I am anymore. I've played so many characters. I've had my heart broken more times in a few months than most people have in a lifetime."

"I'll tell you what I know." Jasper lifted her chin with the knuckle of his first finger. "You're obsessed with developing ways to cure people who are sick. And you have more than one heart to give, when it comes to love. Sometimes you have to throw a few darts that smack the wall before you finally hit the mark."

"But what does it mean that I can throw those darts at people who end up being . . . being . . ."

"Maggie?"

Ruby looked at her shoes and nodded.

"That's why they call it 'falling for someone.' Sometimes, you have to hit pavement—hell, blow it up like a bomb—before you realize the truth."

Her uncle gave her a peck on the cheek, and opened his car door. He put the key in the ignition, then rolled down the window and glanced up at Ruby.

"Look at you." He winked. "You're still standing, aren't you? That's what Cutter women do. Never stop fighting."

Ruby stood there, watching his car drive up Fifth Avenue until it disappeared into the lines of cars that vanished into the infinity of north Manhattan.

The name Sumi Park played in her mind as she watched the sunlight reflect off the buildings. There was still so much to do, so much love in her heart to give, so much grieving to do. The war seemed to be going on forever, but it couldn't last. Could it?

Ruby thought of the sunlight, and the photons reflecting off the window glass, and of its seemingly limitless incandescence. Even the sun, billions of years old, with its atomic fusion reactions creating bounteous amounts of energy, its constant source of light and warmth, would end someday.

"But not today," Ruby murmured. "Not today."

AUTHOR'S NOTE

When I was in college at Columbia University in New York, I took a physics class in Pupin Hall. I remember something like a bowling ball tethered to the ceiling used to demonstrate pendulum motion. I was extremely tempted to sneak in after hours and swing on it. (I did not, for the record. I did sneak into other off-limits spaces and, er, rooftops . . . probably too many . . . but I should stop here so I stay in good graces with my alma mater.)

During a random collegiate moment, someone pointed out Pupin Hall and said, "Hey. They developed the atom bomb in there."

I probably shrugged, made a mental note, and spent the rest of my mental energy strategizing where to obtain my next bagel and schmear.

However, I never forgot that tidbit of American history.

It is actually true that the Columbia football team was enlisted to haul graphite blocks indoors to make a nuclear pile for a test chain reaction. Enrico Fermi, one of the physicists crucial to the project, noted how he'd worked with these "husky boys" on the team, who helped shove the uranium into hundred-pound packs with ease, according to a 1993 interview with the *Columbia Spectator*.

I could practically see William Scripps in my mind when I first read that quote. So, in my desire to place the next iteration of the Cutter family history in New York City, I chose World War II as the time period, and decided that one of those football players would be a main character.

I was also fascinated by the work done at the Brooklyn Navy Yard, and the timeline of my story crystallized when I learned that women were allowed to work at the Navy Yard starting on September 14, 1942. That's when Maggie popped into my head. Several books were key to my understanding of what Maggie's life and what her experience at the Navy Yard might have been like. If you're curious, check out the Brooklyn Navy Yard website (https://brooklynnavy-yard.org/about/archives) for photos, history, maps, and more; *Rosie the Riveter*, by Penny Colman; *Our Mother's War: American Women at Home and at the Front during World War II*, by Emily Yellin; and the Brooklyn Public Library's Oral History Collection on the Brooklyn Navy Yard (https://oralhistory.brooklynhistory.org/collections/brooklyn-navy-yard-oral-history-collection/).

And then of course there is Ruby, and all her poisonous interests. Ruby is a bit like myself, in that we are both completely fascinated by poisons and antidotes. I had a jolly time writing about historical "antidotes" in *Quackery: A Brief History of the Worst Ways to Cure Everything*, cowritten with Nate Pedersen. But I couldn't stop thinking about the subject. I first saw activated charcoal in action as a medical student rotating through the Bellevue Hospital Emergency Department, where victims of poisonings or overdoses often sat in their gurneys with telltale black smudges around their mouths. Lewis Goldfrank's *Toxicological Emergencies* is a staple reference in my house (for writing purposes! I swear!). Dr. Goldfrank is a pioneer of toxicology and has taught at NYU and Bellevue, the nation's first public hospital, for decades. If you know my books, you'll notice Bellevue frequently shows up, for that is where I completed my internal medicine residency training and most of my medical school clerkships. Ruby and Dr. Allene Fielding would have appreciated Dr. Goldfrank very much in their time. And yes, if you want to, you can google how to cook up some activated charcoal in your backyard, but I'm fairly sure it'll be a messy affair, and I really recommend you do whatever is necessary *not* to put yourself in a situation where you need to use it. Stay safe, folks.

Learning about atomic physics wasn't easy for me. I like the realms of chemistry and medicine better, and plus, the history of the atom bomb is incredibly disturbing, considering that the end goal is absolutely horrific. But if this history intrigues you, I recommend a somewhat obscure book, *The Traveler's Guide to Nuclear Weapons: A Journey through America's Cold War Battlefields*, by James Maroncelli and Timothy Karpin. The book was crucial research material. It's a great primer on the history and will show you actual places involved in the making of the atom bomb, all over the country. Also check out the Atomic Heritage Foundation site, which has photos and interviews (https://www.atomicheritage.org/history/manhattan-project), as well as Richard Rhodes's *The Making of the Atom Bomb*.

I stuck closely to the true timeline of the events that occurred in New York, including the storage of tons of pitchblende at the Dean Mill Plant, and Will's understanding of how the Manhattan Project was working toward uranium enrichment via uranium hexafluoride. Many of the names in the book are very real, and very much integral to the development of the atom bomb, including General Leslie Groves, Enrico Fermi, James Chadwick, and Leó Szilárd.

If you'd like to take a historical atomic heritage tour within New York City, here are the ones that have cameos in the novel: The MED, or Manhattan Engineer District headquarters, was located on the eighteenth floor of the Arthur Levitt State Office Building on 270 Broadway (now a condo building). The Dean Mill Plant on Staten Island, which stored the pitchblende early on in the story, no longer exists, and would have been under the setting-sun shadow of the Bayonne Bridge. The Baker and Williams Warehouses still exist, and you can see them (like I did) from a walk on the High Line. The Kellex Corporation Headquarters was in the Woolworth Building. The

Beach-Russ Company in Brooklyn no longer exists; it would have been at 544 Union Avenue in the Northside section of Brooklyn. The Nash Garage building is at 3280 Broadway, about thirteen blocks north of the Columbia University campus. And then of course there is my alma mater, Columbia, at 116th and Broadway, where Pupin Hall still stands. Go visit and see if you can find the hidden owl in the *Alma Mater* statue in the center of campus. I often did, for good luck before an exam!

If you'd like more of a taste of wartime New York City, I highly recommend *Over Here! New York City during World War II*, by Lorraine B. Diehl, and *Helluva Town: The Story of New York City during World War II*, by Richard Goldstein. Both gave fantastic accounts of the blackouts, plane spotting, the very real fear of spies, and the day-to-day life experiences of those years. You can practically feel the city pulsating with patriotic energy and going dark and silent during those blackout drills in these illuminating reads.

One last, long note, and a bit of missing history from this novel.

In August of 1939, about three years before the setting of this novel, Leó Szilárd wrote a letter. Signed by Albert Einstein, it warned President Franklin D. Roosevelt that Germany might develop atomic bombs, and thus urged the United States to begin its very own nuclear program. From thence was born the Manhattan Project, named for the city where much of the planning occurred, in order to mask the true nature of the project.

Six years later, on August 6, 1945, the B-29 *Enola Gay* released an atom bomb that detonated over Hiroshima, Japan. The blast was estimated to be equal to thirteen kilotons of TNT, and an area of nearly five square miles was decimated. Approximately eighty thousand people were killed, including twenty thousand Koreans enslaved by the Japanese. Another seventy thousand people were injured.

On August 9, 1945, another B-29 plane loaded with another atom bomb flew over Kokura, Japan. Because the city was too cloudy, the city of Nagasaki was chosen as an alternate target. The explosion was as powerful as twenty-one kilotons of TNT, killing around forty thousand people and injuring sixty thousand.

Only weeks before, a petition was written and signed by seventy scientists working on the Manhattan Project, begging President Harry S. Truman to use diplomacy to effect the end of the war, before using atomic weapons.

The so-called Szilárd petition never made it to President Truman's desk.

In my heart, I know that William Scripps would have signed that petition.

We humans are such a unique species in our need to destroy each other. We are apt to create things of such beauty and goodness. And we are capable of monstrous hatred and violence. We have but one Earth, and one life; let us all endeavor to create more of the good while we're here.

All my best,
Lydia

ACKNOWLEDGMENTS

As always, an enormous thank-you to my nuclear family, who keep me laughing and well loved when I am in the throes of writing. You are the stars in my sky. And to my extended family, whom I have missed so dearly during this awful pandemic, I love you all so very much.

A big thank-you to the many people in my life who have kept me afloat in many different ways. To the incredible team of fantastic humans in my primary care clinic at Nebraska Medicine—y'all keep me happy, and you keep my patients happy. Thank you always! To my wonderful patients, of course, for being you. To Sarah Simpson Weiss, my assistant extraordinaire, and Felicity Bronzan, who keeps my life from imploding. To my many friends and colleagues, including Sarah Kosa, Peter Kosa, Angela Hawkins, Phil Smith, Gale Etherton and Fedja Rochling, Jasmine Marcelin, Chelsea Navarette, Nate Pedersen and April Tucholke, Tosca Lee, A. H. Kim, Tsui Ling Toomer, Todd Robinson, Lindsey Baker, Heather McIntyre Haas and Eric Haas, Ann Williams, Kelli Van Winkle, Alice Kim Blake and Adrian Blake, Kathy and Bill Lydiatt, Pintip Dunn, and Kate Brauning. There are *so* many more, and I appreciate you all so very much.

To Hannah Rivers and her parents, Susan and Todd, for supporting such a great cause at Fontanelle Forest and letting me put Hannah into my story. To Munk Davis and Keith Wilson for the very useful 1930–1940 car advice, thank you. And to Elizabeth McGorty at the

Brooklyn Navy Yard and Mariane LaBatto at Brooklyn College for all the important historical research help.

And, of course, to my fantastic agent, Eric Myers (who also served as my 1940s slang consultant!) and my editors Jodi Warshaw and Caitlin Alexander. Thank you all for supporting my stories and helping me bring them into the world. And thank you to the entire team at Lake Union Publishing, including Kimberly Glyder for the stunning cover design.

ABOUT THE AUTHOR

Photo © Chelsea Donoho

Lydia Kang is an author and internal medicine physician. She is a graduate of Columbia University and New York University School of Medicine, and she completed her training at Bellevue Hospital in New York City. She lives with her family in the Midwest. Follow her on Twitter (@LydiaYKang) and Instagram (@LydiaKang).